W9-BAO-223

THE CITY'S DARKEST
NIGHTMARE BROUGHT
THEM TOGETHER

FLOOD . . .

Burke . . . He's got bad debts, a few scruples, and Pansy, a watchdog who eats strangers for breakfast. His specialty is survival.

Flood . . . She's a hard-knocks woman who was brought up rough. She loves and kills with equal skill.

FLOOD . . .

"The good guys are bad, but the bad guys are much, much worse . . . For hard-core fans of the hard-boiled school."

> —Roderick Thorp, author of *The Detective*

"What Dostoevsky would have done if he'd been writing in the Mike Hammer mode . . . Vachss has been there, into the dark, steaming streets . . . *FLOOD*'s pace, its dagger-sharp understanding, its moral outrage over the ugliest kinds of criminality make it A CLASSIC KIND OF THRILLER."

> —Les Whitten, Senior Investigator for
> Jack Anderson, and author of
> *A Conflict of Interest*
> and *A Killing Place*

"A STEAMY, FETID WORLD DELIVERED WITH CONVINCING AUTHENTICITY . . . ASTONISHING."

> —*Publishers Weekly*

The Mercenary Recruiters . . . They're looking for the right kind of men . . . who get off on guns, racism . . . and children. Burke would waste them to find The Cobra.

The Car . . . Burke's Plymouth, a lethal fantasy on wheels. The cigarette lighter taps out S.O.S. on the rear lights.

Max the Silent . . . He's huge, mute, a Tibetan karate master. He bends brass knuckles with his fingers. He likes Burke, and that makes Burke lucky.

Michelle . . . the hooker with a heart who does Burke special favors. All she needs is a sex change.

Flood

ANDREW H. VACHSS

POCKET BOOKS

New York   London   Toronto   Sydney   Tokyo

POCKET BOOKS, a division of Simon & Schuster Inc.
1230 Avenue of the Americas, New York, NY 10020

Copyright © 1985 by Andrew H. Vachss
Cover art copyright © 1986 Roger Kastel

Published by arrangement with Donald I. Fine, Inc.
Library of Congress Catalog Card Number: 85-80251

ISBN: 0-671-61905-5

First Pocket Books printing July 1986

10 9 8 7 6 5 4 3 2

POCKET and colophon are trademarks of
Simon & Schuster Inc.

Printed in the U.S.A.

For
Victor Chapin
Yale Lee Mandel
Iberus Hacker (a.k.a. Dan Marcum)
Wesley Everest

very different actors
who all left this junkyard of a planet
to work a better room

———————————

ACKNOWLEDGMENTS

The ultimate poverty is to fail to acknowledge your debts. For the material in this book and in others to come, I am indebted to many people, some as close as my blood, some forever to be my enemies. I will never forget any of them.

1

I GOT TO the office early that morning—I think it was about ten o'clock. As soon as the dog saw it was me, she walked over to the back door and I let her out. I went outside with her as far as the fire escape and watched her climb the metal stairs to the roof where she would deposit her daily load. Someday I'm going to go up there and clean it all up, but in the meantime it keeps the winos from using my roof as a sleeping porch—too many of them smoke in bed.

The dog is a hell of a lot better than a burglar alarm. The cops wouldn't rush into this neighborhood in the middle of the night anyway, and with Pansy on the job the burglar would still be there when anyone showed up. She's a Neapolitan mastiff—about 140 pounds of concentrated hatred for all humanity except me. My last dog was a Doberman named Devil. She bit some clown and I got hit with a $100,000 lawsuit, so she had to run away from home. She never had a license and I'm about as judgment-proof as a man can get, but this lawyer I refer cases to sometimes told me that I should give my next dog a name that wouldn't sound so negative. I thought of naming her the Neapolitan Homicide and calling her Homo for short, but the lawyer told me you never know who is going to be on a jury, especially in New York—so I compromised and called her Pansy. A lot of my clients don't like the dog, but that doesn't amount to a whole hell of a lot of people.

When Pansy came back downstairs, I shut the back door and got out her food. I only feed her the dry stuff, but she still slobbers like a politician near money. That's why I have the floor covered in Astroturf—it handles anything, you just wash it off. A lot of my clients think that's low-class too, but, like I said, there aren't enough of them to make a difference.

I told the dog to stay where she was and went to check the other office. Actually, it's just the next room, but there's no connecting door and the outer door was sealed shut years ago. I just use it when people I don't want to see knock on my door—once I stayed there for three days. It has a private john, a fridge, a hotplate, and even a TV with earphones. Not bad— but the only ventilation is the little window that opens off the fire escape where I climb in so I don't use it too much.

I don't make a lot of money at what I do, but the overhead is no problem—I have my own form of rent control. By accident, I once found out that the landlord's son did something to some people and they've been looking for him ever since. I found the kid too, but his own mother wouldn't recognize him. The landlord bought him a new face, got him started in business, and the kid was golden—except that I knew about him and I told the landlord I did. I haven't paid rent in about four years. There's no ethics problem—nobody ever hired me to find the little weasel.

I checked the mail first—a letter from American Express addressed to one of my other names demanding immediate payment of $3,504.25 or else they would wreck my credit rating for openers, a package on the latest FM transceiver bands from the U.S. Law Enforcement Assistance Administration addressed to the Crime Prevention Foundation, and a check for $771.25 from the Social Security Administration addressed to Mrs. Sophie Petrowski (the unfortunate Mr. Petrowski's only survivor), proving to me that despite a lengthy sojourn in the federal joint the Mouse was continuing his one successful scam. There were also four handwritten letters containing the requisite ten-dollar money order in response to my ad promising information about "mercenary opportunities in foreign lands for qualified adventurers."

I threw the American Express garbage where it belonged, put the Petrowski check inside a handsome envelope engraved with *Law Offices of Alexander James Sloan,* and typed the Mouse's righteous name and institutional number on the outside. Stamped with my bold red *Confidential Legal Mail,* the envelope next went into my postage meter, a machine which could never be returned to Pitney Bowes for service. I understand the Mouse has a friendly guard who will cash these for him, obviously a future roommate. I added the four would-be mercenaries' names to my Rolodex, took a manila envelope for each and enclosed a Rhodesian Army recruiting poster (Be a Man Among Men!), an Exxon map of Afghanistan, two phone numbers for bars in Earl's Court, London, and the name of a hotel on the island of Sao Tome off the coast of Nigeria. As usual, none of them had enclosed the self-addressed, stamped envelope. The world is full of crooks.

The buzzer sounded, telling me either I or the dope-crazed hippies in the lower loft had a customer. I switched the toggle over to *Talk,* and hit the *Play* switch on the cassette recorder. A sweet female voice lilted out of the recorder and into the microphone connected to the downstairs speaker, "Yes please?"

A woman's voice came back from downstairs, "I would like to see Mr. Burke, please."

I hit the second switch on the recorder, and my faithful secretary asked, "Do you have an appointment?"

"No, but it's very important. I don't mind waiting."

I thought for a second, contemplated the state of my finances, and selected another switch from the two remaining. "Very well. Please come up and Mr. Burke will see you shortly."

"Thank you," came the woman's voice.

As soon as I hit the opener for the downstairs door, which also sends down the elevator, I went through the back door to the fire escape and climbed out past the connecting window to the second office. I kept going until I was near the end of the building, where I had a periscope mounted to give me a view of the entire hall from the elevator on down. It was a miserable arrangement even with the floodlights in the corridor—when it was raining or dark outside, you couldn't see that much— but at least you could tell if it was more than one person outside the office door. It wasn't this time and I went back inside.

Pansy growled softly. I adjusted the fake Persian rug on the right-hand wall (the second office is against the left wall) so that it looked as though there were a connecting door, and I opened the outer door just as she was getting ready to knock again. I motioned her to come inside and sit on the low couch next to my desk, activated a switch to open the phony intercom, and said "Sally, hold my calls for a while, okay?" A quick push of the second switch got me "Certainly, Mr. Burke." I then turned to look at my new client.

The low couch usually bothers people but this lady couldn't have cared less. I guess she measured about five feet total (maybe an inch or so less), white-blonde hair, high forehead, thin nose, wide-set dark eyes, and a kind of thick chunky build you would call buxom if you hadn't had a look at her from the waist down. I hadn't yet so I mentally settled for old-fashioned "buxom." She wore wide-legged gray wool slacks over medium-heeled black boots, a white turtleneck pullover covered by one of those unstructured ladies' jackets, no hat, no jewelry that I could see, pale lipstick, too much eyeliner, and some rouge that didn't quite hide the tiny scar just under her right eye. It looked as though someone had engraved a tic-tac-toe crosshatch with a fine scalpel. She crossed her legs and folded her hands over her knee; one of the knuckles had a faint bluish tinge.

Everything fit together on her nicely but you can't always tell what a woman spends on her get-up the way you can with a man—no jewelry, for example, didn't mean she was broke. She sat as calmly as a toad waiting for flies, and the dog's presence didn't seem to unsettle her. It didn't look like a matrimonial to me, but I've made a career out of being wrong. So I just asked, "How can I help you?" in my neutral professional voice.

Now that she wasn't coming over the speaker, her voice sounded like she forgot to clear her throat. "I want you to find somebody for me."

"Why?" Not that I give a senator's morals for her reasons, but this kind of question usually gives you a good clue to how much money the customer wants to spend.

"Is that important?" she asked.

"It is to me. How do I know you don't want to find this person and do some damage to them, for example?"

"If I did, you wouldn't take the job?"

I didn't need sarcasm this early in the morning. Even Pansy grinned appreciatively at her before rolling over and cracking another piece of her marrow bone.

"I didn't say that. But I have to know what I'm getting into . . ."

"So you can fix the price?"

Okay, sure I have to fix the price. But she obviously didn't understand the complexities of my business. If I put a flat fee on the job and I find the guy right away, I make some money.

But if I don't, then I'm out a lot of time and I don't make out so well. And if I set a daily rate and happen to find the guy right away, I still have to keep him under surveillance for a few more days before I turn him over to the client so that I make a decent buck. I do a lot of locates, especially for bondsmen, but I don't bring the people in myself—I have a gorilla I use for that work and I can only use him when he's out of jail. He's such a genius that I once got him to turn himself in on a bail-jumping rap for half the commission. So I said, "I get paid for the work I do and the risks I take, just like anyone else. If I have to go looking down a sewer, I have to be paid for the possibility of rat bites even if I don't get bit, you understand?"

"Yes, I understand quite well. But I don't have time to bargain with you. I'm not a good bargainer. I will pay you a thousand dollars if you will spend one week trying to find him—period."

I pretended to think that one over. It was no contest—a grand a week is more than what some legitimate private eyes make.

"Okay, sounds reasonable to me. I'll just need some basic facts and then I'll get right to work."

"Are you sure you can clear your calendar?" she wanted to know.

"Look, I didn't solicit this business, right? If you would prefer someone more in tune with your social station, just say the word. I'm sure you can find your own way out."

"All right, I'm sorry—maybe that wasn't necessary. But I don't want you to think I'm some dummy you can pull a cop-and-blow on."

(That was a funny one. She didn't look like a hooker—and she couldn't be paying me to find a pimp. If those weasels aren't visible, they're not earning. And if they're not earning, they're hanging around some dummy's apartment, spending the welfare check and planning their big comeback.)

"Where did you hear an expression like that?"

"I read it in a book. Let's cut the snappy dialogue—just tell me who to make my check out to."

"Make it out to cash. Then take it to your bank, hand it to the teller, exchange it for greenbacks and bring them all back to me. I'll be happy to give you a receipt, but we don't take checks in this business."

Kind of hard to take checks when you don't have a bank account, but let her think that her own honesty wasn't exactly certified at my end.

"Okay, I'll be back in a couple of hours." She got off the couch, sort of shook herself so her clothes settled back on her frame without a wrinkle, and went over to the door. Her hips moved the way a woman's do when she's annoyed but not ready to sever the relationship. Even Pansy seemed entranced—she called upon some hidden reserves of energy and raised her massive head a couple of inches to watch the lady leave. I'm not one of those who wants to see a check so he can tell what bank the customer is using—who cares? Anyone with half a brain knows how to get around that dodge, and she looked like she had more than enough smarts.

If I was a detective, I would have spent the next few hours productively trying to deduce what kind of case this was. I never read Sherlock Holmes but I saw all the movies, so I did the intelligent thing and totally analyzed her character from her clothes. I came up with a flat zero. When I checked it out with Pansy, she confirmed my diagnosis.

I picked up the telephone gently to see if the trust-fund hippies downstairs were discussing one of their major marijuana deals again. It's their phone—I simply had an associate hook me up an extension so I could make calls without the inconvenience of monthly bills. But I don't abuse the setup—I have a good supply of slugs for the pay phone downstairs when I have to go long distance. The line was clear, which it usually is until the late afternoon when the hippies get up—it must be nice not to have to work for a living. Thinking about it, I was sure that the lady would be back soon, and I'm not a man to leave money lying around uninvested. So I put in a quick call to my broker, Maurice.

"Yeah?" came the friendly greeting.

"Maurice, this is Burke. Give me a yard to win on the three-horse in the seventh tonight at Yonkers."

"Three-horse, race number seven, at Yonkers—that right?"

"Perfect," I told him.

"I doubt it," says Maurice and he hangs up.

2

I PUT IN a quick call to Mama Wong at the Poontang Gardens (she had serviced the military at Fort Bragg during the Korean War) to see if I had any messages. I do her favors occasionally and she answers the pay phone in her kitchen with "Mr. Burke's office" anytime it rings. I don't get a lot of messages, and her favors aren't any too tough either.

"Mama, this is Burke. Any calls?"

"You have one call, from a Mr. James. I tell him you would be back later, but he wouldn't leave a number. He say he call back, okay?"

"Sure. When he calls back, tell him I'm out on assignment and if he can't leave a number, I won't be able to talk to him for another week or so."

"Burke, you not call him back, okay? This is a bad man."

"How can you tell from his voice, for chrissakes?"

"I know. I hear his kind of voice years ago from a man who say he is a soldier but is really something else, okay?"

"Okay, Mama. But if he wants to find me bad enough he will, right? So take the number and let me call him."

"Not good idea, Burke. But I do it if you say, okay?"

"Okay, Mama. I'll call you later."

I got a small piece of steak out of the fridge and called Pansy over. As soon as she saw the steak, she started drooling quarts and came over to sit next to me, watching carefully. I draped the steak over her massive snout and she sat there looking miserable but not moving. After a couple of minutes I looked at her and said "Speak!" and she snatched the steak so fast I hardly saw her jaws move. Pansy won't eat anything unless she hears me say the magic word. It's not a party trick— no weasel is going to poison my dog. I don't use the usual poison-proofing words the dog trainers favor, like "good food" or "kosher," because I don't figure any freak who wants to take her out of the play will ask her to speak when he hands over the food. And if you try to feed her without saying the word, you get to *be* the food.

Pansy looked pleadingly at me. "I told you a thousand times, *chew* the goddamned food. If you swallow it whole, you don't get the benefit from it. Now try and *chew* it this time, dummy." And I tossed her another slab of steak, saying "Speak!" while it was still in the air. Pansy snarfed that one down too, realized that was all, and rolled back to her place on the rug.

I sat down in front of the mirror and began my breathing exercises. I started them years ago while my face was healing from the repairs. Now I do them sometimes just to help me think. An old man once taught me how to move pain around in my body until I had gathered it in one spot and could then move it entirely outside my skin. It was all in the breathing, and I've kept up the exercises ever since. You suck in a heavy gulp of air smoothly through the nose and down into the stomach, expanding it as far as possible and holding for a slow count of thirty. Then you gradually let it out, pulling in the stomach and expanding the chest. I did this twenty times, concentrating my focus on a red dot I had painted on the mirror. When I climbed into the red dot, the room went away and I was free to think about the girl and her problem. I went down every corridor I could open and came up empty. When I climbed out I heard Pansy snoring away, probably dreaming of a nice crunchy thigh bone. I left her where she was, locked the place up, and went downstairs to the garage.

The garage is actually the first floor of my building, with a sliding door opening into a narrow alley. The best part of it is that I can get to it from inside the building, so I can drive the car into the garage and then just disappear. Someone once followed me all the way to the garage when I was hurt and not paying attention. He just sat there and patiently waited for about six hours. The guy was a real professional. Devil (my old Doberman) took him just as he was making a deposit into an empty Coke bottle he carried with him. Turned out later he knew how to play the game—he never gave any information about me to the cops from his hospital bed. Just some tracker who should have done his work on the telephone.

I climbed into the Plymouth carefully. It can look like a lot of different cars, but I had last used it as a gypsy cab and it was still an ungodly mess inside. I lifted the steel plate next to the transmission hump, found the set screws, removed them, and took out the little five-shot Colt Cobra I keep there. Checked the cylinder, emptied the piece, and pocketed it. I thought it would be best to have a friend with me until I had a better idea of what this woman wanted. I screwed the car's floor back together, climbed out, and went back upstairs.

While I sat waiting for the mysterious lady to return, I went through my latest issue of *Hoofbeats*, daydreaming about the magnificent yearling I'd own someday. Maybe an Albatross colt out of a Bret Hanover mare, a lovely free-legged pacer eligible for all the big-stakes races. I'd name him Survivor, win a fortune, and be rich and respectable the rest of my natural life. I love animals—they don't do the things people do unless they absolutely have to, and even then it's never for fun. Sometimes I'd see the name of a yearling for sale in the magazine and I'd say his name softly to myself and feel like I used to feel in the institution when I was a kid—like I'd never have anything good. But that feeling never lasts.

People won't let you live the way you want to, but if you're strong enough or quick enough, at least you don't have to live the way they want you to. I live, though, no matter what.

The downstairs buzzer bit into my thoughts. I had my secretary answer and sure enough, it was the lady again. Even though I figured she was just coming up with my money, I went backstage and monitored her progress up to the door again. Force of habit.

She walked in wearing the same outfit, so she probably did go to a bank. If she'd gone home to pick up the cash, she would have changed her clothes, at least a little bit. Not all women are like that, I know, but this one seemed to be. The only difference was that the pale lipstick had been replaced with a heavy dark shade. She tossed a thick wad on my desk, wrapped in rubber bands. Just like the gangsters.

"I thought you'd rather have small bills," she said.

"The bank won't care," I replied. She gave me a crooked smile that told me maybe she didn't just select me at random. "Don't you want to count it?" she asked.

"That's all right; I'm sure it's all there." Holding it in my hand, I was sure it was. I took out a yellow legal pad, my imitation silver ballpoint, and began the interview. "Who are you looking for?"

"Martin Howard Wilson."

"Any a.k.a.'s?"

"What?"

"Also Known As . . . an alias, you know."

"Well, he used to be called Marty, if that's what you mean. And he calls himself the Cobra."

"The what?"

"The Cobra, like the snake."

"I know what a cobra is. That's his name?"

"It's not his name, it's what he calls himself."

"Does anyone else call him that?"

She laughed. "Not hardly," and she folded her hands across her knees again. I picked up the faint bluish tinge on the knuckles more clearly this time.

"What does this Cobra do?"

"A lot of things. He tells people he's a Vietnam veteran. He studies what he thinks is karate. He believes he's a professional soldier. And he rapes children."

"You seem to know a lot about him."

"I know everything I need to know about him except where he is."

"Got a last known address?"

"Yes, he was living in a furnished room on Eighth Avenue just off the northeast corner of Thirty-seventh Street."

"How long ago did he leave?"

"He left last night."

"How do you know?"

"Because I just missed him."

"Didn't you ask where he'd gone?"

Another short laugh. "The circumstances made that impossible, Mr. Burke."

"Can you be a little more specific?"

"I had to be forceful with the superintendent."

"A bit *more* specific . . . ?"

"He tried to put his hands on me and I kicked him."

"So?"

"I don't mean kick like *you* would mean it, Mr. Burke. He'll have to go to the hospital."

And then I remembered where I'd seen those bluish knuckles before—on the hands of the elderly kung fu instructor who had taught me how to breathe. "What style do you study?"

Her eyes went flat. "I study no style. For the last several years I have been my own teacher. Years before, many different styles. I don't have a black belt, I don't break boards, and I don't fight in gymnasiums."

Somehow, I already knew that. "You seem like you're more than capable of taking care of yourself, Miss . . ."

"Flood."

"Miss Flood. So what do you need me for?"

"Mr. Burke, I did not come to you for protection, but for information. I understand you have sources of information which would be closed to me. I am a person of honor. I need a service, and I am prepared to pay for that service."

"Look, I don't get it. No offense meant, okay? But the first time you come in here you talk like an Eighth Avenue hooker, and now you come on like Fu Manchu. I think you know some things you haven't told me. I think you think I know this Cobra you're looking for. I don't."

"Mr. Burke, I know you don't. But I know you run a service for fools and misfits who think they want to be mercenaries. I know you know the mercenary scene. This person has to leave the country now that he knows I am looking for him, and it would be right in character for him to try and go down the mercenary pipeline. But he's not mercenary material—he's a freak, a psychopath. And a stupid loser. So I thought maybe he'd turn up in one of your recruitment files and then I'd have him."

"And if he doesn't?"

"Then I've paid for a week of your time to find him out there," a short sweep of her arm indicating the streets outside.

"It could take a lot longer than that to find a guy like you're looking for. He could be anywhere."

Her eyes went cold when she looked at me and said, "I only have a week," but her mouth tightened just enough to show me the truth.

"You only have the grand, right?"

"You are very perceptive, Mr. Burke. I have only one thousand dollars, which I have already given you. It will take a long time for me to come up with that much money again."

"How come?"

"It's not important how come. It's not your business and it won't help you find this person for me."

I looked at her a long moment. Her face went flat again; she wouldn't make the same mistake with her mouth twice. She had lived someplace where an expressionless face was an asset, maybe the same place I lived when I was a kid. I asked her. "You ever do time?"

"Why do you ask?"

"I like to know what I'm working with."

"So do I, Mr. Burke. And I already satisfied myself about you before I came here. I'm hiring you to do a job, that's all. I know you've done a lot of jobs for a lot of people and never asked too many questions. I don't expect to be treated any differently because I'm a woman."

"That's not why I'm asking. It sounds like you're trying to find this guy so you can cancel his ticket, and I don't want to get involved with any number like that. This guy's not registered anyplace. I can't trace him on the phone or through the mail—I have to go in the street. I can't be that subtle about it. If I find him, and he turns up dead, people are going to be asking me questions. I can't answer some of them."

"There won't be any questions."

"I only have your word for that."

"I always keep my word, Mr. Burke."

"I don't know that either. How the hell *would* I know? Give me a name—give me someone to call who'll vouch for you."

"There's nobody in New York—nobody who would talk to you, anyway. You should know about people by now."

"Look, Miss Flood. I've seen some things. I've done some things. I'm not stupid but I'm no mind reader. You want a bloodhound, I've got to know what you want to do with the man after I turn him up."

Her white teeth against the heavy dark lipstick denied what might have been a smile. Very chilly. "What if I tell you that I only want to talk to him?"

"*Is* that what you're saying?"

She looked at me carefully, ran the first two fingers of her right hand softly against the underside of her squarish jaw, then cocked her head slightly to one side and looked at me some more. "No." She stood up. "May I have my money back, please? I don't believe we can do business."

She held out her hand, palm up. The other hand curled into

a tight fist, held just in front of her waist. With legs slightly spread, she shifted her weight below her hips. The gun was in the desk drawer—no contest. I put the money in her hand and she stepped backward, brought both her hands together, bowed slightly and stepped back again. She opened both hands and spread them in front of me, like she was asking for something. The money had disappeared. The office was quiet. I looked to my right, and saw Pansy on her feet—a low growl, almost like a purr, came from deep in her chest but she didn't move. I threw a switch on the desk and the door behind Flood locked with an audible *click*. Flood looked from the dog to me. I took out the pistol slowly and carefully and held it on the desk. I spoke softly, spacing the words.

"Listen to me. I am going to say something to the dog. It will *not* be an attack signal, no matter what it sounds like. Don't do anything stupid, because I'm not going to. Just listen to me, please. You can't do anything to me here. This is my place—I survive here. I am not trying to scare you or make you do anything foolish. I know you want to leave, and you're going to. I'm not your enemy. I just want you to understand that you can't come back. Don't be stupid, and don't get stupid ideas. When I say something to the dog, she'll lie down. Then I'll throw this switch, and the door will unlock. When I put the gun down on the desk, you open the door, go downstairs, leave here, and don't come back. Do you understand?"

She didn't change expression. "I understand."

I looked over at Pansy—the hair on the back of her neck was standing straight up. "Pansy, jump!" and she immediately hit the deck like she'd been crushed with a hydraulic press. I threw the switch and Flood could hear the door unlock behind her. I cocked the pistol and laid it gently on the desk, the barrel facing her. I looked at Flood and bowed my head slightly as she had done. Without a word, she turned her back and walked toward the door. The roll of her hips looked deadly, not friendly this time. She closed the door behind her softly without looking back.

She didn't make a sound going down the stairs, but the red light on the desk glowed to tell me she was three steps from the middle of the staircase. Then another glowed to tell me she was three steps from the bottom. There's a switch if I don't want the staircase to be there anymore, but I didn't put my hand near it. I heard the downstairs door open and close. That didn't mean anything. I went to my office door, opened it, and pointed out into the corridor. Pansy trotted out the door and over to the staircase. I went back to my desk and watched the light. It stayed on. Pansy was holding her front paws on that third step from the middle, like she was supposed to. I waited, heard Pansy's short bark of disappointment, and knew that Flood had actually left.

When I called Pansy she rolled back in the door, looking expectant. I went to the fridge again and got a big slab of steak. "You're a good girl, Pansy. Yes, you're a fine girl, a perfect friend, aren't you?" She happily agreed as I tossed the steak through the air at her, saying "Speak!" This piece was so big she actually chewed it for a second or two before making it disappear. The best things never last.

I went over to the couch Flood had occupied, took off my shoes, laid back against one of the pillows, and closed my eyes.

3

WHEN I WOKE up, it was already getting dark. Pansy was looking at me like she was dying to go out, but I knew that was an act. The dog has the metabolism of a diesel engine— she doesn't move fast but she can go for days and days without stopping. I let her out to the roof anyway, like I usually do at night. While she was upstairs, I set about putting together my props for the night's work. Miss Flood wasn't the only person of honor on this planet. When I bet that hundred with Maurice, I was really betting that she'd show with the money she'd promised. I won that bet, but I didn't expect to be as successful at Yonkers as I was at reading human character. And Maurice would want his money tomorrow. My heart doesn't run a heavy risk of stopping from overwork—I only use it for betting on horses.

Tonight there was a lovely three-year-old going in a C–3 pace who hadn't won all damn year. But he was a colt by Armbro Nesbit, who held the track record. I was there the night he set it. Usually, I have a tremendous bias in favor of horses who run off the pace and then come from behind in the stretch, like I'm always telling myself I'm going to do someday. But Armbro Nesbit always rocketed to the lead, dictated the fractions, and just dared the other animals to come at him. After his four-year-old season, his people put him out to stud, and he only got two crops before he died in his stall. A lot of asshole horseplayers laughed about how he must have died happy, but they don't know anything. He didn't die happy. The only way Armbro Nesbit would have died happy was on the front end of the mile, charging for home.

Anyway, this horse I bet on tonight was his son, and I wanted him to win. And I realized that I'd have to see Maurice in the morning if I wanted to keep that line of credit open.

When I got Pansy downstairs, I called Mama and learned that this James character hadn't called back. I went into the closet next door to dress since I needed to look good for the night's Murphy Game. I fingered my one silk shirt. I love that shirt—it's from Sulka's and it cost me a hundred and fifty dollars. The way it works with Sulka's is that you go in and order a dozen shirts, so they treat you like a citizen. But you have to know up front that they won't make you a dozen shirts until they get one that fits perfectly. So, when I had the money, I went up there and got fitted. The sample they made me up was this beautiful rose silk, with no pockets and french cuffs with my initials ("mb" for Mister Burke) on the left cuff. I paid for the one shirt (a class outfit, they didn't raise their eyebrows at cash), and told them I'd be back in a couple of days to pick out the rest of the colors I needed. I never went back, of course. But I couldn't wear that shirt for this game, so I found a nice blue oxford-cloth buttondown, a plain blue tie, and a dark blue pinstripe that fell off a rack in the garment district along with several others last year. All the department stores have my size—it's called "shrinkage." With my black brogans polished, I took an attache case from the closet floor and was ready to operate. I thought I'd stop by Mama's if I got the chance, so I told Pansy I'd bring her something good when I got back.

I went down the stairs to the garage, put the gun back next to the transmission hump—at least I knew where *this* Cobra was—and hung the suitcoat neatly in the back so it wouldn't wrinkle. I wanted to get to the Criminal Court before they started doing heavy business with the night arraignments.

It's lucky the court's not far from my office. I parked the car illegally in the back, put my PBA card that says "Attorney" on its embossed silver police shield on the dashboard, and flipped the switch in the glove compartment that would keep the car from moving even if some skell tried to steal it. Then I walked around to the front entrance, looking for Blumberg, Artuli or any of my regulars.

As I walked inside the marble-floored slime pit I spotted

Blumberg in his usual position. He was leaning up against the information booth that hasn't been occupied in years and trying not to look like what he is—a fat slob is what he is, but he isn't any worse than Legal Aid for night court. Blumberg won't try a case—but he'll plead you fast and, all things being equal, plead you pretty well. His doughy face arranged itself into a smile when he saw me. "So, Burke, how's the boy?"

"Got anything on tonight, Sam?"

"Well, my boy, I'm not sure. I did have this client call me and ask me to meet him here, but he didn't give a name. He said he would recognize me."

"From the front-page coverage of your last big trial, no doubt?"

"There's no profit in hostility, Burke. You want to work tonight?"

"That's why I'm here, Sam. The usual twenty-five percent?"

"Well, I'll tell you, son. There are guys working for twenty now, and there's one Spanish kid who works for ten, you know?"

"Yeah, I know. Listen, you want a yard in front, right? Okay, I'll get you the whole yard, no percentage, and I keep everything over that. How's that for a deal?"

"Burke, you're sure you're not Jewish? How about twenty-five percent up to two hundred, and a third after that?"

"Right. Look, I got to go to work. Try and at least *look* like a real lawyer for a couple hours, okay?"

He didn't answer and I went to work.

You have to know who to look for—that's always the game. Forget the hookers. They never have a dime anyway, and if they're not already in the pens waiting for arraignment, they're carrying some scumbag pimp's money to pay another girl's fines. And *real* poor people are a waste of time too, for obvious practical reasons. What you want is some lame who thinks a private lawyer is going to do more for him than Legal Aid— someone who thinks he's got an image, even if he was busted for stealing welfare checks. But the best is some parent whose kid has just been arrested. Tonight I couldn't wait for the best, just a fast hundred and out the door. Breaking my ass to get back to zero. The people inside the big building were all worried about getting a sentence—and here I was, already serving mine.

My first customers were a black couple—the man about

forty-five, still wearing work clothes, and his wife, dressed up her Pentecostal best. I stood there looking like one hell of a lawyer, but they didn't move. So I did. "Pardon me, sir, are you here for your son's arraignment tonight?"

"Yes—yes, I am. Are you the man from the Legal Aid?"

A slightly sardonic laugh, "No sir, you'll be able to recognize them easily enough. They'll be the kids wearing blue jeans with the long hair. Just pick out the first one you see who doesn't even *look* like a lawyer."

From the woman, "Oh my God. Harry, do you . . ." As I turned and acted like I was walking away to some important business, the man lightly touched my sleeve: "Sir, excuse me, are you a lawyer?"

"No, I'm a private investigator. I work for Mr. Blumberg. You know, *Sam* Blumberg,"—like the fat man's name should mean something to them. "I'm here tonight on a case with Mr. Blumberg, but I think his last motion to suppress was so effective that the charges will be dismissed, so I won't have anything else to do."

"We don't have a private lawyer. The police said that Henry would have Legal Aid—we didn't have to have one."

That, of course, made me angry, and I let it show. "What a racist pig! What a terrible thing to say to you folks."

"You mean it isn't true?" the mother asks.

"Well, it's true enough that your son will have Legal Aid *if* you don't retain private counsel. But what the cops were really saying is that you're probably on welfare and you couldn't afford a real attorney."

Harry said, "Man, I work. I got a *good* job. Had it for almost fifteen years. What kinda crap is this?"

"Well, sir, I can't speak for the police, but you know as well as I do that they'd rather have you go with the Legal Aid so they have a better chance of convicting your son."

"Yeah, that makes sense. Are there any private lawyers right here?"

"Well, Mr. Blumberg himself is here, on that case I told you about. If it doesn't go forward, I'm sure he could accommodate you."

"Is he expensive?"

"Well, sir, the best costs the most, as you know. But I also know that Mr. Blumberg is especially interested in young people, and what with you working and all, I'm sure something could be worked out. Of course, you'd have to have a retainer to pay him immediately so he could file a Notice of Appearance on your son's behalf."

Now the lady got back into the act. "How much would that be, mister?"

"Well, it generally runs about five hundred dollars, but Mr. Blumberg doesn't expect people to walk around with that kind of money, the way crime in the streets is today."

"Do you know how much he would take?"

"Well, I know he never takes less than two hundred, no matter what. But sometimes he's lucky and the whole case can be disposed of in a single evening."

Momma says, "Oh God, that would be wonderful. They been holding my boy in that jail ever since yesterday afternoon and—"

"Well, let me go and find Mr. Blumberg and I'll get back to you, all right?"

"Thank you, yes."

I was glad to accommodate them—they seemed like nice folks. Odds were that their kid would get held for the Grand Jury, and Blumberg would be filing his notice *For Arraignment Only*, but at least they'd have a private lawyer for their two bills. And it just might work out—who knew? This part of my work isn't really a scam—the people are getting what they paid for. Besides, when it comes to making a quick deal, Blumberg can hang in there with the best of them. He pleads so many cases that he knows what they're really worth, and he's not going to let a kid cop to some outrageous nonsense. Sam doesn't sit in on the games too long anymore, but he can still play a decent hand while he's there. Anything's better than some Legal Aid hippie who'll make some halfass speech about racism or "the system" while the judge doubles the bail.

I quickly found Sam, told him the deal, closed it, brought the good people to him, watched the money change hands, and went along with him to file his notice. I braced him in the hallway, took my fifty bucks, and went back to work.

I told the black couple they should wait inside the courtroom for their kid to be brought up because it would look good to the judge to see them so concerned, and I split. I'm not pleading good Samaritan, but it was an honest dodge. They'd get a fair shake from the fat man.

Business was great that evening. A bullshit burglary charge

that even Sam could get tossed was good for a yard and a half, fifty bucks from some character who kept mumbling about wanting a private lawyer so it wouldn't be like the "last time" and a great score of three hundred from a Puerto Rican whose brother had been held for four days on an attempted murder charge. Sam was in heaven, and I cleared $183. I told him to keep the breakage on the last third (the three-hundred score) and that gave him orgasms.

A couple of hours of intense work and I had Maurice covered plus a good piece of change for the next couple of days. As I walked up to my Plymouth, I saw a couple of uniformed cops leaning against it. They checked my clothes, nodded at the car. "You on the job?"

I smiled at them. "No, private," and they walked off in disgust. Nice guys.

4

I PUT THE key into the door, turned it twice right and once left to deactivate the alarm, and climbed inside. I just sat there for a minute; sometimes I go down to the garage and just sit in it, too. The car is a 1970 Plymouth that cost forty thousand dollars. It was supposed to be the ultimate New York City taxicab. It has independent rear suspension so even the West Side Highway doesn't shake it up; a forty-gallon gas tank, fuel injection so it doesn't stumble in traffic, a monster radiator with connecting tubes to cool the oil and transmission fluid so it can't overheat, never-fade disc brakes all around, bulletproof Lexan instead of glass in all the windows, and bumpers that would turn a charging rhino. It weighs about two and a half tons, so it doesn't get real good mileage, but when it was built that wasn't a consideration. The kid who put it together told me this was the seventh version—he just kept doing it until he got it right. The super-cab was going to make him rich—rich enough so that wife of his could have everything she ever wanted. In the meantime, they went without everything—the cab was hungrier than a dope addict. All the kid did was drive a fleet cab and work on his prototype.

I got into the car when the kid hired me to watch his wife. He had the idea she was seeing someone else, and he got my name from Mama Wong, where he used to eat during his late shift. He told me there probably wasn't anything to it, but he just wanted to be sure, you know. It didn't take me long to find out what his wife was doing. She had a girlfriend in the same apartment house. I watched and listened for a few days, but I didn't want to just go back and tell the kid his wife was making it with a woman—I figured there was more to the story.

I approached the wife one night while the kid was at work. I knew she always waited a couple of hours before she went upstairs to her girlfriend, so I just knocked on the door.

"Yes, who is it?"

"My name is Burke, ma'am. I'm here about your husband."

She flung open the door, quick as a shot. She was wearing an old bathrobe, but her face was all made up.

"What is it? What's happened? Is he . . . ?"

"Your husband's okay, Mrs. Jefko. I've been doing some work for him and I have to talk to you about it."

"Look, if it's about that damn car, you'll have to see him. I don't—"

"It's not actually about the car, ma'am. May I please come in for a minute?"

She looked me over carefully, shrugged, turned her back, and started walking toward the living room. I followed her but I walked past the entrance to the living room and sat down at the kitchen table. She fumbled for her cigarettes on top of the refrigerator and sat down facing me.

"Mrs. Jefko, I'm a private investigator. Your husband hired me to . . ."

"To fucking check on me, right? I knew he would. Marie said he would sooner or later."

"Not to check on you, ma'am. He knew you were unhappy, and he thought that maybe something was wrong with you, something medical maybe, that you weren't telling him about. He was concerned about you, that's all."

She started to laugh but she was out of practice. "Concerned about me. What a beautiful word—*concerned*. All he cares about is that fucking car and the millions and millions of dollars he's going to make with it someday."

"You know why he wants all that money, Mrs. Jefko?"

"No. I know why he *says* he wants the money. For me, right? What bullshit—he don't care about me any more than I care about that car. He never talks to me, never looks at what I wear, doesn't want to do nothing with me anymore. Marie says—"

"I know what Marie says."

"How could *you* know? You got the phone tapped or something?"

"No, but I know what a recruiting pitch sounds like."

"What're you talking about?"

"Marie understands you, right? Marie knows you're really a very sensitive person, with lots of undeveloped talent, right? Marie knows that you were meant for better things than sitting around this miserable apartment waiting for some grease monkey to come home. Marie knows your husband has all the sensitivity of a pig, right? He doesn't even know how to make love, right? Just fuck."

She just sat and looked at me. "Maybe all those things are true."

I looked back at her. "Maybe they are, I don't know. But I know that your husband loves you, that's for sure. I know he could be something, and that he wants you to be too. But he don't have a fighting chance against Marie, does he? He has to work."

"Marie works too."

"You know what I mean, Mrs. Jefko. This has got to end."

"You can't make me do anything—I have my own life—"

"I'm not telling you what to do—I'm saying this has to end. And you know it does too. Sooner or later your husband will find out—or you'll move out to be with Marie, or something. I just mean it won't go on like it has been."

I looked at her face and I saw that she hadn't been thinking that far ahead, although the odds were that Marie had. Then she asked me what she should do, and I said I didn't know. I told her the only reason I was there was that I didn't want to be the one to tell her husband, that I thought she could try again with him, maybe move to a different place. "Talk to someone, the two of you together. I don't know. But something."

"You don't look like Dear Abby."

"What do I look like?"

"You look like a nasty, cold man. And I think you should get out of my house."

I thought so too. There wasn't anything else I could say. I didn't have the right words, and she understood that. I went back downstairs and back to my office. When I saw the kid a few hours later, I told him that his wife wasn't involved with any other man as far as I could tell.

A couple of days later, he grabbed me outside of Mama Wong's. He told me his wife had told him the whole story, even about me being there. His eyes looked bad, and he wanted to go in two different directions. "Mr. Burke, I know why you went to see her. You should have told me yourself. You ain't no fucking marriage counselor. It's my problem, and I can handle it."

"All right, kid. I'm sorry."

"Yeah, you're sorry. You did it all wrong. You should have just told me."

"Look, kid—"

"Hey, fuck you, okay? How much I owe you for the last work?"

"Two hundred."

The kid looked at me, trying to make up his mind. He finally did. "Well, you can go scratch for that money, Burke. I ain't paying you. You didn't do your fucking job. How's that?"

"Okay, kid," I said, and just walked away. I knew he was staring after me but, like he said, I hadn't earned the money.

Mama Wong got a letter for me from the kid a few weeks later. As soon as I saw the return address, I knew what had happened. I went to see the kid in the Tombs, wearing my nice pinstripe with an attache case full of file folders and business cards in case the guards wanted proof I was a lawyer. But they didn't give a damn. They were holding the kid for homicide—his wife. He looked all right when they brought him down to the interview room, calm and relaxed, his hands full of documents. "Mr. Burke, my lawyer says I'm going to trial on this in a few weeks. I wanted to talk to you first."

"What can I do now?"

"Nobody can do nothing now. I did what I had to do, what I thought was right. Just like you did—just like she did. I just got to clear something up first. About my car."

"What about the car, kid?"

"I don't want the lawyer to have it, okay? He already got paid too much by my father. My father don't know any better—he wants me to cop to manslaughter or something, says I'll only get a few years. I don't want a few years."

"You want me to investigate . . . ?"

"I don't want you to do nothing, Mr. Burke. I understand a few things now. Not everything, but a few things—enough. I just want to get everything in order, make things right."

"What things?"

"Those things that are left. Nothing ever would have worked

out with Nancy anyway—I knew that, I guess. But if that scumbag lawyer gets my car . . ."

"What do you want, kid? I can't just—"

"Here's the title. I had my father send it over. I'm gonna sign it over to you. I owe you money anyway. Besides, you'll *use* the car, won't you? I mean, you'll have it on the street, in your work, right? I don't want them to sell my car at some lousy auction to pay that motherfucker."

"Look, you don't have to do this. You're a young guy still. You can do the time. I know—I've been inside. It's bad but it's not impossible. There's ways, things you can do. And then you can come out and finish the car."

"The car is finished, Mr. Burke. It's really been finished a long time, I guess. It never was the money, you understand?"

I do now, but I didn't then. So the kid signed the car over to me, and I went and got it registered. I even found a guy who would insure me—no problem, just minimum coverage. That car doesn't need collision insurance.

It wasn't hard to figure what the kid was going to do. I didn't say anything to anyone—he was a man and he was entitled to that much respect. Even the guards knew what was coming so they put him in a special cell, suicide-proof. It didn't stop the kid. After all, he was a mechanical genius, they said. He hung up a couple of days later. I heard his lawyer was asking questions about the car, but they only found another 1970 Plymouth that the kid was cannibalizing for parts. That was a few years ago. I used to think about the kid every time I drove the car. Then no more until tonight, for some reason.

5

I CRUISED SLOWLY over to Mama Wong's. That Flood broad was going to go about finding her Cobra the wrong way for sure. You can't find a freak by chasing him. You have to use the herd-spook technique and make him show himself. When I was in Africa, I noticed that a lot of the predators would size up a herd and then do something to make it stampede. They used different ways—wild dogs would charge like they were trying to bring down an antelope, and lions would just deliberately piss on the ground. It had the same effect—the antelopes would run like hell and the predators would just watch and wait. Soon you could see at least one of the antelopes couldn't run too good. Maybe it was too old, or too sick, or whatever. But after they saw that, the predators would all concentrate on that one beast, and it would be over soon. The best way to find a particular freak is to get them all moving around, out of their caves, so you can spot them easily. But she wouldn't know that, the dumb broad. She'd probably just go around and ask a lot of fool questions and maybe get herself blown away. Just because she took out some super who was trying to cop a feel from what he thought was a helpless girl didn't make her any certified freak-fighter in my book. She probably was in the can for a while, but she probably avoided the freaks like the plague, if she could. I didn't do that—I watched them. She may have been thinking she was going to a better place when she got out of the joint, but I knew better.

When I got to Mama's, she was at the front cash register like she always is. Like always, she didn't greet me. I just walked past her to the last booth in the back, ordered some duck and fried rice and waited.

She came back after about a half hour and sat down herself. Then she said something in Chinese to the waiter who had appeared a split-second after her. He left and came right back with a large tureen of hot-and-sour soup and two bowls.

"Burke, you eat some of this soup. Very good. Make you feel better quick."

"I feel fine, Mama. I don't want any of that soup."

"You eat soup, Burke. Too much here for just one. Better for you than duck." She filled the bowl and passed it to me. "Chinese way, serve man first always." I smiled at her. She kept stirring soup in the tureen, looked up, smiled back and said, "Not all Chinese ways so good."

The soup was rich and clean at the same time. I felt my nasal passages opening up just putting it near my face. Mama's eyes swept the room, better than any electronic device. She lived in fear of being discovered by tourists and having enough diners in her joint to ruin her business. I was there the night she got an advance tip that the restaurant critic from *New York* magazine was coming. They gave the guy and his date some stuff that was damn close to rancid dogmeat served in embalming-fluid sauce. But she was still scared the clown would like the ambiance of her dump and tell all the Now and Today jerkoffs to come around, so I made a gross pass at the critic's date while he was in the men's room fending off one of Mama's boys, who was acting like he was drunk and needed to throw up—preferably on a human being. Mama was still screaming at me in Mandarin for being so obnoxious to the guy's date when he returned to the table, so I called him a faggot and attempted to belt him. I missed, and fell right across the table instead. We all watched the reviews carefully for weeks, and were relieved to see no mention of Mama's establishment.

I separated a hundred from my courthouse earnings and handed it to Mama. "Mama, please hold this for me. If I call tomorrow, please have Max carry this over to Maurice, okay? If for some reason I don't call," (she started to smile sadly) "hang on to it for me."

Max is one of her relatives. At least I think he is. Max can't hear or speak, but he communicates okay. He wasn't programmed for fear—whoever rolled the genetic dice left that out too. If Mama asked Max to deliver a package to the Devil,

Max would go straight to Hell. Unlike others of my acquaintance who had made that particular trip, I had complete confidence that Max would come back. Max the Silent is one tough boy. In fact, he's so infamous that one time over in night court when he was being arraigned for attempted murder, nobody even laughed when the judge told him that he had the right to remain silent. They all knew that Max never *attempted* to murder anyone.

Mama pulled a scrap of paper from her dress. "This man James call you again, Burke. He leave a number, but he say you only call him tomorrow evening between six and six-thirty. He say he very busy and be out of his office except for then, okay?"

I looked at the number she gave me. I'd have to check it against my list, but the odds were a hundred to one it was a pay phone.

"Maybe you not call him, okay, Burke? He sound on the phone like I tell you. Bad man, okay?"

"We'll see, Mama. I have to work for a living, right? Business hasn't been so good lately. You got a marrow bone for my puppy?"

"Must be big puppy, Burke." Mama laughed. She hadn't met Pansy but she knew my Doberman pretty well.

"Yeah, she's pretty big."

"Burke, if this man who called you has a dog, I know what kind of dog he has."

"What are you talking about, Mama?"

"Burke, I tell you. This man have the dog with the dark color back, you know?"

"No, I don't. How could you know what kind of dog he'd have?"

"I don't say he has dog, but if he has dog, it will be this kind."

I took the marrow bone for Pansy and said good-bye to Mama. With the car back in the garage, I went upstairs and let Pansy out to the roof again. The marrow bone went into a pot of boiling water to make it okay for her to eat.

Sure enough, when I checked the list of numbers I got from the phone company through an indirect route, James's number turned out to be a coinbox over on Sixth Avenue, near Thirty-fourth Street. If I remembered correctly, it was right across from the Metro Hotel.

Pansy and I watched television while we waited for the marrow bone to boil out perfectly. When it did, I cleaned it off, gave it to her, and waited for the first satisfying *crack* before I sacked out on the couch.

6

THE SOUND OF distant thunder woke me—it was Pansy slamming her paw against the back door to tell me she wanted to go to the roof. I got up, opened the door, and went next door to fix breakfast from the food I took home from Mama's.

When everything was on the hotplate, I threw on a jacket and went downstairs for the *News*. My watch said it was about eleven in the morning, so even the thief who runs the corner store would have the four-star edition by now. He does make good egg creams, and I thought I'd treat myself with some of last night's legal fees, so I sat down at the counter and waited for the proprietor. Since I was going to buy the *News*, I took the *Post* off the rack to read through it.

Some kids in the back were hanging around the ancient jukebox, imitating the latest *Godfather* movie. At least they weren't trying to imitate Bruce Lee, like the kids a few blocks east of here. Their conversation drifted over.

"She's got some beautiful body, you know, but her face's ugly as shit."

"Man, you don't fuck her *face*."

The third one added his sage comment. "Hey, where are you from, lame? Kansas?"

Even if I woke up some morning as totally disoriented as the hippies who live downstairs from me, I'd still only have to stagger as far as the corner to know I was in New York. I put back the *Post*, paid for the *News*, collected a sour glance from the owner of the dump, and went back upstairs. My

Chinese food was just about ready. I'm a real gourmet—I know you have to burn pork to make it safe to eat.

Usually when I'm here in the mornings I read the race results to Pansy so I can explain why my horse didn't do as well as expected. So today I called her over and fed her some extra pork scraps while I checked last night's charts. I never read my horse's race first—I start with the first race and work my way down. The seventh was the feature at Yonkers, and my horse won. The goddamned horse won, and the sonofabitch paid $21.40 to do it. I checked the horse's name, checked his position and . . . yeah, it was number three for certain. I was over a grand to the good—damn! I wanted to sit back and read the charts again and again, to retrace my horse's path to victory as slowly as I could. But I knew it was too good to be true— something had to be wrong.

So I bit the bullet and called Maurice, using the hippies' phone. When he told me some reason why my horse wasn't the one that won, I was just going to tell him I'd have Max deliver his money later that day. I'm a good loser—practice makes perfect.

"Maurice, this is Burke."

"Burke, I thought you died—I figured you'd be on the fucking phone as soon as I opened this morning. You got someone else picking 'em for you now?" And I knew I really had won.

"Oh, yeah," I said casually, as though my last big winner was last week instead of three years ago. "Look, Maurice, can you hold on to it for me until later this afternoon?"

"What'd you think, dummy, I'm gonna leave town with this big score?"

"No, I just—"

"I'll be here," says Maurice, and hangs up. What a charmer.

I went back and sat down at the table and read the charts to Pansy until she was bored to tears. My horse just wired the field—he left from the three-hole, got to the top with a 28.4 quarter, kept the pressure on to a 59.3 half, coasted the third quarter in 1.31 flat, and got home handily by a length and a half in 200.4. His best race ever, a lifetime mark—his father would have been proud. It was like the Flood broad had never taken her money back.

For some reason, it took me a long time to get dressed that morning. I put on a suit, got out my overcoat with all the extra pockets in it, and put in my little tape recorder and the clip-on thing for my shirt pocket that looks like the top of a ballpoint pen—when you flick it to the side, about six feet of car antenna comes out like a steel whip. It's only good for people who like to work with knives, and the people I was going to see only worked with guns, but I didn't think it would be a straight path to them. Anyway, I planned to be on the street when I called this Mr. James.

I fixed Pansy up with extra water and left her some dry food in the washtub she uses for a dinner bowl. Then I went down to the garage, got the gun out of its usual place, emptied it, and replaced the slugs with some hollow points that an associate had thoughtfully filled with mercury. Next I dug out the long-barreled Ruger .22 automatic. It holds nine shots, counting the chamber—I put in four filled with birdshot, two mini-flares, and two teargas capsules. Perfect for a roomful of people and no good for much else. The .22 went inside the door panel on the driver's side and the .38 went back where it belonged. I pulled out. The gas gauge said I had half a tank, which meant more than twenty gallons. The garage is always heated so I don't worry about it not starting when it gets low. I'd fill up later when I got my money from Maurice.

Every time I get a little ahead I always buy some clothes, give Mama some money to hold as credit for Maurice and other emergencies, and give the car whatever it needs at the time. A couple of weeks ago I had to go into my stash at Mama's because there was an epidemic of a lethal dog disease called Parvo virus going around. The vaccine was in short supply and I had to go for seventy-five bucks just for two ready-to-inject needles from this vet I know. I always give Pansy her shots myself—the needles don't bother her, but strangers do.

I drove down by the Hudson on West Street near the docks, under what would be the West Side Highway if construction ever got down this far. I cruised over to one of the piers, backed the car in so I was facing the street, and waited. The Plymouth looked enough like the law to keep the locals away for a while, but it wouldn't last. I just sat there, playing the radio softly and smoking. You can't be in a hurry working down here— you have to settle in. One of them finally approached, slowly. She was of medium height and had ridiculously high spike heels topped by black pencil-leg pants, a wide belt to emphasize the narrow waist, a quasi-silk blouse and a shoulder-length red wig. Skinny and pale, even though she worked out here in the sun. A veteran, she walked carefully through the rubble without once tripping on the high heels. She approached the Plymouth. "Hi. Looking for a party?"

"No, I'm waiting for a friend."

"Anybody I know, baby?"

"I hope so. I'm looking for Michelle."

"I don't know any Michelle, sweetheart. But whatever she can do, I can do."

"I'm sure that's true—but it's Michelle I need to talk to."

"Let me see your badge first, baby."

"I'm not the heat. I'm a friend of Michelle's."

"Baby, Michelle don't work anymore."

"That's too bad."

"I'd love to stand around talking to you, baby. But if you don't want to party, I've got to run along, okay?"

"Whatever you say. But tell Michelle that Burke's looking for her—tell her I'm right here."

She turned and wiggled away to show me what I'd missed by opting for Michelle's brand of party, but at least she wasn't aggressive about it.

I sat and waited. Two men walked by, one guy's hand on the neck of the other, and ducked into one of the abandoned buildings on the pier. I'd gone into one of those once, at night, looking for a runaway kid. I didn't find him. I wouldn't go back in there again without Pansy.

About an hour later, I saw her starting to walk over this way again. I eased the .22 out of the door pocket and held it down against the floor with my left hand. She took her time about getting over to me. I didn't move, didn't turn the radio down. I wanted a smoke, but didn't reach for one.

"Remember me, baby?"

"Yes."

"I heard Michelle was going to be down on Pier Forty in a few minutes. Now I don't know if this is straight or not, you know. But I just heard it, you understand?"

"Thank you. I appreciate you coming over to give me the message."

"It's not a message, baby. It's just something I heard, okay?"

"Whatever you say."

She just stood there by the car. I slowly reached out to the dashboard for my cigarettes. Held out the pack to her. She took one and moved closer for me to light it for her. "I heard something else, baby."

"And what's that?"

"I heard that sometimes, if a working girl had troubles with her man, that you'd talk to her man for her."

"You hear that from Michelle?"

"Michelle don't have no man. You know that."

"Yes, I know. So?"

"I do."

"Yeah?"

"And I just heard that sometimes you'd talk to a girl's man if there was a problem."

"You've got to be more specific."

"My man's black."

Not a muscle shifted in my face as she studied it carefully. "So?"

"That doesn't mean anything to you?"

"Should it?"

"There's pressure on now. There's some people moving into things. People who hate niggers."

"Moving into what?"

"Into the Square. With kiddie stuff—pictures, films, like that."

"And?"

"I already said enough—maybe it wouldn't work anyway, it's just stuff I heard. Look, I just did you a favor, right?"

"If Michelle's on Forty, you did."

"She'll be there, baby. I just did you a favor. If I needed one back, could I call you?"

I looked at her, trying to see the face behind the makeup, trying to see the skull behind the face. The sun was in her eyes, bouncing off the dark glasses she wore. I couldn't see anything. Her hands were shaking some.

"You can call me at this number, anytime between ten in the morning and midnight," I said, telling her Mama's pay phone. She didn't say a word, just moved her lips several times memorizing the number. Then she walked away again, without the exaggerated wiggle this time. I started the engine, let it idle a minute, tossed the smoke out the window (you can't use the ashtrays in this car), and took off for Pier Forty.

I spotted Michelle as soon as I pulled up. She was wearing a big floppy white hat, like you'd see in a plantation movie.

It should have looked stupid with the blue jeans and a sweat shirt with some jerko designer's name on it, but it didn't. Before I turned off the engine she was already walking over to me. She jumped in on the passenger side, slammed the door behind her, leaned over to whip a quick kiss on my cheek, and draped herself back against the door. "Hi, Burke."

"What's happening, Michelle?"

"The usual, darling. The bloody usual. It's getting harder and harder for an honest person to make a living in this town."

"I've heard that. Listen, Michelle, I need some information about a guy who's holed up somewhere near here. A stone freak, maybe a baby raper."

Michelle looked over at me, giggled, said, "I'm your man," and giggled some more. She's not too concerned anymore about being what she is, says even the truckdrivers who pay her for some fast work with her mouth know she's not a woman. She says they like it better that way—who knows?

"All I know about this guy is his name, Martin Howard Wilson. He calls himself the Cobra."

Michelle cracked up. "The Cobra! Jesus have mercy—he's not a snake-fucker, is he?"

"I don't know, what's a snake-fucker?"

"You know, Burke, the kind of guy who'd fuck a bush if he thought there might be a snake in it."

"No, that's not our boy. I don't really know too much about him—no description, just the name and the nickname. But I thought you might have heard the name yourself—maybe have something for me."

"Darling, I have never heard of this particular freak, believe me—but that doesn't mean I won't. But I'd have to hear it long distance, you know? The cesspool is even more slimy than usual, if you can believe that. It's no place for a sweet young thing like me, honey. There's people working the place now that make even the freaks look good."

"I just heard something like that from your friend."

"You mean Margot? She's a trip, all right. Comes out here every day and turns down tricks. Can you believe it? Her man's elevator must not go to the top floor. She's smart, though—went to college and all. She's one of the few girls out here I consider my intellectual equal, honey."

"Does she know what she's talking about?"

"If you mean about some new scum moving into Times Square, she sure does, baby."

"Any idea why?"

"Yes, darling. There are people who are into sordid things who are not just businessmen—people who just don't know how to act, if you catch my drift."

"Margot said they hate niggers."

"That's part of it, I guess. There's only a few of them now, and they're Americans. But they all play like they're foreigners."

"From where?"

"Think of a country even more vicious to people like me than this one, baby. Think of a country where half the freaks in *this* country dream of going someday."

"Michelle, come on. Geography isn't my strong point."

"Maybe crime is your strong point—think of a country where they use capital punishment like we use fucking probation."

"South Africa?"

"Give the man a gold star or a quick blowjob, whichever you'd prefer," and Michelle went back to giggling.

"How do you know it's South Africa?"

"Baby, I don't know. It may be Rhodesia, or whatever they're calling it today, or something like that. But it's white men, with this African-soldier rap."

And I thought of Mama Wong, and the dog with the dark colored spine—a Rhodesian Ridgeback, the kind they breed for tracking down runaway slaves. They can even climb trees. Not supposed to be good pets, but some folks are crazy about them. Michelle saw I was trying to catch the tip of a thought and run it down. She kept quiet, smoking. I thought about all the conversations in the yard when I was inside. The guys with the short bits dreamed about parole—the guys with the telephone-number sentences only thought about escape. And the warrior whites, the neo-Nazis, the cons with race war on their minds at all times . . . they always talked about Rhodesia like it was the Promised Land. Where they could be themselves.

"Michelle, what do they want?"

"Honey, God only knows, and *She's* not telling. But they're here and making a lot of trouble for some people."

"What kind of trouble?"

"I can't tell you. I don't get up there much anymore. I just hear it around that they're bad people to deal with, that they don't know how to play the game, you understand?" I just sat there, looking out the windshield to the street. Michelle looked over at me. "You got some more questions, honey, or did you change your mind about the kiss of life?"

"One more question. Will you ask around about this freak I told you about?"

"Anything you say, Burke. Is there any money in this? I still want to visit Denmark and come back a blonde." The giggle again.

"I honestly don't know, Michelle, but there might be. I can give you this twenty on account," and gave her a piece of last night's cash.

More giggling. "On account of what?"

I touched my forehead in a half-salute and she slithered out of the car.

I didn't know which Michelle needed more . . . an operation on her plumbing or her head, but it didn't matter to me. Maybe the guys who paid her twenty-five bucks for a car trick weren't exactly sure what they were buying, but I was. Her gender might be a mystery, but in my world, it's not who you are, it's how you stand up.

7

I FIRED UP the engine. The Plymouth rolled away from the
pier and headed north as surely as though it had a radar cone
dialed to *Sleaze* in its nose. I stayed as close to the river as I
could on my way uptown, looking for someone I knew. Most
of the street signs have long since disappeared once you get
into the West Thirties, but I didn't need them. I stopped for a
red light beneath the underpass and made eye contact with a
youngish guy wearing an army raincoat and black beret. He
walked carefully toward the car, trying for a smile out of his
bloated face. I kept looking at him, didn't move. He opened
the raincoat to display what looked like a scabbard with a long
handle at the top and looked up at me to see if I was still
watching. When he saw that I was, he pulled the handle up to
show me part of a gleaming machete blade. Then he put the
blade back into the scabbard, closed the coat, tried for a smile
again, and held up his open right hand. Flashed it open and
closed three times to show me he wanted fifteen bucks for the
blade, raising his eyebrows to see if I wanted to buy or to
bargain. I reached in my pocket and held up a gold shield—
if you got close enough to read it, you'd see it said I was an
official peace officer for the ASPCA. He didn't get any closer
but he didn't run either. Just stepped backward a few feet until
he disappeared. Like I said, I don't need the signposts.

I drove slowly up and down the back streets in the West
Forties until I found what I was looking for—a parking place,
complete with attendant. The muscular black kid hardly looked
up when I parked, didn't move when I walked over to him. It

wasn't even dark yet and he didn't have to work for a couple of hours. He was already dressed for work in green leather sneakers with bright yellow soles and gold suede stripes, dull green slacks topped off with a broad-banded green-and-gold short-sleeved T-shirt and green knitted tam with a big yellow button. Heavy leather bands studded with brass were on each wrist. He flexed his biceps when I first approached, but switched to flexing his leg muscles when I looked too much like a cop to suit him.

I took out a twenty, finally catching his full attention, and carefully tore it in half. I held out half the bill to him. "I don't want anyone to bother my car for a couple of hours, okay?" He took the bill, gave me a quick look, nodded his head. I smiled to tell him there was nothing worth more than twenty bucks in the car, kept smiling at him until he realized I was memorizing his face, and walked off down the block. I didn't look back—a survivor works with what he's got. This was costing me a lot of cash already, but I figured there was still a thousand-dollar pot of gold at the end of the rainbow.

Without a description, I didn't expect to run into the Cobra on the street, but I knew enough to check certain places first. Once before I was working on a locate and the target was a porno freak, so I dropped into a joint in the Village where I knew the owner. The place was called Leather Pleasure, and the owner was the prime mover in some kind of society where they get together for coffee and consensual torture. I told him my subject was addicted to porn, and the owner told me he ran a specialty house that didn't cater to the general trade. When I asked him what he was talking about he launched into a long-winded explanation that began somewhere with the Roman Empire, touched on his unique brand of nationalism— "The Germans don't understand the creativity in pain, they don't understand that you have to give to get. Only the British genuinely conceptualize human relationships"—and ended up with a generous splat of snobbery. "If you just want *porn*, you know, like dirty pictures and all that, my friend, you must go to Times Square. Down here, each shop has its own unique character, its own personality, if you will. A client will know he's in the wrong place in a minute should he come in here without the proper attitude." Funny place—the owner was this pleasant guy who sounded like a college professor and his merchandise was full of all this violence.

All the porn houses looked about the same from the outside. Only the joints that featured live human beings did any promotion, and they promised anything the mind could dredge up for ten bucks. But the magazine and photo joints just had windows that were painted over or boarded up or were solid-faced storefronts, with the usual menu on the outside—"Bondage, Discipline, Animal Love, Lesbian Love, Latest from Denmark."

Nothing on the covers of these dumps indicated kiddie porn on the inside. I went into the first door I came to, checked the fat guy sitting at a register by the opening, and saw row after row of sterile-looking aisles. Magazines and books, all in plastic shrink-wrap, were neatly arranged according to topic—a sort of Dewey Decimal System of Dirt. But there was no kiddie stuff. I kept walking up and down the aisles, occasionally taking a magazine off the shelves, glancing at the front and back cover, putting it back. It was a good place to work, actually, since all of the other five customers studiously looked down. No eye contact—big surprise. I made two circuits before I found the back section marked *Adults Only*. Maybe the boss had a sense of irony—it had nothing but pictures of kids, books about kids, and magazines with kids. Nice stuff—everything from naked kids romping in the sun to a little boy with his hands and legs hog-tied behind him being double-sodomized.

There was just one guy in this section. Nicely dressed, he had a three-piece suit, polished shoes, briefcase. Wandered from shelf to shelf like he was in a daze, not touching anything. Not my man, I could tell. Over to the left, still further back, were some booths with doors on them marked "Private Reading Area. See Attendant for Key." I knew what the private areas looked like—all plastic and vinyl so the Lysol wouldn't stick to fabric when they prepared for the next customer.

As I walked past the attendant, I pulled my coat open with both hands to show I wasn't glomming any of his merchandise. He gave me a quick glance and went back to whatever he was doing. I thought a moment and decided on the direct approach. No use flashing a phony badge down here. Half the quasi-cops (like the Civilian Patrol, or the characters that carry PBA cards like they're members of a secret society, or the lames who send away to magazines for their International Organization of Private Investigators credentials) in the city hang out down here.

I also know there aren't too many independent operators left in the Pit.

After I loomed over the guy at the desk for a minute or so, he looked up. "I don't want to waste your time," I said. "I'm a private investigator looking for a young woman who's got to be down here. If you can help me, I'll make it worth your while."

"Look, pal. A lot of women come down here—you'd be surprised. I don't take no notice. I just do my job."

"The boss would want you to do this one, friend."

"Huh?"

"Look, she's a member of one of those wacko organizations that want to close down these dens of sin, you understand?"

"So? We get *them* in here all the time too—on tours or something. Don't mean nothing."

"This broad means business, my friend. She just got out of Mattawan for throwing a firebomb into one of these places—killed a guy. She said Jesus told her to do it. Remember, it was on Forty-fourth, about two years ago?"

He looked at me, mentally plodding through his file of potential dangers to himself. Balanced the odds. "So?"

"So Carlo gave me this job, told me to find her and take care of her before she blows up one of his joints, right?"

"So?"

"So I was promised cooperation from your boss, you understand?"

"My boss ain't named Carlo."

"Look, I'm trying to be reasonable. I thought I was dealing with an intelligent guy." I imitated his squeaky voice: "My boss ain't named Carlo!" His head shot up. I said, "You asshole— I mean your fucking *boss,* not the flunky who tells you when to open this dump—understand *now*?"

He looked around behind him like something was gaining on him. Then he glanced quickly over at the pay phone in the corner. I played out the string. "Look, pick up the phone, call your boss, and tell him Tony's here to do a job for Carlo. You think you can maybe do that without getting confused?"

He looked at me again, trying to make up what some un-informed person might call his mind. I said, "Look, go ahead and call, I'll watch the jerkoff artists for you," and got his attention again as I pulled the .38 partway out of the underarm holster.

He rubbed the side of his head. "If you're from downtown, what's my name?" I looked into his eyes, seeing fear. He looked into mine and saw what he expected. I trotted out my whisper-of-the-grave voice. "Don't make yourself more important than you are."

We looked at each other. He blinked, wiped his forehead with a dirty sleeve. I opened the front door slightly as though to throw my cigarette butt into the street, at the same time making a quick gesture with my hand that he cleverly picked up with his sensitive vision. He decided. "You said there was something in it for me?"

"That's what I said."

"A cunt came in here maybe an hour ago—short blonde cunt. Asked me a lotta stupid questions about the kiddie shows over on Eighth. I thought she was comin' on to me, you know? I said something to her and she fucking sapped me—right in the fucking face. I think she broke a tooth or something—hurts like a motherfucker."

"She hit you with a sap?"

"I didn't see it, but it must of been a sap. Didn't even see her fucking hand move."

"Yeah, she sounds like the one, all right. You did the right thing, not trying to stop her—probably carrying one of those firebombs right in her purse."

He looked gratefully at me. "Yeah, I figured she was carrying something, you know? What a sicko bitch."

"You see where she went?"

"No, man. She just zipped out the door."

"You call downtown?"

"Uh . . . no, man. I mean, I figured . . . she was just another sicko, like I said. I didn't know anyone gave a shit."

"Yeah, you did right. Okay."

"You said there was something in it for me?"

"Yeah, I got something for you." Against my better instincts, I reached in my pocket for a pair of twenties, folded the two bills, and stuffed them in the pocket of his knit shirt. He tried to display some class, but he had his hand in his pocket almost before I was out the door.

Back on the bricks I moved away quickly before he got the idea of making a phone call and picking up some congratulations for his cooperation. Flood *was* around. I knew she'd be down here—all guts and no brains—with a lousy interrogation technique and a worse temper. No surprises so far.

But where would she go next? Even someone like Flood would know better than to think she could just slap and kick her way down Forty-second Street until she got some answers. If I stayed on the trail long enough, I'd have to come up with some myself.

I had been walking aimlessly until I looked up and saw I was headed toward the Port Authority Building. Flood wouldn't be there. Plenty of freaks, all right, but not the kind she was looking for. I kept walking—past the whores, the winos, the stud-hustlers, the dope peddlers and the rough-off artists, past narrow alleys. Nothing. I checked faces, looking for whatever—cold neon lights flashing off dead eyes, lost kids, dirtbags looking for lost kids to turn a profit, Jesus freaks, bag ladies, bored cops. Nothing.

Then I spotted a huge Spanish-looking kid sitting on a milk crate at the mouth of an alley, giant transistor radio held next to his head so close it looked like it was growing out of his ear. He was singing to himself. Other street kids walked by in front of me, checked out the Spanish kid, looked over his shoulder into the alley, and kept rolling fast. Something smelled. I walked by too, glancing over his shoulder, and saw a flash of white in the alley, no sound. Too many people around to take the kid out of the play—and I didn't want him behind me if I went past. No time. Past the kid, I turned into the first door, a topless club next to the alley. It was dimly lit, blue smoke inside, disco music, no conversations. Sluggo braces me at the door: "Ten dollars cover charge." Wonderful. Probably took him a week to memorize the words. I threw ten bucks at him and went past, checked out the topless dancers with their sagging bodies and dead brains, and walked the length of the bar. I kept moving like I was looking for a good seat.

Nobody was paying attention. I headed toward the back, my sense of direction distorted by all the twists and turns in the place. Found the door to the men's room and walked in— a guy in a red leisure suit and white shoes was throwing up in the sink. I went past him. No windows. Nothing there. Back out the door, looking for the kitchen. I found a door with No Admittance in red letters, pushed gently, and it yielded. I shoved it open and walked inside like I knew where I was going. The cook looked up from a slab of metal that was once a stove and yelled "Hey!", but I was already past him and up to the back door. It was bolted in three places from the inside. I shot the bolts back, stepped into the alley, and looked to my right where the Spanish kid was still sitting on his milk crate, now with his back to me. The bolts slammed home behind me and high, thin laughter came from my left along with the sound of shoes scraping on gravel. I moved in that direction, slowly now.

I turned the corner carefully and saw four of them frozen, waiting—one kid with a big afro who looked Spanish waving a length of bicycle chain, a smaller one holding an open stiletto, another one just standing . . . and Flood. She was backed against the alley wall, one foot bent in front of the other, one hand a fist, the other stiffened to chop. A door sagged open behind the kids—a basement? Flood stood like a block of marble, breathing quietly through her nose. Her purse, closed, lay on the ground between them. The one with the knife moved forward, swiped underhand at Flood, and grabbed for the purse. Flood stepped back as if she were retreating, spun on her back foot, whirled all the way around, and fired a kick from the same leg at the kid's face. He jumped back just in time. The purse stayed.

The kid with the big afro said, "Come on, mama—ain't no way you gonna keep that bag. Just give it up and get outta here." Flood opened her hands and motioned the kid forward like a prizefighter showing his opponent that the last punch didn't hurt. The kid with the afro faked an advance and immediately jumped back. The kid without the weapon laughed, all the time moving more and more to Flood's left. The kid with the afro was shrill now. "Fuckin' *puta,* fuckin' pig. You ask too many questions, *blanco* bitch." Flood moved at him and he backed away. The kid with the knife started to move to her right, but he was clumsy and she cut him off, getting even further away from the third one.

The spokesman for the pack stopped trying to be polite. "Fuckin' bitch. We take that purse and we take you in the back and we stick a broomstick up your fat ass. You like that, you cunt?" Flood's lips pulled back from her teeth and a hissing sound came out of her. She faked a move forward, spun and lashed out with her left foot at the kid without a weapon, kept spinning and shoved her purse behind her with the same move, then whipped her arms back across her chest down to her sides, and they were back in the same positions as when I first came on the scene.

They all stood frozen—maybe a minute, maybe more. Then the one with the knife tried to circle Flood on her right, moving so that his back was to me. I held the .38 tightly in my right hand, moved in close behind him, and punched him in the kidneys with the barrel. He went down with a nasty grunt. They all turned in my direction. I kicked the kid who was down in the back of the head with my steel-toed dress shoes, stepped around him holding the piece way out in front of me for the others to see. They backed toward the alley wall where I motioned for them to stand together. I cocked the gun so they could see that too and put it about a foot in front of the afro's face. "You know what this is?"

He was quiet now, but his pal knew when to speak. "Yeah, man, we know what it is. We didn't mean nothing." Sure. I backed away to give them room to move.

"Get back in there," I said, motioning toward the open door. They didn't move. Frozen, they were looking past me. I turned slightly and saw Flood had picked up the knife. She was kneeling over the kid on the ground, one fist full of his genitals and the other holding the blade poised to slice.

"Do it," she said, and they both ran to the open door.

I was right behind them. "Turn around and put your hands on top of your heads," I said. "Now!" They did. Flood dragged the knifeman over and flung him inside like he was a light sack of garbage. I told the other two to get inside, and the silent one moved into the doorway. The afro froze. My nose told me he had wet himself. I just touched him with the piece and he followed his friend. I went next, with Flood right behind me.

We were in a cellar room with a cot in one corner, a radio playing—it was too dark to see anything else. "Get on the floor," I told the two who could still move. The other one lay where Flood had thrown him. With the .38 in my left hand, I pulled the .22 from my coat and aimed it at all three of them lying there. It wouldn't kill anyone, but they didn't know that. Neither did Flood. Then I started pulling the trigger as fast as I could.

One of them was screaming even before I emptied the piece. Between the bird shot and the flares and the teargas, the room turned into the hell they permanently deserved—for a few minutes anyway. I slammed the door on my way out and charged down the alley, Flood at my side. The .22 didn't make much noise, especially with those special loads, and it was all inside, but the kid on the milk crate must have known something was wrong. As we came down the mouth of the alley he was carefully putting down his radio before he went to investigate. Flood's flying dropkick caught him in the ribs—I could actually hear the crack. He slammed into the wall, Flood hit the ground, rolled in one motion, and came to her feet. We ran across the street together. There was some crowd noise behind us where the radioman had fallen, but it was probably someone trying to steal the radio and fighting someone else for the privilege. We turned the corner and headed for the car. I wanted to ditch the guns, but they'd be hard to replace. Besides, every window had a watcher—to see if one of the fish in this cesspool went belly-up.

I was out of breath, a stabbing pain in my chest and cramps in my legs—two more blocks to go. Flood wasn't even breathing deeply.

The black kid with the T-shirt was sitting on the hood of my car. I took out my half of the twenty and held it out with my left hand. He looked at me, looked at the twenty, looked at Flood. "Seems like I should be getting a bit more, somehow." He smiled at me. I was running on empty by then, reached for the .38, and cocked it in his face, my hand shaking. "You want some more?" He held up his hands like a robbery victim and started to back away. I watched him for a second, glanced over at the car, and he broke into a run. I opened the driver's door and Flood jumped in ahead of me, sliding over to her side. I had the car rolling into a fast, quiet U-turn before I had the door closed. I headed back toward the river. Checked the mirror—no pursuit. We rolled north, heading for Harlem on the West Side Drive, exited at Ninety-sixth Street, hooked Riverside south to Seventy-ninth, then went crosstown to the FDR. I didn't relax until we got deep downtown, heading for the Brooklyn Bridge.

Flood was breathing deeply through her nose, sucking the air in and holding it for a long count like I do when I'm trying to relax. With her, it was like watching a battery recharge.

8

I DIDN'T LIKE the way my hands felt on the wheel, so I got off the FDR at the Manhattan Bridge exit, took a sidestreet and parked the Plymouth on Water Street just off Pike Slip. No law-enforcement types come to that neighborhood. I shut off the engine, rolled down my window, and reached in my pocket for a smoke—but my damned hand wouldn't fit in the pocket. After a couple of tries, I just put both hands on the wheel to stop their trembling and stared straight ahead. Flood had both feet on the floor, hands clasped in her lap, head slightly back. She was dead calm. Putting her hand on mine where I had grabbed the wheel, she said, "Want me to light one for you?" I nodded. She reached into my shirt pocket, pulled out the pack, knocked a butt free, put it in her mouth, reached for the push-in lighter on the dash.

I had enough presence of mind to bark *"No!"* at her, and she pulled her hand back so quickly I could almost see the vapor trail. I wanted a cigarette, not the damn taillights to start spelling out "SOS" over and over again. This was one of the kid's brilliant inventions for the super-cab—in case someone was sticking him up, he could just hit the lighter and anyone behind the car would see something was wrong. Supposedly that would bring the cops on the double. I don't know if it would work or not (I kind of doubted it), but it was a bad time to experiment.

Flood didn't seem surprised. She just sat back with the cigarette in her mouth. "Do you have a lighter that lights cigarettes?" There wasn't a hint of a smile on her mouth but her eyes crinkled slightly at the corners. I felt better already, and got out my transparent sixty-nine-cent butane special. I've got a few just like it back at the office that are full of napalm, and look so much like this one that they scare me to death. The lunatic who sold them to me swore you could use them just like regular lighters if you wanted, even demonstrated one for me. I never believed him.

Flood fired the lighter, sucked in smoke, blasted it out her nose like a little blonde dragon, and handed it to me. She didn't smoke now, I guessed, but it wasn't as if she never had. I smoked and looked out the car window. I could feel Flood next to me, but she didn't say anything for a long time. Finally she asked, "You just happened along, huh?"

I looked her right in the eyes. I can lie to anyone—when I finally get to Hell, I'm going to convince the Devil he got a wrong shipment. But it didn't seem worth it to lie right then. "I was looking for you. I decided that I'd take the case even without the information."

The smile around her eyes dropped to her broad mouth for just a second. "That's funny. I was going to look you up and give you the information you wanted."

I was feeling better. "You still got the grand?"

That brought a happy little laugh and, "Yes, Mr. Burke. My own investigations were quite inexpensive."

"Yeah," I said. "I could see that."

She lit another cigarette for me. I could have done it for myself by then, but what the hell. We had to get moving—the Plymouth was as anonymous a car as you could want, but Flood and I hadn't made any friends in the last few hours and you never know. "Where to?" I asked her.

"I think you should come with me," she said, "I have the information you want, but I can only show it to you where I live." I nodded and she gave me directions. She knew the city better than I expected.

It was an old factory building on Tenth Avenue, south of Twenty-third. The sign over the entrance said *Lofts Available for Any Commercial Purpose. Raw Space. No Living,* and gave the name of some broker to contact. The directory board showed a variety of businesses, most of them the kind that cater to the twits who eat wine and cheese for breakfast and brag about getting the latest in venereal diseases.

Flood had a key and we took the freight elevator to the

fourth floor. A small hand-lettered sign proclaimed this the Yoga Plateau, and Flood produced another key. Inside was a huge empty room, gym mats on the floor, plain white walls, stereo set in one corner, and speakers all over the place. One whole wall was industrial windows. A sprinkler system hung down from the ceiling, pipes all painted white. There was a tiny white plastic desk and white push-button phone. Even the bulletin boards were white. In the middle of the linoleum floor was a large square marked off with wide black industrial tape. Flood walked toward the square, then veered off to the side. I stepped into the square, and was stepping back out of it even as Flood shook her head no. She headed toward a door against the side wall away from the windows. She had the key for that one too. I followed her inside.

We were in a tiny private apartment. The stove had a large wok covering the only two burners; the waist-high refrigerator had a white wood cabinet on top; and there was a chest of drawers with an armoire standing next to it, both painted white. Through an open door, I saw a stall shower, sink, and toilet. The room next to the little kitchen had rattan mats on the floor, probably for sleeping. There was no other furniture.

Flood left the door open behind us. She tossed her purse on top of the chest, shrugged out of her jacket, spread her hand to indicate I should sit on the floor. I looked carefully around the little room—no ashtrays. She caught my eye, took a small red-glazed bowl from next to the sink and handed it to me. "Use this."

I sat and smoked through a couple of cigarettes while Flood busied herself around the place. She asked me if I wanted tea, and seemed unsurprised when I said no. Finally, she came over to me and sat across from me in the lotus position.

"Mr. Burke, I have to explain some things to you. And I have to show you some things so you'll understand why I have to find this person who calls himself the Cobra. Let me just tell you in my own way and when I'm finished you can ask any questions that you like." I nodded okay, and Flood rose to her feet without using her hands, like mist coming off the ground. Standing about five feet from me, she reached down and took off her shoes, one at a time. She was wearing slacks of some kind of dark silky material—the legs were wide and loose, but tightly fitted from her upper thighs to her waist. A dark jersey top was so snug it had to be a bodysuit. She had the traditional hourglass shape, all right, but hers was so densely packed that she looked powerful and beautiful all at the same time.

She did something at her waist, and the silky pants floated to the floor. I was right—it was a bodysuit underneath. She stepped away from the shiny puddle at her feet, bent in half at the waist and I heard the snaps pop on the bodysuit. She pulled the suit over her head in one motion and tossed it gently on top of her pants. Her bra and panties were of some smooth material that matched; the combination looked more like a fairly modest bathing suit than underwear. She hooked her thumbs inside the waistband of the pants and slid them down and off, one leg at a time. I just sat there watching, not smoking now. She stood there for a moment, hands on hips, staring down at me. She looked like a lot of things to me then, but vulnerable wasn't any of them. She turned slowly to her right, half her back on the left side coming into view. Even her rump looked like muscle covered with pale skin. I heard my own breathing.

She kept turning until she was facing completely away from me, and then I saw it—halfway down the right cheek and partway down her thigh was a dark red stain—the skin under the stain was raised and rough. I knew what it was instantly—fire scars. She bent forward slightly as if to show me the whole thing, then turned back until she was facing me again. She walked over until she was right in front of my face and turned again. The scar was ragged and uneven as though she had sat down in a fireplace—not a surgeon's work. Maybe skin grafts would have worked years ago, but it clearly was too late now. When she turned again to look at me, I nodded to show I understood what it was. She walked away from me toward the bathroom. The scars didn't affect the muscles underneath. She walked with that independent, up-and-down movement of her cheeks that even most strippers never get right. I sat there looking at the puddle of her discarded clothes and heard the hiss of spray. She didn't sing in the shower.

She came out in a few minutes wearing a yellow terrycloth robe, gathered the pile of clothes from the floor and threw them in a large wicker basket near the dresser. Then she came over and sat down next to me. It was dark in her place, but the white walls from the studio bounced enough light inside for me to see her face. I lit another cigarette and she began to talk.

"I don't remember much about my mother, but I know I

was taken away from her when I was just a little kid. I lived in foster homes at first, but then they put me in an institution when the family that had me moved out of the state. When I was fourteen, they found another foster home for me, and they let me out to go live there. The man in that home raped me. I told the social workers and they asked him about it. He said that we had sex, but that I had come on to him and he couldn't help himself. He went into therapy, I went into a home for girls. I ran away and they caught me. I kept running away. I always got caught after a while, and they'd put me in an empty room with nothing in it, not even a book to read. The social workers told me it was all right to be sad, but not to be angry. It wasn't healthy."

She took a deep breath. "I had a friend, my best and greatest friend ever. Her name was Sadie. Her mother was Jewish and her father was black. She was so smart. She told me she wouldn't have ever been put in the institution except that she wasn't fashionable. I never understood that, at first. But she was my friend. We did everything together. We always shared. Everything. We fought the bull dykes together and the matrons too. I didn't know how to fight then, but I was strong and I was always angry. Sadie couldn't fight at all but she always tried. Once they put us in the Quiet Room for two weeks together and it only made us closer—better than sisters, because *we* decided. We ran away together once, to New York. We wanted to go to the Village. Sadie met this guy on a motorcycle who said he had a crash pad where kids could stay. I didn't trust him—I didn't trust anyone. But Sadie had charm. She said even if he was a bad guy, he wouldn't have to be bad to us. I never had charm."

An expression I couldn't read flashed across her face and she went on, "We went with him and he was nice at first. But that same night, he brought in some other men from his pack. They told us to take off our clothes and dance for them. We wouldn't. I could have gotten away, but I fought them with Sadie. I broke a bottle and cut one of them in the face. They beat us, badly. When I woke up, there was an old man there with a suitcase. He was arguing with the pack. He said something about how he couldn't do it—we were too young. One of the pack came over to us and said he was sorry for what the others had done. He said the man was a doctor and he'd fix us up. He gave us each something to drink. I don't remember anything except reaching for Sadie before I passed out.

"When I came to, I saw Sadie lying next to me. We still had no clothes on and Sadie was bleeding between her legs. I checked, but I wasn't. My whole face was swollen so bad I could hardly talk. I think it was another day or so before we both really woke up. There was a dirty bandage on my hip, one on Sadie's too. I thought it was maybe where the doctor gave us a shot, but it was a big bandage. I crawled out into the hall. The pack was all asleep in the next room. It was like a cave of devils—filthy and smelly. Sadie and I found some clothes and we made it down the stairs. A policeman found us, and took us to a place for runaways because Sadie told him we were sisters from Ohio. She was smart—I couldn't think of anything to say. When they took the bandages off in the runaway place to give us showers, we saw what they had done, why they brought the old man up there. We each had a tattoo on our bottoms. Just the name of that pack, but a real tattoo. When I saw it on Sadie, I cried for the first time in years. She cried too. The nurse at the runaway place told us that they were permanent—they would never come off. When they left Sadie and me alone, we talked—and we decided what we had to do. I wasn't afraid. I didn't care anymore after what they did to us.

"Sadie and I just walked out of the runaway place. They didn't even try to stop us. Sadie panhandled in the Village until we got some money, then we bought four of those five-gallon cans and went to a gas station and filled them up. We just sat outside that building where the pack was until it was late at night and then we went upstairs. The pack was all zonked out on booze and dope. It was easy. Sadie and I knew what would happen to us, but it didn't matter. We poured the gasoline all over the place—all over those sleeping devils. Then we each lit matches and threw them into the gas. We didn't even run out of the building, just walked away. They screamed a lot—I wish I could have been there to see them. The papers said eleven people died. No people died. They weren't people. It could have been eleven hundred for all we cared.

"Then Sadie and I went to this flophouse. We paid for the room with what was left of the panhandling money and walked right upstairs carrying one of the cans with a little gasoline left in it. In that room, we kept our promises to each other. We took off our clothes and we laid down on our stomachs and we poured gasoline over each other's bottoms. We had the sheets all soaked in water, like a swamp. We said that we loved each other. We knew we couldn't make any noise or it wouldn't work. I kissed her. We were crying, but we did it. We put some of the wet sheets in our mouths, and we held hands and we lit the matches and put them on ourselves. We said we would count to ten before we rolled over onto the sheets. Sadie tried, but she pulled away before I got to three in my head. I held onto her like I promised—she fought me, but I held on. We rolled onto the sheets and spit the mess out of our mouths and it was okay to scream then. The cops got us when they came to the flophouse. They said we were too young to be tried as adults. We knew that before, but it wouldn't have made any difference.

"The ambulance man was this big fat black guy. He looked so fierce, but he cried when he saw me and Sadie. After we got out of the hospital we went to some court and they put us away like they had before. I had a lawyer—some young kid. He asked me why we killed those devils and I told him, and he said if I pleaded insanity maybe they'd send me to a state hospital instead of the institution. I tried to get at him too, and they kept me handcuffed after that.

"We were good in the institution. Nobody bothered us anymore, not the other girls, not the matrons. Nobody. Everybody's afraid of fire—everybody has respect for revenge. And they all knew we were stand-up people—I told the judge the whole thing was my idea and I made Sadie do it, but she told them the same thing, it was only her, so we both went to jail. We always said that when we got out we would never come back—we would do things. Sadie was so smart, so charming, even after the fire. I wanted to be a gymnast. Sadie read books all the time. They let us out when I was twenty-one. She was older than me but she stayed so we could leave together.

"We got an apartment and jobs. Sadie went to college. I met someone who began to teach me the martial arts. Sadie got married, she was going to teach school when she graduated. I lived with her and her husband, saving my money to go to Japan. My teacher said there was nothing more for me to learn here—I had to go to the East to finish my studies.

"Sadie had a daughter. She sent me pictures in Japan. The baby was named Flower because that was the only part of my

Japanese name she could translate into English—the other part means fire. She and her husband were doing so good—only he had cancer and they didn't know it. I was with Sadie and Flower when he went. She was strong. She still had her child and she had her work. I helped her cry it out and then I went back.

"She found a daycare center for Flower, at a church that was active in all kinds of stuff—gay rights, peace marches, welfare reform. There was a man, a Vietnam vet, who worked in the center. He was a very violent man, but gentle with children, they said. A man damaged by the war, but good inside. This man also did babysitting for some of the church members when they wanted to go out.

"One day the police came looking for this man. He had sodomized some of the children he was supposed to be caring for—they got him when he tried to sell some of the pictures he had taken of the children. He wasn't at the daycare center that day, he was taking care of Sadie's child. He must have known the police were getting close to him. Later they said he was under great psychological pressure. Sure. While the police were looking for him, he raped Flower and he choked her to death.

"Sadie sent me a wire, but she was dead before it arrived—a car crash—nothing to do with Flower. The man who raped and tortured Flower to death gave the district attorney a lot of good information about the child pornography business. At least that's what I was told. He was found incompetent or something. He never went to trial. He went into some hospital for a year and he's supposed to get outpatient therapy. He doesn't talk about how he sodomizes children, but he does talk about his military skills and how he expects to hook up with a mercenary outfit and fight in Africa.

"His name is Martin Howard Wilson."

9

FLOOD DIDN'T SEEM to have anything more to say. By then it was so dark in her place that all I could see was her outline, the highlights from her hair, and the glint from her eyes. She must have been breathing but you wouldn't know it from looking at her chest. She sat like someone waiting, but waiting without expectations. Like when you're in the joint and it's years to parole.

It was a lot of information to absorb. I needed time to think, so I said, "You said I could ask questions." She nodded. I lit another cigarette. It wasn't nervousness—they always taste better after a jolt of adrenaline, which is my own particular euphemism for fear. "I need to know *how* you know some of the things you said."

"Why?"

"Because I don't want to rely on information that might be no good."

"All right. What do you want me to tell you?"

"You said that he was a Vietnam vet, that he made a deal with the D.A.'s office, that he was in a hospital, and that he wants to hook up with a mercenary outfit, right?"

"Yes."

"Well, who told you all that?"

"One of the other women at this church group. She said she knew Sadie, so she told me what she knew."

"You believed her?"

"I knew she was telling me the truth because I told her I would come back and see her if she did."

"That doesn't make any sense to me. I could understand if you told her you'd come back to see her if she *didn't*, but—"

"She saw a different side of me than you have, Mr. Burke."

"You mean she never saw you crack people's skulls?"

"I mean she was a lesbian."

"And you?"

"I said I would come back to see her—a promise that I will keep. That's the *only* promise that I made."

"But maybe she didn't see it like that."

Flood shrugged her shoulders so slightly that her breasts didn't even move. "I don't know what she saw. Some people wouldn't see a shark in their own swimming pool."

"How did this woman know about the court stuff?"

"The mother of one of the other children—another child that this devil raped—she was planning to sue the church for negligence or something. She hired a lawyer and this lawyer did an investigation. He paid some money to a detective, and the detective paid someone in the court, and they put all this together."

"The lawyer took a case like this on spec?"

"On spec?"

"Without any money up-front—you know, like in a contingency arrangement where he doesn't get anything unless he wins—like with a car accident or something."

"Oh. Yes, he apparently did."

"It doesn't add up. A case like that's awful hard to prove in court. Besides, those churches never carry any decent insurance. Now if it was the archdiocese . . ."

"The lawyer just said he wanted to help this woman." Flood shrugged her shoulders again, just the way she did before. I was beginning to understand what it meant.

"So this clown thought he was going to have a very grateful lady on his hands?"

"Yes, I think he did."

"But you found out about it through this woman who was a friend of hers, who told you because she liked you."

"Yes."

"And that woman and the woman who went to this lawyer are good friends?"

"Very good friends."

"So the lawyer isn't going to get any luckier with the second woman than the first got with you?"

Flood chuckled. It was too throaty to be a giggle, but it was close—and her breasts moved, bounced this time. Finally: "I don't think so," she said.

I sighed. "Nobody's honest, huh?" Flood started to make a hard face to disagree but figured it wasn't worth it and went back to another shrug.

"Okay, let's assume this information is all true for a minute. Do you have a good description of this Wilson? A picture would be perfect."

"I have a description but not a really good one. And I have no pictures. I know they must have taken his picture when they arrested him—a mug shot, right? So I thought maybe you could get a copy."

"I might be able to if the D.A.'s office didn't arrange to have it destroyed."

"Could they do that?"

"Sure. But they probably wouldn't unless he was in the Witness Protection Program. You know, like if he gave the *federales* some dynamite information and they gave him a new identity, relocated him and all that. But it doesn't sound like they would for this guy. He's still around, trying to link up with a mercenary team, you said?"

"Yes, that's why I came to you in the first place. I heard that you were a recruiter for one of the mercenary armies, that people who wanted to go overseas and fight had to be cleared by you first."

"Where did you hear that?"

"There's a bar in Jersey City, just on the other side of the river, a really weird place. It looks like a roadhouse in West Virginia or something. They play country-and-western music up front and I know they have all kinds of strange meetings in the back rooms."

"Strange meetings? Like dope deals, guns, what?"

"No—like the KKK or the American Nazi Party."

"Oh—that kind of strange."

"Does that scare you?"

"Yes and no," I said, and it was the truth. The freaks individually don't scare me—they're usually terminal inadequates. But the idea scares the hell out of me. It's unnatural, you know what I mean? Freaks are supposed to stay by themselves—in furnished rooms, with their picture books and inflatable plastic dolls. We're in bad shape when they start forming fucking affinity groups. "But I have done business with them in the past. I know a few of them."

"What kind of business could you do with people like that?"

"Purely professional, nothing personal," I said. No point telling her about the genuine recordings of Hitler's speeches I sold them. Real expensive, exclusive stuff, pirated out of the bunker where Adolf the Asshole waited for his final reward. Only one other like it in the whole world, and that (of course) was in the archives of a neo-Nazi party in West Germany. Yeah, I had it on the best authority from an old Nazi who escaped to Argentina, where he's recruiting mercenaries to attack Israel. I couldn't sell the defectives on that particular venture, but they lapped up the tapes and paid the going rate. They apologized for not being able to understand German (although one of them told me he was studying it by correspondence), but they said they had the exact translation of Adolf's final speeches which they had purchased from some other enterprising businessman. What the hell—Yiddish sounds a lot like German anyway, and the six hours of Simon Wiesenthal's address to the German crowds at a Holocaust memorial rally only cost me twenty bucks. A little reel-to-reel work, some Iron Cross lettering, a swastika or two, and I was ahead well over two grand. I gave them a discount price, of course, because after all, they were true believers. But Flood would never understand what a man has to do to make a living.

She gave me her shrug. "Like the professional recruiting business you do with mercenaries?" Maybe she did understand.

"Yeah, exactly like that. What about that bar?"

"I went there a few times and listened. Your name came up more than once."

"Just about the mercenary scam?" There was no point in euphemisms anymore.

"Yes, nothing else. You're quite a legendary figure to those people, Mr. Burke."

"Yeah—to others too. I'm surprised you didn't use your famous interrogation tactics on them to get more information."

Another shrug. "I guess I did with one of them. He told me he had your telephone number in his car. I went out to the parking lot with him to get it and he tried to be stupid."

"What happened?"

"I left him there."

"Alive?"

"Certainly he was alive—do you think I walk around murdering people?"

"That action in the alley when you grabbed that kid's family jewels is liable to stay on my mind for a while."

"Why?"

"Well, it's not your everyday act, right? Would you really have given the kid the chop?"

"That's not important. It was important that the others understood they had to move, had to obey. It took away their will to fight any more."

"It almost took away my will to hold on to my lunch. Would you really have done it?"

"Do you remember what the one with the bushy hair said he was going to do to me? Do you think he was just trying to frighten me?"

"He *was* trying to frighten you." I paused, recreating the scene in the alley. "But he would have done it, that's right."

"So I would have done it—but only because I threatened to do it and those are promises you must always keep. I would rather have just killed him."

"Yeah, what the hell, a few more killings shouldn't be any big deal."

"Why do you try to sound sarcastic, Mr. Burke? I was willing to kill to live, not for the pleasure of it. You killed those three vermin just to kill them. They couldn't have come after us."

That knocked me over. "What? I didn't kill anybody. What the hell are you talking about?"

"Those people we put into that room—you fired the gun so many times, right at them. You must have killed them."

And that started me laughing. I must have kept laughing for a while, because the next thing I remember was Flood holding the lower part of my face in one hand and pressing the other against my stomach. I looked up at her—she was only inches away. She asked, "Okay now?" and I let out a breath and tried to explain.

"I was just laughing because . . . well, it's not important. But I didn't kill anybody in that room. The pistol was full of a special mixture a friend makes up for me. Look," I said, and pulled out the .22 and the spare clip. "Here's the gun I used, and here's the bullets." I popped them out of the clip one at a time and showed her the tiny mini-flares, the teargas cartridges, and the flat-faced slugs with the birdshot inside. Flood opened her mouth slightly in concentration as I explained.

"Watch. First you use a couple of the mini-flares so it looks like rockets are going off inside the room, then some birdshot for the stinging effect, which they think is shrapnel. They usually hit the floor and use up all their air holding their breath or screaming. Then you fire some teargas to start them choking and then some more mini-flares and birdshot to keep them down. It turns any closed space into hell, but it's all in the mind—you can't die from it. I wouldn't kill anybody like that—that's not my game. You couldn't kill anybody with this gun anyway, loaded the way it is, even if you blasted them right in the face. It's just to keep people where they are for a while, that's all."

Flood fingered the cartridges carefully, then smiled. "You're just a man of peace, aren't you, Mr. Burke?"

"That's me. I'd have to be damn scared to kill anyone—it's not worth it. I survive. I'm not looking for a whole lot more."

"Was the other gun loaded with this stuff too?"

"No. With .38 specials—two wad-cutters, two hollow points, and one high-pressure load."

Flood gave me that chuckle again. Maybe she thought she had me figured out, but I was way ahead of her. I noticed her breasts only bounced when she chuckled, not when she shrugged—very appropriate.

"I have to start looking," I said.

"Is it safe for you?"

"I guess so. But I need some sleep first and to get a few things from my office—make a few calls—you know."

"I know." Flood shifted out of that damn lotus position so she was sitting next to me. She reached out that death-dealer of a hand and brushed my cheek with the back of it. I knew it was time to go.

10

THE OUTSIDE OF Flood's studio was deserted, no action in the halls. I rang for the freight elevator and went to the stairs when I heard it start to move. Checked the elevator entrance, nobody around. The Plymouth was sitting untouched where I'd left it. I didn't expect anything else—any fool who tried to take off the tires would have to be wearing razor-proof gloves, for openers.

I got back to the office just as the sun was breaking over the Hudson. A few solitary men were standing on the piers with fishing tackle, setting up for the day. The fish in the Hudson aren't much to look at, never grow too big or have bright colors. But the guys who fish down there tell me they put up a hell of a fight. I figured that any fish who could survive the Hudson River would have to be tough, like a dog raised in the pound. Or a kid raised by the State.

I put the car away, making a mental note to do some cosmetic surgery on it before this case with Flood made it too visible. Went upstairs, deactivated everything, and let myself in. Pansy gave me a halfhearted growl just to let me know she was on the job, then charged over, wagging her stump of a tail. Even without the security systems I knew there hadn't been any visitors. Pansy was cut from the same cloth as my old Doberman, Devil, and nobody would get in here without war breaking loose.

That had happened once, and it gave Blumberg his big chance to act like a real lawyer. I was hiding a certain gentleman in my old apartment. He told me people were looking for him, but said nothing about those people wearing blue coats and badges instead of business suits. Anyway, while I was out trying to square some other beef, the cops arrived and decided to serve a Smith and Wesson warrant on my premises. They smashed in the door, and Devil met them head on. My client had more than enough time to leave by the back window, and Devil nailed two of the cops before they got smart and retreated until the ASPCA arrived. Those clowns blasted my dog with a load of tranquilizers and carted her off to the pound. By the time I found out what went down, she was already behind bars waiting for adoption or execution, whichever came first. Just like a lot of kids in orphanages.

The ASPCA wouldn't return her to me at first, saying the Major Case Squad wanted her held for evidence. The jerks— I knew she'd never talk. Anyway, by the time I proved the Doberman was really my dog, they told me she was being held for adoption. I figured they might have been sincere about that, since she was too fine an animal to just stuff into the gas chamber, but I wasn't ready to give her up that easily. So I went to see Blumberg.

Fortunately, it was already late afternoon by then and night court would soon be in session. I explained the matter to Blumberg and he opened with his usual sensitive probing, "Burke, you got the money, kid?"

"How much, Blumberg?"

"Well, this is a major case, my boy. I know of no legal precedent which covers the issue. We'll have to *make* law, take this all the way to the appellate courts, maybe even to the southern district. You and your fine dog have constitutional rights, and there are no rights without remedies. And, as you know, remedies are not cheap."

"Blumberg, I've got a flat yard, period. Not a nickel more. And I want a guarantee I get my dog back."

"Are you crazy? No guarantees—that's a rule of the profession. Why, I could be disbarred for even mentioning such a thing."

"You mean you're not?"

"That's not funny, Burke. That matter was dismissed. All the baseless allegations of misconduct on my part have been expunged from the record."

"What about the allegations that weren't baseless?"

"Burke, if you're going to have a negative attitude about this, we simply cannot do business."

"Sam, come on, I'm serious. I know you're the best in the business when you want to be. This isn't some skell who's going to Riker's Island for a year. My dog didn't do anything—and those bastards at the ASPCA are liable to gas her if I don't get her out."

"Oh, a death penalty case, is it? Well, normally I charge seven and a half for capital cases, but seeing as it's you, I'll take the case for the five hundred you offered. You got it on you?"

"Sam, I said a yard, not five. I'll make it a deuce—that's the best I can do. Half in front, half when it's over."

"Are you completely insane, my boy? Be reasonable. Where would I be if I allowed my clients to withhold half of the fee until they were satisfied?"

"You'd be working on fifty percent of your usual gross."

"I'm going to ignore that comment in view of the fact that you are obviously grief-stricken over the potential loss of your beloved pet. And, my boy, it just so happens you're in luck. Justice Seymour is sitting in criminal court tonight because of the crowded calendar. Since he's a judge of the supreme court, we won't have to wait until morning to bring on your Application for Relief."

And it went just like Blumberg said. He was too slick to try and put the case on the calendar since night court is only for arraignments, so he waited until he was in front of the judge on a shoplifting case. Before the poor defendant even knew who his lawyer was, Blumberg, the D.A., and the judge had swiftly converted the case to Disorderly Conduct. The defendant was hit with a $50 fine and a conditional discharge and was led over to the clerk's bench while still trying to thank Blumberg for saving him from the ten years in prison the fat man had assured him was a distinct possibility. Then Blumberg pulled his vest down over a bulging stomach, cleared his throat with such authority that the entire court quieted down, and addressed the judge in a resonant baritone:

"Your Honor, at this time, I have an extraordinary application to make on behalf of my client, who is, at this very moment, incarcerated and awaiting execution."

The judge looked staggered. His cronies over at the supreme court had told him anything could happen at night arraignments, but nothing he had heard prepared him for this. He looked up sharply at Blumberg, and in a voice designed to display a mixture of pure contempt laced with intimidation, said, "Counselor, surely you realize that this court is not the appropriate forum to bring such a matter."

Blumberg was not deterred. "Your Honor, if the court please. Your Honor is a supreme court justice and, might I add, a most eminent legal scholar. Indeed, I know from personal knowledge that Your Honor's landmark legal opinions have been required reading for students of the law for many years. As a sitting supreme court justice, Your Honor has jurisdiction over properly presented extraordinary writs, and Your Honor should be aware that this matter is one of the most dire urgency, threatening, as it surely does, the very life of my client."

The judge attempted to intercede, saying, "Counselor, if you please," but he might as well have been trying to keep a hungry rat away from cheese. Blumberg brushed aside the judge's feeble attempts to halt the lava-flow of his rhetoric, simultaneously firing his masterstroke.

"Your Honor, if the court please. A life is a sacred thing— it is not to be trampled upon or trifled with. The public's faith in the criminal justice system must be ever vigilantly protected, and who is better cast in the role of protector than a justice of our supreme court? Your Honor, my client faces *death*—a vicious and ignominious death at the hands of agents of the State. My client has done no wrong, and yet my client may die this very night if Your Honor does not hear my plea. The members of the press"— here Blumberg indicated by a sweep of his hand the single *Daily News* stringer as if the poor kid were an entire gallery of eager scribes—"questioned me about this matter before I entered this august courtroom, and even such hardened men as they wondered how such a thing as summary execution without trial could actually take place in these United States. Your Honor, this is America, not Iran!" At this, the ragged collection of lames, losers, and lumpen proletariat began to stir, their mumbled snarling energizing Blumberg like a blood transfusion. "Even the lowliest cur is entitled to due process—even the poorest among us is entitled to his day in court. If Your Honor will only permit me to expound upon the facts in this case, I am certain Your Honor will see fit—"

"Counselor. *Counselor, please*. I have yet to understand

what you are talking about and, as you well know, our docket is quite crowded this evening. But in the interests of justice, and upon your representation that you will be *brief*, I will hear your application."

Blumberg ran his hand through what was left of his mangy hair, took a deep breath, paused to be certain every eye and ear was focused on him, and then shot ahead. "Your Honor, last night the premises in which my client was working were invaded by armed police officers. These officers were *not* armed with warrants; they were *not* armed with probable cause; they were *not* armed with justification for their acts. But they *were* armed with deadly weapons, Your Honor. The door was kicked in—my client was forcibly and physically attacked—and when he valiantly sought to resist an illegal arrest, the police called in additional agents and brutally shot my client with a so-called tranquilizer gun, rendering him insensible and unable to resist. My client was then dragged down the stairs and into a cage, and is now being held against his will. I am told that my client will be summarily executed, perhaps even this very night, unless this court intervenes to prevent a tragedy."

"Mr. Blumberg, this is a shocking accusation you make. I know of no such event. What is your client's name?"

"My client's name is . . . uh, my client's name is Doberman, Your Honor."

"Doberman, Doberman. What kind of . . . what is your client's first name, if you please?"

"Well, Your Honor, I am not actually aware of my client's full name at this time. However, my client's owner is present in court," gesturing over to me, "and will provide that information."

"Your client's *owner?* Counselor, if this is your idea of a joke—"

"I assure you it is no joke, Your Honor. Perhaps you have read about this case in the late papers?"

Suddenly, the light dawned. "Counselor, are you by any chance referring to the police attempt to apprehend a fugitive from justice early this evening on the Lower East Side?"

"Exactly and precisely, Your Honor."

"But the fugitive escaped, I read."

"Yes, Your Honor, the *fugitive* escaped—but my client did not. And my client is being held at the ASPCA, through no fault of his own, and will be executed unless he can be returned to his rightful owner."

"Mr. Blumberg! Are you saying that your client is a *dog?* You invade my courtroom with a writ of habeus corpus for a *dog?*"

"Your Honor, with all due respect, I prefer to refer to this extraordinary application as a writ of habeus canine, in view of the unique nature of my client herein."

"Habeus *canine.* Counselor, this court does not sit as a monument to an individual attorney's perverted sense of humor. Do you understand that?"

"Your Honor, with all due respect, I understand it fully. But were I to proceed along the conventional civil channels, I have no doubt but that my client would be deceased before I could even get on the calendar. Your Honor, no matter what we *call* a court, be it criminal court, supreme court, surrogate's court, or family court, they are *all* courts of law and of equity. They are forums through which we the people exercise our right to justice. My client may be a dog—and I can say freely that I have personally represented individuals so characterized by this very court even when they possessed both first *and* last names— but my client is still a living creature. Is not life itself sacred and holy? Can an attorney asked to protect the life of a beloved pet refuse on the ground that some procedural nicety stands in the way?"

By now, Blumberg was riding the groundswell from the packed courthouse—humans who normally wouldn't blink at accounts of babies tossed into incinerators were outraged at the tale of animal abuse. In the rare position of representing a popular cause, the fat lawyer pounded ahead. "Your Honor, I say to you at this time, I would rather be a dog in America than a so-called citizen of countries that do not enjoy our freedoms and our liberties. My client herein is not the first client I have represented who does not understand the procedures of this court and he will not be the last. My client did his job. He gave his all for his owner—must he also give his life? My client is young, Your Honor. If he made a mistake, the mistake was an honest one. How was he to know the people battering down his master's door were lawful agents of the police? Perhaps he thought they were burglars, or armed robbers, or dope-crazed lunatics. Surely there are enough of *those* people in our fair city. Your Honor, I beg you, spare my client's life. Let him go forth once more to frolic in the sunshine, to work at his chosen profession, perhaps to sire offspring that will carry on the proud name of Doberman. A life is sacred, Your Honor, and no man should tamper with another's. That, Your Honor, I respectfully submit, is the work of the Almighty, and His alone. I beg this court, let my client go!"

Blumberg was actually weeping by then, and the watching crowd was clearly on his side—even the court officers' ever-present sneers were replaced with looks of compassion for a young life threatened with extinction.

The judge tried once more, knowing he was doomed to failure. "Counselor, can you cite one single legal precedent in support of your arguments?"

"Your Honor," Blumberg rang out, "every dog must have his day!" And he got perhaps the first standing ovation ever given in New York City night court.

The judge called me up to the bench, satisfied himself that I was the dog's owner, and took us all back into chambers. He made a quick call to the ASPCA, informing a thoroughly cowed attendant of the potential liability they were facing if they killed my dog. Just to make sure, I typed a release order on engraved stationery from the secretary's desk while the judge was being congratulated by Blumberg on his judicial wisdom. I picked up my dog and took him to the Mole at the junkyard, where he could join the pack. Nobody knows the name on the Mole's birth certificate, but he lives under the ground and he's reliable as death. I heard later that Blumberg picked up half a dozen cases from the gallery while I was gone. Most guys don't even have the guts to reach back into themselves when they have to, but Blumberg actually had something there when he did.

While the Doberman's successor prowled her rooftop, I set about making preparations for the coming hunt.

11

THE FIRST ISSUE was identification. If Wilson was really a Vietnam vet, he must be wise to the grab-bag of goodies Uncle Sam makes available. If he was scoring from the VA on a regular basis, for instance, he had to be using his righteous name. And that name would have to be connected to an address somewhere in the government computers. I knew a guy who specialized in that racket for a long time—a computer wizard who just liked to play with keyboards and telephones. He was the same guy who gave the Mouse the idea for his big social security scam (which, from my recent mail, was obviously still working). Unfortunately, finding that guy would be tougher than finding Wilson. He'd done me a lot of favors over the years, so when he came to me for help in disappearing, I showed him how to work the game and he vanished. He should have been satisfied making regular little scores, but he talked too much. One of the mob guys overheard him bragging in a singles bar about how he could get access to any government computer and approached him to get inside the Witness Protection Program. The mob guy wanted to find out the new identities of some of the informants who had been relocated by the government. It worked to perfection, but when people started turning up dead all over the place (especially in California—for some reason, most of the gangsters who opt for relocation have to try the Holy Coast), my friend decided to exit the stage. The mob made so much noise looking for him that they tipped off the feds—or maybe, in a touch of perfect irony, one of the mob guys leaning on my friend for information was a rat himself. Who knows?

Since the guy was a friend, I didn't send him down the Rhodesian pipeline, but recommended Ireland instead. They've got no extradition treaty with the U.S., and he should be all right if he keeps his head down. Israel is another good choice, especially since my friend had such marketable skills, but those people are too serious and I don't think they would have tolerated his nonsense. The guy had bad personal habits and no real sense of surviving by himself. Between the need to talk to the wrong people, which means *any* people, and the need for computer toys and telephones, he probably won't last.

I sell a lot of identification, mostly to clowns who want the option to disappear but never will. The stuff looks pretty good—all you need are some genuine state blanks, like for drivers' licenses, and the right typewriter. IBM makes a special typing element—one of those things that looks like a studded golf ball—designed for computer reading. They call it an OCR element and you can't buy it over the counter but this is something less than a significant deterrent to people who steal for a living. I have a complete set in the office. A white dropcloth, a Polaroid 180 with black-and-white film, some state blanks, and I can put you in the driver's seat in about half an hour. I also sell discharge papers from the army, draft cards (although there isn't much business in them anymore), social security cards, marriage licenses, and a variety of firearms permits.

But none of that crap is really any good. The proper way (and the way I fixed up my computer-junkie friend) is simply to find someone who died soon after birth with an age and race similar to the person you want to fix up. Then you apply for a duplicate birth certificate in that person's name, which becomes *your* name when it's issued. This perfectly legitimate piece of paper opens the door to all the rest—driver's license, social security card, you name it. And that paper is perfectly good. To get a passport, for example, all they want is a birth certificate, which you can get certified at the Health Department for a couple of bucks, and a driver's license or something similar.

The finishing touch is to hire some local lawyer and tell him you want to change your name for professional reasons, like you want to be an actor or something equally useful. Then you put an ad in the paper announcing to the world, including your creditors, that you want to change your name. Most dead people don't have too many creditors, especially those who have been in such a state for a couple of decades or so. When nobody comes forward to object to the change of name, the court will give you a certified order so you can change your name legally on all the other documents. This adds another layer of smog to what was phony to begin with, and it's more than enough to keep a step ahead. The whole package costs less than $500 from start to finish. It's a bargain—you'd pay more than twice that just for a phony passport.

The next thing you do is run up some credit accounts. It doesn't take much—most of the charge card companies will issue one of their pieces of magic plastic to someone on welfare. Then you pay the bills, not exactly on time but close enough. When a cop stops you, there's nothing like the American Express Gold to make him think you're a solid citizen, especially if you're outside New York.

People used to use post office boxes as a mail drop, but that's out of fashion now. Any process server can get the Post Office to disclose the home address of anyone who took out a box if he says he has no other way to serve legal papers. Anyway, all anyone has to do is watch who comes to the box and follow them home. I work mine a bit differently. The return address I put on any correspondence is a box, all right, but no mail ever goes there. As soon as I opened it (using another name and an address that would be somewhere in the East River if it existed), I put in a change-of-address card that got my mail forwarded to a place in Jersey City. The guy there sends it on to a warehouse that Mama Wong owns, although her name doesn't appear on the incorporation papers. They put all my mail in this old battered desk in the back, and Max the Silent picks it up once every couple of weeks or so. Then he gives it to me or to Mama. The delivery isn't fast, but I don't get any personal mail anyway. If anyone came around the warehouse asking questions, they'd be told that mail comes there for me regularly and they just as regularly throw it in the garbage. If the investigator asked why they didn't notify the post office that I don't live there, he'd get either a lot of broken English laced with Cantonese or an unbroken stream of hostility, depending on his attitude. But no information. The guys who work there would never rat on Mama Wong—it wouldn't be worth it to them. Anyway, Mama doesn't have my address.

So Wilson could be using a post office box to pick up VA checks, if he was getting any. That would be the easiest way. You'd think the government wouldn't allow you to get checks at a post office box, but you'd be wrong. First of all, in New York a lot of folks on welfare and social security get their checks at the post office because their own apartment mailboxes are considered withdrawal windows by the local junkies. Secondly, the VA doesn't want to know who's getting the checks— it would just depress them. Remember that Son of Sam freako who killed all those women a while back before the cops stumbled onto him? Well, there's a contract out on him in prison, I heard. Not because the cons hate a sex offender—that doesn't happen anymore—but because some reporter found out he was getting a VA disability check every month while doing about seven life sentences. That snapped out the public, and a later investigation revealed there were literally thousands of prisoners getting checks while they did time. Some of the cons noted the media explosion about this, and figured Son of Sam was to blame, so there's a lot of hostility. (They should save their energies for scamming the parole board—no politician is going to vote to take away a government benefit merely because the recipient is locked up. It would hit too close to home.)

If Wilson was using a box anywhere between lower Manhattan and the Village, I could find him sooner or later if I knew what the hell he looked like. Flood wouldn't be much help there either. I halfheartedly checked through my resume file (from applicants for mercenary work), but none of them had a picture attached and none of them sounded or smelled sufficiently like my man to make me think we'd get lucky there.

Pansy trotted downstairs while I was still going through the files, and I put together some breakfast for her. Then I went to the phone, checked to be sure the hippies hadn't become early risers in my absence, and dialed the number Flood gave me.

"Yoga School."

"Is that you, Flood?"

"Yes, what's happening?"

"Some things—I can't talk long on this phone. You know where the Public Library is, on Forty-second Street?"

"Yes."

"Meet you inside the doors, all the way to the right, at about ten o'clock, tomorrow morning, okay? The doors off Fifth Avenue, with the lions?"

"I know where it is."

"Okay, listen, you have a pair of white vinyl boots, like go-go dancers wear?"

"Burke! Are you crazy? What would I want with things like that?"

"For the disguise."

"What are you talking about?"

"I'll explain when I see you, Flood. At ten, right?"

I could almost hear the exasperation in her voice but she kept it under control and just said, "Right."

12

AFTER I FINISHED talking to Flood, I spent some time just sitting by the open back door looking out toward the river with Pansy next to me, explaining the whole mess to her. Part of me just wanted to stay where I was, where it was safe. But I had already thrown too many pebbles into the pool for that. If I just wouldn't get involved with any other people—if I could just live like the Mole. But it's not too good to start thinking like that. It makes you crazy. Scared is okay—crazy is dangerous.

Some people get so scared of being scared that they go crazy from the fear—I saw a lot of that in prison. When I was only about ten years old there was this dog the Boss Man kept in the dormitory—a fox terrier named Pepper. He kept Pepper for the rats in the place. Pepper was a lot better than some miserable cat—he really liked rumbling with a juicy rat about half his own size—and he knew his work. Pepper would just kill the rats—he didn't play around with them. It was his job.

I never would have had the guts to run away from that joint except that Pepper went with me. I ended up by the same docks I use now. Sitting there, scared of everything in the whole world, but not of the waterfront rats—I had Pepper with me for that. I stayed out for almost six months until some cop picked me up because he thought I should have been in school. I could have gotten away but I didn't want to leave Pepper.

I thought they would put us both back in the same joint, but they didn't. They put me in some place upstate—the judge said I was incorrigible, and I didn't have any family. She was a nice judge, I guess. She asked me if I wanted to say anything and I asked her if I could have Pepper with me and she looked sort of sad for a minute—then she told me that there would be another dog where they were sending me. She was a liar, and I haven't trusted a judge or a social worker since then. I hoped they put Pepper someplace where there were rats, so he could do his work. There were plenty of them where they sent me.

I went into the side room, found a good dark conservative suit, a dark blue shirt, and a black knit tie. I set Pansy up for the day and went off to the docks to find Michelle. For once it didn't take long—she was in the back booth at the Hungry Heart, sipping some evil-looking potion and eating a rare steak with some cottage cheese. I walked right on through to the back, feeling the looks and giving off businessman vibes like I was Michelle's date. No problems—I sat down and a waiter appeared, looking at Michelle to see if I was trouble for her. She extended her hand like a bloody countess, smiled, and the waiter withdrew. Nobody came there for the food.

"Michelle, can you do a phone job for me?"

"Starting today?"

"In a few hours."

"Honey, it's a known fact that I give the best phone in all New York. But I suspect this has nothing to do with someone's love life, is that right?"

"That's right."

"You're going to tell me more?"

"When we get there," I said.

"So mysterious, Burke. Is this a paying customer?"

"How much do you want?"

"Now don't be like that, baby. *I'm* not like that. If you're on a budget, just say so. If this is a money-maker for you, I should get something for the time *my* money-maker's out of action, yes?"

"Yes. But I can't pay you what you're worth."

"They never do, sweetie, they never do."

"It's a bit downtown from here, Michelle. We're setting up a temporary office—you know what I mean?"

"Not in that damn warehouse."

"In the warehouse."

"And this involves . . . ?"

"I'm still looking for that freak I told you about."

She thought about it for a moment or so, then reached over and tapped my arm. "We have to stop at my hotel, Burke."

"For how long?"

"Just long enough for me to get my makeup case and some clothes."

"Michelle, this is strictly a phone job, you know? Nobody's going to *see* you."

"Honey, *I'll* see me. If I want to sound right, I have to feel right. And to feel right, I have to look right. That's the way it is."

I grunted my annoyance at this delay, all the time knowing she was right.

Michelle wasn't intimidated. She just widened her eyes, looked at me, and said, "Baby, you came to me for this work— if you don't like my peaches, don't shake my tree."

I just looked at her—I'd said more or less the same thing to Flood, but not as well.

"It's important," said Michelle, in a serious, no-nonsense voice. And there was nothing I could say to that. We all know what we need to do our work.

She was as good as her word. Less that fifteen minutes after I dropped her off she came tripping down the front steps of the hotel carrying one of those giant makeup cases like models use. I had been sitting in the car with a newspaper over my face—a newspaper into which I had punched a clean hole with the icepick I always keep in the car. It gave me a clear view of the street ahead and the mirror did the same behind. I never turned off the engine, but the Plymouth idled as quiet as an electric typewriter. I kept it in gear, with my foot on the brake, but the brake lights didn't go on. As soon as Michelle opened the door, I lifted my foot from the brake and we moved off like smoke into fog.

13

MAX WASN'T AROUND at the warehouse. I pulled the car all the way in, and Michelle and I went into the back where I keep the desk and phone boxes.

While she was changing into her outfit, I tested the equipment the Mole had set up for me. It was perfect—the Mole's work made Ma Bell look like the crooked old bitch she is.

Michelle came back inside, straightened out the desk to suit herself, and began to page through the loose-leaf book I gave her. The damn book costs about five hundred bucks a year just for the updates—it's cheaper to buy military secrets than direct-line numbers for government employees. She found the number she was looking for and punched it into the Mole's contraption. I could hear it ring through the speaker box—both ends of the conversation came through loud and clear.

"Veteran's Administration," answered the bored voice at the other end.

"Extension Three-six-six-four, please," came Michelle's executive secretary voice. It buzzed four times before it was picked up.

"Mr. Leary's office," answered a flat female voice.

"Mr. Leary, please—Assistant United States Attorney Wayne calling," said Michelle, now with a clipped, upper-class tone. If Leary was around, it was clearly expected he was to get his ass over to the telephone—pronto.

A pause, then a voice: "This is Mr. Leary. How can I help you?"

"Hold for Mr. Wayne, please," said Michelle, hitting the

toggle switch and handing the phone to me with a smile. I took the instrument, smoothed out my voice (all those Strike Force guys went to Ivy League schools), and opened the dialogue. "Mr. Leary? Good of you to speak with me, sir. My name is Patrick Wayne, Assistant U.S. Attorney for the Southern District of New York. We've had a situation come up here that I hope you can help us with."

"Well . . . I will if I can. Are you sure it's me you want to talk to?"

"Yes, sir—allow me to explain. We are interested in an individual who is currently receiving VA benefits—and our interest frankly concerns traffic in narcotics. We are in the process of preparing an informational subpoena for your payment records so we can determine the extent of this individual's ability to support himself."

"A subpoena . . ."

"Yes, sir. It would be delivered to you personally, and would encompass the full range of your activities pursuant to . . . but, let me explain. That's why I'm calling you. The subpoena—and the Grand Jury testimony, of course—may not be necessary if we can secure your cooperation."

"Cooperation? But I haven't done—"

"Of *course* you haven't, Mr. Leary. All we *really* need is the opportunity to speak with this particular individual. You see, we have learned that he has no permanent address—that he comes directly to the VA for his check every month. All we want you to do is put a temporary stall on that check the next time he comes, and give our office a call. Even a day's delay is more than sufficient. Then, when he returns the following day, we will be able to pick him up and speak with him."

"And then there'd be no subpoena?"

"No, sir—there'd be no need for one." First the pressure—then the grease. "Of course, I realize you probably have no interest in such things, but it is the policy of our office to award governmental commendations to those who assist us as you will be doing. If you are shy about the media we could avoid all publicity, but our office does feel you should have official recognition in some way."

"Oh, that's not necessary," chanted the bureaucrat, "I just do my job."

"And we *appreciate* it, Mr. Leary—rest assured that we do. Our man's name is Martin Howard Wilson."

"What's his service number?"

"Sir, I'll be frank with you. We only have an old number, and we're fairly certain he's been collecting under a new one. We assumed your computer network—"

"Well, we *are* fully computerized. But searching for just a name takes longer."

"Would his last known address help you?"

"Certainly," he snapped back, now officially on the job.

"We have Six-oh-nine West Thirty-seventh Street, but we understand he's long since departed that location."

A sly note crept into Leary's civil servant's voice as he said, "This will take just a few minutes to check—can I call you back?"

"Certainly, sir, please take down our number," and I gave it to him.

We said good-bye on that note. I smoked another couple of cigarettes and Michelle went back to her Gothic romance novel, popping a stick of gum into her mouth. In about fifteen minutes, the phone box buzzed.

Michelle threw the switch, bit down on the wad of gum. "United States Attorney's Office," she said in a pleasant, bouncy receptionist's voice.

"Could I speak with Mr. Patrick Wayne, please?" asked Leary.

"I'll connect you." Michelle flipped a switch, silently counted to twenty on her fingers, flipped the switch open again, and said, "Mr. Wayne's office" in the earlier voice.

"Could I speak with Mr. Wayne?" asked Leary again.

"Who is calling, please?"

"Mr. Leary, from the Veteran's Administration."

"He'll be right with you, sir, he's been expecting your call." She flipped the switch and handed the phone to me.

"Patrick Wayne here."

"Oh, Mr. Wayne. This is Leary. From the VA?" he said, like I might have forgotten him already.

"Yes, sir. Thank you for getting back to me so promptly."

"Mr. Wayne, we have a problem here."

"A problem?" I asked, my voice taking on an edge.

"Well, not a problem *exactly*. But you said that this Wilson picks up his check here every month. But our records show that it's being mailed to his home address."

"His home address . . . ?" I tried to keep the eagerness out of my voice. "Perhaps it's a different Wilson."

"No, sir," assured the bureaucrat, now on familiar ground. "It's the exact same name you gave me, and the address is the same too."

"You mean . . ."

"Absolutely. Martin Howard Wilson's checks are mailed to him at Six-oh-nine West Thirty-seventh Street, Apartment Number Four, New York City, New York One-oh-oh-one-eight. He's on three-quarters disability, as you know. That address has been used for . . . let me see . . . the past nine checks. He would have received the last one only last week or so."

"I see." And I was beginning to—and cursing myself for a fool as I did. "Well, sir, our information leads us to believe he has abandoned that address. Let me ask you this, Mr. Leary—will you agree to hold his check one extra day if he should appear in person? You don't forward those checks to new addresses, do you?"

"Certainly not, Mr. Wayne. In fact, it says Do Not Forward right on the envelope. If he has moved the check will be returned to us. We don't change the address unless we get a formal notice from the veteran himself."

"All right, sir. Now, assuming the check is returned, couldn't he just come to your office and pick it up—assuming he had proper identification, of course?"

"Yes, he could do that. Some of them do."

"Well, sir—will you agree to hold his check one extra day if it *is* returned to you? All we want you to do is tell him to come back the next day and give us a call here at the office. Will you do that for us?"

"Well, it's a bit irregular—couldn't I just stall him for a while and give you a call?"

"Well, sir, we would prefer the course of action suggested to you. But we do appreciate your efforts and I believe the solution you devised would be more than satisfactory."

"Yes, that would be better—I mean, those guys are *used* to waiting for their checks, you know? Another few hours won't make any difference. But a whole day . . . well, I'd have to get approval all up the line for that."

"Would a letter on official stationery from my superiors be of assistance to you, sir?"

"Yes, *sir*, Mr. Wayne. That would be perfect."

"Very well, it will be sent out to you later this week. You know how it is getting the boss to sign anything." I chuckled, one-on-one.

"Don't I," he agreed, now at ease with a fellow schlub.

"All right, sir, shall we leave it like this? If Wilson shows up before our letter arrives, you stall him for a couple of hours and notify my office immediately. And if your letter arrives first, I'm sure you'll have no difficulty securing approval to hold the check for a day or so."

"That would be fine, Mr. Wayne."

"Sir, on behalf of our entire office, I appreciate your assistance. You'll be hearing from us."

"Thank you, Mr. Wayne."

"Thank *you*, Mr. Leary," I said, and rang off.

14

I SAT THERE for a minute, absorbing the impact of my own stupidity. Some blonde bimbo comes into my office and tells me she spooked a heavyweight freak by kicking a building superintendent in the chops and I take her word for it. It was like when I was back in the joint—all the young guys wanted to know what being on parole was like: how to get over on the P.O., what you could get away with, how close they checked on you . . . all that stuff. So who would they ask? Naturally, the only guys inside with us who knew anything about parole were chumps who were back inside on a parole violation. All over this world we keep confusing repeated failures with lots of experience. Maybe this Wilson slipped the super a few bucks and told him to tell anyone who came around looking that he'd moved out a few days ago. But maybe he was still there.

I didn't want to brace a character like that without Max for backup, but I didn't know where he was and there was no time to find him. I told Michelle to pack up the place and make herself scarce. If Wilson was still there, he might be on his way out the door right this minute.

It was only a couple of miles to the address the VA gave me, but that was a couple of miles through the city and it was nearly one in the afternoon. Michelle would call Mama and tell her to have Max come to the Thirty-seventh Street address, but I didn't know when she'd make contact. Max can do a lot of things, but he can't use a phone.

The big Plymouth hummed along, eating up the streets, moving through the packed traffic like a good pickpocket at work. Maybe Wilson was there all along—sitting in some furnished room surrounded by kiddie-porn magazines and take-out food containers and thinking he was safe. Or maybe the address was never any good—maybe he had the brains to use an accommodation drop or he had a forwarding address permanently in place. Or maybe he was packing his bags even as I was heading over to him. Too many maybes, and no time to sort them out. I'd have to hit alone—no Max, no Pansy. It'd have to do.

The Plymouth wheeled crosstown onto Eleventh Avenue and past the giant construction site where another multimillionaire was building another building for his brothers and sisters. I found Thirty-seventh Street and nosed down the block looking for a place to park—I might have to get out of there quickly. Nothing. Back to Thirty-eighth, the parallel block, where I finally found an empty spot.

I put the car into reverse and started to back in when I heard a horn blasting at me—some miserable piece of garbage wanted the spot for himself. I ignored him, but the scumbag shoved the nose of his Eldorado into the spot ahead of me. Stalemate— he couldn't fit all the way in but it was enough to keep me out. Ram him out of the way or talk? I jumped out of the Plymouth like I was mad enough to waste him, grabbed the gold shield from my jacket pocket, and fingered the .38 with the other hand. I charged the Eldorado—the driver pushed the power window button and sat there in his pimp hat smiling, showing me a gold tooth with a diamond set in its center.

"Police! Move that fucking car! Now!"

And then I caught a break as the pimp raised his hands in a calm-down gesture and backed out without another word. Bad move on my part—maybe I called too much attention to the Plymouth, but it looked close enough to the unmarked cars the Man used in Midtown South. I put the Plymouth into the space and hit all the switches in case the pimp decided to return and act stupid. It would be a bad idea—I had his license number.

I hit the street. The block was dead at that hour—the working people were gone, the thieves were still asleep, and the welfare cases were watching television. Number 609 was on the corner, just where Flood said it was. Six-story tenement, brick front. Two glass-paneled wood doors, unlocked, a row of mailboxes inside, most of them with no names—no buzzer either. The inside door was locked. One bell was marked Super so I pushed it. Waiting for an answer, I was thinking how to play this next part. If it was a more middle-class joint I'd be tempted to come on as Detective Burke of NYPD. I looked enough like it, I was dressed right for a middle-class mind, and I could talk that talk. But any citizen of this neighborhood would see right through it.

Detectives never work alone anymore—the department won't let them. And they don't dress as well as I was either if they're not on the take—I had left the double-knit disguise home in the closet where it belonged. If I had time I could have taken one of the quasi-cops with me—you know, one of the badge-freaks who likes to pretend he's a real cop. He joins some bullshit organization, gets an honorary badge, and immediately goes out and buys himself a set of handcuffs and a blue light for his car. He hangs out in the cop bars and talks like he's on television. I'm the founder and sole beneficiary of the Metro Detectives Association, which has enrolled dozens of these losers. We don't charge a fee, of course, since all our men are doing important volunteer law-enforcement work. But you'd be amazed at how many of them purchase the optional framed certificate, bumper plaque, laminated plastic photo I.D. card complete with their picture, gold badge in genuine leather case—all that. It costs them an average of a grand per man. You tell a card-carrying disturbo that he's a genuine "peace officer" and he goes straight into major orgasm, maybe for the first time. Not a bad deal for me, but this time I didn't have one of them around when I needed him.

I rang the bell—and waited. I rang it again—it was probably as dead as my chances of finding Wilson sitting upstairs. The door lock was almost as tough as cottage cheese. I was inside in a few seconds. I walked down the corridor, looking for the basement where the super would be. If he took money from Wilson to lie, he'd take more money to tell the truth. The hall lighting was as dim as a subway tunnel—more than half the bulbs were missing.

I found the right door, knocked, got nothing. I hit it again, putting my ear to the door. Nothing—no radio, no TV, no voices. In a dump like this they wouldn't use the super to collect the rent.

If I had stopped to think about it I wouldn't have gone any further. I could have tried to find a pay phone where I could watch the door and call Mama to have her send Max over. But there was no sense in spoiling a perfect record.

Where the hell was Apartment 4? Fourth floor? Fourth apartment on the second floor? Okay—six stories, figure four apartments to each floor from the layout, total of twenty-four units. There was no elevator. I found the center stairway, listened for a second. Nothing was moving. It smelled bad—not dangerous, just the way these buildings smell after enough years of abuse. On the second floor landing I saw I was right—two apartments to the right, two more to the left. I spotted the number 3 in what was left of a faded gilt decal on one door. On the other side, the Number 6, again on a decal, black number on gold background—very classy. If the numbers went all the way to 6 on this floor, with four apartments in all, numbers 1 and 2 had to be downstairs. So Number 4 had to be on this floor—right next to 3.

I put my ear to the door—nothing. I slipped on my gloves and rapped softly—still nothing. Pick the lock? No—try the other apartments first. Number 3 was a no-show too. It was still quiet when I crossed the hall to 5 and 6. As I raised my hand to knock I heard the sound of an open hand on human flesh and a yelp—I moved closer and heard a young black man's voice, rapping in that hard-edged ghetto whine that the players think distinguishes them from the citizens. "Who's your daddy?" (slap) "I can't *hear* you, bitch" (slap). A mumbled sound from someone else. "Bitch, I'm not playin', you hear me? I'm serious—you understand?"

More mumbling. Another sharp slap. Sounds of crying.

"You run away from home, you find *another* home, right, little bitch? You got a *new* daddy now, right?" And some more slaps. I knew what was behind that door, and it wasn't Wilson. I walked back to Number 4, pulled my tools, and worked the lock. I stepped inside like I belonged there.

One glance told me nobody belonged there. It was just like I had pictured in my mind—a convertible couch opened into a bed with grayish stained sheets, a round Formica-topped table in one corner, two padded chairs with the seats torn, fast-food cartons all over the place. There was a moldy stack of magazines in one corner—*Nymphets at Play, Lolita's Lollipops*—like that. Nothing in the closet but some dirty jersey underwear thrown in a corner.

Tacked to one wall was the Cobra's collage of socially

acceptable porn—ads for bluejeans with little girls sticking their little butts into the camera, underwear ads from the catalogs with children strutting their undeveloped stuff for the photographer. Some of the photos had been scissored out—maybe there were also some adults in the ads and the Cobra had been offended at their intrusion into his maggoty fantasies.

On the bathroom wall was one of those pressure-point charts of a human figure showing the correct spots to kill with a single blow. There was a filthy tub, no shower—a can of shaving cream was the only thing left in the medicine cabinet over the sink. Plaster covered the walls, sweating in the heat from the radiators—he must have split very recently or the super would have been up to shut them off.

I moved through the Cobra's den, but it was no go—he was gone and he wouldn't be coming back here. Flood had spooked him away somehow and he was running. I checked the whole apartment again, cursing myself—if I had just listened to my experience instead of that damn blonde, I might have had him on a plate. A waste—it told me nothing I didn't already know.

I walked out the Cobra's door into the hallway, pulling the door shut behind me just as the pimp walked out of Number 6 across the hall, pushing a little girl out in front of him. I got just a quick flash of them as I stepped forward—a skinny girl, maybe thirteen years old, wearing an ankle-length maxicoat opened to display tiny white hot pants and a red top, thick-soled high heels—her face was closed behind a thick mask of makeup. The pimp wore a maxicoat too, his an imitation leopard. He had a safari hat with a leopard band—I caught the glassy flash of a fake diamond on his hand. The pimp caught my eye and then quickly looked away, but it was too late—by then I was on top of them. The pimp was yelling "Hey, man!" but I had the little cylinder of CN gas in my hand and I blasted him full in the face. I could see the gas turn to liquid on his skin right between his frightened eyes.

"Hey, mister—hey, *please*. Man, I didn't know nothin', man. I thought she was legal age, you know? Hey, man—I didn't *know*." He was screaming and clawing at his face at the same time.

I dropped the gas canister in my pocket and grabbed hold of two fistfuls of the pimp's cheesy coat, jerking him off his feet and back into his apartment. He tried to stand against the wall, but a knee to the testicles doubled him over. I clubbed him sideways across the face with a forearm as he slid to the ground.

I dropped to one knee, still holding his coat with one hand. "Fuckin' *yom*. You know who the fuck this is?" indicating the little girl who was huddled in a corner, watching with wide eyes. "That's Mr. G.'s daughter, asshole."

And then he realized this was more than a statutory rape beef—he was on trial for his life and the jury wasn't too deeply committed to civil rights. He looked for a way out, tried to speak, but nothing came out. I leaned down so I was real close to his face, slipping my hand around a roll of nickels I keep in my coat, my voice a harsh jailhouse-whisper. "Go back to Alabama, nigger. Never let me see you again in life, you understand? I see you again and I got to bring Mr. G. your fucking face in a paper bag. Got it?" punctuating each unanswerable question with a punch to his side until I felt a rib go. I pulled his face right into mine and spat between his eyes. He never moved—he would remember my face—I wanted him to. The closer the better for work like that.

I got to my feet and switched the roll of nickels for the .38. I pulled the hat off my head and wrapped it around the barrel. The pimp knew what was coming next as I knelt next to him, he could hear the pistol cock. "Mister—mister, I'm gone. I *swear* . . . I swear to *God*, man! Please . . ."

I acted like I was making up my mind, but of course it was no contest. His life wasn't worth the ninety days in jail it would cost me. The girl was still in the corner, her painted mouth open and slack, but she wasn't going to scream. I grabbed her arm and shoved her out of the apartment in front of me, half-throwing her down the stairs. A white face stuck itself out of a first-floor apartment as we went past—I showed the .38 to the face and it disappeared behind a slamming door. We hit the sidewalk—me walking fast and pulling the kid along with me. Her arm felt like a twig in my hand. She didn't say a word.

I found the Plymouth untouched, pushed her inside ahead of me and climbed in behind, punching down the switch so she couldn't unlock her own door. We were rolling in seconds, heading for the highway.

I pulled into one of the parking areas under the overpass where I know the manager. I told the girl, "Sit fucking *still*," locked the car, and walked over to the little booth where the manager sits. I tossed a twenty on his desk and he walked out like he had an appointment someplace. I picked up his phone, dialed the number of NYPD's Runaway Squad, for my money the only damn cop operation in New York worth the price of a city councilman.

"Runaway Squad, Officer Morales speaking."

"Detective McGowan around?" I asked.

"Hold on," said Morales. Then McGowan's strong Irish voice came over the wire. "This is Detective McGowan."

"Burke here. I got a package for you—about thirteen. She just left her pimp, okay?"

"Where's the kid?"

"At a parking lot under the West Side Highway on Thirty-ninth. Can you move now?"

"Be there in ten minutes," he said, and I knew I could count on it.

In the car waiting for McGowan, I lit a cigarette, looking over at the girl. A real baby—her skinny legs hadn't even grown calves yet. I couldn't do McGowan's job—I'd end up doing life for wasting one of those dirtbag pimps. McGowan has four daughters—twenty-five years on the job and he just made detective last year. I heard the brass was going to close down the whole Runaway Squad too. I guess they need all the cops they can get to protect visiting diplomats. New York's got an image to protect.

The girl said, "Mister—"

"Just keep your little mouth shut and your eyes down. Don't look at me—don't say *nothing*." Maybe I should have been a social worker.

She kept quiet until McGowan and his partner, a guy they call Moose for good reason, pulled up. I unlocked and he reached over and opened the girl's door. He held out his hand and she took it immediately. McGowan put his arm around her shoulders and started crooning to her in that honey-Irish voice and walking her back to his car. By the time they got back to the stationhouse he'd know where she had run away from— and probably why. I put the Plymouth into gear and pulled out. If anyone asked McGowan, he'd say he got an anonymous call and never saw the deliveryman.

But the Cobra was running—and I didn't know how far

he'd gone. I used a pay phone on Fourteenth and called the warehouse number.

"United States Attorney's office," came back Michelle's bubblegum voice.

"I thought I told you to clear out," I told her.

"I called Mama—she's going to call me when Max shows." Did *any* woman in the world do what I told her?

"Okay, babe—stay there. When Mama calls, tell her to send Max by, okay?"

She blew a kiss into the phone and hung up.

15

THE PLYMOUTH PURRED its own way back to the warehouse, oblivious to my depression. This case was certainly
going to do wonders for my reputation—a bit more of my
skillful detective work and I'd be known as Burke the Jerk.
Fuck it, I thought (my theme song), no point crying over spilt
milk. I had seen babies in Biafra too weak to cry, and mothers
with no milk left to nurse them. I had gotten out of that—I
could get out of this.

When I let myself into the warehouse Michelle was sitting
by the phone box with her legs crossed, reading her book next
to an ashtray stuffed with about two packs' worth of butts. Her
eyes flashed a question and my face gave her the answer.

"Thank God you're back, anyway," she said. "This place
was beginning to smell and I didn't want to leave the phones."
She picked up the ashtray and headed for the bathroom in the
back. I heard the toilet flush, then a rush of air as she opened
the ventilation shaft for a minute to clear out the room.

When she came back, patting her face with one of those
premoistened towelettes every working girl carries, she asked
me, "So?"

"He was there—and now he's not. Gone. I have to start
over."

"Too bad, baby."

"Yeah. Well, it wasn't a total loss. I found another kid for
McGowan."

"McGowan's a doll. If I was a runaway I'd turn myself in
to him in a flash."

"You were never a runaway?" I asked, surprised.

"Honey, my biological parents packed my bags and bought me the bus ticket."

There was nothing to say to that—I knew what Michelle meant by biological parents. Once I had a teenage girl come to my office and offer to pay me some money to find her "real" parents. She said she was adopted. It made me sick—these folks adopted her, paid the bills, took the weight, carried the load for her all her life, and now she wanted to find her "real" parents—the ones who dumped her into a social services agency that sold her to the highest bidder. Real parents. A dog can have puppies—that doesn't make it a mother. I took her twenty-five hundred and told her to come back in a month, when I gave her the birth certificate of a woman who had died from an overdose of heroin two years after the girl had been born. The phony birth certificate said "Unknown" next to the space for "Father." I told her that her father had been a trick, a john. Someone who paid her mother ten bucks so he could get off for a few minutes. She started to cry and I told her to go talk it over with her mother. She wailed, "My mother's dead!" and I told her that her mother was home, waiting for her. The woman who had died had just been a horse who dropped a foal, that's all. She left hating me, I guess.

Mama still hadn't called, which meant Max wasn't at the restaurant. I told Michelle I'd drop her wherever she wanted, and we packed up the stuff together.

When I pulled the Plymouth up in front of her hotel Michelle leaned over and kissed me quickly on the cheek. "Get a haircut, honey. That shaggy look went out *ages* ago."

"You always told me my hair was too short."

"Styles *change*, Burke. Although God knows, you never do."

"Neither do you," I told her.

"But I'm going to, honey . . . I'm going to," she said, and bounced out of the car toward the steps.

Michelle had a place to live, and so did I. But we had the same home. I drove past mine to the place where I live.

16

YOU CAN WALK out of prison and promise yourself you'll never be back, but it's not such an easy promise to keep. You always take some of the joint with you when you go. The last time I got out, I told myself it would be great to get up when I wanted to—not when the damn horns went off in the morning. But it's still hard for me to sleep late. Besides, Pansy isn't the kind of cellmate who's willing to sleep in and forget about hitting the chow line.

While she was out on the roof I looked out the back door toward the river. It was quiet up there, but I knew things were happening on the street. I'd never be able to live high enough up to not know that.

I went back into the living space next to the office and put together the stuff I'd need. All the firepower went back into the compartment in the floor of the closet except the .38, which would go back into the car. I put the clip-on car antenna into the breast pocket of an old tweed sportcoat, put it on over a plain gray sweater. Some tired corduroy pants, a battered felt hat, and a pair of desert boots completed the professor's outfit. The hat didn't really fit in with all the other stuff, but I don't like to play stereotypes too rigidly.

I put the microcassette recorder inside the special pocket in the lining of my leather overcoat and connected the long flexible wire the Mole had made for me to the remote microphone sewn into the inside of the sleeve. Then I connected the remote-start wire to the switch in my overcoat pocket, the same one that would hold my cigarettes. I used a handy police siren from down by the river to test the recorder for treble, patted Pansy's head until she purred to test for bass—it was as sensitive as the Mole had promised. I had ninety minutes of uninterrupted recording time—voice-activated, although it was so sensitive that it would run all the time once I touched the switch. I'd have to pay attention when I started it working.

I got Pansy all set up, activated the security systems, and went downstairs. The desert boots don't have steel toes like my other shoes, but they're rubber-soled and I don't make a sound.

I let myself into the garage, put the .38 back where it belonged, and got out some old chamois cloth. The Plymouth had to be thoroughly cleaned before I put on its disguise. A couple of concealed hinge pins the kid had installed were all I needed to remove the entire front outside section. Next I took the precut sheets of heavy vinyl with gum backing and proceeded to turn the Plymouth from a faded blue to a brilliant two-tone red and white. I smoothed the vinyl on very carefully, like the guy I bought it from showed me, then went over the whole thing with a soft rubber block to get rid of all the little bubbles. It wouldn't pass a serious inspection, but I wasn't planning on anyone getting a close look.

Then I put on new license plates. They're perfectly legal dealer plates from a junkyard in Corona. I own a ten percent interest in the junkyard, which I paid for in cash. In return, the old man who runs the thing carries me on the books at minimal salary so I have something to show the IRS, and lets me carry a set of dealer plates with me in case I see something worth salvaging. I cash the checks every month and get the cash right back to the old man. No problem. I suppose if some citizen got a reading on the plates the cops could trace them back to the junkyard, but they'd collect their pensions before I ever showed up there. And finding Juan Rodriguez (I told the old man that my parents were Spanish Jews, not that he gave a damn) in the abandoned building on Fox Street in the South Bronx would be a hell of a feat too.

I still had some time before I had to meet Flood, so I guided the Plymouth, resplendent in its new clothes, over to the warehouse to check on the mail. It looked empty as usual, but I rolled the car inside, turned off the engine, and waited. Max materialized at my window. I never heard him coming—they don't call him Max the Silent just because he doesn't speak. He twitched a muscle in his right cheek, parted his thin lips about a millimeter—that's his idea of a friendly smile—and motioned for me to follow him into the back room. He gestured to the old wooden desk to indicate that there was some mail. I scooped it out and pulled a cigarette out of my pocket, offering Max one.

You ever watch an Oriental smoke a cigarette? They really know how to get something out of it. Max touched the butt to his lips with his palm facing in, drew a deep breath and reversed his grip so that he was holding it with his thumb on the bottom and his first two fingers on top. Then he gradually pulled the cigarette away as he inhaled, a gesture that meant I should tell him what was going on. I pointed to my eyes, then spread my hands wide to show I was looking for somebody but didn't know where he was. Max touched his own face, held his hand in front of his eyes to show me a mirror, then gestured as if he were describing someone's physical characteristics. I pretended I was taking a picture, then beckoned as if I were inviting someone to enter. Max understood that I was expecting to get a photograph of the target soon. Then he held his hands out in front, turned them slowly back and forth, and looked up expectantly. I pointed to my eyes again and made a no-no gesture with my palms down—I only wanted to find the guy, not hurt him. Max shrugged, then made a glad-to-see-you-pal gesture with his hands and face to ask me if the guy would be happy when I did find him. I made a sad face, indicating he would not. Max looked at his hands again. I shrugged my shoulders to show that maybe he was right, or would be right when this all came down.

Grabbing an elbow with each hand as if I were rocking a baby, I crossed my arms—did Mama Wong have anything for me? Max picked up an imaginary telephone, spoke into it, touched his finger to his forehead like he was making a mental note to remember something. So I had gotten a call at Mama's, someone very insistent. Okay.

I buttoned up the coat to show Max I was leaving, and he glided out into the front area to make sure nobody was around. Max is a bona fide member of the warrior class—he doesn't need combat to prove what he is. A lot of clowns who spend half their time slobbering about "respect" should see how the rest of the world treats Max.

As I pulled out of the garage, Max gestured that I should let him know if things got difficult. Implicit in his gesture was the belief that almost anything was too difficult for me to do alone.

17

THE DRIVE OVER to Mama's was uneventful. The Plymouth was running smooth as a turbine. I checked the tape recorder hidden inside the dash to be sure it was working, then switched over to some cassette music. Charley Musselwhite's version of "Stranger in a Strange Land" came back at me through the four speakers. He was a perfectionist once, but he'd left his best efforts in Chicago a dozen years ago—I don't play any of his latest stuff. Too bad you can't keep people's best performances on tape cassettes like you can music. It wouldn't matter in my case, though—I haven't had my best shot yet, I hope.

I parked next to the dumpster in Mama Wong's alley. It's perfectly legal to park there, but nobody does. There's some kind of Chinese writing on the wall, courtesy of Max the Silent. I don't know what it means, but nobody parks there. I knocked twice on the steel door to the back of the restaurant, heard the peephole slide back, and one of Mama's alleged cooks let me in. Mama was sitting at her tiny black-lacquered desk, sipping a cup of tea and writing in her ledger book. I guess a lot of people would like to take a look at that book—I guess a lot of people would like to be rich, happy, successful, famous, secure, and healthy too. They've got about the same chance. Mama greeted me with her usual blend of Far Eastern subtlety and politeness.

"Burke, why you wearing that silly hat?"

"It's a disguise, Mama. I'm working on a case."

"Not so good disguise, Burke. You still look like European." (Mama likes to pretend all Occidentals look alike to her.)

"Max said you got a phone call for me?"

"Burke, you only one that can talk to Max except for me. Max like you. Max say that you are a man of honor. How come he say that?"

"Who knows why Max says anything?" (Meaning: That is between Max and me—he may work for you but he and I are a separate thing. Mama knows this but never stops trying. She thinks all secrets are dangerous except her own.)

"Burke, you get phone call from same man. James, he say. I tell you before, this man not good, okay?"

"What did he say this time?"

"He say I better tell you to call him. That this mean good money for you and you be mad at me if I don't tell you."

"Did he scare you, Mama?"

"Oh yes, very frightened. Many people killed over the telephone, right?" (Meaning: The phone number I give people rings in Mama's restaurant, but the actual instrument is located in the back of the warehouse, with the bell disconnected. It's hooked up to a diverter, which bounces the signal to the junkyard's pay phone in Corona, where another diverter picks it up and rolls it back to the pay phone in the kitchen. Bribing a phone company employee will eventually get you the address of the warehouse, but that's as close as you'd get. And going there with threats for Mama Wong would be fatal.)

"He leave a number, Mama?"

"Same number as last time. He say you can call him between six and seven tonight."

"Okay. Anything else?"

"No, nothing else. You want something to eat, some hot-and-sour soup?"

"You got it prepared already?"

"Always ready, always on stove cooking. Cook adds things during the day, but same soup, okay?"

I nodded yes and sat down at one of the front tables. The place wouldn't open for another couple of hours, and the curtains were drawn across the windows. One of the cooks came out with a big bowl of soup and some hard noodles, the *Daily News* and tonight's *Harness Lines*, which is the working-class version of the *Daily Racing Form*. It was a perfect breakfast, sitting there with the hot soup and the papers. Quiet, peaceful, safe. I couldn't concentrate on the racing form, so I let my mind drift off and slowly finished the soup. If this James was up to something in Africa, it had to be diamonds, ivory, or soldiers. A connection with Wilson? No, Wilson couldn't know I was looking for him. Besides, James had been calling Mama's even before this business with Flood started. It wouldn't come together.

I cleaned off the table and took out a pack of cigarettes, arranging ten of them in a star formation with the filters pointing toward the open center, then stared deep into the center until the cigarettes disappeared and walked around in the empty space in my mind for a while. Nothing came. Tendrils of thought licked at my brain but nothing ignited—I would have to wait for it to surface when it was ready. I'd already taken too many chances with the Flood thing.

I got up, returned all the cigarettes but one, stuck that one in my mouth unlit, went out to the kitchen with the plates. "See you later, Mama."

"Burke, when you call this man on the telephone, you meet him at the warehouse, not your office, okay?"

"Mama, I'm not going to call him. I don't need the work right now. I already have a case."

"You meet him at the warehouse, okay? With Max, okay?"

"How do you know I'm going to meet him, Mama?"

Mama just smiled. "I know." She went back to her ledgers.

I made the alley, fired up the car, and headed for the library to meet Flood.

18

I GOT TO Bryant Park around nine-thirty. This little plot of greenery located behind the Public Library is supposed to enhance the citizens' cultural enjoyment of their surroundings. Maybe it did once—now it's an open-air market for heroin, cocaine, hashish, pills, knives, handguns—anything you might need to destroy yourself or someone else. There's a zoning law in effect, though—if you want to have sex with a juvenile runaway from Boston or Minneapolis, or to buy a nine-year-old boy for the night, you have to go a few blocks further west.

Not too much activity when I first got there. The real scores are at lunchtime. But the predators and the prey were already doing their dance: broads walking through with gold chains and swinging handbags, solid citizens hustling to get to whatever hustle they do for a living, amateur thugs who wouldn't know an easy score from a steady job lurking as subtly as vultures in a graveyard, small packs of kids moving through fast on their way to one of the porno movies in Times Square, some old lunatic feeding the pigeons so bloated from slopped-around junk food that they couldn't fly, a bag lady looking for a place to rest her body for a few minutes before she nomads on.

I looked around carefully. There were no real hunters on the set (like someone who got burned in a dope deal looking for the salesman). I sat down on a bench, lit up. Like always, I was early. Sometimes if you come late for one of those meetings, you never leave.

I was smoking my cigarette and watching the flow around

my bench when I saw the Prof approach. He was making his way carefully through the clots of people, occasionally stopping to exchange a few words but moving steadily in my direction. Not quite a midget, he was maybe four-and-a-half feet tall, even with the giant afro that shot out of his skull like it was electrified. Maybe forty years old, maybe sixty. Nobody knows all that much about the Prof. But he knows a lot about people: some say "Prof" is short for "Professor," some say it stands for "Prophet." Today he's wearing a floor-length cashmere overcoat that probably fit the guy who originally brought it from Brooks Brothers and was dumb enough to hang it on a restaurant coathook—it trails behind him like the robes of royalty. The Prof speaks from the streets or the skies, depending on his mood:

"Today it is seven-twenty-seven. That's the plain truth, and that's no pun."

"How's business, Prof?"

"Do you hear the word, Burke? The number today must be seven-twenty-seven."

"Why?" I asked, not looking up. The Prof was standing to one side, not blocking my view. No matter how he talked, he knew how to act.

"Not what you think, Burke. Not what you think. Not the airplane seven-twenty-seven, but a doom dream in reverse."

"Yeah, that makes sense."

"Do not mock the Word, Burke. Last night I dreamed of cards and death. Not the Tarot cards—gambler's cards. You know the Dead Man's Hand?"

"Aces and eights?"

"This is true. Aces and eights. And death means time, and time means hope, and to hope is to reject death, is it not?"

"Time don't mean hope when you're *doing* it, Prof."

The Prof doesn't like to be challenged when he's talking nonsense.

"Who you talking to, chump? A tourist? Hear what I got to say before you go on your way."

"Okay, Prof. Run it down," I told him. That was a cheap shot about time anyway: small as he was, the Prof had stood up when we were inside.

"See the face of a clock in your mind, Burke—the reverse of one is seven, and the reverse of eight is two. The Death

Number is one-eighty-one—so the Life Number must be seven-twenty-seven. And today is Life."

"And you know this how?"

"Every man has a life sentence, brother. I know because I know. I know things. When I appeared, you were listening to a song in your mind."

"So? What song?"

"A song of aces and eights."

"I was listening to 'Raining in My Heart.'"

"By Slim Harpo?"

"The very one."

"And some mock the words of the Prophet! I know what I see, and what I see others do not know. Play seven-twenty-seven today, Burke, and be wealthy for a week to come."

I reached in my coat pocket and came out with a five, slapped it into his upturned palm. The money vanished.

"You may count on me, Burke. For it is written: those who cannot be counted *on*, may not be counted *in*. I will hold the proceeds for you until next we meet."

"May it be in a better place," I said, bowing my head slightly.

The Prof said nothing, just stood there sniffing the air like we were back inside, on the yard. And then, from the side of his mouth: "You working?"

"Just waiting for the library to open up so I can do some legal research for a client."

"How's Max?"

"The same."

"I heard your name a couple of nights ago."

"Where?"

"In a pub near Herald Square— two men, one with a loud voice and a red face, the other better-dressed, quiet. I didn't get everything they said, but they spoke British."

"British? You mean English?"

"No, Burke. Like British, but not quite the same. Like with a British accent or something."

"Hard guys?"

"The loud one, maybe, and only if you let him. Not city people."

"What'd they say?"

"Just that you were being cute with them, and that they had to meet with you to do some business."

"How'd you get so close?"

"I was on my cart." He meant a flat piece of wood with some roller-skate wheels on the bottom. When he kneels down on this and propels himself along wearing his long coat, you'd think he had no legs. It's a living.

"If you run across them again, I'd like to know where they live," I said, handing him another bill—a ten.

The Prof took the money, but more slowly this time. "I don't like those folks, Burke. Maybe you should stick to your legal research."

"It's all part of the same case, I think."

The Prof nodded and put his hand on his forehead as if he were getting a message. Instead, he gave me one: "If there's a reason, there's a season," he said, and flowed back into the crowd.

I watched him disappear into the murk, checked both sides of the street, and got up to meet Flood.

19

FLOOD WAS STANDING right where she was supposed to, just inside the doors past the entrance guarded by stone lions. She had her back against the wall, pocketbook over one shoulder, left hand in front of her, right hand holding the left wrist. She was wearing another one of those loose jackets with a bodysuit underneath, pale gray this time, with floppy wide-legged pants so loose at the cuffs I couldn't see her shoes underneath. Her hair was piled into a chignon at the top of her head but it didn't make her look any taller.

She didn't see me and I stayed in the doorway a minute to watch her. I still hadn't figured out how she could breathe without moving her chest. Flood had her eyes nailed to the door I was supposed to use. Human traffic flowed around her, but she never moved. Some professorial-looking person with an open book in one hand stopped and said something to her. He might as well have been talking to one of the stone lions out front—her big dark eyes never flickered. The professor shrugged elaborately and moved on.

I went in the door and Flood spotted me but stayed where she was. "Nice disguise, Flood," I said, and reached down to take her hand. She pulled it away but rose up on her toes and kissed me quickly on the cheek to show she wasn't telling me to get lost. Then she moved her hand toward her waist so fast I only saw the vapor trail, smiled like a little girl who'd just done something clever and held her hand out for me to take. She had small, chubby hands, not what you would expect if you'd seen her use them.

We walked down the lion-guarded steps hand in hand, me being careful on the steps and Flood bouncing along like she was on level ground. Maybe we looked like some graduate student who had stayed in school too long and his date. Hard to tell what we looked like but I guess we didn't look like a survival expert and a deadly weapon. So maybe the disguises weren't so bad after all.

It was good walking with Flood in the sunshine, so I made a complete circle of the block just to make it last—and to see if anyone was more interested in us than they should have been. As we turned into the park, I dropped Flood's hand and slipped my arm around her waist, squeezing her side to get her attention. She looked up at me. Quietly, out of the side of my mouth, I said, "What did you have in your hand?"

Flood looked at me, shrugged, and opened her closed hand. I hadn't seen her hand move back to her waist, but that was where she must have stashed it—a flat piece of dull metal shaped like a five-pointed star with a hole in the middle, about the size of a half dollar. When I reached for it, it sliced into my finger so cleanly that I didn't feel the pain until I saw blood—the goddamned thing was nothing but a star-shaped razor. Flood pulled it out of my finger, bent over to look at the wound, put my finger into her mouth, sucked sharply for a second, spit some blood onto the ground. "Hold it closed with your other hand for a few seconds and it'll stop bleeding. It's a clean cut." The star went back into her waistband someplace. I squeezed Flood's waist again to see if I could make her body bounce a little bit. She was so much fun. "What the fuck is that thing?"

"It's a throwing star. A defense tool when your opponent is beyond your hands and feet."

"You *throw* that thing?" By then we were walking toward one of the old trees that somehow had managed to survive the steady diet of wild dog urine, alcoholic upchuck, and junkie blood for which the park was justly famous. She rolled her shoulders slightly and I heard a faint whistling noise and then a tiny *snick* like when a knife snaps open. Flood tilted her chin toward the tree and I could see the throwing star sticking out of the mangy bark. We walked over and I tried to pull it out without defingering myself—no go. Flood put her thumb against the side of the star, pushed hard to the right, then shifted her hand and carefully removed it with two fingers. It disappeared again. I didn't know what the future was going to be for Flood, but I was reasonably certain she'd never be a battered wife.

We walked through the park to the car. I saw one of the local denizens looking at Flood's pocketbook and was tempted to let her walk on alone just so at least one miserable purse-snatcher would meet justice head on, but it wasn't worth it. Actually, I wouldn't have minded Flood walking ahead of me just to watch her walk.

When we got to the Plymouth, I checked it quickly, opened my door, and Flood slid in first. We drove over toward the East Side Drive, down to the Park & Lock joint near the river. I wanted to approach the Daily News Building on foot. I turned off the engine, rolled down the window, lit a cigarette, and waited. It's always good to wait. Most people lack patience, especially when they're doing something they really don't want to do.

It was quiet and dark in the lot, even in the middle of the day, and Flood didn't seem in a hurry. She just sat quietly, watched me smoke, and finally said, "You're not carrying guns today, are you?"

I turned away from the window. She was sitting with her legs crossed, elbow on one knee, chin in her hand. "Why do you say that?"

"A person walks differently when he's carrying a weapon. He moves differently. You can always tell."

"You learn that in Japan?"

"Yes."

"Well, they told you wrong. I don't walk differently, I don't move differently."

"Burke, you're not carrying those guns."

"I'm armed."

She looked at me, smiled, and said "Bullshit" in a merry voice. I looked as injured as possible under the circumstances.

"You want to search me?"

Flood gave me a throaty laugh, said "Sure," and put her hands inside my coat, under the arms, down my ribcage, around to my back, into the waistband of my slacks, dropped her hands to my ankles. Came up empty. She raised her eyebrows, patted my groin and round the inside of my thighs. Back to the groin again. "Is this what you mean?"

I tried to look serious, settled for a kiss on the tic-tac-toe scar instead and lit another cigarette. Flood looked pouty.

"Look," I said, "those folks in Japan don't know everything. I'm not trying to put them down, but you won't survive long if you believe everything someone else tells you."

"I still don't see any guns." Flood tapped her fingers on my knee as if she were patiently waiting.

I tightened my right fist, brought it up against my shoulder, flexed my bicep hard until I popped the Velcro flap inside the sleeve at the elbow joint. I pulled my fist rapidly away from my shoulder, opening it just in time to catch the short metal tube as it slid down my sleeve through the silk channel into my open hand. It wasn't as smooth as Flood and her star, but her mouth popped open like she'd just seen magic. She clapped her hands delightedly. "Burke, what's that?"

"What's it look like?"

"Like a big fat lipstick."

I held it in my hand and told her to look closely. The tube was perfectly machined steel, about two-and-a-half inches long. Inside was a .357-magnum hollow-point slug. All you do is press hard on the back of the tube and the slug comes out the front. The Mole wouldn't guarantee accuracy over five feet but he did guarantee it would work. Flood reached for it but I jerked it away from her.

"Can't you unload it and let me look at it?"

"You can't unload it. Once you force the slug in against the spring, that's it."

"Can you reload it after you use it?"

"Nope. You shoot it once—it blows up a piece of your hand and whatever's in front of your hand, and that's all there is."

"What a crazy thing."

"You just searched me. Did you find it?"

"The star is better."

"Better for *you*. It takes skill to throw that damn thing. All it takes for this is the guts to push the button."

She sat there for a while, obviously thinking it over. Like she knew something was wrong but couldn't get a grip on it. I smoked another cigarette while she was thinking. Finally she said, "It's no good. It doesn't even look like a gun. You couldn't hold it on anyone and make them do anything. It wouldn't scare anyone."

"It's not supposed to scare anyone. Nobody's even supposed to see it, much less get scared by it. It's just in case."

"In case of what?"

It was my turn to shrug. I took off the jacket, put the tube back inside, refastened the Velcro flap, tried it back on, and moved around inside the jacket until I was comfortable again. "Ancient philosophy covers everything, right? People have evolved since those Japs went into the mountains to study the fine art of breaking other people into little pieces. We got all kinds of freaks walking around this planet who didn't even exist a hundred years ago. This is for them, not for me. You have a reason to be here, but only for a while. Then you'll go back to wherever you came from and do whatever you did before. I have to stay here—it's a life sentence for me. So don't tell me how a man looks when he's carrying a gun— you don't know, little girl. You may be the toughest broad on this whole earth, okay? But in this little section of it you're ice cream for freaks."

Flood looked like her whole face went flat except for her eyes. I didn't let it stop me. "Don't get an attitude, Flood. I'm not trying to be your daddy. If I was in fucking Japan looking for someone I'd at least have enough sense to find a translator first, right? We've got work to do, and I can't have you stomping around like a fool—you'll fuck things up. And I'll get my ticket cancelled."

Flood tried to sound bitter. "That's the real issue, huh?"

"Ah, kiss my ass." I threw my hand up in disgust and opened the door to get out. Flood's hand turned into a grappling hook as she hauled me back inside like I was a featherweight and slammed me back against the driver's seat.

Still holding the lapel of my jacket, she thrust her square little face right against mine, growled "Maybe later," and giggled. Then she leaned over and kissed me hard on the mouth. "Let's be friends, okay?"

"I *am* your friend," I said, "I just don't want—"

Flood made a shut-up gesture with her hands. "That's enough. I'll listen to you—you'll listen to me. Let's do it."

I nodded my head. We both got out of the car and started up the block to the Daily News Building.

20

AS WE WALKED up Forty-second Street I kept my hands in my pockets. Flood rested her left hand on my forearm, keeping the other one free and loose. There's something about that street that makes you think a freak is going to jump out of every alley, even when you're way over on the East Side. Now that we had some of the ground rules straight, Flood decided to ask some questions. "What are we going to do at the News Building?"

"*We're* not going to do anything. I'm going inside to see someone—you're going shopping."

"Look, Burke—"

"Flood," I said wearily, "I'm not leaving you out of anything. There's no reason for this guy I have to meet with to see your face, right? And besides, you really do need some kind of disguise if you're going to go around with me. We don't know what's going to come down when you meet up with this Cobra freak. There's no need for people to see you."

"We *are* going to find him, Burke?"

"We are going to find him, yes. For damn sure if he's still in the city. And eventually even if he's not. Okay? But you've got to loosen up. Let me do what I can do—then you'll get your shot at him."

Flood smiled. A genuine, happy smile. "Okay!"

"All right, listen. You have to buy some clothes and some other stuff. You got money?"

"Yes, I have some."

"Here's what you need. A good black wig, about medium

length, some instant-tanning lotion, any kind you want, some gold eyeliner and eye shadow, some dark lipstick, the darkest you can find. Then either a low-cut blouse or a V-neck sweater, some spike heels with dark stockings or pantyhose, and the tightest pair of bright-colored pants you can squeeze yourself into. Oh yeah, and a wide belt with a buckle in front. Get a cap that'll help you hold the wig on, some color that matches the rest of the outfit."

"Forget it."

"Flood, there's no *forget it* going down here. I thought you said we'd work together on this."

"Where do I get to work, some massage parlor?"

"Hookers in massage parlors don't wear junk like that, Flood—they wear cheesy nightgowns and body powder."

"I'm sure you're a real expert on the subject."

I slowed down to light another cigarette. Opened my mouth to explain the reasons to Flood, who said, "You smoke too much," and slapped the butt out of my mouth. She turned away so I couldn't see her face. We both stopped in the middle of the block. She said nothing, just kept looking away from me. I was about ready to give up. "You're a goddamned baby."

She whirled around to look at me. Her eyes were almost bright enough to have tears in them. "I'm not a baby. But I'm not going to just *do* things. You have to explain them to me."

"Flood, there's a good reason for every single damn thing I told you to get. But we don't have to fight about it out here in the street, okay? I've got to see this guy to get things ready. You can do one of three things: go and buy the stuff and meet me at the car; go and wait for me in the car so I can fucking *convince* you to buy the stuff; or go back to the Land of the Rising Sun."

"I could find him myself."

"You couldn't find this freak if he was listed in the Yellow Pages."

Flood faced me, held out her hand, palm up. I gave her the spare key to the door (it won't work the ignition), told her how to work the lock, and she about-faced and marched off. I went up the block to the News Building and dialed the guy I wanted from the pay phone on the corner. He was in. I told him what I wanted on the phone—there's no way I'm walking into a newsroom with all those nosy clowns around. Most of the younger reporters do all their investigating over the phone, but there're a few veterans around who'd make my face and have it filed away forever. I told the guy I'd meet him in his favorite Irish bar in an hour and hung up.

I called Mama and told her to tell Mr. James that I'd be calling him that evening at the number he'd left, unless he wanted the number changed. Then I sat down with the racing form again for a half hour before calling Maurice with twenty across the board on a trotting mare I fancied, just to let him know I hadn't left town. When I strolled into the Irish bar I found the reporter in a booth with a folder full of newsclips. I like this kid. He graduated from Harvard, has *two* master's degrees, makes fifty grand a year, and talks like a mildly retarded working-class dropout with a philosophical bent. Maybe it works on women.

"Burke, here's the dope you wanted. What've you got for me?"

"Got nothing now, kid" (he hates to be called kid) "but I'm working on a real scandal over at the courthouse."

"Yeah, sure."

"I gave you that habeus canine piece, right?"

"Big fucking deal."

"What do you mean, big fucking deal? I bet you copped a raise for such a sensitive piece of investigative reporting."

"Look, Burke, don't jerk my chain. You wanted the clips, I got you the clips. I know there's a story in this someplace, so all I'm asking is that I get in first."

"Kid, you know I don't talk to reporters, right?"

The kid nodded—he thinks I'm in organized crime, one of the few Irishmen to break through the Italian barriers. The closest I ever got to a mob was at a wrestling match—some lunatic paid me good money to learn the true identity of the Masked Marvel for him.

I looked through the newsclips the kid got me from the morgue. My man was there, all right, just like I thought—Martin H. Wilson, arrested on charges of rape and sodomy of three Puerto Rican kids. No more on that story. Then Martin Wilson arrested on rape, sodomy, and murder charges of Sadie's kid, D.A. asks $100,000 bail at arraignment. Then later on, court orders competency hearing after Wilson's defense attorney says he's a victim of Agent Orange poisoning in Vietnam. Then the other clips—I had a hunch about why Wilson wasn't in the can waiting on a trial. Yeah, there it was: Elijah Slocum, major kiddie-porn dealer, arrested at his mansion in Riverdale by detectives from the Bronx D.A.'s office following a six-month investigation by undercover operatives. Slocum posts $250,000 bail, claims he was set up by his "enemies." Slocum moves to reduce bail; several prominent citizens testify as character witnesses; case still pending.

Good enough. There was no picture of Wilson but I didn't expect one. A *Daily News* photo would never be good enough anyway. All I really wanted were the dates. I put them in my memory, shook my head sadly, and handed the clips back to the kid. "Well, it was a long shot anyway."

"This stuff is no good?"

"You got me what I asked for—I just came up empty, that's all. Listen, I still figure I owe you one, okay?"

The kid nodded glumly, swallowed his beer in a single throw and signaled to the barmaid for another as I was getting up to leave. I said I'd give him a call. He mumbled "God bless" and started on another brew. I walked four blocks west, caught a cab, told the driver I wanted the U.N. Building, and got off near Forty-ninth Street and First Avenue. Then I walked down to the river and south to the car where Flood was sitting in the front seat reading a newspaper.

I let myself in, noticing the packages piled on the back seat. So far, so good. Flood looked at me expectantly. "I'll explain when we get to the office," I said, eased the Plymouth into gear, and set off for downtown.

21

HALFWAY DOWN THE drive I realized that I wasn't acting like I'd been trained to—I couldn't really bring Flood back to the office without showing her too much. And I wasn't ready to do that. "Flood, is anyone using your studio this time of day?"

"Why?" She was obviously going to stay hostile until I came up with some answers for her.

"Well, I can't bring you back to the office without deactivating the dog, and that could take a couple of hours. Besides, I don't want to do any business with clients until we've wrapped this thing up. I just want to concentrate on this."

"There's nobody there. They only have classes two nights and one day every week. But why can't we go to your place?"

"I live in a hotel and there's no way to get past the front desk without a lot of people noticing. I don't want anyone to notice you until you've gotten into the disguise."

"It must cramp your style, not being able to get by the front desk."

"It cramps everyone's style. That's why I live there."

Flood didn't seem surprised that I knew the way to her place. I told her to go on upstairs and that I'd call her in a few minutes to see if anyone had been around asking questions. She made no move to take the packages out of the back seat when she got out.

I gave her ten minutes and called. A frigid voice just barely identifiable as Flood's informed me that everything was as it had been and that I could come up when and if I decided to.

I carried the packages in, rang for the freight elevator, and waited until I heard it start to groan its way downstairs. Then I stepped back outside. When it came down empty. I pressed the switch to send it two floors above Flood's place, and took the stairs—quietly. There were no sounds except the elevator. Waiting in the corridor on Flood's floor, I heard the elevator creak to a stop somewhere above me and stepped into the studio. It was empty, the same as when I was there last. I walked back to Flood's private place where she was sitting on the floor in that lotus position waiting for me. And my story.

I tore open the packages—tanning lotion, eyeshadow and eyeliner, a lustrous-looking black wig, a pair of pink toreador pants, a black jersey V-neck pullover, a black patent-leather belt, some black mesh pantyhose, and a pair of four-inch spikes in black pseudo-leather. Cheap junk, except for the wig. Flood said nothing, watching me.

"Okay, here's the story. You can't change your face, not really. But you're going to have to be seen by some people—you dress like this and people will notice everything but your face. All they'll remember is some pink pants and maybe black hair. Besides, you have to look kind of sexy and incompetent at the same time, because you have to ask some people for help. They won't remember what they don't see."

"Burke, what the hell are you talking about?"

"Flood, for chrissakes, what's wrong with you? You weren't raised in a convent. The average man takes one look at you shaking it down the street in these pants and that's all he'll remember. What's so goddamned hard to understand?"

"I don't care if people know who I am or what I'm looking for."

"Yeah, that's right, you don't. Either you're going back to Japan or you've got some *kamikaze* plan—you'll do your job and then you just don't give a damn what happens after that. That's not me. I *do* care—I don't want people looking for me. If they have to look for you, for Flood, and they connect us up, they'll look for me too. Get it? You just look too strange the way you're dressed now—the way you look."

Flood held up the pink pants. "These *don't* look strange?"

I tried again. "Flood, this isn't a question of good taste, okay? People are going to notice you no matter what, see? But there's no way a man's going to look at your breasts bouncing around in that sweater and at your face at the same time."

"My breasts don't bounce when I walk."

"Flood, I don't care if you're the world's greatest martial arts expert—I don't care if you're fucking Wonder Woman. You wear that sweater and no bra and your goddamned breasts will bounce."

"Burke, you're a lunatic. No bra with that outfit? I'd look like some moron's version of a whore."

"Now you got it."

"I won't do it."

"The fuck you won't. I made some major sacrifices to do this job—you can too."

"What sacrifices did you make?"

"I had plastic surgery."

"You had *what?*"

"Plastic surgery. I'm telling you the truth."

"For this job."

"Goddamned right. Before I took this job I used to be a male model."

Flood tried like hell not to giggle, gave it up, tried to get a straight face again. Gave that up and started laughing. It was a great laugh—peeking between her fingers at my former-model's face, she just plain cracked up. Finally, she came over to sit down next to me and picked up the pink pants. "Burke, I'll look like the fat lady in the circus if I wear these."

"You'll look beautiful."

"Burke, I'm serious. Some women can wear these things, but I'm not built that way. It took me about fifteen minutes to get them on in the store."

"Oh, you already tried them on." Flood looked down, said nothing. "Flood, you vain bitch. All this crap about clothes and it's only because you think you don't look good in them."

"It's not just that."

"So what else is it?"

"I can't move in them."

"Put them on and let me see, okay?"

Flood jumped to her feet, flung off her jacket, untied the sash at her waist, and stepped aside as her slacks fell to the floor. She popped open the snaps in the crotch of her bodysuit, ripped it over her head, and grabbed the pink pants out of my hand in one vicious motion. That took about three seconds. Then she grunted and strained for about five minutes, trying to get the pants over her hips, muttering curses at me all the while, but she finally got them closed over her waist. It looked like bright new pink skin. With her hands on her hips, she glared at me. "See what I mean?"

"Can you bend over?"

"Bend over? I can't even *walk.*"

"Just try, okay?"

She turned and walked away from me. It was the finest combination of sex and comedy I'd ever seen. From the ankles to the upper thighs, she was sheathed in pink metal, and from there on up it looked like pink Jello bitterly resisting confinement. Flood spun around. "Burke, if I even see so much as a smile on your ugly face I'm going to put you in the hospital."

My face was as flat as a pane of glass. Unfortunately it was equally transparent and Flood charged with both fists clenched. Thank God by the time she made it over to where I was sitting, she was laughing herself. She laughed even harder when I tried to help her get the pants off. She struggled to her feet, and swished her way over to the bathroom with the rest of the outfit. When she came out she was perched on the spike heels, wearing the wig and the jersey top. Even *trying* to watch her face with all that flesh bouncing around was impossible, and I could tell she knew it too. With her face made up, we'd be home free. She pranced around in the middle of the room, making a few experimental passes with her feet, twirling them in small circles a few inches off the ground.

"I can kick in these things, but no high kicks, no round-houses."

"Forget about that. It isn't a fighting outfit, Flood, it's a damn disguise, right?"

"What if I have to kick someone?"

"Take the pants off first."

Flood gave me a look, and started to roll the pants down over her hips. By the time they got halfway down, I knew she wasn't going to kick me.

22

WHEN I WOKE up a couple of hours later, Flood was still out like she'd been drugged. I wish I could sleep like that—maybe it was because her conscience was so clear. We still had a bit of time so I got out my cigarettes and sat by the big window looking down at the street. I held the butt below the windowsill and blew the smoke down in case there was some freak out there looking for a tiny red light in the darkness that meant *go* instead of *no* to him. I still had to think of a plan that would get Flood her raw meat and keep me away from the government. Nothing came to me.

The sounds of the shower brought me back inside, where I waited for Flood to come out. When she did she was wearing some big fluffy white towel and walked past me to the large room where I'd been smoking. I followed her and watched while she dropped the towel, walked nude over to the wall with all the mirrors, and started her workout—a complicated *kata* with spinning kick-thrusts and double hand-breaks, knife-edged and clenched fist. A *kata* is a martial arts exercise: some of the Japanese styles use them to qualify for higher degrees, like a black belt; some use them as stylized practice. When an amateur does a *kata* it's like watching a spastic robot, but Flood's was a death dance. I watched her quietly, not moving. The only noise was the occasional hiss of breath through her nose.

Flood's *kata* was steel-edged white smoke. She finished by landing into a split any cheerleader would envy. Stayed perfectly still on the floor, concentrating on something. Then she looked up at me. "Can you throw me those pants I bought?"

I went back into her space and brought them out. Flood worked them back up over her hips. Her body had a light sheen of sweat and it was still a struggle. It didn't look funny this time. She zipped them up, snapped the front button closed, walked over to the wall, and took down a pair of heavy leather gloves, something like catcher's mitts. She tossed them to me. I knew what she wanted me to do, so I took off my shoes and walked out onto the gym floor. Standing in a semicrouch, I held the gloves out toward Flood, one at my right knee, the other at my left shoulder, the palms facing her.

Flood came to me with her hands open in front of her, bowed slightly. I nodded that I was ready. She approached with small, light steps, floated up on her toes and sideways into a cat-stance, and suddenly lashed out with her left foot at my right knee. She caught the open glove squarely with a harsh *pop*, spun on her right leg, planted her left foot, and whipped the right up at my right shoulder. It never came off—the skin-tight material held her legs together at the crotch and she fell, immediately rolling to the side, hands clasped near her head, elbows out.

I knew what she was going to say. "It's no good. I can't get any speed or leverage above the knee. We have to get something else."

"Okay, Flood, I don't want you to feel helpless."

"It's not a joke."

"It doesn't bother you to fight with no clothes on, but—"

"I had to train for a long time before it didn't. We all have to practice like that, so that we don't think about ourselves, just about the task."

"So didn't you ever train to fight wearing clothes?"

"Burke, listen to me. I could fight no matter what, yes? At least I could defend myself. But I need room to move or I can't develop any power."

"So when you fight this Cobra freak . . ."

"Yes."

"Flood, I'm not promising it will end like that."

"You just find him for me."

I went back to the window and sat down on the floor, lit up. Flood padded over to me, floated down into a lotus position, sat there quietly for a while. Maybe keeping me company, maybe thinking too. She didn't understand a fucking thing.

"Flood," I said, "you know how to fight an attack dog?"

"I never have."

"There's just one secret, okay? When he bites you—and he *is* going to bite you—you have to ram whatever he bites back into his mouth as deep and as hard as you can."

"And then?"

"And then you use whatever you have left to cancel his ticket."

"So?"

"So the dog expects you to do just one thing—pull away as hard as you can. He's a hunter and that's what his prey is supposed to do. Panic and run."

"So?"

"So there's no such thing as a fair fight with a dog."

"Wilson's not a dog."

"You know what he is, Flood?"

"No."

"Well, I do. So you do it my way—you listen to me."

Flood's eyes narrowed, then relaxed with a calmness that reflected through her body as she spoke. "There's a right way, a correct way to do anything."

"There's a right way to rape little kids?"

"Burke! You know what I mean."

"Yeah, I know what you mean—and you're out of luck, kid. The only way to do anything is to do it so you walk away from it."

"And if I don't agree?"

"Then you walk *into* it alone."

Flood's eyes bored into my face, looking for an opening. There was none. I didn't know why I'd even come this far, but I wasn't going past my own limits. The only game I play is where winning means you keep playing. She smiled. "You're not so tough, Burke."

"Endurance beats strength. Didn't they teach you that over in Japan?"

She thought about it for a minute, then flashed a lovely, perfect smile. "You think they make these kind of pants in some stretch material?"

"I don't know. Why don't you check it out early tomorrow morning before you go to court?"

"We're going to court?"

"Not me, just you. I have something to do on my own and besides, I don't like to go to court in the daytime."

I lay down on the floor, put my arms behind my head, and blew smoke rings at the ceiling. Flood leaned on one elbow and rubbed the side of my face with her knuckles while I told her how you look up a docket number in the Criminal Court Building. It was quiet and peaceful there, but I had to make that call around six. I kissed Flood good-bye, got my stuff, then climbed the stairs to the roof, where I checked the street. Nothing. I rang for the elevator and hit the stairs down as soon as I heard it move.

The car was just as I'd left it. Must be a pretty crime-free neighborhood—this was two times running.

It was almost evening and I wanted everything secure before I called this James character, so I stopped at a pay phone on Fourteenth Street to reserve a ride for the night. I have this arrangement with the dispatcher—I call him, he gives me a cab for the night shift, and I don't have to return it until morning. I keep whatever I earn for the evening on the meter and he gets a flat hundred bucks. I also keep a hack license for Juan Rodriguez (the same guy who makes his living working in that Corona junkyard) behind the false wall at the rear of the Plymouth's glove compartment.

You have to be fingerprinted to get a hack license in New York. It costs you an extra fifty to bring your own fingerprint card already made out for the inspectors. I have a couple of dozen cards stashed, already fingerprinted, but with no names or other information on them. I don't know the real names of any of the guys who would match those prints, but I know the cops would have a hell of a time interviewing any of them.

The old man who works as a night watchman in the city morgue told me how the cops sometimes fingerprint a dead body while it's still fresh so they can make an identification. He showed me how it was done. I got the blank cards easily enough, waited a few weeks, and the old man let me make a few dozen prints from a corpse that came in on the meat wagon one night. Nasty car accident—the guy was headless, but his fingers were in perfect shape.

Driving a cab in New York is the next best thing to being invisible. You can circle the same block a dozen times and even the local street-slime don't look twice. The cops do the same thing in their anticrime cars—only trouble is their union won't let them work the cars alone, so when you see two guys in the front seat of a cab, you know it's the Man. Very subtle.

I drove past Mama's to check her front window. Usually there are three beautiful tapestries of dragons on display—one red, one white, one blue. Tonight the white one was missing— undercover cops of some kind were inside. If the blue was gone, it would mean the uniformed police. I kept rolling like I was supposed to do. I could have gone inside, since only the red dragon standing alone meant danger, but I needed to find Max and he wouldn't be inside, at least not upstairs with the customers. When Max wanted to leave he climbed down to the sub-basement, below the regular storage area. It was pitch-dark down there, and dead quiet. I was there once when two uniforms came looking for him. The young cop wanted to go down there after him but his partner had more sense. He just told Mama to ask Max to stop by the precinct because they wanted to talk to him. Going down in that basement after Max would be about as smart as drinking cyanide and have the same long-term effect.

I pulled into the warehouse with the headlights off, rolled down the window, lit a cigarette, and waited. It was quiet there, so quiet that I heard the faint whoosh of air before I felt the gentle thump on the car's roof. I stared straight ahead through the windshield until I saw a hand press itself against the glass, fingers pointed down. I told Max that one day he would break his fool neck jumping from the second-story balcony on to the roof of cars. He thought that was hilarious.

We went into the back room and I pointed to one of the chairs, then spread my hands to ask "Okay?" When he nodded, it meant he'd wait there for me. He knew I'd explain when I got back.

The basement of the warehouse was my next stop. The only light down there came from the diffused rays of a streetlight through one of the dirty narrow windows, but it was bright enough for me to find the exit door behind a pile of abandoned shipping pallets. Inside one of the pallets was a rubber-covered dial telephone with two wires ending in alligator clips and a set of keys. One of the keys let me into another basement halfway down the alley, and the second got into the telephone wire box for the commercial building on the corner. It was peaceful—the collective of Oriental architects who inhabited the place in the daytime never worked at night. I checked my watch. Another three or four minutes until James would be expecting the call. I opened the telephone junction box, hooked up the handset, checked to see if anyone else was on the line, got a dial tone, and waited. At fifteen seconds to six I dialed the number James had given to Mama. Someone answered on the first ring.

"Mr. James's wire."

"This is Burke."

"One moment please." I was supposed to think I was calling an office. James came on, another voice, so at least two of them were in on the game. "Burke. I've been trying to reach you. You're a hard man to catch."

"Why didn't you just stop by the house, pal?"

"I don't know where you live."

"That's right, you don't. What do you want?"

"I've got some business for you; something right up your alley. There's a considerable sum involved. Can we meet?"

"You know somebody I know?"

"I don't want to say names on the phone. But let's say I know your reputation, and this would be something you would want to do."

"I don't think so."

"I do think so," his voice turning what he thought was hard and forceful, meaning that he was going to be a continual pain in the ass and stay on my case. It was better to meet him once and have done with it.

"Okay, pal. Tonight—all right?"

"Tonight's fine. Just tell me where."

"I'll send a cab for you. The driver will bring you to me."

"That's not really necessary."

"Yeah, it is."

There was silence as he thought for a minute, not that there was much for him to think about. He was probably going to tell me to send the driver to some fancy hotel and he'd be standing out in front like he belonged there. It was time to show him we weren't going to spend the evening being stupid. "Look, here it is. The cab will be there at ten o'clock on the dot. You and your friend just get in the backseat, don't say anything. The cab will have its off-duty light on and it will blink its lights twice when it comes up on you. Just get in and it'll bring you where I am. You get out when the cabby stops, wait on the corner, and I'll pick you up and take you to the meeting place."

"That sounds a bit complicated."

"Suit yourself."

Another short silence. Then, "Okay, Burke, tell your cabby to meet us at—"

"Never mind all that. The cabby will be at the same corner you're standing on right now. And don't waste your time trying to talk to him, he won't say a word. Yes or no?"

Silence, a muffled conversation. Then, "Yes, we'll—" I unhooked the alligator clips, terminating the conversation. If they weren't on the same corner as the pay phone when the cab rolled up, that would be the end. I went back the way I'd come, returning the equipment and the keys, and rejoined Max in the warehouse.

When I put the hack license on the table in front of Max his face broke into a joyful grin—he loved to drive the cab. I got out paper and a marking pen, showed him the corner where he'd pick up the two clowns, and gestured that he should bring them back to this neighborhood. He nodded and I diagrammed that he should bring them only to the far corner, make the turn, stash the cab in the back of the warehouse, then go back and escort them inside.

Max patted his face with both hands, shrugged his shoulders, and spread his palms out wide, asking me if they wouldn't recognize him as the driver of the cab when he brought them inside. I held up one finger, got up, and walked over to the big trunk where we kept our supplies—hats, wigs, false beards, face putty, stuff like that. Max was in seventh heaven now. This was perfection—not only would he get to drive the cab, but he'd have a disguise too. We brought the mirror out from the bathroom and tried on a few different versions of Max's face. His favorite was the Zapata mustache, which, together with mirror-finish sunglasses and a fat cigar in his mouth, made him impossible to recognize. I added a jaunty beret in a dashing shade of pink. Max wasn't crazy about the color but he did smile at the sight of the hat, no doubt remembering the would-be mugger who had donated it to our collection one dark night last summer.

We found Max an old army jacket and some regulation combat boots, very comfortable for driving. Everything went fine until I got out the gloves—Max never wore gloves even in the dead of winter. But his hands were more recognizable than most people's faces. I didn't know how observant these guys were, but I wasn't taking any chances.

Max slammed the gloves down on the table in a gesture of total refusal. I grabbed the gloves in one hand and balled the other into a threatening fist, telling him to put on the damn gloves or I'd break his face. His face broke all right, into silent laughter. Then he lightly touched the first two fingers of his right hand to his forehead and to his heart, and opened his two hands in front of me. This was an apology, not for refusing to wear the gloves but for laughing at me. Max thinks I'm more sensitive than I am. At least I think he does.

We went to examine the cab. It was typical of the breed, a battered old Dodge with hundreds of thousands of no-maintenance miles on the clock. The trunk, as expected, was empty, since fleet owners don't want the cabbies to sell the spare tire and claim it was stolen. We spread a heavy quilt on the floor of the trunk, checked to make sure the exhaust system was free of leaks, and Max punched a few tiny holes in the trunk lid with an icepick. I'd be wearing a one-piece padded refrigerator suit while I rode along in the trunk, the kind guys use to work inside meat lockers. That, plus the quilt, would keep me from breaking a few bones when Max slammed the cab around like I expected.

While Max finished checking over the cab, I got the giant portable tape player (another mugger's donation) and a supply of tapes for Max to play while he drove. It was a little after eight when we finished, so I put some Judy Henske tapes in the player and Max and I continued our game of gin. We had previously agreed to play until one of us won a million dollars from the other. We'd been playing almost ten years and Max had all the score sheets from our first game in the Tombs to last week's. I was a good seventy bucks ahead. We sat there, playing gin, smoking—me listening to the music, Max feeling the bass lines through his body. It was good to be sitting in the one club where I was always welcome. I think Max felt the same, although we never talked about it.

23

JUST PAST NINE we loaded up the cab and pulled out, me driving and Max as the passenger. We rolled the cab into my own garage. Max stayed there while I went upstairs, let Pansy out, and got her something to eat. Then I climbed into the trunk and Max took the wheel. No way I was going to let these people get a look at my face until I was sure it was going down like it should. If there were cops on the corner, Max would just motor right on by. We headed for the pickup point near Thirty-fourth Street. Although Max loved to drive, he generally behaved himself when he was at the wheel of a cab. Cabs were too sloppy for him—they didn't respond to a delicate touch. The Plymouth was another story—every time I let him drive that beast he'd happily tear chunks out of the pavement, corner in four-wheel drifts, break 125 on the West Side Highway, and generally act like the city was a giant demolition derby. A lot of cabbies drove like maniacs but there was a purpose to it—making money. Max was immune to money.

I could feel the streets slip by—I could tell where we were just from the sounds and smells. I lay there wrapped in the quilt, looking like so much garbage in the filthy refrigerator suit. If anyone were to open the trunk, it would take them more than a second or two to figure out there was a live human being in there. By then they'd have mace, if not stars, in their eyes. We had checked the trunk light to make sure it wasn't working.

The cab slowed to a gentle stop and the engine revved sharply—once, twice. It meant we were a few minutes early and Max didn't want to turn the corner until he could do it right on the money. Okay.

We started up again, turned a corner, drifted over to the right, and began slowing down in a long gradual slide. By now Max was blinking the lights like we had arranged. I heard someone say "That's it" and people approach the cab. The back door opened and a voice said, "Are you the guy from Burke?" The cab lurched as Max took off—the body of one of them slammed backward from the acceleration and the cab shot straight ahead, heading for the West Side Highway.

One of the passengers started to say something, but gave up as the shrieks and screams of contemporary disco pounded through the cab's interior from Max's ghetto blaster. There was no hope of them getting any kind of look at Max—the interior light hadn't gone on when they'd opened the door, Max had kept his high beams on while picking them up so they couldn't see through the windshield, and the protective screen of plexiglas between driver and passenger was black with years of nicotine and grime.

Max sped downtown, obviously ignoring several red lights, judging by the occasional gasps of the passengers and the un-interrupted flow of our passage. When he got near the Division Street underpass, he slammed to a stop. There was no action from the backseat, but when Max turned off the cassette player they got the message that this was the place. They got out and the cab was moving again before the back door was closed. We were out of their sight in less than ten seconds, around the corner and heading for the warehouse.

Max pulled the cab in the back, I let myself out of the trunk, and we both covered the cab with one of the tarps we always kept around. You never know what you might have to cover in an emergency.

I set up the meeting table in the side room while Max removed his disguise—he changed into a pair of chinos, sweat-shirt, and black leather shoes so thin they could have been ballet slippers. While I sat at the table with the light behind me and waited, Max faded out the side door to bring on the clowns. If they had split the scene, Max wouldn't bother to look for them. Unless they got out of the area real fast, one of the roving packs of kids would take them quickly enough.

It was about twenty minutes before they came back. Max led them inside to the table, ushering them over to a pair of chairs facing me, then floated over and took the chair to my left.

Two men. One beefy-faced and bulky, close-cropped hair, a thick drinker's nose, steel-frame glasses. A fringe of whitish hair poked out of the top of a white sportshirt worn outside his pants. Omega chronograph on his left wrist, dial facing out, short, fat hands, flat-cut nails. Expressionless face, piggy eyes. The other, taller with a heavy shock of blond hair parted on the side, suede sportcoat, mobile clean-shaven face, two thin gold chains around his neck, hands clean and well-cared for, a metal case protruding just slightly from his breast pocket.

We looked at each other for a moment or so, then the taller one spoke. "Are you Mr. Burke?"

"Yes."

"I'm James. This is my associate, Mr. Gunther."

Gunther leaned forward so I could see his little eyes and clenched one of his hands into a fist. The heavy. "Who's this?" He pointed a fat finger at Max.

"This is my silent partner."

"We're just dealing with you. Nobody else."

I looked back at him pleasantly. "It's been a pleasure talking to you. My driver will be happy to take you back to where he picked you up—"

James broke in. "Mr. Burke, you will have to pardon my friend. He's a soldier, not a businessman. There's no reason why your partner can't sit in if you wish."

I said nothing. Max said nothing. Before James could continue, Gunther spoke up again. "He's a gook. I don't like fucking gooks—I saw enough of them. What kind of white man has a gook for a partner?"

"Look, asshole," I told him, "I'm not buying any master-race stock this week, okay? You got business, talk—you don't, walk." I was pleased at the rhyme.

"You do all the talking for the two of you?"

"Yep."

"What's the matter with the gook, he don't talk?"

"He doesn't do any talking. And so far neither have you."

James put his hand lightly on his pal's clenched fist and patted him. A tender gesture. "Mr. Burke, I must again apologize for my friend here. His family was killed by terrorists back home. They were blacks, of course, but we later learned that they had Chinese leadership. You understand . . ."

"You think my partner was one of the terrorists?"

"Don't be silly. I just mean—"

"I'm not silly, just confused. Are you people cops, journalists, businessmen, or just a couple of thrill-seeking faggots?"

Gunther was on his feet, opened his mouth to say something, then focused his eyes sufficiently to notice the double-barreled sawed-off I had leveled at his face. He closed his mouth and sat down. James hadn't moved. I turned the shotgun sideways so they could see it didn't have a stock. It didn't have much of a barrel either, just about enough to sheath the shells waiting inside. I moved it lightly from one to the other.

"You call and pressure me until I finally agree to meet with you. I send a cab for you, bring you to this place I had to rent for the evening. You cost my partner and me a lot of time and some money too. Then you come here and talk a lot of garbage—now you want to threaten me too? You have business or not?"

"We have business, Mr. Burke, serious business. Business that could make you a rich man, if you'll just allow me to speak."

"Speak. First, you carrying, either of you?"

James said no, but Gunther reached in his pocket and took out a pair of brass knuckles. Laying them on the table in front of me, he said, "That's all."

"That's all?"

Gunther wasn't finished with his heavy act yet. "That's all I ever need," he said, and settled back into silence.

"Let's just start over," James said. "We have a buyer for certain goods in our home country, and we have a seller of those same goods. What we need is for those goods to reach the buyer, and when they do, there is a handsome commission available to the individual who expedites matters. We understand that you have the means to accomplish this, and we simply want to put that proposition on the table."

"What goods?"

"Fifteen hundred long arms, about half-divided between Armalites and AK–47s, two thousand rounds for each weapon, five hundred bulletproof jackets, four dozen SAM–7s, some pump-action .12 gauges, and some other miscellaneous items."

"To where?"

"That's not important."

"How do I move them if I don't know where to?"

"You don't have to move them, Mr. Burke. That's the beauty of this. All we want from you is a valid End Use Certificate from your friends in Africa. We'll do the rest."

"And the money?"

"Half a million, U.S. Payable anyway you say."

"What makes you think I can get an End Use Certificate?"

"Mr. Burke, suffice it to say that we are aware of your services to the former Republic of Biafra. We are aware of an exile government now operating in the Ivory Coast and your friendship with that government."

"I see."

"It would work like this. We would purchase the goods and stockpile them in this country. You obtain the certificate, valid in the Ivory Coast. How we get the goods from there to our home country is our problem—we simply trade the certificate for the money."

"Sounds simple."

"It is simple."

"And you'd purchase the goods simply on my say-so?"

"Well, of course, we'd have to have a deposit on your end. We're risking all the goods, and we have people to answer to. But it's important enough to our cause to take the chance and trust you substantially—"

"How substantially?"

"I don't follow."

"How much of a deposit?"

"As you know, ten percent is traditional. But in your case, because of your reputation, we would accept only two percent."

"Of the total value of the goods?"

"Certainly not, Mr. Burke. We realize that individuals don't have that kind of cash available. Only two percent of the value of the commission you are to receive for the certificate."

"So ten thousand?"

"Exactly."

"So I put up ten thousand, and you put up what?"

"Mr. Burke, we put up title to the goods—in your name or in whatever name you desire. Title to the goods in your name, F.O.B. London. Of course, the goods will never leave the States until you hand us the certificate, but you will have title."

"So what would prevent me from just selling the goods on my own?"

That was Gunther's cue to role-play again. He leaned forward. "It wouldn't be worth it to you." Picking up the brass knuckles, he rapped them on the table for emphasis.

I sat back like I was thinking about it but then Gunther had to overact again and spoil everything. He looked over at Max. "What's the matter with the chink? How come he don't talk?"

James looked pained, as if Gunther were a dangerous madman just barely under control. A good act, but the wrong stage.

"He talks," I said. "I interpret for him."

"Oh yeah? That's real nice. Ask the chink what year this is."

"What year?"

"Yeah, you know. The gooks all have names for years, right? Like the Year of the Dragon or the Year of the Horse. Ask him what year this is—I got a feeling this is the Year of the Pussy."

I knew I shouldn't have made that crack about faggots, but it was obviously too late now. Max looked at Gunther, smiled, tapped his forehead, and shook his head negatively. I was in it anyway by then, so I translated. "He says he knows what year it *isn't*."

"What year is that, wise guy?"

Max repeated his earlier gestures, then reached out onto the table with his hand like he was groping for something, stopped when he found it, and turned his palm over. Then he made a disgusted face, gently turning his palm over again, and shook his head once more.

"He says it's not the Year of the Maggot," I told them.

Gunther glared over at Max, who gave him a beautiful soft smile in return. When he spoke he accented each word with vicious precision. "Tell that slant-eyed punk that one day I'm going to meet him when you're not around with that scattergun to save his ass. Tell him that I'm going to make him polish my boots with his tongue. Tell him that."

Max smiled even more sweetly. Taking the brass knuckles in his two hands, he rotated them against each other. His forearms looked like twisted ropes of heavy telephone cable, his face was flat—lips parted just enough to show a tiny gleam of white. His nostrils flared, his ears flattened against his head and the flesh moved away from his eyes. The deaf-mute gook had become the Mongol warrior lord as though the metal in his hands had flowed into his face and upper body. The brass knuckles resisted, then yielded, bending almost double in his grip.

Gunther's face lost its blood, but he couldn't look away from Max. I put the shotgun on the table butt-first toward Gunther, shoving it right into his hands. "Want to try this?" I leaned my chair back against the wall. A smell that you can find in the lobby of most any housing project suddenly filled the room. Gunther got up, backing away from the table and the shotgun as if they were radioactive. James slowly pushed his own chair back and walked over to Gunther. The shotgun and the brass knuckles lay untouched on the table.

"Don't ever come back," I told them. "Don't ever think about coming back. I'll call you at your number three nights from now, at six o'clock, and tell you if I'm interested in your deal. You understand?"

James mumbled yes and they walked out the door, his hand on Gunther's arm.

Max and I sat there for a second, then got up to get away from the aroma. Max put his hands together and flicked them back and forth to show me he would clean up. I went over to the cab to get my cigarettes, lit two, and let them burn in the glass ashtray. Max came over, took one. He touched his hand to his heart to thank me for showing him respect by putting a loaded shotgun in the hands of his enemy. I made an it's-nothing gesture to indicate that even with the shotgun Gunther was no match for him. Max drifted to the front of the warehouse to see if they might have some crazy idea about coming back. While he was out front I took up the shotgun and exchanged the blank shells inside it for some real ones in case they did.

24

MAX WAS BACK in a couple of minutes to let me know James and Gunther had vacated the immediate area. He touched his eyes and made a circle in front of his face, parallel to the ground, to let me know he was going out to see what happened to them. I told him I'd wait right where I was and sat in the empty warehouse. I didn't enjoy the quiet. My first thought was that Gunther's reaction had been unprofessional, that they were amateurs who had blundered their way into a weapons contract and didn't know how to move from there. But it wouldn't wash. They were professionals all right—but professional scam artists, not gunrunners.

If I could get my hands on a valid End Use Certificate, I wouldn't need the likes of Gunther and James to do the merchandising for me. Any damn fool with money can buy all the weapons he wants in this country. The real money was out there for transportation and delivery, not outright purchase. The ten-grand deposit was all the money that they meant to change hands—sort of an international version of the Pigeon Drop game, except instead of an envelope stuffed with newspaper I'd get a phony Bill of Lading, F.O.B. London, telling me I was the proud owner of a bunch of nonexistent weapons. You can't really cheat an honest man, someone once said, and they were right. Those lames thought I'd make the deposit an investment in my own ripoff scheme and steal the guns for myself. It told me two things—they thought I had some real contacts in Africa from the Biafra episode, and they thought I was a thief. Like most losers, they were about half-right.

So why did I tell them I'd get back to them? One reason was that I didn't want them to do anything stupid, and James might have thought the con was still running for them. But there was something else, something I couldn't isolate in my mind. They must be good for something, maybe something connected to this whole Cobra business, but I didn't yet see exactly what or how.

I knew one thing, though: in the joint, the major child molesters and the neo-Nazis had one thing in common: they all wanted to be part of "law enforcement." One of them—he had been running a school "for disturbed kids" with sodomy as therapy—told the Prof that he was working for the FBI. When the Prof played him along, he said he had a code name and everything—that the lawyer who came to see him regularly was really a Bureau agent. He told the Prof that he was gathering information about rival kiddie-porn dealers and passing it along. Just a good citizen. I didn't think anything about it—it was just good information to have. But when I saw this creep buddy-up with a guy who called himself Major Klaus, I knew they had to have something in common. One of the mistakes I make sometimes is to lump all freaks together in my mind—like there are brand names for certain kinds of humans. I should know better. My survival instincts told me to keep James and Gunther on the hook, but a connection to the Cobra wouldn't come to the front of my thinking. It was just lurking somewhere in the back. I didn't press it. Whatever instincts, intuitions I had had kept me alive so far. From experience, I figured when it was time for the connection it would come to me.

While I was trying to dope out how they came to connect me with African work (and giving it up as a bad job because a lot of people knew something about that craziness—diamonds that weren't there and starving kids that were), Max rolled back. He gestured that the two losers had been picked up in a cab about ten blocks from our base. He didn't bother to find out where they went since it wouldn't mean anything to us. I could see Max was still up for battle, pumping fire inside but handling it well. If you didn't know what to look for, you wouldn't see anything, but I did—this hadn't been the first time. He followed the cab back to the taxi garage in the Plymouth. I turned in the hack, picked up my four hundred bucks from the half-a-grand deposit with the dispatcher (he returns all but a yard as the rental fee), and we headed home.

I could see Max wasn't down to normal operating temperature yet, so I started telling him about this Cobra freak and Flood and what I wanted to do. The more we talked about how we'd pull it off, the calmer he got. Except when I told him how it all started, with me hitting that horse at Yonkers for a grand from Maurice. That he simply refused to believe, so I told him to go to Maurice's and pick up the money himself and hold it for me. I wouldn't even have to call Maurice and let him know Max was authorized to make the pickup—Max the Silent has a better reputation for honesty than the Orthodox Jews in the diamond industry. Max is often used as a courier for that reason, plus the fact that ripping him off would be past the capabilities of your average SWAT team. Max only moves money or things like money—jewels, paper, computer printouts. He won't move dope, and people know better than to ask him anymore. He's not bonded, so all you get for your money is his word. To a warrior like Max, that means you get your stuff or his life. Uptown when they want stuff delivered, they have guys in fancy uniforms who have passed polygraphs, given their fingerprints and all that—down here we have Max the Silent.

I told Max that finding the Cobra would be the real problem, and he made the sign of maggots under a rock again, then shook his head, held his hands toward the sky, and snapped his fingers like a magician pulling things from thin air. I got it. Maggots don't come from outer space, they're on the earth for a reason. They only move in the direction of decay—they help it along, eventually make it disappear and then they move on again. Like an old-time burglar told me once, explaining why he never worked with dope fiends, "Dead meat brings flies." The Cobra had to be swimming in slimy waters or he'd stick out like an honest man at a political caucus.

That didn't narrow the search much. Some people think slime is subject to zoning laws. They pick some part of a city and call it the Tenderloin, or the Combat Zone, or the Block, or even the Red Light District if they have a blue nose. Assholes. You don't need a Ph.D. in sociology to understand slime. Slime needs fresh meat to live, and if you don't bring it around, the slime goes shopping. The uptown glitzo who gets ready for Saturday night by slipping a vial of cocaine into the glove compartment of his Mercedes can't see the slime lapping at his hubcaps. He pays his money and the money gets passed around until it coagulates into a movable mass. All money moves. Dope money moves into a pipeline, and at the other end you get loan-shark cash on the streets and kiddie-porn operations in the basements. The glitzo goes to his hip party and whips out his vial of nose candy and shows the other jerks that he's connected—he's down with the program.

A few blocks away, some dirtbag pimp passes his vial around in an after-hours joint. He got the money for his dope out of the body of some thirteen-year-old runaway who thought the smooth-talking man in the Port Authority Bus Terminal was going to make her a star.

Yeah, they're both connected—to each other.

I move through slime like a poacher on some rich man's estate. I take what I can. Whatever money's out there is as much mine as any dirtbag's. Some of them don't like it—most of them don't know it. I guess some people are still waiting for a man to walk on water. I wish them a lot of luck—I walk on quicksand. One time when I was a kid in the juvenile prison I made the mistake of telling one of those halfassed counselors what a bitch it was growing up in the orphanage—the miserable punk told me you have to play the cards they deal you, like that was supposed to bring on a flash of insight and make me into a good citizen. As I got older and kept doing time I began to realize that maybe the counselor had been right—you do have to play the cards they deal you—but only a certified sucker or masochist would play them honestly.

I asked Max if he would ride with me over to the piers to see if Michelle had learned anything. He nodded okay and I drove the Plymouth west. I told Max to stay in the car no matter what he saw going down. One time when I was looking for someone on the docks Max saw this freak all dressed up in a stormtrooper outfit standing out on the abandoned pilings. He was waving a giant bullwhip around like he was getting ready to drive some galley slaves. A bunch of locals were standing around watching the show—just entertainment for them, I guess—but old Max decided that they were all terrorized by this freak, and he slid out of the car and kicked the poor fellow into the Hudson River before I could stop him. When he pivoted to the crowd like he was expecting applause, the audience ran like they'd just seen their future up-close. Max isn't desperate for recognition, and the locals weren't exactly his peer group, but you could see he wanted some acknowledgment of his feat.

So I told him he was now the undisputed champion of that pier.

Max doesn't have a big ego about that kind of thing, but I didn't want him suddenly deciding to defend his title, so I repeated the deal about staying in the car no matter what.

The piers were dark and murky, like they always are. Couples walked to empty buildings, hustlers waited, predators watched. No Michelle. No Margot. No cops either.

I drove Max back to the warehouse, waved good-bye, and watched him disappear into the interior. Drove back to my office, put the car away, went upstairs. As I put the key into the floor-level lock I heard Pansy's low growl. When I got the door open she was poised about three feet away, the hair on the back of her neck standing straight up and her fangs, like they say, bared. Somebody had been around to visit—maybe a visitor for the hippies upstairs who got the wrong address, maybe someone with some bad ideas. I asked Pansy, who didn't say. Whoever it was hadn't gotten into the office.

I got some marrow bones out of the fridge and put them on to boil while I changed clothes and listened to the news. I switched to the police band for the local precinct, using the crystals I wasn't supposed to be able to buy over the counter. The radio runs into an antenna lead, and the antenna itself runs up through the useless chimney stack on the roof, protruding about a foot. I got perfect reception, but all it picked up were routine crime-in-progress calls and cops telling the desk man they were going off the air for personals, which could mean anything from a bathroom visit to a shakedown.

I used a strainer and poured the boiling water off the marrow bones to let them cool. Pansy came down from the roof, a lot calmer now—whoever had come around hadn't come over the rooftops. I started thinking about the roof and how I'd like to have a garden up there someday—there was sure as hell enough fertilizer already in place. I could tell I was getting tired because I was starting to think like a citizen. Putting down roots, even on a city roof, is blubber-brained. Roots are nice, but a tree can't run.

When the marrow bones cooled I gave one to Pansy and

sat patting her massive head while she crunched it. Maybe real private eyes make up lists of things to do and places to go, but I like to work them out in my head—an old prison habit. Trees can't run and people can't Xerox your thoughts. If they could, they never would have let me out of that orphanage when I was a kid.

25

WHEN I WOKE up the next morning I was still in my chair. It didn't look like Pansy had moved either. My watch said it was almost nine. I opened the back door to let Pansy out and went next door for a quick shower and shave. By the time Pansy trotted downstairs to supervise my work with the razor, it was just about time for my phone call. I went back into the office, picked up the receiver to check for hippie-interference, noted their usual early-morning silence, and dialed the direct line for an assistant D.A. I know in Manhattan. Toby Ringer was a real hardnose, with no political hooks, who battled his way up the bureaucracy by being willing to try cases that scared most of the other D.A.'s. You know the kind I mean—where the bad guy's a hundred percent guilty but there's no solid evidence and the odds are you're going to lose it in front of a jury and get a black mark against your record. Some of those wimps won't even touch a case unless there's a videotaped confession and four eyewitnesses. Toby's no cowboy—he doesn't have fantasies of some death squad wiping out all the vermin in the city someday, but he has a genuine hate for the real slime, so we've been able to help each other out on occasion. He's not State-raised, but he's been around long enough to know how to act.

All the D.A.'s answer their phone the same way. "Mr. Ringer's line."

"Good morning, Toby. I got a present for you."

"Who's speaking?"

"Your friend from the Gonzales matter, remember? I don't

want to talk on the phone, okay? But I got a gold-plated chance for you to nail a baby-raper, and I'll throw in a homicide to boot."

"In exchange for what?"

"For justice. I don't want anything—I just want to tell you something that I can't tell the cops."

"This is Mr. B., I presume."

"I'm your man. Can I meet you someplace tonight?"

"My office. That's it—no other place. Deal?"

"Deal. What time?"

"Make it around eight. Everybody's gone home by then and the night crew will be downstairs working the Complaint Room."

"Want me to see the man at the front desk or just bypass him?"

"Go to the desk. I'll leave word—what name?"

"Tell him Mr. and Mrs. Lawrence."

"Who's your friend?"

"You'll see, Toby. Tonight, right?"

"Right." And we hung up simultaneously. I keep all my calls on this phone under one minute; this one had barely qualified.

I sat down at my desk planning to compose a suitable recruitment ad for the mercenary journals. It might bring the Cobra around but that would be a last resort, especially since it takes three or four months for the ads to get into print. He might be long gone by then—forget it. I locked the place up and aimed the Plymouth for the docks, figuring Michelle would be easier to find in daylight.

I backed into my usual spot facing West Street, lit up, and waited. There were plenty of hustlers working, but no Michelle. Waiting isn't hard for me, though. Different people use different tricks to make the time go by, but it all comes down to the same thing. You can't make anything happen, you just have to be ready when it does. Sometimes you have to hide the fact that you're waiting so you use something like a taxicab and sometimes you find yourself a job to do while you're waiting so if someone is looking they see the worker, not the watcher. Some places you stand out only if you *don't* look like you're watching, like in the cesspool—Times Square. If you're tracking a man in that pit, the only thing to do is really gawk around and be obvious as hell about it. Then they only wonder what you're looking for, not who. This job was like that. All the freaks parading by knew I was waiting for something or some-body. And after I was there a half hour or so, word would get around; they'd talk, compare notes. They'd know I wasn't law, but they couldn't be sure I wasn't trouble.

In some neighborhoods, especially Italian or Hispanic ones, the young bloods would try their luck with a stranger just to be doing it. Not down here—everybody down here already knows their luck is permanently bad, and the nice-looking man in the cashmere topcoat coming down the block might just have gotten so bored reading muscle magazines every night after his frigid wife went to bed that now he's stalking the streets with a handgun in his pocket and exorcism on his mind.

When I wait like this I usually listen to some of my tape collection. I started it by accident. I'd gone to a meeting that I wanted to record and the Mole had rigged me up with one of his devices, using sequential blank-tape banks with mini-cassettes. It was voice-activated and would record for six hours straight. I kicked it in before I even got out of the car, but I forgot to turn it off. So when I dropped by this cellar club later to unload a couple of gross of phony tickets to a rock concert, the tape was still running. They had a kid playing at the club that night who looked like he left Kentucky to work in the Chicago steel mills, but he was a blues singer, pure and simple. Someone once said the blues are the truth—maybe that's why I listen so close when I hear that music . . . truth's in short supply in my line of work. Anyway, when I got back to the office and played the tapes I found a couple of the kid's numbers at the tail end. The Mole was right about the perfect fidelity—listening to the tape was exactly like being back in the club. And listening to the music was exactly like being back in my own life, like the blues are supposed to be. The blues don't make you think—they make you remember. If you've got no memories, you can't have the blues. I avoid physical pain like a vulture avoids live meat, but I call up the past sometimes and let it wash over me on purpose. Maybe it helps me survive. Maybe it makes me believe that survival isn't a waste of time. I don't know.

When the tape broke into the cellar club's sounds I heard the rattle of glasses and the voices of the waitresses hustling drinks and the muted electric hum that meant nobody was listening to anyone else. The kid fronted a classic Chicago-style blues band: he sang and worked a mouth harp off the same microphone, a piano, a slide guitar, rhythm guitar, electric bass, drummer. The kid didn't have much of a rap—he didn't have the years and confidence for that yet. But he understood that if you could make people in a basement club stop boozing and snorting and hustling long enough to listen, you had something real. Whatever that something was, the kid wanted it— bad. He leaned a bit into the microphone, said "This is 'Bad Blood Blues,'" and the piano man started into a series of rolls and falls, going with just the bottom line from the bass player. It wasn't loud, but it was intrusive, insistent—impossible to ignore. So much so that by the time the guitarists and the drummer were there, too, the crowd was waiting to hear what the kid had to say. He cupped the harp around the microphone, then appeared to change his mind and just got to it. Unlike most white blues singers, the kid didn't try to sound black. The words came out firm and clean, not covered by the band:

> I always tried to do right,
> But everything I did seemed to turn out wrong.
> I always tried to do right,
> But everything I did seemed to turn out wrong.
> I didn't mean to stay with that woman,
> At least not for very long.

and you could hear the crowd shut down and shift over to a listening stance. By the middle of the second verse the kid was getting shouts of agreement when he sang:

> Oh I knew that she was evil,
> People told me she was mean.
> Yes, I knew that she was evil,
> And people told me she was mean.
> I knew that she was evil . . .
> But I always thought that she was clean.

Then the kid bridged into a hard, anticipative harp solo, taken against the bass and rhythm guitar, letting the crowd know he was going to explain the mystery to them in just a little while. And he did:

> Well, she never gave me nothing,
> She just about ruined my life.

You know she never gave me nothing,
She just about ruined my life.
And when she finally gave me something . . .

(By then, we all knew what he was talking about.)

I brought it home to my poor wife.

And behind shouts of "That's right!" and "Had to be!" the kid picked up the harp again and the blues came out. Just that simple, and damn-near perfect. By then the people knew where he was going, where a story like his had to go:

Now my life is so empty,
My wife don't want to see my face.
My life is so empty,
And my wife don't want to see my face.
I got to walk this road alone,
Bad blood, it's my disgrace.

And the kid rolled the harp down with the rest of the band and finished. He had them all moving now and he went uptempo but stayed with the blues. The harp barked into a fast lead, the piano floated off the top, and then the kid sang his own road song:

I got a long way to travel, honey,
I'm sorry you can't come

And people in the crowd who knew what he meant chuckled in agreement.

I got a long way to travel, honey,
I'm sorry you can't come.
You are all used up, babe,
And I have just begun.

Like a lot of the blues, sex got mixed up with everything else. The kid grabbed a breath:

I got a long way to go, babe,
And I know that you don't care.

> I got a long way to go, babe,
> And I know that you don't care . . . just where
> You wouldn't like it anyway, babe,
> They ain't got no suburbs there.

And the harp barked its challenge to the crowd, wailing out the don't-mind-dying credo of all bluesmen as the tape finally ran to its end.

That was the first tape in my collection—I've added dozens since. I got some early Paul Butterfield, Delbert McClinton, Kinky Friedman (and if you think this guy's just a quasi-cowboy clown, listen to "Ride 'Em Jewboy" just once), Buddy Guy, Jimmy Cotton—all live. I had a Muddy Waters tape too, but it sounded like he was playing Prom Night in the suburbs someplace, the same way Charley Musselwhite did when I caught him at some college hangout near Boston. I don't blame either of them, but I erased the tapes. I have some stuff I didn't record myself too, some Hank Williams, Patsy Cline, stuff like that. I keep the tapes in the Plymouth to help me do the waiting— I've got more sense than to listen to them inside a closed room.

About an hour later I saw a black Lincoln Town Coupe pull up under the elevated portion of the West Side Highway, the part they're never going to finish building. Saw a flash of nylons as a woman climbed out of the front seat, working before she hit the ground. She disappeared into the shadows and the Lincoln pulled away. I thought I recognized the woman, but it was long distance and I didn't have time to put the monocular to my eye. I turned off the tape, set the system up to record instead, lit a smoke, and waited.

I was right. Margot approached from the far right. She must have crossed the street under the El, doubled back to the side, and walked along the river's edge by the piers. She was swinging her purse like she was planning to do business. It might have fooled the pimp in the Lincoln if he was watching her, but it wouldn't have fooled anyone who'd seen me sitting there for a couple of hours.

As Margot got closer, I saw she was wearing giant sunglasses that covered half her face. I slowly rolled down the window in time with her approach so that she arrived as the glass disappeared.

"Waiting for me, Burke?"

"I don't know, Margot, am I?"

"Listen, I think he's watching me, okay? Let me in the car—I'll get on the floor like I'm giving you head and talk to you."

"No good. I've been here too long. Other people have seen me—they know I'm not waiting this long just to get off."

"I got to talk to you."

"Go back where you were, okay? I'll meet you—"

"No. Forget it—no, wait. Let me get in the car and just drive away. They'll think you *were* waiting for me, right? A hotel job."

"What's the rate for that?"

Margot lifted up the sunglasses so I could see her face. One eye was swollen shut and there were traces of dried blood over a plucked eyebrow. She spoke in a flat, deliberate voice. "It used to be fifty, but now Dandy says I'm a full-fledged three-way girl so it costs a yard." I just looked at her face—her eyes were dead. Her voice didn't change. "And he says if I don't make a success of myself going three-way I can try the Square and do some chain jobs. He gets two yards a night or I get worse—get it?"

We had already talked too long, in front of too big an audience.

"Get in the car," I told her, and fired up the Plymouth. Pulling out of my slot, we rolled onto the highway, heading south toward the World Trade Center, hooked a deep U-turn, and rolled back north toward uptown. Nobody following.

I motored around for another twenty minutes to make sure. Still nothing. So I drove over to a basement poolroom with the dirty neon sign that said *Rooms* over the entrance and got out. Told Margot to come with me and keep her mouth shut no matter who said what to her. I handed her an empty attache case I keep in the back seat and said to hang on to it like it was full of money.

We went down the short steps to the basement and stopped by the wire cage, where an old man was watching a small-screen color TV with his back to us. To the right of the cage was a flight of steps leading upstairs, to the left was the basement with the pool tables. I rapped my knuckles on the counter. The old man didn't even turn around from the TV. "No vacancies, pal."

"It's me, Pop," I said, and he turned around, looked at me, saw Margot, and raised one eyebrow. "It's business." I pointed at the attache case. The old man reached under the counter, took out a key with the number 2 on the attached paper tag, and I handed him two fifties. He turned his back to us and went back to the TV set. I motioned Margot upstairs in front of me and we climbed in silence.

Pop only rents rooms to certain people and only for business. The key says #2, but it really means the whole second floor. When you're finished you leave the key on the hook by the door, leave the door unlocked, and go down the fire escape. The rate is a hundred bucks until the next morning, no matter when you check in. And nobody stays past the next morning, no matter what they want to pay—house rules. Pop uses Max the Silent for evictions, but they don't happen often.

When we got to the first-floor landing we saw the steel door with no doorknob. I told Margot to wait, and in a few seconds it buzzed and popped open. I pulled it closed from the other side, knowing there was no way to go back through it. If anyone else tried to come through the door legit, Pop would buzz once like he just did and they'd get through. But if someone was forcing him to do it he'd hit the buzzer a few times rapidly. That wouldn't open the door, but it would seem like he was trying to—anyone in the building would know it was time to split. Even if the law hit the door with the usual fireaxes and battering rams you'd have at least fifteen minutes to get out. More than enough. Pop didn't allow any dope-dealing in the place, but anything else went, and guys sometimes went up and down these stairs with enough explosives to put the whole block into orbit.

I used the key to open the first door on the second floor, and Margot and I went inside. Large, barely furnished suite of rooms, two bathrooms, convertible couch, empty refrigerator. If you wanted it, you had to bring it. I found an ashtray and lit up. Margot let out what sounded like a groan and sat down on the couch. I looked over at her. "So?"

"I've got a job for you."

"I don't need a job, Margot. I need to talk to Michelle."

"I already talked to her. I've got a message for you."

"Which is?"

"First I want to talk about the job."

"Hey, what is this crap? Just tell me what Michelle said."

She took off her glasses again, gave me a dead smile to go with her eyes. "Don't be tough, Burke—don't be a hard guy.

Don't threaten me. I've had everything that can be done to a person done to me except killing and I don't care about that. Don't threaten me, just listen to me, okay?"

I said nothing, smoking. Margot lit one of her own.

"Something has to be done about Dandy."

"Your pimp?"

"My pimp."

"I don't know him, never heard of him."

"He's from Boston. He just came down here."

"What has to be done?"

"Murder."

"You're talking to the wrong man. That's not me."

"That's not what I heard."

"Then you heard wrong."

"How much?"

"Forget it. You're a fucking dummy—you don't want this creep, get on a bus and split."

"I can't leave."

"Bullshit."

"It's not bullshit—first he has to die."

"Don't even tell me about it."

"Would five thousand do the job?"

I got up from the couch and walked over to the window. Layers of filth made it impossible to look through, even in the daylight. I still needed that message from Michelle, so I gave Margot some free advice. She listened like it was worth what I was charging. "Look, dummy. You pay a man five G's to knock off some halfass pimp and he takes your money and says thank you and never does it. *Then* what the fuck do you do?"

"I earn some more money and now I have a list of two people."

"At that rate you'll be on social security before you find someone who's for real, and he'll want a million dollars for your whole list."

"I can make a million dollars if I have to—I got my money-maker right here," Margot said, slapping herself on the rump and smiling her dead smile. We were getting nowhere.

"Look, I don't do that kind of work. Just leave him and be done with it."

"He has to be dead first."

"Because he'll come after you or what?"

"The first."

"If I could—and I'm not saying I can—arrange it so he never comes near you again in life, would that do it?"

"You don't know him."

"Yes I do."

"I thought you said you'd never heard of him."

I blew an attempt at a smoke ring at the ceiling, went back over to the couch and motioned her to come over and sit next to me. Margot hesitated, biting her swollen lower lip. "What the fuck's the matter with you?" I asked her. "You come into a strange place with a strange man, you ask him to kill someone, and now you're afraid of a couch?"

It didn't even get a smile out of her, but she did walk over and sit next to me. And listened.

"Look, let's say a man works in a maggot factory. You know, where they dig up maggots from under rocks and put them into little containers for people who need maggots, like fishermen and scientists and abstract artists or whatever. Okay, he works in this factory for twenty years, right? He watches maggots work, he watches them play, he watches them breed. He sees them individually and in groups. He observes their every fucking characteristic, all right? Now you find a man like this and you ask him if he knows your *personal* maggot. And he says no. But he knows maggots, you understand? And one maggot's not a hell of a lot different from the other maggots? Okay?"

"Yes."

"So I never heard of this Dandy."

"I got it."

"Okay, now what's the message from Michelle?"

"Wait. You'll do something with Dandy?"

"For five thousand dollars. But I won't kill him—and you'll have to participate."

"Why? How?"

"The why is so you don't end up testifying against me and my people. The how I don't know yet."

"This is straight?"

"You tell me."

Margot looked into my face like there was something she could learn. There wasn't, but she was satisfied, I guess. She nodded okay.

"Now . . ."

"This is the message from Michelle, word for word. She said, 'Tell Burke that the man who knows the Cobra made a movie star out of a corpse.' That's all."

"That's the whole thing—that's all she said?"

"That's it. She made me say it twenty times until I got it down perfect."

"What's she think I am, Sherlock-fucking-Holmes?"

"Burke, I don't know. That's what she said. Not like it was a riddle but like you'd understand."

"Okay." I told her I'd drop her off wherever she wanted.

"It doesn't matter. I've got to be off the streets for a few hours. I'll tell Dandy I turned a freak trick for two bills. That's what he wants anyway. He says that's where the money is."

"So?"

"So can I stay here and have you got the two bills?"

"You must be crazy. You go through all this to offer me five grand and you haven't got two hundred?"

"I got it, Burke. I just don't have it here. I couldn't carry it around with me, could I?"

"I already laid out a yard for this place."

"I'll have your money tomorrow—meet you here at noon?"

I just looked at her, her eyes were still dead. But Michelle must have trusted her if she gave her that message to pass on. "Burke, if you do this, I swear you'll never regret it."

"I already regret it."

"I got nothing here to give you, nothing except my body— and I'm sure you don't want that." And suddenly, damn her, her dead eyes got wet and she started to cry.

And so Burke the great scam artist, the never-suckered city poacher, sat on a couch and held a crying whore for almost three hours and then gave her two hundred dollars and drove her back to the streets. Before I went into that room, Dandy was a maggot. Now he was a maggot who owed me money.

26

AFTER I DROPPED off Margot I kept thinking about how her eyes didn't look dead anymore. Maybe they were alive with hope, maybe with the joy of ripping off another sucker. There was only one sure way to find out, and that meant I had to find the Prof and Michelle both. There was only one place in the whole city where I might hit that exacta, a midtown joint called The Very Idea. So I stashed the Plymouth back at the office, walked a few blocks, and caught a cab uptown.

The Very Idea isn't exactly closed to the public, but it's not the kind of place where a citizen would stay very long. It's supposed to be just for transsexuals and their friends—no trans-vestites, drag queens, fag hags, or hustlers—and most espe-cially no tourists. It's over near First Avenue, just a snort away from some of the heaviest singles bars. I heard that the folks in The Very Idea used to get together and practice their routines on each other before they tried them out on the citizens. They're all supposed to do this while they get the hormone injections—Michelle told me you have to cross-dress for a year, stay in therapy, and get a clean bill of psychiatric health before they let you have the sex-change surgery. But the citizens are too easy to fool, and it's not a good test. The club was the idea of a few of them, a private subscription deal. They didn't expect to make money, just to have a place to hang out in peace. But somehow the joint caught on and now it does a good business. It's not frantic like a gay bar, and I can see why folks like to just drop in to spend a few bucks and enjoy the quiet. But, like I said, most people aren't welcome there.

I had the cab let me off a few blocks away, walked over to the river, and doubled back to the club. There was a middle-sized lunch crowd already in place and it looked more like Schrafft's than a gay bar. Well, like Michelle said, it *wasn't* a gay bar.

I didn't see Michelle so I headed for the long counter. As usual, Ricardo was in place. He serves as sort of a maitre d' and bartender at the same time, selected more for his courtly manners than anything else, I suppose. I know for damn sure they don't need a bouncer in that joint. One time some jerkoff sailors found their way inside and started some trouble with Ricardo. He didn't participate personally—just watched while his customers made short work of the sailors. I don't know if the Shore Patrol declared the place off-limits after that or what, but I do know the sailors' threats to return and demolish the place never came to anything. "Ah, Mr. Burke," Ricardo greeted me, "a pleasure to see you again, sir. Will you have the usual?"

I said sure without the slightest idea of what he was talking about. Ricardo thinks questions like that add a lot of class to the joint. He put some silly-looking glass filled with dark liquid and a slice of lime in front of me. I didn't touch it—I don't drink. I put a twenty on the bar, Ricardo made it disappear and threw a bunch of bills back in the original spot. I let them ride and asked, "Seen Michelle?"

"Today?" A blank look on his face.

"Ricardo, you know me—what's the problem?"

He let his eyes drift down to the money on the bar. Sure—if I was there as a friend, why would I have to bribe this guy just to find out where she was? Ricardo wasn't as dumb as he acted. So I said, "For my drinks . . . and hers, right?"

He smiled. The man had about twice the normal allotment of teeth. "She's in the dining room, sir."

The dining room crack just meant she was around someplace, and that he would let her know I was here. I don't know how they do that, and I never asked. But the system works—in less than five minutes Michelle swished through the door of the ladies room and took the stool next to me.

"Looking for company, handsome?"

"Actually," I told her, "I'm looking for the Prophet."

"Aren't we all?"

"No, baby, I mean *Prof,* you know?"

"Oh, *that* Prof. He'll be here. This place is on his regular rounds. But I guess you knew that."

"Yeah. Look, I have to ask you something about your friend Margot."

"Ask me what, honey?" said Michelle, her face calm but her eyes alert.

"Is she straight?"

"She's a who-ah, sweetie, a pros-tit-tute."

"That's not what I mean, Michelle. She told me some things, and maybe she asked me to do some things. I don't want to get it caught in a wringer."

"One of my friends got it caught in a wringer. It cost a lot of money—she should have gone to Sweden. You know they don't do the operations at Johns Hopkins anymore?"

"Yeah, I know. Do you know Margot's pimp?"

"Dandy? Yes, I know the swine."

"A swine because he's running girls or—?"

"A swine, darling. A pain-freak—there's a lot of them around nowadays. I don't even think he's a righteous pimp, you know? Like he marks the girls in the face—what kind of pimp does that?"

"What's his weight?" I asked.

"Strictly fly, baby. He came from Boston where he was working some runaways. That's his real thing, you know. He has some boys too. I heard he was even pimping when he was in the joint."

"Why would he come down from Boston?"

"Baby, don't you know the way it works? It's harder to pimp in a small town. You have to be in good with the locals, and you can make enemies *so* easily. Here in the Rotten Apple there is room for everyone—you don't have to be connected to work street girls, you don't have to make payoffs, don't even need a trick book. All you need is meat on the street, just some meat on the street. Maybe he had some trouble back in Boston—who knows?"

"You saying Margot is good people?"

"Honey, for a biological woman, she's all right."

"Okay," I said, "now what about the message you gave her for me?"

Michelle leaned against me, put one hand on the back of my neck to bring me closer to her lips, and whispered, "I heard about a freak who did some kids, did them real bad. And when he got popped he dropped a pocketful of dimes, okay? I don't know if he's your man, but he sounds right. And one of the heavies he is supposed to have given up is this man who makes ugly movies. Burke, I won't even say this man's name—get it from someplace else."

"Where?"

"Honey, I don't know. I already said too much, even to you. This is the man you have to see if you want a snuff film, okay?" Michelle released her grip. "I love you, Burke," and she leaned over to kiss me on the cheek. She swung off the stool and disappeared back into the club without another word.

I asked Ricardo for a roast beef sandwich and got some three-decker nonsense on toast with the crusts neatly trimmed off. I was eating and checking the paper when the Prof appeared in a floor-length raincoat and carrying an umbrella. The city was in for a long dry spell.

"It's going to rain?" I asked the Prophet.

"It will rain," he promised.

"What happened to seven-twenty-seven?"

"It was the wrong plane, my son. The number came seven-forty-seven. When you work with me, you have to think big."

"So it was my fault?"

"God gives the word—mortals interpret the word of God. There is more than a single version of the Bible, and for good reason."

"Do you think you might be persuaded to give the word to an individual here on earth?"

"This is always possible," he said. "Are you going to finish that sandwich?"

"No," I said, and shoved it across, signaling to Ricardo to give him whatever he wanted to drink. Ricardo appeared, looked questioningly at the Prophet, who asked, "Buttermilk?" smiling his sweet smile.

Ricardo served it up like he had a call for buttermilk every day. Maybe he did.

I turned to the Prof. "You know a halfass pimp named Dandy?"

The Prof handled the segue back to the prison yard without breaking stride. "I got the slant on the whole plant, Burke. He's a new boy, green to the scene—talks a tough game but he hasn't been with us long."

"The word is he won't be with us much longer if he doesn't change his ways."

"Talk to me," said the Prof.

"Let me put it this way," I said. "Sometimes you have to play the same hand you deal to other people."

"What goes around, comes around—true enough. Who's down on his case?"

"Among others, Max the Silent."

"Max? Max the life-taking, widow-making, silent wind of death?"

"The same."

"I got the message, Burke. The Prof will not be around when the shit comes down."

"No, that's not it, Prof. I want this fool to understand what he's playing with, okay? I want to send him a message."

"Which is . . . ?"

"Clean up his act or take it on the road . . . alone."

The Prof thought for a minute. "Leave his string behind, is that it?"

"As far as I know, he's got no string—just one lady, and he's working her too hard."

"I got it. And I'll give him the word. Can I tell him in public?"

"Why?"

"Look, Burke, I got to survive on these streets too. If I lay the message on him and he doesn't listen, then Max moves on him, right?"

"Right."

"So people connect *me* with Max—that's a better insurance policy than Prudential."

"Good enough. But he's supposed to be a nasty bastard, Prof—he may not take the message too well."

"If he wants to play, he's got to pay," said the Prof, and I put a pair of tens into his hand. He slid off the barstool, turned, and said: "What's the word?"

"If there's a reason, there's a season?" I ventured.

"Yes, and if it's truth, it can't be treason," he replied, and vanished into the daylight outside.

I left a ten on the bar for Ricardo and followed in the Prophet's footsteps. At the rate this case was going I could end up on welfare—or veteran's assistance, or disability, workman's compensation, unemployment, or any of the other government paths to a regular income. I hoped not—it was a drag keeping track of all that paperwork.

27

I WALKED A few blocks through the sunlight, found a pay phone, and called Flood. Someone else answered. "Ms. Flood is instructing." I hung up while she was saying something about leaving a message. Walked another few blocks to another phone and called Mama. I told her I'd be over and hung up on her too when she started going on about being careful with bad people. After walking crosstown all the way to the West Side I got into a cab and told the driver to cruise down West Street. I got off near the World Trade Center, bought a copy of that night's *Harness Lines,* and took my time strolling back to the office.

I passed an OTB parlor on the way. I don't do business with them—at least I don't place bets—but I do have one of those plastic credit cards that says I have a telephone account. Very useful. Not for betting on the phone, but for using the City of New York as a courier service. Here's how it works: let's say you're rolling down the street carrying cash and some people know about it. They'd like to talk to you. So you duck into an OTB and make a cash deposit to your telephone account. You fill out a deposit slip just like in a bank, and they give you a stamped piece of paper for a receipt. Then you light a cigarette with the receipt and go back outside. If the people waiting ask you to step into their car and they search you, there's no cash. They conclude you weren't carrying the money on that particular occasion. Then, when you want your cash, you go to the main OTB branch on Forty-first Street, give them your account number and code word, and they give you a check that's as good as gold. You can either mail the check to yourself or walk a half-block and turn it into cash. It's a fine way to move money around the city, and OTB doesn't charge a cent for the service. Even the checks are free.

When I got back to the office I let Pansy run on the roof again. She looked as calm as usual but that didn't mean much—dogs don't have long memories. The phone line was clear so I tried Flood again.

"Ms. Flood, please."

"Who's calling?"

"You're great at disguising your voice, Flood."

"Burke?"

"Yep."

"I went to the court and—"

"Save it. Not on the phone. I'll—"

"But listen—"

"Flood! Give it a rest. I can't talk on this phone, okay? I'll pick you up tonight, your place, at seven, okay?"

"Yes."

"Can you wait in the lobby downstairs? Move out when you see the car?"

"Yes."

"Don't sound so depressed, kid. It's coming soon."

"Okay," as flat as ever.

"Later, Flood." I hung up.

I cruised over to Mama's in the Plymouth, parked around the back, and went through the kitchen to look through the glass. The place was empty except for some dregs from the late lunchtime crowd. Stepping through the kitchen door sideways I entered the restaurant from the back like I'd been in the bathroom. I sat down at the last booth in the rear, the one with the half-eaten food standing around on the plates, and one of Mama's waiters approached. "Will there be anything else?" I don't know how Mama trained them, but they were good—I'd obviously been here for the past hour or so. I told the waiter I was satisfied and lit an after-lunch cigarette.

When the rest of the crowd moved out Mama left her place by the cash register in front and came over to sit with me. The waiter cleared off the table and I ordered some eggdrop soup and Mongolian beef with fried rice. Mama told the waiter to bring her some tea. "What is happening, Burke?"

"The usual stuff, Mama."

"Those men on the phone—bad men, right?"

"Not bad like dangerous, Mama—just bad like lousy, you know?"

"Yes, I know, I hear in their voice, okay? Could be very bad people if you afraid of them, right?"

"Oh yeah, fear would make them tough for sure."

"Max help you?"

"Sometimes."

"I mean with those men, okay?"

"Max is my friend, Mama. He would help me and I would help him, understand?"

"I understand. Beef good?"

"The beef is perfect."

"Not too hot?"

"Just right."

"Cook very old. Sometimes you do thing long time you get very good, right? Some things you do too long, not so good."

"Like me?"

"You not so old yet, Burke." Max suddenly materialized at Mama's elbow. She slid over in the booth to make room for him and signaled for more tea. Mama thought tea was important to Max's continued growth and development. Max seemed indifferent to the entire issue. "Do all Chinese people believe in tea?" I asked her.

"All Chinese people not same, Burke. You know this, right?"

"I just meant, is it a cultural thing, Mama? Like when the Irish drink beer even when they don't like it?"

"I don't know. But Max like tea too. Very good for him." I looked at Max. He made a face to say the stuff wouldn't hurt him so what the hell. He reads lips so well that sometimes I think he only pretends not to hear.

"Well, that's kind of what I meant. You're Chinese, Max is Chinese, you both like tea . . ."

Mama giggled like I'd said something funny. "You think Max Chinese?"

"Sure."

"You think all people from Far East Chinese?"

"Mama, don't be—"

"Maybe you think Max *Japanese*?" Mama giggled again. Don't ask me why, but Chinese people don't like Japanese people. In fact, the only subject on which I've seen Orientals agree is that none of them seem to like Koreans.

"I know Max isn't Japanese."

"How do you know?"

I knew because one night Max and I were talking about being a warrior and what it meant, and I mentioned the samurai tradition and Max said he had nothing to do with that. He told me a samurai must fight for his lord and Max had no lord. I didn't get all of it, but I knew he wasn't Japanese. It made sense to me—if you're going to do crime for a living, the only way is to be self-employed. But I just told Mama, "I know."

Max looked over at Mama, bowed his head to show great respect for all things Chinese, and then made great mountain peaks with his hands and pointed at his chest. Mama and I said "Tibet" at the same time and Max nodded. What the hell, Max wasn't any more of a citizen than I was.

Mama said she had to get back to business, and Max stood up to let her out of the booth, bowing and sitting back to face me again all in one motion. Mama looked at me, then at Max, and spread her hands in a gesture of frustration. Max nodded sharply to tell her that I would be all right, and she seemed satisfied. Then he put twenty fifty-dollar bills on the table next to my copy of the racing form. I pocketed eighteen of them, left the remaining two for him—ten percent is his usual transportation fee.

Max wasn't going for that. He crooked the first two fingers of his right hand in a come-here gesture and I put my money back on the table. Then he extracted another two bills from my pile and motioned I was free to pocket the rest. Okay, so we *each* had a hundred on the table. So what?

Picking up the racing form, Max indicated that I should pick out a horse for that evening and we'd both invest. I made a variety of gestures to show him that I couldn't always be expected to pick winners, but Max put his hands together in a prayerful attitude, pointed at me, and tapped his pocket. He was saying that I must be especially skillful since, after all, I'd won all this money.

The last thing I needed was Max's silent sarcasm. Thus challenged, I whipped out a felt-tip pen and went to work on the form. Max sat down next to me and we spent the next hour or so going over the charts. I used some blank paper to demonstrate that although Yonkers and Roosevelt were both half-mile oval tracks, Yonkers had a much shorter stretch run. So a horse that fired late but lost at Yonkers because he just ran out of racetrack would have a shot at Roosevelt. Then I showed him the bloodlines of certain animals that seemed to run better in cooler weather. (You have to look for Down Under horses, from Australia or New Zealand—their biological clock is different from American horses because their summer is our winter.) I told him about high humidity making horses go faster, and the importance of post position. For pure guts, I told Max, all other things being equal, you have to go with a mare rather than a male horse.

When I finally checked my watch, hours had flown by. Max was as intent as ever. Finally we found a horse that had been running strong at Rockingham, up in New Hampshire, and was shipping in for the first time. A three-year-old that hadn't been heavily staked, he was trying the older horses in a $27,000 claimer. He had a good driver, decent but not spectacular breeding, and he looked tough as nails. And Rockingham was a couple of seconds slower than Roosevelt, track for track. Looked good to me—I thought he was maybe in a little cheap, and leaving from an inside post to boot. The horse was named Honor Bright, but I don't bet on names. Max took our two hundred and used my pen to circle the horse on the racing form. Then he nodded at me, bowed, smiled, and split.

It was about time to meet Flood, so I did the same.

28

IT WAS ALMOST seven when I poked the Plymouth's nose down Flood's block the way a ferret sticks his nose down a hole before taking the plunge. Everything seemed quiet, so I rolled down my window and snaked out the hand-held spotlight so it was pointed across the windshield directly at Flood's door. When I flicked the switch the night turned into day—nothing happened, nobody jumped from the shadows. Flood walked out the door wearing an ankle-length maxicoat with a big pocketbook slung over one shoulder. She climbed in the car without a word and I set it rolling downtown.

As soon as we straightened out, Flood started pulling pieces of paper out of her bag and talking at the same time. "I did exactly what you told me. I looked through everything. There's no name even *like* his anywhere. I even asked the clerk to help me and he did and we still couldn't find anything."

"Just calm down, Flood. It's no tragedy. Did you write down all the docket numbers from the days I told you to check?"

"Every single one. There's no—"

"Never mind." I already had an idea about the Cobra, and if Flood had done her job we'd know soon enough. We still had a little time so I pulled into a parking place, got the pocket flash from the glove compartment, and took Flood's notes out of her hand. I was trying to concentrate but I was slowly being knocked unconscious by Flood's perfume—it smelled like Eau de Whorehouse and it was thicker than flies on a corpse.

"Flood! What the hell is that stuff?"

"What stuff?"

"That fucking perfume! It smells like a used motel room."

"I thought it would go with my outfit," she said bitterly, and the maxicoat fell open to reveal Flood. Revealed her because the clothes she had on obviously did nothing to cover her—a jersey sweater clearly worn without benefit of a bra, and pink pants so tight I could see the muscles of her thighs. Even the black wig said Slut.

"Flood, what are you doing?"

"Well, you said I had to wear this nonsense, so I thought—"

"Flood, for chrissakes, I said to wear the outfit to court, right? Not for the rest of your life."

"You didn't tell me I should change, so—"

"Don't you have a fucking grain of common sense?"

"First I'm a dumb broad because I don't listen to you—now I'm a dumb broad because I do. Which is it?"

"Flood, the outfit was for court, so they'd look at your body and not pay any attention to your face. Tonight we're seeing an assistant D.A."

"You think he won't look?" Flood pouted like a real brat. I would have given her a smack if I wasn't afraid of permanent injury.

"Sure he'll look. But he's a professional, not like those rumdums at the courthouse. He'll remember your face anyway. And it won't matter—he's a straight citizen, not one of the bad guys."

"Oh."

"Yeah, 'Oh.' Wonderful."

"You want me to go home and change?"

"There's no time. We can't be late for this. Besides, you'd have to take a bath for a month to get that smell off."

"I only did it because—"

"Bullshit, Flood. You're not that dumb. I think you like wearing that get-up."

Flood got a dangerous edge to her voice when she said, *"What?"*

"You heard me. This isn't a game, right? Use some sense."

"I'll keep the coat buttoned, Burke. Okay?"

"Keep your lip buttoned too."

In a sweet little-girl voice, Flood said, "Please don't get mad, daddy," and reached over to squeeze my hand. Then she moved over against the passenger door like some high-school girl rejecting a pass. By the time the Plymouth was turning into Baxter Street behind the courthouse I felt some life come back into my hand. Actually, I'd thought it was paralyzed for life, but I'm too tough to scream. I've got my pride too.

I parked the Plymouth where I could move it easily if I had to. I told Flood, "That was childish. You're a real adolescent. Give me your coat."

"What for?"

"Because we're going to walk up the steps, and people besides the D.A. will be watching, right? Maybe it wasn't such a bad idea to wear that outfit after all. But stop being a baby, okay?"

Flood said okay, handed me the coat, and turned to go. I checked to see nobody was around, then dropped an old business card on the ground. My arms were full of Flood's coat and briefcase, so I said, "Grab that, will you, Flood?" When she bent at the waist to pick it off the ground, I gave her a healthy smack with the hand she'd squeezed. It was like slapping a side of beef—the pain shot from my hand right up my arm. Flood straightened up like nothing had happened, giggled and said, "Used the wrong hand, huh?" She wiggled off ahead of me and after we got about ten feet said, "Want to give me my coat back now?" I did and I wouldn't think Flood was dumb anymore. At least not about some things.

Toby stood up when we came through his door. He always dresses the same day or night, whether he's on trial in Supreme Court or sitting around his office listening to political discussions: Brand X three-piece suit, solid-color buttondown shirt, striped tie, wingtip shoes. Toby has a thick mustache but it doesn't make him look any older than he really is—late thirties, I'd guess. His image is perfect for juries: solid, respectable, middle-class, not flashy or arrogant. Toby's not a man with major resentments about his life. He's not crazy about the fact that some defense attorneys who couldn't carry his briefcase make five times the money he does, but he lives with it. No politician, his rise through the office has been steady if not spectacular. He doesn't like criminals much, but he doesn't stay up nights planning how he's going to stop them all by himself. But he doesn't like baby-rapers a whole lot. Maybe because he has little ones of his own—I don't know. I do know he's sincere about it—I've worked with him before. Toby held out his hand.

"Mr. Lawrence, good to see you. And this is Mrs. Lawrence?"

"Yeah, this is the little woman," I said, carefully keeping clear of Flood's reach.

"What's on?"

"There a guy, Martin Howard Wilson, who rapes babies for fun and profit. Without boring you with a long story, we'd like to find him."

"Why come to me?"

"He was indicted over here for sodomizing a kid. The kid died. So did the indictment. I figure he rolled over on somebody and maybe there was good enough reason for your people to let him go, okay? But he didn't pay for what he did and I represent some people who think he should."

"Can you be more specific?"

"About the people, no. About the maggot, sure. I got a decent physical description, approximate age, last known whereabouts, even an alias. Calls himself *The Cobra*, if you're ready for that."

"What else?"

"Toby, he's got a blank docket number."

Toby said "Oh," and sat back to think. I'd checked Flood's lists and there was a complete run of docket numbers in sequence for the arraignment and indictment days when Wilson made his appearances, but one number was missing. Both Toby and I knew what that meant, and if the *federales* didn't have this freak holed up in their so-called Witness Protection Program the Manhattan D.A. should know where to find him, or at least what he looked like. But it was a lot to ask, and Toby and I both knew it.

"Your people who want to find this guy . . . he steal money from them or something?"

"Something."

"Why should I do this, Burke?"

"Lawrence."

"Lawrence. Why should I do this?"

"Because this guy has a special racket. He works the daycare centers, the babysitting gigs, the foster-care scam, the runaway-youth hostels, the sheltered workshops, the group homes. You know the routine—he's a disaffected Vietnam vet with a story to tell, and the liberals just fucking eat it up. Then he swallows their kids. And he walks off the charges for some reason. He *has* to be rolling over on someone to do that. And now he's loose again and he *will* take out some more kids as sure as we're all sitting here having this debate. He's a dangerous, vicious degenerate who got a free pass from the government to do his filth. You want more?"

"You wouldn't be working for the people this man allegedly rolled over on, would you, Mr. Lawrence?"

"No. I thought you knew better, Toby."

"I know you—at least I know something of you. And I know you walk pretty close to the line all the time."

"There's some lines I wouldn't cross."

"So you say."

"My references are in the street, right?"

"Some of your references are doing time."

"How many for baby-raping?"

"Okay, I get your point. Now let me think a bit." He turned to Flood. "Are you uncomfortable like that? Would you like me to take your coat?" Flood the genius favored him with a dazzling smile and handed it to him. Toby approached to take the coat from her and the combination of Flood's perfume and her dancing chest almost knocked him back into his chair. But you don't get to be a top criminal trial lawyer without some degree of composure, so he just took the coat and turned to hang it on a wooden rack—only his reddened ears gave him away. We all sat in silence, Toby smoking his pipe, me smoking one cigarette after another, and Flood taking deep breaths every time she thought Toby or I looked bored.

Time passed. Nobody talked. Phones rang down the hall, sometimes fifteen or twenty times. They always stopped eventually. Maybe someone picked them up, maybe somebody gave up—who could tell? We all jumped when the phone on Toby's desk rang. He snatched the receiver, barked "Ringer!" into it, and Flood and I listened to his half of the conversation, obviously with a new D.A. in the Complaint Room:

"What's the cop say?" Pause. "What about the complaining witness?" Pause. "Guy have a record?" Pause. "Okay, don't get worked up. It's no big deal. It'll never get past the grand jury. Write it up as Assault Third and put a note in the file, *No ACD at Arraignment*. At least we'll make him sweat a bit. Tell the Arraignment Part A.D.A. to ask for five hundred bail. Yeah." Pause. "That's all." And he hung up.

ACD just means Adjournment in Contemplation of Dismissal, a six-month walkaway for the defendant—if he doesn't get busted during that time, the whole case against him is dismissed. All Toby meant was that the guy was going to get a play at some point, but they'd jerk his chain at the first appearance. Standard stuff.

Toby turned to face me. "You'll answer for Mrs. Lawrence here?"

"No question."

"She from here?"

"Related to someone from here."

"Anybody I know?"

"Max the Silent."

"She doesn't look Chinese."

"Doesn't talk much either, have you noticed?"

"Is that the relationship?"

"No. And Max isn't Chinese."

"Okay. I'll have to go and see if there's a file. I'll read through it if there is—then I'll decide. No discussions, okay? If it looks right to me, maybe we can talk. If not, time for you to go."

Toby excused himself and went down the hall. Because of our relationship I didn't use the opportunity to add to my collection of official stationery. Toby knows Max. I had to bring him in once when the police were looking for him and Max had to testify in front of the grand jury. I got to go inside with him since I'm a registered interpreter for the deaf. It says so on the official letterhead of the appropriate city agency. Max wasn't indicted.

As soon as Toby went out the door Flood opened her mouth to say something. I motioned her to be quiet. I believe Toby's honest, but I don't believe any city office isn't bugged. If it was we hadn't said anything that would get us in trouble, but with Flood's mouth you could never be sure. I winked at her to show confidence I didn't feel, and we sat there waiting.

Toby's phone rang again. I ignored it. Flood was good at waiting—she just went into some kind of breathing exercise and made the time go away. Her eyes were focused, but she was meditating—in a resting phase, like a battery storing up energy.

Toby didn't get back until it was almost nine-thirty, but when he walked in the door carrying a thick manila folder, I knew we'd won.

"I can't show you what's in here, but you're right about your man. I'll tell you some things. Don't ask me any questions—just listen and then leave, okay?"

I nodded yes and Flood became as rigid as a setter on point.

"Martin Howard Wilson, d.o.b. August 10, 1944. Arrested and indicted as you already know. Agreed to provide specific evidence on the kiddie-porn operations of several individuals, including Elijah Slocum, Manny Grossman, and one Jonas Goldor, the last of which purportedly included the use of children in active prostitution and the sale of children across state lines. This Goldor, I've heard, is a very bad guy. He almost makes a religion out of pain, seems to believe in it somehow. I'm told he can be so persuasive that he actually talks people into trying it of their own free will, but that's just hearsay. Lots of rumors that he's killed some of his playmates, and Wilson claimed he even knew where the private graveyard was.

"There's an old address for Wilson, but it's strictly n.g. now. We checked. We're looking for him too. We didn't actually give him immunity. We *promised* him immunity when and if he made a case against Goldor and actually testified before the grand jury and at trial if necessary. His lawyer said he couldn't be in protective custody and still make the case for us, and we bought it. Wilson seemed to really get into the whole undercover thing, like he always wanted to be a cop or something. He was going to set up a preliminary buy—a truckload of kiddie porn coming in from California. We were going to use those guys as rollovers too, make as strong a case as we could against Goldor. The buy never went down and Wilson disappeared. But he's still out there. He calls in every once in a while and claims he's working on the case for us.

"There's a warrant out for his arrest. Murder Two. Sodomy First Degree. Kidnapping. The works. The A.D.A. running the case doesn't know himself if Wilson's really trying to make a case for us, but when Wilson gets popped he's going down for the homicide. Period. The only other thing I can tell you is that Goldor's listed in the Scarsdale phone book, he's got no mob enemies and a lot of powerful friends. Big political contributor, owns a lot of good real estate, even pays his taxes on time, I'm told. But there's one funny thing . . . even though we don't have real good intelligence operations in the Hispanic community we do know that Una Gente Libre—you know, that Puerto Rican terrorist group—has the word on the street that they're going to whack this guy. Goldor, not Wilson. We don't know why, or anything about them. And Goldor, we know for a fact, doesn't believe it for a second.

"Now that's it. I've told you everything I can, and I've told you with the understanding that you're looking for this individual and if you locate him you will promptly report his whereabouts to our office. Understood?"

"Understood," I said, and blasted Flood with my eyes so she'd keep the disappointment that was trembling around her mouth from erupting into words. Toby got up to shake hands. The interview was over. I palmed the piece of paper he slipped me without saying a word, and Flood just nodded curtly at him, snatched her coat off the rack, and we left.

I could feel Flood steaming beside me as we walked to the car. She yanked off her coat, flung it into the back seat, folded her arms, and stared through the windshield. We drove to her place in stony silence. I parked the car, got out with her, and reached for her hand as we walked down the block to her loft. She pulled it away, said nothing. The door to her studio was slightly stuck—probably the humidity—and Flood hit it a shot with the palm of her hand that practically knocked it off its hinges. She stalked through to her own place and was ripping off the jersey top even before I got to sit down. Then she pulled off the rest of her clothes, put on a rose silk robe, and sat down directly across from me.

"Nothing. *Nothing*. We don't know a goddamned thing we didn't know before—"

"Flood, shut up. We know all we need to know now."

"You're a fool, Burke. And I'm a bigger fool for listening to you. He told us *nothing*, don't you understand?"

"We know the name of a group interested in Goldor, right? Maybe Goldor knows where to find our man."

"And maybe he doesn't. And maybe he won't tell us. And what do you know about Puerto Rican terrorist groups anyway? It's *nothing*."

Flood looked like she couldn't decide whether to cry or kill. For as long as I knew this woman I kept overestimating her or underestimating her—maybe I'd never know her long enough to get it right.

I took the piece of paper Toby had slipped me out of my coat pocket, smoothed it out carefully, and turned it around so it was facing her. It took a second for Flood's eyes to focus on the black-and-white standard mug shot, one full-face view and one in profile. It showed a man just over six feet tall, with a face that was broad at the top and narrowed down to a pointed chin. He had dark hair, dark, bulging eyes, a narrow nose with a too-large tip. The head was slightly jug-eared, and there were old acne scars on both cheeks. His hair was on the long side, but cut close in front so his entire forehead was visible. On the back of the Xeroxed mug shot there was a typed notation: "4-inch scar outside left thigh. Tattoos: right bicep/ Death Before Dishonor with Eagle, left outside forearm/ initials A.B. in a blue circle—wears contact lenses."

Flood stared at the mug shot like she was going to climb inside the paper. I broke her concentration when I turned the paper over. She read it slowly and carefully, moving her lips, memorizing.

"Him?"

"It's him, Flood."

And her face became a sunburst and her eyes sparkled and I'll never see a more radiant smile—it turned the whole room warm. Flood held the mug shot and chuckled to herself, smiling that smile. She threw off the robe, turned around, and bent over, looking back over her shoulder at me.

"You want to try that trick of yours again?"

"Do I look stupid?"

"It won't be the same. Promise."

"How come?" I was suspicious.

"Ancient Japanese technique."

So I gave her a halfhearted smack and she was right. It was like patting soft, bouncy female flesh—the best there is.

"See?"

"You know any other Japanese techniques?"

Flood looked back over her shoulder with that same wonderful smile and said, "Oh yes." It turned out she was right.

29

WHEN I WOKE up it was early morning, still dark outside. I reached for Flood but she wasn't next to me on the mat. Some things I guess you never learn. I got up and made enough noise moving around so I wouldn't surprise her. Not a sound from Flood's room.

I found her back in a corner sitting in the lotus position, staring at a tiny table completely covered with a white silk cloth that reached to the floor. On the tabletop was a small picture in a plain black frame of a young woman holding a little girl on her lap. The woman was smiling into the camera and the little girl looked very serious, like kids do sometimes. Next to the picture was the mug shot of Wilson. Flood had something propped up behind it, so the two pictures faced each other.

Hearing me behind her, Flood turned and said, "Soon, okay?" I went back to the mat. In a minute or two she came out and sat down next to me.

"It was wrong of me to go through the ceremony alone— I just didn't want to wait any longer. You have the right to watch if you want." She held out her hand and pulled me to my feet.

I followed her back inside to the corner where she'd set everything up. She motioned to me to sit down a few feet away from her and flowed into the lotus position again. Soon she began to say something in Japanese. It wasn't repetitious and didn't sound like a prayer, but when she finished she bowed to the tiny table. Then she got to her feet, took off the robe she'd been wearing, and put on a long red robe with dragons on both sleeves. From a dark-red lacquered box she took a piece of red silk and what looked like a six-inch metal spike with a dark wood handle. The spike went between the two pictures and the red silk was placed over the picture of Sadie and Flower. Then Flood said something in Japanese again, pulled the red silk from the photograph, and carefully wrapped it around the spike. Taking the covered spike in one hand and her friend's picture in the other, she held them both in front of her face for a minute, knelt and placed them in the lacquered box.

Only the mug shot remained on the little table. She stood facing it and smiled—if Wilson could have seen that smile he would have found a painless way to kill himself. Flood bowed deeply toward the table, spun around, and flowed out of the room. I followed her to the mat and sat down. She brought me an ashtray and I lit a smoke. She waited until I stubbed it out before speaking.

"Do you understand?"

"A sacred weapon that you just blessed?"

"That is how he will die."

"Flood, listen to me, okay? I'm already in this too deep. I see he has to die but that's really no punishment. Prison is worse, believe me—I know. If you have to kill somebody, then that's what you have to do. You start worrying about *how* you're going to do it, start putting restrictions on yourself, then you get caught. What's the difference if you blow up his apartment building or drop him with a rifle at a hundred yards or poison his coffee? He'll still be just as dead."

"Did you ever kill anyone?"

"I never killed anyone who wasn't trying to hurt me like you want to do to him."

"He already hurt me."

"He doesn't know that."

"So he's innocent?"

"No, he's a maggot, Flood. He can't be rehabilitated or reformed or even contained, okay? But you're taking a job and making it personal. That's bad enough—but with all this religious stuff you're going to lead the law right to you when it's over."

"And to you, right?"

"Right."

"You think I'd ever talk, ever tell anyone about you?"

"Never in a thousand years. If I ever met a person in my life who'd stand up, it's you."

"So?"

"So listen to me, you crazy bimbo. I'm not saying I'm not going to help you. I'm just not going for all this religious nonsense so we can get ourselves caught. I'll help you find him, even help you cancel his fucking ticket, okay? But if we have to drop him some other way, that's the way we're going to do it, understand?"

"Go find yourself an alibi, Burke. Get out of here and find yourself a good alibi for the next couple of months," she said, turning away from me.

I got to my feet. "Give me the picture, Flood," I said in a calm voice, knowing what was coming. "Not a chance," she said. I started toward the corner where she'd set up the table. Flood spun into a fighting stance, the robe swirling around her. "Don't," she said, no emotion in her voice. I sat down again, lit another cigarette.

"Flood, come here and sit down. I'm going to leave, okay? I'm not going to try and take the picture from you. But you owe me something so you're going to come over here and listen to me talk. When I'm finished I'll disappear. But first you listen."

Flood approached warily. The little mace canister in my pocket might have taken her out of action long enough for me to get the mug shot—or it might not. Anyway, she knew where I could be found and she'd never quit. "You can't find him, Flood. You know what he looks like so you think you've found him. But he's still just another maggot in a big slime pit. You couldn't find him in a hundred years. You understand combat, that's all—you don't know anything else. I can find him. If it wasn't for me, you wouldn't *have* that picture. Right?"

"I know what you're saying."

"And I know what you're thinking—now that you've got the mug shot you can track him down with some jerkoff private eye. All they'll do is take your money. Or your body, if you want to trade that."

"I can find him."

"Flood, let's say I wanted to get to someone who was living in your temple in Japan. Could I do it?"

"You'd never find the place, never get through the mountains. You'd never get in the door if you did."

"It's not *my* place, right?"

"I'm an American."

"This isn't America out there, you dummy. This is a running sore loaded with dangerous maggots. And you don't have a passport, don't speak the language, don't know the customs. You're a permanent foreigner in the world Wilson lives in. You couldn't find a cop, much less a freak like Wilson. And you probably couldn't tell the difference if you did."

"I found you."

"And you came to me because whoever sent you to me told you I was the man to find a missing maggot. And if we hadn't worked something out, you'd be dog food by now."

"I'm not afraid."

"I surely fucking know you're not afraid. So what? *I'm* afraid all the time, but I can find him and you can't. It's that simple. You blunder around trying to find him and he'll spook and run."

"He has to stay on this planet."

"You know what I think? I think maybe you don't want to really find this freak after all—I think you're full of crap. You like the chase, right? Your bullshit *honor* and all that. You talk tough but you make so much noise I think you want the freak to run. You're a phony, Flood. This isn't for Sadie and Flower, it's just for your bullshit Japanese ego games. You don't give a flying fuck for your friend at all, you—"

Flood backhanded me across the mouth so fast I only saw the flash of her robe. I tried to roll with it, turned a somersault, landed on my knees with my hands crossed in front of my face. Flood was just a blur—I felt her foot crack against the side of my head and I slammed into the wall and bounced off, clawing for my gun. But Flood wasn't on the attack anymore—she just stood there looking at me.

"You don't understand," she said, not even breathing hard.

I didn't say anything.

"Burke . . ."

I didn't say anything.

"I'm sorry. Sadie is my friend. Maybe I should have stayed in the temple. He won't fight, will he? Will he, Burke?"

"Flood, he'll run if he can, or he'll kill you if he can. But fight?" I shrugged.

She came over to me then, sitting down and reaching for my face. I put up my hand to block her but she slapped it away like it was made of feathers. Taking my face in her hand, she turned it back and forth. It felt like pulp to me.

"You're going to need some stitches."

"Lucky for you I'm a gentleman, Flood, or I'd kick your ass all over this room."

"Oh, I know," she said, without a trace of a smile or sarcasm. "I know where I can get this fixed up. Then I have to see some people, get some things, and we'll go and see this Goldor."

"Can I keep the picture where it is?"

"How tight is this place? Would other people come into your room when you weren't around?"

"The people here are from my temple. It's not permitted to look at another person's altar."

"But might they do it?"

"No. There's no chance. Honor counts for everything. All the people here have been together in the temple for many years. I'm the youngest one here."

"I'm sorry I said that about you."

"No, you're not. I understand—you have to stay here after I'm gone. It's all right. I know you love me."

"Flood! I never said I loved you. You don't—"

"Shut up, Burke—you're not so smart. Not so tough, either. But you didn't show bad form when you did that first tumble. Did you ever study?"

"My brother is a master. He's been trying to teach me for years but he says I'll never be any good. I think that's true. My mind's not right for it—every time I hit the ground I'm looking around for some blunt object to use instead of my hands."

"Your brother is really a master?"

"Yes."

"You understand what that means, Burke? He's as good as me?"

"He's better, Flood. I mean it. No contest."

"I'm sure he's stronger—but faster?"

"Believe me—I don't demean you, but there's no one better."

"Then he's not American."

"No."

"Japanese? What style does he fight? Does he—"

"He's from Tibet."

"Tibet. I heard stories . . . more like legends. From our temple. A man who studied with our old master many years ago but he wouldn't accept our ways. But it's probably not . . . I mean, your brother. Did he . . . ?"

"He's called Max the Silent. I don't know his deep past."

"I only know the name in Japanese. It means Silent Dragon. It doesn't make sense—he couldn't be your brother . . ."

"We have the same father."

"I don't understand."

"The same father you had, Flood."

"The fucking *State* was my father. I told you."

"I know."

Flood said nothing. Just sat there absently patting my face like it was a mound of clay and she was trying to decide on the shape of the sculpture before she really went to work. Finally I nudged her with my shoulder. "Flood?"

She snapped out of it. "What? Oh, Burke . . . Okay . . . I can put it together now. And it's all right. It makes sense. I just didn't see it." She shook her head as though to clear her vision. "I'll go with you. I'll do as you say. And I'll find this devil and I'll put the stake into his heart like I'm supposed to. You'll see—it will be the way it should be." She looked at me, focusing on my face for the first time. "And you can have the picture too, all right?"

I just nodded. The side of my face was beginning to swell—I could feel it growing—and I'd need to do some talking soon. I told Flood to go get dressed and she dutifully went off. I sat there smoking until she was ready to leave. It was still dark as we slipped out her front door and into the waiting Plymouth.

30

AS WE DROVE back toward the office I felt Flood staring at the right side of my face where she'd done her work.

"You've had some real training, haven't you?"

"Why would you say that?"

"It has to be hurting you, but you're breathing properly."

"That's not training—it just hurts to breathe through my damn mouth."

Flood slid across the seat until she was right up against me and gently squeezed my thigh. "Maybe you're just a tough guy, Burke."

I'm not a tough guy. If I could figure out a way to run from pain I'd do it at Olympic speed. I can't do that so I let it just move through me like I was taught. But I couldn't do it and drive the damn car at the same time. Actually, I couldn't do it that well at all.

I put the Plymouth away and walked around to the front with Flood holding onto my arm. When we walked in the entranceway I leaned against the mailboxes like I was dizzy. She immediately threw her arm around my waist and pulled me against her, supporting me up the stairs. When I touched the mailbox the red-and-white lights the Mole had strung all around the office would start to flash in sequence. It was the signal for Pansy to stop whatever she was doing. Her aggressive juices would start flowing when she saw the flashes, she would pad over to her designated spot to the left of the door so she'd be just out of sight when it opened. There's also a light switch that sets off a monster strobe light the Mole had mounted in what looked like a stereo speaker, blinding whoever walked in the door. If the strobe fired so would Pansy. She'd also fire if I walked in the door with my hands up, strobe or not. But I'd only hit the downstairs switch to keep her working and alert. Any dog will lose whatever conditioning you've put into her if you don't reinforce and reward constantly.

When we got to the top of the stairs I told Flood to take my hand. She did it without questioning—I think she finally understood that my office wasn't the place to act stupid. I opened the door, pushed the light switch down instead of up and walked in holding Flood's hand. Pansy was standing to the left—chest out, fangs bared, and trembling with eagerness. She was supposed to wait in silence but a low rumbling growl escaped. Still, she didn't move and she let Flood and me walk in hand-in-hand. I told Flood to sit on the couch, turned around and told Pansy "Good girl."

She came loping over to me and I patted her hard enough to make a normal dog lapse into unconsciousness. Her giant tongue slobbered out and covered my face. Ignoring Flood, I told Pansy to stay and went next door to get her a slab of steak—small compensation for not being able to chew on a human being, but she would have to make do for now. I opened the back door and let her onto the roof and told Flood to stay just where she was until Pansy came back downstairs—you can only train a dog so much.

When Pansy came down I gave her the hand signal for *friends* and she ambled over to her spot on the Astroturf and lapsed into the semicoma that's her normal waking state. I got out my medical kit and told Flood to give me a hand.

With everything laid out on the desk I turned on the overhead light so Flood could see what she was doing and leaned way back in my chair. Flood looked at the equipment. "You'll have to tell me what to do."

"First, spray some of this Xylocaine completely over the area."

"What does it do?"

"It's a nerve deadener. You may have to probe around in there and I know how clumsy you are."

"I wish you had some real anesthetic here."

"Flood, let me tell you something. Anesthesia isn't like going to sleep the way the goddamned doctors tell you—it's a disease the body eventually recovers from, that's all. I've got some stuff like that but it's not for working on myself, you understand?"

She said nothing, just tested the spray against her hand, then turned and shot it into my face where she'd kicked me. The spray stung, burned, then turned cold like it was supposed to. I reached in and removed the upper right-side bridge. It came out easily, covered with blood and some flesh, so she was right about me needing some stitches.

"Flood, take the swabs and the orange stuff there and clean out the whole thing so you can see what you're doing."

She did what I told her. She was breathing shallowly through her nose, and I tried to match my rhythm to hers. She saw what I was doing and gave me a quick smile of encouragement.

"Now take those little scissors and trim away anything that's hanging loose. Just the part that looks like it's going to be dead skin."

Flood worked carefully but quickly. She would have made a great surgeon, but I guess her calling in life was to make work for the medical profession—or the undertaker.

"See if you can press the edges together—do they match up?"

"Almost." She grimaced.

"Okay," I said out of the good side of my mouth, "can you hold the edges together and sew with one hand?"

"I don't think so." She sounded upset.

"All right, all right, no big deal. Take my hand and show me where to put it, I'll hold everything together. You take this needle"—I pointed to the tiny curved piece of shiny steel— "and put some *small* stitches in as careful as you can, okay? Remember, they have to come out. Make sure the edges are together firmly so it'll knit. You understand?" Flood nodded, still concentrating. She threaded the tiny needle as easily as putting a pencil in a donut hole. "Work from one end across to the other. Don't overlap, I'll have to take them out later. Tie a big knot at the end. That's where we'll cut them off."

Flood put the stitches in silently, occasionally motioning me to move my hands so she could see better. When she finished I held up the mirror to check. Lovely work. I smeared the gauze pad liberally with Aureomycin ointment and put it in place. It didn't taste too sporty but it would drain well and stop any infection in its tracks. I poured alcohol over my bridge and let it sit in the glass—I wouldn't be using it for a while—then flicked off the overhead light and lay back in the semidarkness with my eyes closed. Flood lit a cigarette from my pack. "Can you smoke?" She touched her own mouth. I nodded, took it from her. Smoked silently, watching the red tip glow illuminating Flood's blonde hair.

She shifted her hips, sat down on the desk next to me and asked in a matter-of-fact tone what was next. She was still afraid I'd panic. I took another drag, handed the butt to her, and she stubbed it out for me. "I have to call someone about Goldor. Can't do it until seven in the morning when they open up."

Flood glanced toward the still-open back door. "That's still a couple of hours, just about. You have any pain-killers here?"

"No good—they put you to sleep, slow you down. Have to do a lot of talking soon. Work things out for Goldor."

"And you're a tough guy, right? Don't need 'em."

"Right—that's me."

Flood stood up, took off the jacket she was wearing, and pulled the jersey top over her head. Her breasts looked like hard white marble in the dim light. She came back over to me, sat on the desk again.

"Does next door have a shower or a bath?"

"Why?"

"I want to make love to you, Burke. And if there's no shower here, I'll never get these damn pants on again afterward."

"There's a shower, but—"

"It doesn't matter. I don't need to take them off."

"More ancient Japanese techniques?"

"I don't think so, but it'll work just as well. Make you nice and sleepy, yes?"

"You sure?"

"Would you rather that way . . . or are you afraid I'll hurt you if we . . . ?"

"Both," I said.

"Sold," said Flood, and reached for my belt.

31

WHEN I CAME to, I was still in the chair. Pansy was muttering at me. I told her to go on the roof—the door was already open. I needed a shower and a change of clothes. I figured I couldn't shave my face the way it was and I was glad of the excuse— I hate shaving. But Flood, who looked as fresh as new flowers, said she could shave me painlessly as long as I got my face warm and wet. It was awkward in the tiny bathroom, but Flood sat on the sink facing me and did a beautiful job. I never felt a thing. While she was shaving me I watched her breasts bounce ever so slightly in the morning light—she was biting her lip in concentration, and I thought how fine it would be to have her around all the time. I realized I'd been hit harder in the head than I'd thought.

At a little past seven in the morning I sat down at my desk again, checked the phones to make sure the hippies weren't changing their ways, and dialed. It was picked up on the second ring. *"Clinica de Obreros, buenos dias."*

"Doctor Cintrone, por favor."

"El doctor esta con un paciente. Hay algun mensaje?"

"Por favor llamat al Señor White a las nueve esta mañana."

"Esta bien." And we both rang off.

Flood was staring at me. "I didn't know you spoke Spanish."

"I don't. I just know a few phrases for certain situations."

"You asked him to call you tomorrow?"

"Today, Flood. *Mañana* just means morning—like in German *morgen* means tomorrow, but if you say *guten morgen* it means good day."

"Oh. So who's this doctor?"

"Nobody. You didn't hear that conversation. That knock on the head you gave me is making me stupid. I'll do this, not you. Okay?"

Flood shrugged.

"I have to go out and see someone. I'm not sure when I'll be back. You want to wait here, at your place, or what?"

"Would it be a problem to take me back to the studio? You could call me there."

"No problem, I need the car anyway."

I set out some food for Pansy, hung around a few moments until she snarfed it down, set up the office again, and we went downstairs to the garage. I moved quickly to get Flood home, and she seemed to understand that I was working on a schedule now. Jumping out of the Plymouth while it was still rolling to a stop, she threw me a quick wave over her shoulder and ran into her building. I had to be at the pay phone on Forty-second and Eighth at nine on the dot. That's what the Mr. White message would mean to Dr. Pablo Cintrone, director and resident psychiatrist at the Hispanic Workers Clinic in East Harlem.

Pablo was a towering figure in the city, a graduate of Harvard Medical School who turned down a small fortune when he went back to where he came from. He's a medium-sized, dark-skinned Puerto Rican with a moderate afro, a small beard, rimless glasses, and a smile that made you think of altar boys. He worked a twelve-hour day at the clinic, six days a week, and he still found time for his hobbies, like leading rent strikes and campaigning against the closing of local hospitals. The rumor that he went to medical school to learn how to perform abortions because the cost of the pregnancies he caused were going to break him was untrue. Other people thought he was dealing prescription drugs out of the clinic or that he was a secret slumlord. All bullshit, but he allowed the stories to circulate because it kept the focus away from things that were really important to him—like being *el jefe* of Una Gente Libre.

Una Gente Libre—A Free People—didn't operate like most so-called underground groups. No letters to the newspapers, no phone calls to the media, no bombs in public places. They had been blamed for a number of outright assassinations over the years—a mixed bag of sweatshop owners, slum landlords, dope dealers, and apparently some honest citizens. But infiltration was impossible—they'd never applied for a government grant. The word would go on the street that UGL wanted someone—and someone would die. UGL was a dead-serious crew.

You can't hang around Forty-second and Eighth. It's a trouble-corner, especially after dark. But early in the morning there's still a few citizens around. And, of course, plenty of whores in case the citizens want their cocktail hour a bit early. But the phone booths were empty, like I expected. I'd rather have used someplace else, but the rule is you can't ever make calls from Mama's. This conversation wouldn't last long anyway. I knew where I had to go—I just had to be sure I could go there safely.

I rolled up on the phone with a minute or so to spare. It rang right on the money.

"It's me."

"So?"

"Have to meet you. Important."

"Hail a green gypsy cab with a foxtail on the antenna in front of the Bronx Criminal Court tonight at eleven-thirty. He'll ask you if you want to go to the Waldorf."

And that was the whole conversation. Time was running short—I could put off the business with Dandy, but I'd given the phony gunrunners a deadline. I put the Plymouth in gear and rolled.

32

WHEN YOU'RE RUNNING, you have to pace yourself. I hadn't had a chance to see the morning papers yet and I wanted to study last night's charts so I'd be able to give Max a good, solid excuse for the failure of our joint investment. I needed something to eat and a place where I could work out some of the angles in peace and quiet.

Since I had to meet Margot at noon I thought I'd run over to Pop's basement, shoot a few racks, have a sandwich, and calm myself down. Nothing really to do until this evening. A man of leisure.

I parked, went downstairs, got a box of ivory balls from the guy in charge, carried it over to a back table, and went over to the private racks for my cue. When I took it down I unscrewed it at the joint in the middle, put both halves on the table and rolled them back and forth to see if the balance was still true. I unscrewed the cap at the butt to see if anyone had left a message for me—not this time. By then the old man who's always there had the balls racked up for me. I gave him a buck, told him I was just going to be practicing, and he moved off. In a game for money the old man racks each round and the players throw him something each time. For a big match he gets paid a flat fee. Some of the cheapskates won't pay him anything when they're just going to practice. Stupid— who knows when the old man's going to give you a bad rack when some money is on the line?

I tried a hard approach shot to the full rack, slamming into it from behind. The object was to bank the head ball off the left long rail into the short rail where I was standing and then into the right side pocket. I can make it sometimes—this wasn't one of them. But my shot scattered the balls sufficiently and I gently nudged them around the table for a few minutes until my stroke came to me, then started working on sinking them. It was quiet, just the click of the balls and the occasional muttered curse from one of the other tables. The poolroom had a giant No Gambling sign over the entrance which was universally ignored, but the other rules were religiously observed: no loud talking, no fighting, no weapons, no drugs. If you wanted conversational pool, you could shoot down at one of the front tables near the door. The back tables were for money games or for practice, and they were in much better shape.

Three tables down from me one of the professionals was practicing. The same shot each time—cue ball to the eight ball lying on the long rail into the corner pocket with the cue reversing the short rail and smacking into the area where the rack would be. Over and over. He tried dozens of variations on the cue ball, but the shot itself never varied. The black eight ball dropped in each time. Our eyes met and he raised his chin slightly to see if I was interested in losing some money. Not today. He went back to what he was doing. At a buck an hour you can practice for days at these tables without hurting yourself.

Pool is a fascinating game. I know a structural engineer who took years to figure out a way to make a shot if the cue ball was exactly in the spot where the head ball would be if there was a full rack. It looks damn near impossible, but he could do it every time. He's been waiting years for the situation to come up in a game—when it does, he'll be ready.

I dropped the balls in their pockets and they rolled down their runners to be collected at the head of the table. Like this caper—a whole lot of balls and a whole lot of pockets. I kept shooting, occasionally trying to imitate the subtle, relaxed stroke of the professional three tables down. It would never come to me. He had the technique perfect—he never looked up. Once you do you lose your concentration and you have to refocus your eyes. I can't do that, can't keep my eyes only on the table. Probably cost me a few games over the years, but I've won the ones that count. Every morning I wake up, I beat the system. And every morning I wake up and I'm not in jail, I beat the hell out of it.

I saw it was getting close to eleven-thirty so I called Mama's from the pay phone and asked her to have Max drop by the poolroom later on. She said there were no calls for me so I had to assume Margot was still coming. If she was and if she wasn't running a con, I'd need Max to move the cash for me. I told Pop I was expecting to do some business and I'd need the room. He said sure, but didn't make a move. When the other person showed up he'd hand over the key, not before. Pop wasn't going to be a concierge for anyone. I turned in the balls and paid for the table, then went into the lobby to wait for Margot, munching on a package of chocolate-chip cookies Pop had for sale at the counter. They weren't any older than me, and not as sweet.

She was on time, carrying a big purse and wearing one of those huge floppy hats that belong in midtown. I gave Pop the money, took the key, and we went upstairs.

Margot couldn't wait to open her mouth. "Burke, I've got to tell you this . . . Dandy said—"

"Have you got the money?"

"Sure. Now listen, I—"

"Where is it?"

She snapped open her purse, took out a wad of hundreds wrapped in a rubber band, tossed it over to me. "You want to count it?" She seemed unsurprised when I did. It was all there. On surface inspection, it was all good too. Used bills, but not ready for the shredder, no consecutive serial numbers, the right paper, clean inking, no engraving problems. Even if it was bogus I could move stuff this good without any problems.

I still checked it carefully though—some counterfeiters are lunatics and you never know what they'll do. I was watching that TV show about Archie Bunker in a bar one night waiting for a client's husband to come in and make a fool of himself with the go-go dancers, and they had this bit about funny money. Seems the counterfeiter had engraved "In Dog We Trust—instead of "In God We Trust." Everybody watching thought that was hilarious, but the counterfeiter watching from the barstool next to me thought it was blasphemy. He muttered to me that the buffoon who'd done that job had no class. It was okay to do something on the front of a bill for a joke—a spit on the system—but the lame on TV was just a guy who couldn't spell. I nodded like I understood, and the guy pulled out a beautiful twenty-dollar bill and asked me to look it over.

The bill was real as far as I could tell, but instead of "In God We Trust," it said "By God We Must." Now *that,* the counterfeiter told me, was a genuine act of social commentary. I asked him how much he wanted for the bill and he said half face-value. I said that was too much, so he bet me the ten bucks he could shove the bad bill by the bartender even if I warned him.

As he paid the bartender I made some crack about a lot of queer twenties making the rounds. The bartender checked it over carefully, pronounced it perfect and shoved it in the till. So I paid up the ten bucks for the bet and another ten for one of the special twenties, fair and square. Later that night, I gave the twenty as change to the woman who'd hired me to check her husband. It's not often you can get your money back after the race is over.

I pocketed Margot's money. No problem doing that—with the coats I wear, I could make a lot more than that disappear. Now I'd listen. "Dandy said some old nigger came into the Player's Lounge and told him he was the Prophet himself, right? And that Dandy should walk in the ways of righteousness or his offenses would rise up like a tidal wave to drown him."

"So?"

"So Dandy'd been doing a bit of coke, right, and he was high and feeling good. So he kicked the old nigger's ass out of the club and they all had a good laugh, he says."

"So?"

"So *listen,* Burke. He keeps talking about it, right? Like he wants to laugh it off or something but it's almost like he's scared—I mean it was just some old wino or something."

"He didn't work you over?"

Margot smiled, a tiny bit of her dark lipstick showing on her teeth. "Dandy doesn't hurt me anymore hardly at all, Burke. I know it's going to be over soon so I just go into my stash every day and give him money. All he wants is for me to tell him what the trick did to me and then fuck him. He doesn't hurt me himself much. He's like a trick too, you know—some of them just want you to talk. Only he doesn't pay."

"He will."

"That's what Michelle said."

"You told Michelle I was doing something?"

"No, I'm not stupid. But I told her what happened in the

Lounge and she said this old nigger really *is* the Prophet. Weird, huh?"

"You think Michelle is crazy?"

"Man, I know she's not even *close* to crazy, but it doesn't make sense to me."

"Then don't worry about it."

"You're going to do the thing with Dandy?"

"We agreed that the object was to get Dandy to stop his action with you, to let you walk away and not come after you, right?"

"Right."

"That's *all*, right?"

"Well, it doesn't seem like a lot for five grand."

"Since when? That was the deal—there's no more coming to you."

"I'm not saying anything. Just when—"

"When it happens it happens, Margot. You'll know because you're going to be in on it, right?"

"Yes, I know." She seemed tired all of a sudden. Walking over to the blackened window, she tapped her nails against the sill. I asked her if she had the *News* with her, and she pulled a copy of the *Times* from her giant purse. Did they have the race results in that uptown rag? I sat down to check while Margot kept up a steady patter of insights about the streets and the life. It wouldn't take a genius to figure out how she ended up with the likes of Dandy, but that wasn't my job. I used to dream about how someday people would pay me to think, but it hasn't happened yet.

Nodding occasionally to Margot so she'd keep talking quietly, I was left pretty much to myself. I hadn't expected anyone in the poolroom to comment about how my face looked, but I'd thought Margot would say something. She never saw it—obsessions give you tunnel vision. I should know.

I finally found the race results, appropriately displayed in lower-case (and upper-class) type. Damn! Honor Bright, ninth race, the winner, paid $11.60. That was all the information the sissy *Times* would give me, but it was enough. I was now on the longest winning streak of my life with the horses. Come to think of it, with anything at all. But I didn't want to spoil the moment by dwelling on it, and I didn't want to share it with Margot either. So I said, "Okay, I won't be able to reach you, I guess. So you can call me at the number you have in a couple of days and we can make a meet. By then we should have everything in motion."

Margot was drumming her nails against the face of her watch.

"I don't want to go back on the streets right away—Dandy might see me or something. You going to stay here long?"

"No—I got to go to work."

Margot leaned forward, partially blocking my way. "You think it shows?"

"What?"

"On me—you think it shows . . . being a hooker?"

"No, when you're not one."

"I don't get it."

"It's not important. Your eye's healing, right? My face's going to heal, right?" She noticed my face for the first time.

"What happened?"

"I got bit by a baby dragon."

"Where?"

"It's not important. Look, you call, okay?"

Margot stood up. "Burke, as long as I've got to be here anyway, you want . . . ?"

I looked at her, tried to smile, not sure if it came off. "It's the best offer I've had in a long time. But not now, I got to work. Can I raincheck it?"

Margot looked like she'd expected the answer. "I shouldn't be thinking about tricking all the time, huh?"

"If I was you, I'd think about something else."

"Like what?"

"Like how I'm going to solve my problems."

"*You're* going to solve my problems."

"I'm going to solve one of your problems, kid. But you make problems for yourself—you do wrong things."

"Like what?"

"Like calling the Prophet an old nigger," I told her, getting up to walk her to the door.

33

MARGOT HAD NO sooner walked out the door than Max appeared—he waits as silently as he does everything else. I gave him four grand, holding out one for myself for the running expenses of this case, and told him to stash it for me someplace. Less four hundred for Max, this thing still had the chance to show a decent profit if it worked out.

I asked Max if he wanted something to eat, purposely avoiding the subject of horseracing, and I saw a tiny flicker pass across his face. So he thought I already knew the results and wasn't admitting anything. Okay, just for that I'd torture him until he demanded to know the truth.

I didn't have long to wait. As soon as we got to the restaurant Max made the sign of a galloping horse to ask me what happened last night. Instead of telling him I showed him that harness horses don't gallop—that's against the rules. In fact, they're called *standardbreds* instead of *thoroughbreds* because they're bred to a standard gait, either a trot or a pace. They evolved from working horses, not from rich men's playthings like the useless nags who run in the Kentucky Derby. I showed him with my fingers how pacers move their outside legs together and then their inside legs together in rolling motion, while trotters put one front leg and the opposite rear leg forward at the same time. I showed him what it meant to break stride, or go off gait, and why pacers were generally faster and less likely to break than trotters.

Max sat through this entire explanation with the patience of a tree, figuring he would outwait me. But he finally cracked under the strain, just as I was explaining about new breeds now being developed in Scandinavia, how they aren't as fast as American-style trotters but they have tremendous endurance. Jumping up, he stalked over to the cash register for the *News* and fired it over to me hard enough to break bones. Then he folded his arms across his chest and waited.

As I opened the paper I had a momentary flash of panic. What if the goddamned *Times* was wrong? But there it was in greasy black and white. We won. I showed Max the chart of the ninth race—Honor Bright had left cleanly, grabbed a quick tuck fourth at the quarter, moved outside with cover at the half, then fired with a big brush on the final paddock turn to blow past the leaders and win going away by almost two lengths. Max insisted I show him what the charted race would have actually looked like if we'd been there watching, so I got some paper and diagrammed the whole thing for him. Max really showed class. He never asked how much we had won—the victory itself seemed enough. Of course, he could have already figured it out. But the real class showed when he agreed to pick the money up from Maurice and never said a word about making another bet. I'd proved something to him, and that was enough—he didn't think he'd found the key to the vault.

I dropped Max at the warehouse where I used a pay phone to call Flood and tell her I wouldn't be seeing her until very early the next morning. I told her I'd ring her from downstairs before I came up.

My face hurt a bit and I wanted to change the dressing—and I wanted to sleep. But when I got back to the office I had to explain the whole race again to Pansy and feed her too, so it was after four in the afternoon when I finally lay down.

34

THE TINY BATTERY-POWERED alarm woke me just past eight. When I picked up the desk phone to call Flood I heard some freak yell, "Hey, Moonchild, are you on the line?" and hung up quietly. I could have used another shave for cosmetic purposes but it wasn't necessary for the role I had to play. I had to be a guy waiting around the night court for a friend or a relative. I didn't want to look too much like a lawyer—I don't work the Bronx courts (neither does Blumberg or any of my regulars—you have to be bilingual to do it), and I didn't want people talking to me. I didn't want to look too much like a felon either—some smartass rookie might decide to ask me if there were any warrants out against me. There weren't but I had to time things right. I had to be in front of the court at eleven-thirty like I'd been told, so I had to get there earlier to make sure. But not too early—I didn't want to be hanging around there either.

I got out a pair of dark chino pants, a dark-green turtleneck jersey, a pair of calf-high black boots, a fingertip leather jacket, and one of those Ivy League caps. I changed quickly, shoved a set of I.D. in my pocket, added three hundred bucks, and snapped a second set of I.D. papers into the jacket's inner sleeve. No weapons—the court's full of metal detectors and informants, and Pablito's people might have even a worse attitude than the law. So no tape recorder either, not even a pencil.

Now for the bad part—riding the subway without nuclear weapons, or at least a flamethrower. But it was early enough and I walked until I came to the underground entrance. I played with the local trains for a while, backtracking and crisscrossing until I got to the Brooklyn Bridge station. I found a pay phone there and called Flood—she said she was doing okay and she'd stay there until I called her, sounding subdued but not depressed. It's bad to be depressed at night—that kind of thing is easier to handle in the morning. That's why when I've only got a couple of bucks in my pocket I get some action down on a horse or a number or something before I go to sleep—something to look forward to. And if it doesn't come through for me, at least it's another day where I beat the system—it's daylight, I'm not looking out through prison bars, the suckers are getting ready to go to work, and there's money for me to make. It works for me, but I don't think Flood's a gambler.

I grabbed the uptown express, rode it to Forty-second Street, and crossed the tracks like I was looking for the local. I took a look around. Lots of freaks working the second shift tonight—chain snatchers, child molesters, flashers and rubbers, the usual. No Cobra, though. Sometimes you get dumb-lucky, not this time. I waited for two more express trains to come on through and took the third one.

A guy in the seat across from me was wearing a tattered raincoat buttoned to the neck, denim washpants, new loafers with tassels, no socks. He had neatly trimmed hair and crazy eyes. Nice disguise, but he'd left the plastic hospital tag around his wrist when he'd gone over the wall. He had one hand in his pocket and his lips were moving. I got up quietly and moved to another car.

A kid about the size of a two-family house was standing in the middle of the next car, playing his giant portable stereo loud enough to crack concrete. Everybody was looking the other way. A citizen with a delicate beard and a belted trenchcoat was complaining to the girl next to him about noise pollution. The kid watched the whole conversation with reptile eyes. I moved on to the next car.

A young transit cop with the obligatory mustache walked through the train listening to his walkie-talkie and nodding to himself. I saw a skinny Spanish kid about fourteen years old practicing his three-card monte moves on a piece of cardboard. He had very smooth hands, but his rap was weak—I guess he was an apprentice. Two blacks in Arab robes with white knit caps on their heads moved through the cars, rattling metal cups, looking for donations with a story about a special school for kids in Brooklyn. Some people went in their pockets and put coins in the cups.

I moved through a couple of cars again. Sat down next to a blond kid wearing only a cut-off sweatshirt, no jacket. He looked peaceful. I checked his hands—one large blue letter tattooed on each knuckle. H A T E. The letters were set so they faced out. I moved on before the fellows collecting money asked this boy for a contribution.

The last car had nothing more troublesome than some kids staring out the front window like they were driving the train, and it lasted all the way to 161st Street.

The South Bronx—not a bad place if you had asbestos skin. A short walk to the Criminal Court Building, almost eleven now. The Bronx Criminal Court is a brand-new building—the juvenile court is in the same building, just with a different entrance. I guess the city figured there was no point making the delinquents walk a long distance before they reached their inevitable destination.

I found a quiet bench, opened my copy of the *News*, and kept an eye on my watch. Nobody approached. It was getting near the end of the arraignment shift and only a few losers were waiting around. I spotted one of the hustlers, a young Spanish guy with a lawyer's suit. I'd heard about this one— he works Blumberg's game, only in the Bronx. Next to him, Blumberg is Clarence Darrow.

I left the bench with five minutes to spare, climbed out of the basement to the first floor, and went out the 161st Street exit. I lit a cigarette and waited. At eleven-thirty a dark red gypsy cab with the legend *Paradiso Taxi* on the door and a foxtail on the antenna pulled up. I walked out of the shadows, smartly said, "Hey, my man," and the driver looked me over. "Where to, *amigo?*"

"Oh, someplace downtown, you know?"

"Like the Waldorf?"

"That's it." I climbed in the back without further negotiations. The cab shot straight up 161st like it was headed for the highway to go downtown and I leaned back and closed my eyes. Rules are rules. The local cops aren't too bad, but some of the federal lunatics don't believe the Constitution applies to banana republics like the South Bronx. If I ever got strapped into a polygraph, I wanted the needles to read *No Deception Indicated* when they asked me where Una Gente Libre had its headquarters.

35

EITHER THE DRIVER really worked a gypsy cab as a regular job or he was a hell of an actor. Even with my eyes closed I could feel the lurch of the miserably-maintained hunk of metal every time we floundered around a corner. Normal potholes put my head against the ceiling, and each genuine home-grown South Bronx edition almost knocked me unconscious. He had the radio tuned to some Spanish-language station at a volume that reminded me of the holding tank at Riker's Island—and for an added touch of authenticity he screamed *"Maricon!"* and waved his fist out the open window at another driver who had the audacity to attempt to share the road with us.

We turned a sharp corner; the driver doused the radio. He switched to a smooth cruising mode and spoke distinctly without taking his eyes from the windshield. "At the next corner, I stop the cab. You get out. You walk in the same direction as I drive for half a block. You see a bunch of *lobos* in front of a burn-out. You walk right up to them and they let you through. You go into the burn-out and someone meet you there."

I said nothing—he obviously wasn't going to answer questions. *Lobo* may mean wolf in Spanish, but I understood he was describing a street gang that would be in front of an abandoned building.

The cab stopped at the corner and got moving again as I was swinging the rear door closed. I looked at the cab as it moved away—it sure looked like a gypsy cab, but someone must have stolen the rear license plate. I marched the half block until I spotted about a dozen kids—some sitting on the steps of the abandoned building, some standing. Only about half of them were looking in my direction.

The *lobos* came fully equipped—they all wore denim cut-offs with a winged and bloody-taloned bird of prey on the back—the birds had human skulls instead of heads. I spotted bicycle chains, car antennas, and baseball bats—one kid had a machete in a sheath. No firearms on display, but two of them were sitting next to a long flat cardboard box.

As I got closer I could see they weren't kids at all—none of them looked under twenty years old. They wouldn't fool a beat patrolman too easily either—no radios playing, no wise-cracking among themselves, just quietly watching the street.

I glanced up and saw a gleam of metal at one of the windows—there wouldn't be any winos sleeping in that building tonight. A car turned into the block from the other end and came toward me. The *lobos* moved off the steps and I stepped back in the shadows. The car was a year-old white Caddy—it never slowed down but I glimpsed three people in the front seat—two girls and a driver with a plantation hat. Some pimp was on his way to the Hunts Point Market, and suddenly I knew just about where I was in the South Bronx.

When I got within fifty feet of the building I saw hands go into pockets but I kept on coming. It wasn't bravery—there was no place else to go. When the hands came out of the pockets with mirror-lensed sunglasses I figured I was going to be all right. Nobody needs a disguise to take your life.

I approached the gang. They looked briefly at me then past me to see if I had come alone. I kept walking up the broken steps, heard movements behind me, didn't turn around. I went through the door into a black pit—and stopped. A voice said: "Burke. Don't move, okay? Just stay where you are."

I didn't. I felt a hand on my arm. I didn't jump—it was expected. The hand groped, found mine, and a heavily knotted rope was pushed into my palm. I grabbed one of the knots and felt a gentle tug. I got the message and followed along in the direction I was pulled. I couldn't see a damned thing—the guy leading me must have been using sonar or something.

The same voice finally said, "In here," and I stepped through a door covered with dark blankets. Now I could see a dim light ahead and I followed the back of the man leading me down a long flight of stairs until we came to another blanket-covered door at the bottom. My guide felt his way through the blankets until he found a bare spot, knocked three times, waited patiently, heard two raps from the other side, rapped once in response, waited, rapped one more time. He gently pushed against my chest to indicate that we should stand back, and then from the other side of the wall bolts sliding, metal scraping, something heavy being moved. I wanted a cigarette but I didn't want to move my hands. After a couple of minutes the door slid open and a large man parted the blankets and stepped out. I couldn't see him too well but there was enough light to catch the highlights bouncing off the Uzi submachine gun he held in one hand. He stood there covering us both for what seemed like a long minute, saying nothing.

Then I felt a breeze on the back of my neck and heard Pablo's voice behind me saying, "This way, Burke," and I turned and entered the door behind me, my back now to the man with the Uzi. By the time anyone broke down the blanketed door and confronted the guard, the people in the room I was stepping into would have been long gone.

The big room was as anonymous as a cell block—a round table in the center, several couches and old stuffed chairs scattered around, concrete floor, plasterboard walls. A light fixture dangled from someplace in the blacked-out ceiling, hanging so low it was almost touching the table—no windows that I could see. There was a large TV set in one corner on a metal stand with a videotape deck hooked up below it. The rest of the room was in shadow. The chairs and the couches were occupied but I couldn't see anything except shapes.

I didn't need anyone to tell me where I was to sit. As I approached the table I noticed a large ashtray on top and a green plastic garbage bag sitting underneath. When we all left this room, it would be as if nobody had ever been there. Fine with me.

I sat down. Pablo sat directly opposite me. He gave me the two-handed handshake he always uses. He made no motion that I could see, but the shadows moved closer as he spoke, especially those behind me. "I'm going to say some things in Spanish to my people now. After I finish I'll talk with you in English, okay?"

"Good."

Pablo launched into rapid-fire Spanish, only some of which I understood. I caught *"amigo miò,"* not *"amigo de nostros."* He was saying this man is a friend of *mine,* not a friend of *ours*. He would be vouching for my character, not my politics. Most of the rest got past me but I caught *compadre* more than once and couldn't tell if he was referring to me or someone else in the room. When he'd finished he looked around. Someone asked a soft-voiced question—Pablo appeared to be giving the matter some thought, then said "No!" in a flat voice. No more questions. Pablo turned to face me, and the shadows moved even closer.

"I told them it would not be necessary to search you, that you were not of the *federales*. I told them you were not with the police, and that you would be here for your own reasons. I told them that you have helped me in the past and that you would help me again in the future. And I told them that we would help you if it did not conflict with our purpose. Okay?"

"Sure. Okay to smoke?"

Pablo nodded and I slowly, carefully took out the cigarettes, left the pack on the table, reached for the wooden matches, and lit up. I heard one of the watchers in the shadows mutter something and I reached out for the cigarette pack, tore it open and laid out the smokes one by one. I tore the wrapping paper into small bits and put the whole mess into the garbage bag. I heard *"Bueno"* from one of them, a short laugh from another. Pablo took it up. "My friend, you said that it was necessary for us to meet. So?"

I picked my words and the pace of my speech carefully, trying for a show of dignity they would respect and that would show my respect for them. You have to talk a lot of different ways in my business. You don't throw in a lot of references to Allah when you're talking to a Black Muslim, but you don't offer him a ham sandwich either.

"There is a man named Goldor"—the room went dead quiet so suddenly that my voice sounded like it was echoing—"that I need to speak with. He knows something I need to know. I understand that he is a person with whom you have a dispute. He is not the target of my inquiries, but he is *not* my friend and I would not protect him. I come here for two reasons. First, I must talk to him and I do not want you to believe that this talk means we are doing business—I would not do business with someone you dislike. Second, if you dislike him you must have good reason. If you have good reason, you have good information—and if you have good information, you can perhaps assist me in getting an audience with him. That's all."

No one spoke, but the tension level had tripled since I said Goldor's name. It stayed quiet until Pablo spoke again. "How do you know we dislike Goldor?"

"This is something I heard from a good source."

"A source you trust?"

"As to reliability of information, yes. That is all."

"So your source is in law enforcement?"

"Yes."

"Have you been told if Goldor has any protection?"

"I have been told that he does not take street rumors seriously, and that he does not believe himself to be in any danger."

Pablo smiled. "Good. Do your inquiries about Goldor involve a woman?" Nothing showed in my face, but it felt like a punch to the heart—did that goddamned Flood ever stop making trouble? "In some ways, yes," I told him, "but I am not looking for a woman. I am looking for a man, and Goldor may know where he is."

"This man is a friend of Goldor?"

"Possibly. It is also possible that he may be an enemy."

"An informant, then?"

"He may be."

"If you find this man, will it help Goldor?"

"No."

"Will it hurt him?"

"Most likely not."

Pablo paused for a moment, looking at me. Then he got up from the table, disappeared back into the shadows—they blended around him until I was alone in a pool of light. I couldn't make out a single word of what they said this time, but it didn't sound like an argument. After few minutes Pablo came back to the table and the shadows followed him again. "For me to tell you what we know about Goldor it is necessary to tell you some other things, some things that otherwise you would not know. But first I tell you this, and I tell you out of friendship only. Goldor is dead. His body is still moving above the ground but his death is certain. If you go and speak with him it may be that later *el porko* will want to speak with you, understand? You must be able to say *another* reason to have spoken with him. Agreed?"

"Yes."

Pablo took another deep breath, reached over and took the cigarette from my hand, put it to his lips, took a deep drag.

"Goldor is not a human being. You have no word for him in English, nor do we in Spanish. The closest we could come is *gusaniento*, you comprende?"

"Like rotten—full of maggots?"

"Something like that, yes. He is the head of an industry which sells the bodies of human beings for the pleasure of others. But not like a whoremaster or a common pimp. No, Goldor is special—he sells children in bondage. If you buy a boy or a girl from Goldor's people, that child is yours to keep—to torture, to kill, whatever you want. Goldor is above the street. He is like a broker of degeneracy—you tell him what you want and he finds it and delivers it to you. Goldor is not human, as I told you. He is a demon, a thing who worships *el dolor,* the pain of others. He *believes* in pain, my friend. Where he finds women who share his beliefs we do not know, but we do know that many of his victims are volunteers. The police know of him but he cannot be touched. To the authorities, his hands are not dirty."

"He's not alone in this."

"Compadre, you come right to the point. Why would we want to deal with such a man when there are so many others like him? I will tell you. On the Lower East Side you know we have a community. It is a bad place to live but survival is possible—you know about survival. We have many operations down there, as we do in the Bronx. We hear many stories about young Puerto Rican boys who just disappear, but with no complaints to the police. So we look for ourselves. We see that some of those boys are in foster care—but not foster care like with the city. Some kind of informal arrangement, we are told. Some of the mothers believe that their children will have a better way of life, more opportunities—at least they say so to us. But some—and we know this for certain—they have just sold their children. We look, we ask questions, we spend some money until we are sure. It is Goldor doing this. Not personally, but it is him.

"We have a meeting about what is to be done—by then we know much about this Goldor. One of our people, a brave *jibaro* not too long in this country, she volunteers to get with Goldor to learn the whereabouts of the children he has taken. Her name was Luz; we all called her Lucecita, which means Little Light. Lucecita was not a child, Burke. She knew that she would have to have sex with the demon, but it was a price she was willing to pay. We are a disciplined people, not like the newspapers think. Her man is sitting right in this room. He fought with her in front of all of us. He wanted to kill Goldor, not to send Luz to him. But we as a group decided that killing him would not find the children—it would not kill the thing he does. Lucecita got a job in a restaurant where Goldor eats, and it was arranged that they would meet. She was invited to his home, and she went. We never heard from her again."

"Did you—?"

"Wait, Burke. Please. The next day Goldor left on a plane for California. We have people there, he was followed. Some of us went to his house in Westchester but we found no sign of Luz. We thought she perhaps had been taken for sale too, but we knew he only sold children—so we assumed she was dead. Then our people in California told us that some of Goldor's people were dealing in films—videotapes. Sex films, torture films. We arranged to buy all of the films, one of each, and they were sent here. When we viewed the films we were looking for clues to where they might have been made, thinking we might find a way to locate Lucecita. We found the answers and we swore by our blood that Goldor would die. There are some things one cannot say in any language. Some things you must see yourself."

Pablo gestured to the shadows to bring the videotape monitor close to the table. I heard the sounds of a cassette being inserted, heard a switch flip, and the screen began to flicker. The overhead light went out. Sitting in the darkness, I saw:

A starkly lit room, all in black and white, with a shot of a long-haired woman seated on a straight chair in the center. The camera zoomed in and I saw the woman was held to the chair with a thick band around the waist and two more thinner ones crossing over her exposed breasts like bandoliers. She was naked except for a dark ribbon tied around her neck. The woman was saying something—biting off the words. There was no sound except for the hum of the machine and a slight tape hiss.

Suddenly she lunged forward, but the chair didn't move. The camera panned down to the chair legs and you could see they were bolted to the floor, held down by metal brackets.

A man entered the frame, wearing a black executioner's mask that extended down almost to his chest. He had a dog's collar in one hand and a short three-lash whip in the other. The woman's hands were free, and the man extended the dog collar to her. She spat on the extended hand, and the whip cut down across her exposed thighs. The woman leaped in the chair, bucking against her bonds, her soundless mouth wrenched open in pain.

The man approached again, holding out the dog collar. The woman flashed out her nails at him but he was too quick. He put down the collar and the whip and came closer, almost within striking distance. He was talking to her, using his hands in a be-reasonable gesture. The woman appeared to calm down, her eyes dropped to her waist.

The man came back to her with the dog collar. She shook her head no. He put it on the floor, shaking his head, then picked up the whip and came to her again. Another slash across her thighs, again she bucked and silently screamed. He tossed the whip aside and walked away from her, turning his back.

The screen flickered and I wondered if parts had been edited out. Then I saw the man close in on the woman until he was just beyond her reach. He crouched in front of her, like he was negotiating with a stubborn child, then gestured that he would set her free, pointing to something out of the camera's view. The camera followed his hand to a leather-covered sawhorse, like carpenters use. He came over to the woman, unsnapped the bindings, and set her free. Again the sweeping gesture with his hand toward the sawhorse, like a headwaiter showing you to your table. The woman started in that direction, shaking her head to clear it—then suddenly the camera blurred as she tried to run. The man grabbed her by the hair and slammed her to the ground, driving a knee into her back—he punched her repeatedly with one black-gloved fist while holding her down with the other.

He stood up—legs spread, standing over her. His stomach moved in and out rapidly like he was breathing hard through the mask. He half-lugged, half-carried the woman back to the chair, positioned her in it like she was before and refastened the bindings. He stepped out of the picture, the camera zoomed in to the woman's face. There was blood in the corner of her mouth, her eyes were scars. The man came back into the picture, again holding the dog collar and the whip. This time the woman didn't move as he approached. He put the collar around her neck, and she sat there, slumped forward. Broken.

He said something to her and the whip flashed down again.

The woman reached her hands up to her neck and buckled the collar, the masked man stepped forward and attached a bright metal chain to the collar. He stepped back, hands on hips. Taking the chain in one hand, he jerked the woman's head, first in one direction, then another. He was showing the camera he could move her head with just a flick of his wrist.

Again he approached and knelt to unfasten the bindings again, all the time talking to the woman. But then he appeared to change his mind and got to his feet. He stepped out of camera range, and the camera came in to a close-up on her face again. Her eyes were dull.

When he stepped back into the camera's view, he was naked from the waist down, standing out erect. His legs were muscular and altogether hairless. His feet were bare.

The camera went from the woman's mouth to the man's groin several times, panning slowly so the viewer couldn't possibly miss the point. The man held the dog leash in one hand and the whip in the other as he walked closer to the woman. He jerked the leash so her head was yanked toward him, holding the whip ready in the other hand—she was being given a choice. She made her decision—her mouth opened and her nails flashed out and the camera blurred again.

The next shot showed the woman with her fingers still extended, breasts heaving. The screen also showed the man holding his testicles with both hands, bent at the waist. Then it went dark.

I reached my hand toward my cigarettes and was trying to get my breathing straight when the screen flickered into life again and the man approached, this time with only the whip in his hand. It came down, again and again, right through the woman's upraised hands. Then the man threw down the whip and walked slowly out of the room, leaving her body running with blood.

The masked man returned, erect again. Two minutes later? A half hour? No way to know. But this time he was holding a black Luger in one gloved hand. Again he approached. Cautiously. Slowly.

The gun was leveled at the woman's face. He must have said something because she appeared to reply. The camera moved in close so all we could see was the woman's face with the shadow of the pistol across one cheek. The gun pulled back and the camera pulled back with it, and then we just saw the woman tied to the chair, looking straight ahead, her lips pressed tight together. There was a bruise showing in one corner of her mouth. Suddenly she was slammed back against the chair, bounced forward, and lay still. Her head dropped against her chest. Her body jerked spastically, once, twice.

The man in the executioner's mask entered the picture again—he walked over to the woman's side and jerked the leash, pulling her head back so it was facing the camera again. Her mouth was open, so were her eyes—there was a starburst hole in her forehead. The screen filled with her face so the viewers would know they had paid for the real thing. And then it went black.

I reached for a cigarette as they pushed the videotape monitor back into the shadows, but my hands wouldn't work. Pablo came back to the table, looked across at me.

"Lucecita?" I asked.

"Si, hermano. Comprende?"

"He *sells* this?"

"He sells this, and more like it. We are told he has some in color and some even with sound."

"How does he get people to film this? It's a cold-blooded homicide, not some sex rap."

"He does it himself, *compadre*—that was Goldor in the mask."

"Then he's bought himself a life sentence."

"How? We cannot prove a thing. We can prove that it was our Lucecita who died, but how to prove that it was Goldor himself? Besides, a life sentence is insufficient."

"So is a death sentence."

"I agree, we all agree. We have discussed this and there was debate. But we will not imitate our oppressors. We are Puerto Ricans, not Iranians."

"I understand. You'll tell me where to find Goldor?"

"Oh, yes—and we will do better than that. We have a dossier, complete. It will be handed to you when you get out of the cab later on. And then there is no more from us, you understand?"

"Yes."

"We are not in a race, Burke. We will not interfere with your work. But you must move quickly—we are almost ready."

"Understood."

"In return you will tell us anything you may learn. That is all we ask."

"Agreed."

There was nothing more to say. We shook hands, the overhead light went off, and I followed Pablo out the door into the corridor. Another man took me up the stairs to the front door where the *lobos* still prowled. I started to walk through them as I had done before, and found myself held in place. I didn't resist, just stayed within the group until I heard a car come down the block. The gypsy cab again.

The pack parted and I climbed in the back. The driver didn't ask me where I was going and I didn't say anything. I didn't open my eyes until I felt the cab crossing the Third Avenue Bridge into Manhattan. The driver took the East Side Drive to Twenty-third Street, turned over to Park Avenue South, spotted an all-night cab stand, and pulled over to the curb. As I got out, he handed me a legal-sized envelope and drove off.

I walked over to the cab stand, checked the first cab. I gave him an address within half a dozen blocks of Flood's studio.

I tried to close my eyes during the ride, but the videotape kept replaying inside my eyelids.

36

THE LEGAL ENVELOPE full of Goldor information had disappeared into the side flap of my jacket by the time I got out of the cab. The pay phone was right where I remembered it, and Flood answered on the first ring.

"It's me, Flood, I'll be there in a couple of minutes. Come downstairs and let me in."

"Are you okay? What's wrong?"

"I'll tell you when I see you—just do it," I said, and hung up.

I looked at my watch to avoid thinking about what Flood had heard in my voice—it was past three in the morning.

I walked right up to Flood's door like I had a key, reached for the handle and it opened. I was so distracted that I didn't bother to ring for the elevator, just let Flood walk up the steps ahead of me—but I snapped out of it and stopped her halfway up the first flight and motioned her to be quiet. It stayed quiet. We were alone.

We walked through the studio to Flood's place without talking. I found a place to sit down and lit a smoke, trusting Flood to find an ashtray for me someplace. I took out the Goldor file and stared at the cover—I didn't want to open it just yet. Flood sat down across from me on the floor. "Burke, tell me what's wrong."

My hands were all right by then but I guess my face wasn't. I didn't say anything and Flood just let me smoke the cigarette in peace. She moved closer and just leaned her body weight against me without saying anything. I felt her warmth and strength next to me and the calmness that came with it. After a few minutes I handed her the cover of the file.

"Everything about Goldor's in here," I told her.

"Isn't that good? Isn't that what you went to find?"

"Yeah, but I found something else too. I think he's our man, the man with the lead to Wilson."

Flood looked questions at me, gave me her soft smile. "Don't smile, Flood. He's not someone we can make a deal with."

She said, "Tell me," and I did the best I could. She sat there not moving a muscle while I took her all the way through that videotape. She didn't ask me how I got to see it—she could see it wasn't important anymore, if it ever had been. She absorbed the story like a good boxer taking a body punch—she moved into it to get something she could understand, something that would make sense. "The woman knew she was going to die." It wasn't a question.

"I don't know."

"She did. She died with honor. You must have seen that, Burke."

"If she did what the freak wanted, would she have lived?"

"Would she have wanted to?"

"We'll never know, right? She has people—she won't have to worry about resting in peace wherever she is. That's why we don't have a lot of time. Goldor is on the spot—he's marked. If this city had vultures, they would be hovering over his house right now, you understand?"

"Yes," said Flood, "but does *he* understand?"

"I'm told not—I'm told he doesn't believe anything can get to him. Everything about him is supposed to be in this file. We'll see."

"What do you want to do?"

"I want to make it like I never heard of this freak," I told her. "And I want to cancel his ticket—watch him die, have him understand that he is going to die just like that girl did—find the field his tree grew in and dig up the roots and pour salt in the ground."

"It's not wrong to be afraid," Flood said, thinking she understood.

"Flood, for chrissakes, I know that—I probably know that better than anyone you'll ever meet. You ever watch a pro football game—ever see how those guys come over to the sidelines and take a hit off an oxygen bottle so they can go back and do their work? That's what I do with fear. It makes me smart—it's the fuel I run on. You don't understand—you didn't see the tape."

"I don't want to see it."

"That won't help. Damn it, Flood—I didn't want to see it either, but even if we never saw it it would still be—it will always be, even if this maggot is dead and gone."

"Like Zen?"

"If a tree falls in the forest . . . maybe so—I don't know."

"I'm not afraid of him," she said, "he's just a man."

"Flood, there is just no place for people like you where I live. Good for you, you're not afraid—you going to protect me?"

"I can."

"Not from this—it's inside of me, it's inside all of us. What he did—people do it. Rich people pay for it with money and poor people just do it and pay the freight in some mental hospital or prison. *People* do it—not animals, not birds—people. If you're not scared of it, it just means you can't see yourself there. It doesn't mean it *isn't* there."

"Maybe it's because he's so rich—there's so much strength when you have money . . ."

"It's not money, Flood, it's power. When I was in Africa once, in Angola before they kicked out the Portuguese—I was near the airport in Luanda and the rebels were getting closer and it was time to get out. The soldiers were all over the place and they were searching luggage, you know, to find contraband—ivory carvings, diamonds, hard currency. Two of them opened my bags on the ground. Nothing in there, but they found the malaria pills I had with me. One of them opened the bottles and just poured them out on the ground, right in front of me, smiling in my face all the time. There was nothing I could do except act stupid and confused. That made them happy—I would get malaria and I wouldn't even understand how it happened. That was enough for them, that much power—for some people, it's not enough. There's a line you cross—and once you cross it you never get back. Then you're not human anymore."

"All soldiers act evil," Flood said. "That's the way they're trained. Everything is black and white, friend or enemy. They don't think, they just obey—"

"And when they rape some helpless woman after a battle, is that obedience?"

"That's evil too. A lot of soldiers do evil rotten things, but when they're no longer soldiers there's no need for them to be evil. They can stop."

"Goldor is no soldier, Flood—his marching orders are in his head."

"You talk like you know him. You were only watching an evil film—you don't know him."

"I know him, all right . . . There was a kid once, a few years ago. A sort of halfwit, you know? Halfass burglar. The Man kept catching him, kept putting him in the can—like meat on a hook in a freezer, hanging up to be cured so it's fit for people to eat. And every time he goes to the joint he listens to those degenerates talk how about they're going to kick some woman's ass until she gets on the street for them and makes them some money, or how they're going to pull a train on some retarded girl down the block—every sicko fantasy in the world. And this kid listens—he don't say much, not because he has enough smarts to keep his mouth shut but because nobody ever listens to such a lame. So he gets out again, right? As soon as he gets on the street he hits a housing project to do another of his dumb penny-ante burglaries. He goes in a window and it turns out to be a bedroom. There's a woman sleeping there and she wakes up. If she'd screamed or tried to fight him he would have run away. But this woman, she read too many books— she tells him, 'Don't hurt me, I'll do anything you want, but please don't hurt me,' and for the first time in his pitiful life he's in control—he's got *power*. He is a fucking god right there in that bedroom—and every evil thing he ever heard about in the joint floods his tiny brain. He puts the woman through every kind of change he can think of. He stays there for hours with her, just power-tripping. And when he leaves there's a Coke bottle sticking out of one side of the woman and a wooden spoon sticking out the other. He doesn't kill her, doesn't take a thing from her apartment. And the *next* time he goes prowling, he's not looking to steal—you understand me? He crossed that power-rush line and he can't *ever* step back over it—he has to live on that other side until he stops living. He's not a man anymore, not a person."

"How could you know this?"

"I knew that kid," I told her, "I talked to him."

"In prison?"

"No. He was in a juvenile prison, one of those dumps they call a training school for delinquents. No, I met him on the street—and I talked to him just before he died."

"Couldn't he have been locked up for the rest of his life?"

"There's no such thing. He'd sit in his cell and draw pictures of women with blunt objects sticking out of them—or he'd do like another freak, a guy I *did* know in prison. This guy had a little tape recorder and he'd prowl around the blocks until he heard some kid being raped and then he'd just roll up and record the sounds and go back to his cell and play the tape and giggle to himself and jack off all over the walls. Sooner or later the parole board's going to cut that freak loose too. And then he'll do some cutting-loose of his own."

"How did that other kid die?"

"He jumped off a sixteen-story building," I said, letting her think it was suicide.

"Oh. And Goldor . . . ?"

"What he does is more addictive than any heroin. But there's more to him than just being a sicko. He *believes* in what he does—you can tell. The way he smashed that woman—it was because he was so angry. So much hate because she wouldn't see the Way—you know, like the Tao. The perfect way—pain for life. And we have to find a way to make him tell us something," I said, thinking how hopeless it was.

"Maybe if we—"

"Forget it—I know what you're thinking. He would beat us, Flood. You could kill him easy enough, but could you really torture him? He could outwait us—he'd know we don't have his feeling for pain—he'd know he could survive. He just wouldn't believe we would kill him."

"You remember that guy in the alley? When I—"

"You going to castrate him, Flood? The problem's not in his balls, it's in his head—he wouldn't be any different gelded. Even the threat wouldn't make him talk to us."

"We have to try."

"We are going to try, but first we have to read all this stuff and then make it disappear. Then I have to sleep, and then see some people. And then I have to—"

"Burke, you want to sleep first?"

"I can't—can't sleep. This stuff . . ." I held out the Goldor file.

Flood stood up and shrugged off her robe. She held out her hand. "Just come and lie down with me. Sleep first—I'll put the papers where they're safe."

I got up with her and went inside. She took my clothes off and pushed me back against the mats. She lay across me with her warm body, her chubby little hand rubbing the side of my face. She kept rubbing me, whispering that Goldor wouldn't win . . . that it would be us, that she believed in me, that I would find a way for us. I got calm and quiet but still not sleepy. And Flood understood the last door for me to go through before I could fight this freak—she helped me inside her and softly and slowly took me past the murky darkness of my fears and into a gentle place where sleep finally came.

37

FLOOD AND I woke up together in the morning. My left hand was buried somewhere beneath her so I couldn't see my watch, but the light outside told me it was well past sunup. Flood stirred against my shoulder, mumbled something I couldn't understand. I bounced her gently with my shoulder until she came around. She opened her eyes and blinked at me. "You okay, Burke?"

"Yeah, and I'm ready to go to work. Let me just get cleaned up a bit, and I want to start on Goldor's file."

She rolled over onto her side so I could get off the mat, then lay back and closed her eyes. I watched her practice her breathing for a minute before I walked into her tiny shower. My face in the mirror startled me—it was healing but the lower jaw was all bluish-yellow—it would probably stay discolored for another few days. I used some of Flood's mouthwash and then examined my teeth in the mirror—the stitches were holding.

When I went back inside, Flood was lying on her back, her legs in the air, toes pointed up. She was doing some kind of exercise where she split them until they were nearly parallel to the ground, then brought them together again, lowered them almost to the floor but didn't touch it—she held them for a few seconds like that, then broke them again and started over. Her movements were so smooth they looked effortless, but they couldn't have been. I waited until her legs were straight up again and grabbed an ankle in each hand. "You have thick ankles, Flood," and moved my hands away from center to spread her legs again. They didn't budge—I increased the pressure and watched the long muscles flex on the inside of her thighs. I could feel the strain in my forearms, and finally her legs started to yield. I pushed harder and suddenly her legs shot open and I fell forward right on top of her. But before I could land she whipped her legs back, doubled up her knees, and caught me on the pads of her feet. And then she tossed my entire bulk into the air like a seal playing with a ball. She caught me on the way down, giggling like a little kid. The second time I was headed down I flipped my shoulders back, landed on my feet, grabbed her ankles again and pulled her upside down and erect, facing away from me. But before I could do some giggling of my own she slammed into my ankles with the heels of her hands and I toppled over with her underneath. This time her damn laughing fit made it feel like I was lying on top of some rocky Jello. I rolled off, reached for a cigarette—she was still chuckling.

"Flood, you're a clown, you know that?"

"What did I do?"

"Never fucking mind," I told her, and tried to keep from laughing myself. She got up without using her hands and floated off to the shower. I got dressed, lit up another smoke, and took out the Goldor file. It was everything Pablo had promised: full name (Jonas James Goldor), date of birth (February 4, 1937, in Cape May, New Jersey), height (5'11"), weight (175), rap sheet (two arrests for assault, the last one in 1961, no convictions), military service (none), marital status (never married), mother's maiden name, father's occupation at time of Goldor's birth (note that both parents were deceased. Too bad—I hated to have anything in common with him). A long list of corporations and partnerships in which he held an interest. Location of two known safe-deposit boxes in commercial banks. Copies of driver's license, ownership registration certificates for four cars (a Rolls, a Porsche 928, a Land Rover, and a 500-series Benz sedan), copies of some cancelled checks written on two of his corporations, a copy of his 1979 IRS return (showing a gross income of $440,775 with a net of $228,000, all from a series of subchapter-S corporations, a pass-through tax trick so that he could be the sole stockholder and not be taxed corporately and individually). Also a floor plan of his house in Scarsdale, complete with all the switch-box locations for the electronic protection system. A note that said Goldor kept nobody but himself on the premises at night, but that he had a silent alarm setup connected directly to the local police station—and another note that said they didn't know all the locations for the switches that would set it off. They even had a copy of a New York City carry-pistol license. Other random notes: Goldor was a health-food freak, gobbled tons of vitamins and supplements every day. Worked out regularly, had a complete gym with Nautilus equipment and a sauna in his basement. He had all his clothes custom-made, even his shoes. A gun collector, but not of modern weapons.

And that was it, except for some blue onionskin pages typed with an ancient IBM Model-B using italic type. A psychiatric profile, obviously prepared by Pablo at long distance from the subject. I scanned it once quickly, then settled down to read:

"Goldor from relatively wealthy family, sent to British boarding school from age nine to fifteen, when he returned to the States. Return probably occasioned by death of his father. Managed a variety of his father's holdings, gradually at first, then took exclusive control just prior to death of his mother when he was about twenty. Obsession with hairlessness probably traceable to preoccupation with bodybuilding (note: body builders routinely shave all body hair so as to better display muscular development and vascularity). No validatable information concerning early development. Runs a variety of sex-oriented businesses concurrently with more legitimate enterprises. Projects image of power and dominance in business relationships."

Then came these underlined words: "What follows is, at best, an educated guess. This represents theorization absent sufficient data and should be so weighted." Then a lot of mumbo-jumbo about "homosexual ideation," "situational impotence," "unresolved Oedipal conflicts," "sadistic obsessions which the subject believes he tightly controls," "suspect enuresis, fire-setting, cruelty to small animals, classic triad," "possibility of iatrogenic therapy prepuberty," "grandiosity bordering on belief in omnipotence," "utterly self-contained," and "functioning psychopath."

I was still reading when Flood came back wearing one of her robes, this time a bottle-green job with wide black piping on the sleeves. I handed her the stuff without a word and sat and smoked while she read through it. It didn't take her long. "You know what this stuff means?" she asked.

"Yes—remember, a lot of it is just guessing."

"I understand some of it—enuresis is bed-wetting, right? But what's this classic-triad stuff? And what does iatrogenic mean? And—"

"Hold up a minute, Flood. The classic triad is the kid who wets the bed, sets fires, and tortures small animals, especially his own pets. If all three things are going on with the same kid the odds are in favor of him pulling a homicide or two before he grows up. And iatrogenic means a therapeutic treatment that makes a disease worse, like pouring salt on a wound. The whole thing boils down to Goldor being a confirmed degenerate, someone who can never get better no matter what you do with him—or to him."

"Is this just words, or does it help us?"

"I don't know. Most of the time it would mean a lot of nothing, but the people who put this together know what they're doing."

"They say he's a functioning psychopath. I thought all psychos were just loony—you know, off the wall."

"You know what a psychopath is, Flood?"

"I guess not."

I got to my feet, walked over a few paces and turned to face her. "Imagine you got thrown into a totally dark room, okay? You can't see a thing. What's the first thing you do?"

She didn't hesitate. "Reach out my hands to see where the walls are."

I reached out my own hands. "Right, you want to find the limits of your environment. Less fancy—you want to know where you stand, what's going on. That's why some kids act so bad when you put them in institutions . . . they don't know the limits and they don't know how to ask, so they act up so people will step in and show them. But a psychopath, you throw *him* in a blacked-out room and you know what he does?"

As Flood looked up at me I wrapped my arms around my biceps like I was giving myself a hug. "A psychopath has everything he needs right inside himself. He doesn't need an environment, doesn't have to work with it. He doesn't see people, he sees *things*. And he could move these things around or throw them out and break them the same way you might rearrange furniture."

Flood looked at me, her face calm and composed. "A whole lot of words."

She had me there. I got my things together, and then Flood and I got out her wok and burned up the whole Goldor file. Pablo wouldn't want it back and I wasn't about to be walking around with it either. We sat together and watched the flames eat Goldor's dossier. No answers rose with the smoke.

I told Flood that I had to make some arrangements before we could go and visit Goldor, that it might be that very night, and she was to stay home and wait for my call. She nodded absently—her thoughts were somewhere else. She walked me to the door, stood on her toes to kiss me goodbye.

38

IT TOOK ME a while to get back to my office. I never go there in a straight line anyway, but ever since I watched that videotape I had the feeling that Goldor somehow knew I was coming for him. The more I thought about it, the more I was convinced Pablo's profile was on the money. Goldor did think he was untouchable. "The man who knows Wilson made a movie star out of a corpse," Michelle had said. Maybe she didn't know the name, but his product was on the street for everyone to see. We were all just so many bugs to him. He wouldn't lose a minute's sleep worrying about a Wilson rolling over on him. Sure, he would know the Cobra—he would know anyone in the kiddie-sex business, but the lion doesn't fear the jackal.

I checked the office carefully this time, but nobody had come calling. Pansy was as glad to see me as she usually was— once she satisfied herself that it was really me she went back to sleep. I made enough noise moving around the office so she realized I would be there for a while, and I let her out onto the roof while I sat at my desk and went over everything one more time. I would have to go back to the Bronx, but this time to the other end of the world. I couldn't use Max for this one— who knew how much protection Goldor would put on himself? Flood was in it to the end because it was her beef.

Too much time had passed without a strike. I would have to call back the phony gunrunners tonight with a way to take some of their money or lose that pair of fish. Time was compressing in on me, I needed room to breathe. I guess when big executives get like this they go to the country, or even out of the country if they're big enough. I could go them one better—one short trip to the Bronx and I could go right off this planet.

The Plymouth was waiting for me, kicked over on the first shot like it always does. I worked my way over to the East Side Drive and took the Triboro to Bruckner Boulevard and 138th Street, then nosed the Plymouth into the maze of abandoned side streets and kept driving until I was sure I was flying solo. When I spotted the rusty old cyclone fence wrapped with razor wire I edged the Plymouth along its perimeter until I found the open entrance, drove in a few feet, shut the engine, and waited.

I didn't have long to wait. I saw a flash of dark fur, heard a thump on the hood and found myself looking through the windshield at the ugliest Great Dane in the world—a battered old harlequin, black and white, missing an eye and with teeth broken in front. He just sat there on the hood like he was some kind of bizarre ornament, bored with the whole thing. I kept my eyes straight ahead, but I could sense the other dogs gathering around the car. No barking, just low-pitched grunts like wolves nosing the body of an elk they had just downed. The dogs came in all shapes, sizes, and colors. I could recognize traces of their original breeding in some of them, but they were all one version or another of the American Junkyard Dog—loyal, tenacious, intelligent, and dangerous—and most of all, good survivors. I saw what looked like a bull mastiff, several variations on the German shepherd, some smaller terriers, another, darker Dane, even what looked like a border collie. All with thick heavy coats that looked like they had been liberally groomed with transmission fluid. Some circled the car, while the others sat on their haunches and waited.

I couldn't drive any deeper into the junkyard because I knew there was a ten-foot drop lying straight ahead. And I didn't get out of the car—those dogs had never seen a can of Alpo in their lives. It wasn't even noon yet but the place was dark. It always is.

When the dogs saw I knew the procedure they all sat back and waited expectantly. The monster Dane on the hood of the car pointed his snout toward the sky and let out a wail that sounded like Kaddish for canines. There was no other sound.

The Dane hit his aria again. One more time, then stone silence.

I badly wanted a cigarette but I just sat there, hands on top of the wheel. If things weren't as they were supposed to be I could just throw the Plymouth into reverse and make believe I had never seen the place—that is, if the Mole hadn't added some new nonsense since the last time I had visited. I wasn't anxious to find out.

I watched the Dane. When his head swiveled sharply toward the side I knew what was coming. The brindle-colored dog bounded into the clearing about ten feet ahead of the car, effortlessly clearing the deep ditch. A mastiff-shepherd cross from the looks of him—a handsome bastard with a bull's body and a wolf's face. He had the same fur coat as the others but with a broad, arrogant tail that curled up over his back toward his neck. Perfect long white teeth flashed in a lupine grin. He slowly cruised the outside of the circle the other dogs had formed, moving with the delicacy and strength of a good welterweight, in no hurry. I heard answering grunts and growls from the other dogs, but they each made way for him. He shouldered his way through the pack until he was standing right next to my window, cocked his massive head, and gazed up at me. It was time. I slowly and evenly rolled down the glass, letting my face emerge so he could see me. But this beast was no sight-hound, and I had to use my voice—fast, before I couldn't use it anymore at all.

"Simba, Simba-*witz*," I called out. "What a *good* boy. How's by you, mighty Simba? You remember me, pal? Simba-witz, I'm here to see my *landsman*, the Mole. Right, Simba? Okay, boy?"

I kept a running patter of stuff like that until I saw that Simba remembered my voice. I knew he wouldn't attack if he heard his full name called, but I wanted to be sure. Calling him Simba would get his head up and paying attention, but Simba-witz was his full Hebrew name and only the Mole's people would know that. The Mole once told me that Simba looked too much like a German shepherd—so even though he was the smartest of the pack, a natural leader and the father of dozens of the pups that were born in the junkyard every year, the Mole couldn't love him until he figured out a solution. And thus Simba became the very first Israeli shepherd, dubbed Simba-witz, the Lion of Zion. The Mole told him this stuff so often that I think the beast believed the legend. I don't really know if he thought he was a lion, but I did know he didn't have to worry about a goddamned thing—he had his first pick of the food and his first pick of the women. A beautiful life, although the accommodations left a lot to be desired.

Simba gave me a short bark, rose up until his gnarled paws were resting on the rolled-down window. I kept talking to him, leaned forward, and he licked my face.

I slowly opened the door and climbed out, patting his head. I would have liked to throw some of the dog biscuits I keep in the car to the other dogs to make friends, but I knew what they would do if they were offered food without the magic word, like I have for Pansy. I didn't know the word, and I didn't want to be the food, so I left it alone.

Simba listened to me say "Mole" about ten times and then just turned and walked away. I followed as carefully as I could. The rest of the pack brushed against my legs, without malice— sort of herding me in the right direction. We walked until I found a solid piece of ground, then I went back to the Plymouth and pulled it around until it was out of sight from the street. I followed Simba and the pack deeper into the junkyard. When we finally came to a huge shack made of tarpaper and copper sheeting somewhere near the back fence, I stopped. I knew what to do from there, and Simba did too. He went off someplace into the artificial darkness, and I stood there waiting.

The pack hadn't exactly lost interest in me, but you could tell they weren't going to get excited. Most of them probably hadn't seen anybody get this far before. I kept my eyes on the shack as though the Mole would emerge any minute. I knew better, but I knew the rules too.

I heard Simba grunting behind me and knew the Mole was coming, but I didn't turn around until I felt his hand on my shoulder. I turned, and there he was. The Mole—even in the dim light, his skin looked transparent, the blue veins corded on his hands like there wasn't enough skin to cover everything. Short, stubby, clumsy-looking Mole, blinking his tiny eyes rapidly at the unaccustomed light of day. He was wearing one of those one-piece coverall outfits like mechanics use in gas stations and carrying a toolbox. In spite of his pale skin he was so dirty from his work that he looked like he was prepared for night surveillance. He moved close to me, bumping Simba aside like the beast wasn't there. And Simba, with that respect for genuine lunacy shared by all animals, moved aside without even a growl.

The Mole put his hands in his pockets, looked carefully at me for a moment or two, and mumbled something to Simba, who immediately trotted off. Then he motioned that I should walk ahead of him to the shack.

As soon as I got past the hanging door I smelled muscatel, urine, and old wet rags. There was an orange crate in one corner with some old newspapers on top and a dirty raincoat lying open on the ground like it was a wino's bed. Some empty bottles, candy wrappers, a broken piece of wood that had been a chair once. The Mole walked past the stuff like it wasn't there, and I breathed through my mouth as I followed him.

At the very back of the shack he fiddled with some levers and pulleys, then bent and yanked something and there was an opening in the ground. He sent me in first, climbed down after me, reached back and made some more adjustments. I felt the Mole slip past me in the dark, then he led the way through the tunnel. We must have walked a hundred yards or so until he found the door and stepped through, and then we were in his den.

I'm not sure how he worked it, but it's like a half-underground, half-above-ground bunker. The top is covered with the bodies of wrecked and rusting cars, but there was some way that light filtered through because the place wasn't that dark. It was as clean as the shack had been foul, and much bigger inside.

The room we entered was like the Mole's parlor, or whatever the equivalent would be for underground bunkers. He had an old leather easy chair with matching ottoman in one corner, a two-person sofa facing it on an angle. I think the floor was hard-packed dirt but it was covered with several sheets of flattened linoleum and there was an oval throw rug in the middle. I had never gotten past this room but I knew there were others—a place to sleep and some kind of bathroom in the back, maybe even a kitchen. It smelled clean down there, but the air was sharp, like the filtered stuff you get in operating rooms. The Mole had some way to vent everything to another part of the junkyard, but I don't know how he did it.

The junkyard itself wasn't open to the public. The Mole and the dogs and God knows what else lived there in perfect symbiosis. We all pick our ways to survive, and the Mole decided this was his way a long time ago. He never left the place except to do his work. I thought I knew the city as well as anybody, but I would never have known of the Mole except for one of my forays into bounty hunting. A man from the Israeli secret service (at least that's what he told me) found me a few years ago and asked my price for locating a Nazi concentration camp guard who had come to the States after the war and gone underground somewhere in Manhattan. You could see the Israeli was a professional, but he didn't know what he was looking for. He came to me because I had done some business with a neo-Nazi group out in Queens and he figured all Nazis were alike. Anyway, I did find the old freak and gave the information to the man who said he was from Israel. I watched the papers for a few weeks after that, but I didn't see anything.

I met the Mole when the Israeli took me out to the junkyard and told him I was working for their cause on a special assignment and to help me if he could. He couldn't then, but he has a few times since, as I've already mentioned.

The Mole will do anything to hunt down Nazis, but he's not interested in too much else—so most every time I come back to see him it's about Nazis. I'm not a political analyst, but it seemed to me that Goldor qualified, and Wilson was a likely candidate too. It didn't matter—the Mole never asked for details. Each time I went to him you could see him balancing the risk that I would bring the heat back with me against the chance that there could be one or two less Nazis doing the looking. Each time I caught the green light.

The Mole flopped into his chair without ceremony, took some gadget out of his overalls, and started fiddling with it. Finally he looked over at me, blinking. "So, Burke?"

"I need a car, Mole. Some license plates. And some help with a power system."

The Mole just kept looking at me, nodding and blinking. There was no question but that he would do it—he always had. If there's one thing I know about it's how to survive, and here was one of the few people living who could teach me something more on the subject. But the Mole had his survival down so well he never talked about it. He looked up. "I'll see you outside. Wait for me. Sit, have a smoke, talk with Simbawitz. I'll come soon."

I stumbled my way back through the tunnel to the shack—the doors to the outside were already open. I don't know how he does that. I found my way outside, sat down on an empty milk crate, and lit up. Simba came back into the yard and stood there looking at me. He approached slowly. When he got close enough I scratched him behind his ears—even his growl of contentment sounded life-threatening. I told him, "Simba-witz, have I got a girl for you! Her name's Pansy and she is a thing of beauty—a face like an angel and a body that just won't quit. I told her all about you and she's anxious to get together. What do you say, pal? Down for a little action?"

Simba snarled, which I took for agreement. Depending on how this caper came out, I might have to go someplace for a few months, and if I did I wanted to be sure Pansy had a home. And the puppies would be beautiful, no doubt about it.

The Mole materialized from the shadows. When he was just a kid he used to read *Scientific American* like it was a comic book, and his teachers said he was wasting his time in school— that he should be in a doctoral program somewhere. But his parents thought he was a strange kid and that he needed to be socialized, so they kept him in the public school.

He was the target of a lot of freakish games by other kids, and he got beat up a lot. He would come home all battered and his father, a dockworker, would tell him to go back and fight it out with the kids or he would give the Mole worse than what he got from the bullies—very creative psychology on a kid with a genius I.Q. The Mole built some kind of homemade laser gun in his basement, went back to school, and blew away half a wall instead of the biggest tormentors—even then, his eyesight wasn't too good.

The police came to his house, there was some kind of confrontation with his father, some talk about therapy, and the Mole ran away from home. He's been out here ever since, first in an apartment over on Chrystie Street and now in the junkyard. I guess he will stay here until he dies. I know this much— if they ever come to take the Mole to a psychiatric ward, he is going to put his own personal Middle East policy into effect. I'm not sure exactly what this is, but one time the Mole asked me if I could get him some plutonium.

When it became obvious that the Mole wasn't going to be any more conversational than usual, I told him what I wanted. "I need you to take out the security system in this house I have to visit."

The Mole blinked a lot of times. "What kind of security system?"

"I don't know exactly. I'll draw you what I have from the plans, but I think there's also a hookup to the police station. I want the whole damn system to go down, and only at a certain time. Like at eight o'clock, bang! nothing works . . . okay?"

"You want a bang?"

"No, Mole. That's just an expression."

The Mole stared at me as he would any lower form of life. "Does it have to be restorable?"

"No, I don't care if the system stays down forever. You set it up so you can kill the whole thing at a certain time, right? Then you do it, and you leave. That's all."

"In the city?"

"Westchester County."

"Multiple dwelling?"

"No, a big house."

"Access?"

"Up to you. No guards, no dogs that I know of. But a wealthy neighborhood—the Man will be around all the time."

"How about a Con Ed Total?"

A Con Ed Total is when the Mole shuts down the utilities for an entire community, but it wouldn't play here. I just wanted Goldor disarmed from calling help, not the whole neighborhood alerted that something was going down.

"No," I told him, "just this one house. And not the lights either, just the special communications systems and especially the phone lines. Can you do it?"

The Mole refused to acknowledge such a stupid question. He came closer and I knelt in the dirt and began to draw the plans of Goldor's place that I had gotten from Pablo and his people. I gave the Mole the exact address and he nodded like he already knew it—maybe he did. He asked an occasional question, and we finally settled on nine o'clock that night. I would have to take a chance on catching Goldor at home, and alone, because once the Mole was programmed to act there was no way to stop him.

We walked through the junkyard until we found a steel-gray Volvo sedan, somewhat battered around the edges but apparently quite serviceable. The Mole said he had good papers for it, but it was actually a cannibal job of several cars and impossible to trace even if I had to leave it on the street when I was done. We kept walking until we found two current license plates, which the Mole sliced up with his cutting torch. He then welded the halves together to make a single license plate with nonexistent numbers. If somebody did manage to read the plates while I was working, the computer wouldn't help them.

The Mole gave me a set of keys to the car, kept one for himself, and said he could drop it off by late afternoon near the Twenty-third Street parking garage I use for alibi operations. I gave the Mole five hundred bucks and we had a contract. I was as sure of the car being there and Goldor's communications system not being there as I was of anything in this world.

The Mole went back underground or wherever he goes and Simba-witz walked me back to my car. In twenty minutes I was climbing over the Triboro to the East Side heading for my office to give Pansy the good news.

39

AS SOON AS I got back in the office I checked for hippies and dialed Flood. I told her to be ready to move out at around four that afternoon and hung up on her questions. When Pansy came down from the roof I told her I didn't have a lot of time to screw around just then, but I had lined up a date with the famous Simba-witz for her, to take place on his suburban estate sometime later in the year. She gave me a lot of crap about blind dates but she finally said it was okay so long as I didn't plan to leave her there.

The four corners of time were coming in hard, cramming me into a narrow box. I needed space to think it all out—how to approach Goldor, what it would take to pry his information loose, how dangerous he was, would Flood distract him? If I waited too long Pablo's people could roll up on him and then he wouldn't be talking to anyone. Or this Wilson, the Cobra, could actually turn up something for the D.A. and they would haul him in. A guy like Goldor had to have some major enemies. I couldn't bring Max in on this, and I would have to keep the gunrunners on hold because there was just the ghost of a chance that they could lead me to buried treasure if they were better at scamming other people than they were me.

I finally decided—just a straight frontal approach, offer the maggot some serious money or maybe if that didn't work let it leak that I could square the snuff-film beef with the *federales* if I was paid enough. I would have to improvise on the spot, so I didn't pack any weapons at all except for the usual stuff in my overcoat. I put on a set of G.I. fatigues over a red

T-shirt, some soft old boots, a tired felt fedora. I slipped a pair of thin suede gloves and some tinted glasses into the coat pockets, gave Pansy some food, and went back down to the garage.

I didn't have much time, so I used it trying to add another layer of protection—but a quick run down to the docks came up empty, and the Prophet wasn't in any of his usual spots. You can't always find a Prophet in New York. I drove over to Mama's, had something to eat, and got the first part of my alibi established. I sat down at my table and wrote out everything I knew about Goldor to leave for Max, just in case. Besides survival I don't believe in much, but I have a soft spot in my heart for revenge.

Mama knew something was up, but she just took the paper I left for Max and put it someplace safe. If things went wrong, Max would go to the office, put Pansy in the Plymouth and deliver her to Simba-witz—he would keep the car. I hadn't bothered to tell him where I stashed any of the emergency money he didn't already know about, and I knew he would strip the office without me telling him. Not much of a will, but then I don't have much of an estate to worry about.

As I turned the key in the ignition in Mama's back alley I got hit with a fear attack. I get them sometimes—everything starts to break up inside of me and I want to find a hole to crawl into. I never get one when I'm in a situation, just sometimes before and sometimes after. I knew what to do, so I let the fear wash through me and fly around my nerve endings until it finally went out my fingertips. I held my hands in front of my face and I could almost see the fear-bolts jump from my fingers. You have to breathe very shallow, no movement. The fear would never really go away, but sooner or later it would move to someplace where I was more comfortable with it. As always, when it finally moved out my brain felt like it was washed clean and sensory perceptions flooded in—the texture of the leather cover on the Plymouth's steering wheel, the tiny imperfections in the windshield glass, the muted sounds of a Chinese argument several doors down from me. When I finally turned the key I could feel the bicep muscles send a message to my wrist, and I actually heard the exact moment of ignition before the Plymouth rumbled into life. I pulled out of the alley with less concern than usual for the narrow opening—even my depth perception was enhanced. My brain started to flicker in and out and around the edges of ideas—warming-up exercises before it was to be tested in combat. I kept it flickering, not wanting to focus until I hit something solid. I just let it flit around in the open spaces until it hit on something—no pressure, no suggestions from my so-called intellect to screw things up.

Max once told me that there is a martial arts style of fighting that closely resembles my way of dealing with fear. It's called the Drunken Monkey, and the object is to have the fighter so completely dehumanized that he operates purely on instinct. Max told me this style is not the best for doing damage to an opponent—it's not efficient. But it's almost impossible to defend against because it's completely unpredictable—you can't telegraph what you don't know. Once my brain goes into full fear-response mode it's a lot like the Drunken Monkey, I guess. I may not come up with any good ideas, but if you tried to read my mind all you'd get would be vertigo.

When I pulled the Plymouth around Flood's corner I caught a flash of white near her door and then she was moving toward me. The white was a pair of vinyl boots, skin-tight, calf-length with about four-inch heels. The bottle-green stretch pants flowed out of the boots, topped by a V-neck jersey in some sort of lemon-lime color. Flood's pale blonde hair was in two thick braids, tied with green ribbons near the ends. I slowed the car, letting her walk to me. I watched all that fine female flesh bounce around and a thought raced across my mind, something about the Prophet and a goat staked out to catch a lion, and then I heard the screech of brakes and I snapped out of it—some poor chump had wrecked his car watching those bottle-green stretch pants swish down the block.

I rolled the Plymouth over to Flood, shoved open the door, and got moving before she attracted any more attention. I didn't turn to look at her until I was moving out of a U-turn to get crosstown to where the Mole would have left the car for me. Even the Plymouth's gentle movement was making Flood bounce around inside the jersey top, but at least she'd left the Eau de Whorehouse at home—she smelled like soap.

Flood looked about eighteen with her hair pulled back like it was, and her face glistened like she'd just stepped out of the shower. We stopped at a long light and my eyes traveled from the tips of the white boots up the length of the stretch pants, across the expanse of her jersey, and stopped dead at her throat—

she had a dark green velvet ribbon around her neck. I looked again, just to make sure my mind wasn't still dancing on me. "Flood, could I ask you a question?" I said sweetly.

"Sure." She smiled.

"Are you *completely* fucking crazy?"

"Why?"

"What's the ribbon for? I told you about the videotape and you put on a fucking *ribbon*. What's wrong with you?"

"I know what I'm doing."

"That would be a fucking first."

"Burke, you were right, okay? This is a disguise—I walked around for a couple of hours before you came and it really works. If you asked anyone who saw me what I looked like they would never get above my neck. Don't you think these pants make me look slimmer?"

"The only thing you come off as is dim, Flood, not slim."

"Look, I thought about it and—"

"And nothing—you drew your usual total blank. The woman in the videotape wasn't *wearing* that ribbon, you dummy—it was part of Goldor's sicko trip. He probably has a drawer full of them—keeps them next to his fucking executioner's mask or something."

"I know that. And when he sees this, he'll think of her."

"And that's your idea of smart?"

"You'll see."

"No I won't—because you're taking it off, right now."

"Listen, Burke—I know men, I know about them. This will really help. You'll see."

"Take it off, Flood."

"Maybe later," she said, and tried to smile, but I wasn't buying any of that. We had a staring contest and I won. She put her hands to her throat, unsnapped something, and it came off in her hand. With characteristic maturity, she immediately sank into a heavy pout.

We drove toward the parking garage in silence. Finally I said, "Flood, on this trip I am the captain and you are the crew—period. You want to sit there and bounce those D-cup extravaganzas in this freak's face until he can't see straight, that's okay. But don't do any *thinking*, understand?"

Silence from Flood.

"You want to sit there and pout like a goddamned brat, or do you want to hear the plan?"

"I want to hear the plan, oh mighty captain."

Now it was my turn to be silent.

"Okay, Burke. We'll do it your way—what's the plan?"

"The plan is we go and pick up another car. Actually, I pick up the car and you wait in this one. Then we drive out to Goldor's house and we walk up and knock on the door, right? Then after he invites us in, you sit there and be quiet and I talk him into giving up Wilson."

"That's the plan?"

"That's it."

"Don't you think it's a bit too elaborate?" She even curled her lip when she said it.

"Maybe you're right. Okay, let's do it this way—I stop the car at the next corner, Miss Smartass gets out and wiggles her way home, and I go out to Scarsdale by myself."

"It won't work."

"Why not? You couldn't find your way home?"

"Don't be so wise, Burke. We have to have a way to make this Goldor tell us about Wilson."

"I'm working on that."

"Don't you think we should work it out first?"

"Flood," I said, looking at her, "there is no time." And she listened to my voice and looked at my face and believed me.

When we got near the garage I pulled the Plymouth over near the wall and told Flood to get out. She looked at me suspiciously. "You can't wait in the other car," I told her. "I'm not even sure where it is and you have no papers for it. I have to leave this one inside and the man there doesn't get to see you, okay?"

She just looked at me. "Flood, if I wanted to cut you out of this deal I wouldn't have picked you up in the first place. Now just get out—stand over where I showed you and be quiet."

She switched away, holding her jacket in one hand. I opened the window on her side and called out to her. "Put that damn jacket on, will you?" and she must have understood because, for once, she just did like I said without a big argument.

I rolled the Plymouth into the underground garage and pulled it over to the side to make sure Mario had seen me come in. In a few minutes he came over to my window, said, "Same as always?" and I nodded. Mario motioned for me to get out, leave the key, and come with him. I followed him back to the cubicle he called his office and we conducted our business.

"What time on the stub?" he asked.

"Anytime between eight-forty-five and nine this evening."

"Pick it up when?"

"Late tonight, early tomorrow," I said, trying to sound indifferent.

"It's still fifty plus the parking charges, right?"

"Right."

We then walked over to the time clock where all the entering cars are punched in. Mario reached halfway down into the pile of fresh tickets, pulled one out, tore off my stub and put the other piece in his pocket. He would clock me in at the right time later that night. The number on my stub would match the check-in time—that's what cost me the fifty bucks. I pocketed the stub, slipped Mario the fifty, and walked out into the afternoon.

Flood was waiting near the wall. "Any problems?" I asked her.

"No."

I started to walk over to where the Mole was going to leave the Volvo, glancing down at my watch to keep on schedule. Just a couple of minutes shy of six, I would have to call the jerkoffs about the gun deal like I said I would. Flood didn't need to know any more about my business than she already did, but listening to my half of this conversation wouldn't do any harm.

I found a pay phone, watched the second hand of my watch until it was ten seconds short of six, and punched the buttons. James answered on the first ring. "Yes?"

"I like the deal," I said, "but I wonder if it couldn't be upped a notch or two?"

"Meaning?"

"Let's say the deal you proposed is one unit, okay? Now I know some people who want another one-and-a-half units, making two-and-a-half units all told, right? Could your people supply the additional amount? I would be responsible for it."

"I'd have to ask."

"Do it," I told him.

"If it can't be done—"

"Then the original is okay, but I would like more if possible."

"Same guarantees?"

"Yes."

"Can I reach you?"

"I'll call same time tomorrow."

"Fine. And listen, about that problem my associate had with your—"

"We had no problem," I told him.

"I just wanted to say—"

"We had no problem," I repeated in a deliberate voice.

"Great. Tomorrow, then?"

"You got it," I said, and hung up. Dopes.

I walked away from the pay phone like it was diseased. You never know. Blumberg once told me that the law has to get a specific warrant to tap a phone and then it's only good for a certain period of time, and even then they can't be listening to every conversation, just the guy they got the warrant to bug. That's all bullshit. Blumberg also told me that it's illegal for a private citizen to tap a phone, but if he does any evidence he gets is admissible in court. What a joke—between the D.E.A. and the Special Narcotics Unit they probably have half the pay phones in this city tapped, but anyone who wants to buy dope can get it by the goddamned carload.

A gull swept by low over the East River, screeching his anger at the humans who kept snatching pieces of his river to build luxury apartments. I turned the phone conversation with James over in my mind and nothing really computed . . . I didn't know if I would ever need him and his faggot friend again. My mind was wrestling with dancing images, but Goldor kept cropping up every fifth frame or so. Wearing his mask. I was way past choices.

I turned away from the river and Flood fell into step beside me, matching me stride for stride. After a block or so she put her hand on my arm, gently. As we walked I slipped my hand around her waist, moved it down and patted her hip. "Behave, okay?" She nodded that she would.

The Volvo was where the Mole said it would be. My key fit, a clean set of papers was in the glove compartment. I got onto the East Side Drive, getting the feel of the car and heading for the bridge and Route 95. The idea was to drive north of Scarsdale, then drop down back into it. We had plenty of time but I wasn't anxious for visibility and we couldn't hit Goldor much before nine if the alibi was to work. I told Flood we would have a picnic first—as soon as we got into Westchester County I changed jackets with her and sent her inside a deli to buy some cold cuts and soda and cigarettes.

With my jacket covering her, Flood looked like a rich-bitch teenager playing some silly game, the kind you would never notice in the suburbs. When she got back I drove to what was left of an old industrial park in Port Chester and we sat in the front seat and nibbled at the food. We weren't too hungry. I lit a smoke, leaned back against the seat cushion.

"Is this our last chance?" Flood wanted to know.

"No, but it may be our last *good* chance. Wilson can't hide forever, but we don't *have* forever either."

"What does that mean?"

"You know."

"That I have to go back . . ."

"To Japan, am I right?"

"You know that," Flood said.

"Yeah . . ."

"Burke, do you want—?"

"Right now—right now I want Wilson."

"Yes."

"That's enough for now."

"I understand," she said, then asked, "Burke, are you afraid?"

"Yes."

"I'm not."

"I know." And I did.

"You know what that means?"

"It means you're still a virgin," I snapped at her.

And Flood slid over next to me and just held my hand until I saw it was time to go.

40

THE VOLVO HAD been the right choice for this run. It was old and dull and anonymous-looking, all right, but it still fit into the neighborhood somehow. Kind of quiet and substantial looking, an appropriate second car for the kind of mouth-breathers who wouldn't live in the city but still sucked their living from it.

I knew exactly where to find Goldor's house—I hadn't wanted to cruise around the area drawing attention to us so I'd checked with the street maps in the City Planning Office. But the maps hadn't told me he lived on top of a short hill or that the semicircular driveway in front of the house would be lit up like a Christmas tree. My watch said 8:47, no time to modify anything. The Mole was already in place, getting ready to do his work—now I had to do mine. I'd gone over the thing with Flood a dozen times and I'd just have to rely on her to act right.

I pulled the Volvo into the drive, rolled just past the front door so it was on the driveway's downward slope, cut the lights, and killed the ignition. There was no reaction from the house to our approach. I opened the car door, walked around to the passenger side, and held the door for Flood in case someone was watching. The front door was set back inside a small archway with a heavy brass knocker in the shape of a lion's face in the middle and a small button ringed with a halo of light on the right panel. Which one? I opted for the lion's face. I banged twice—firm but not too insistent. No sound came from behind the door.

I felt Flood vibrating next to me but I counted to ten and rapped twice more—still nothing. I shrugged my shoulders like I'd come back another time and turned as if to go back to the Volvo, giving Flood a look when she opened her mouth to say something. I started back through the archway, reaching my hand back out to Flood to make sure she came along, and the door opened—Goldor was standing there. I could tell it was him from the shape of his body and his bald head but I couldn't make out his face in the light that was pouring out strong and harsh from behind him. He could see us, though— the setup was no accident. Flood stepped aside to let me talk.

"Mr. Goldor?"

"And who are you?"

His hands were clasped behind him so that he was standing in an almost military posture—chest out, stomach in, shoulders back. He was using an old bodybuilder's trick to make himself look even more massive—squeezing his hands together behind his back to pump the blood through his arms and into his chest and neck. His voice was rich and full—friendly and confident, masterful, relaxed. Whatever else we'd done, we sure as hell hadn't spooked him.

I knew I'd only get one shot with this guy. "My name is Burke, sir. And this is Debbie. I have something I would like to discuss with you, a matter of great importance, and I didn't want to speak on the phone."

No response from Goldor, he just held his pose, letting me go on. "So I took the liberty of calling on you like this. I apologize if it's an inconvenient time and, if it is, I'd appreciate the opportunity of an appointment at your earliest pleasure."

Goldor stepped just slightly to the side, still holding himself erect. He nodded his bald head toward us. "I see. Please come in, Mr. Burke. And you too, uh . . . Debbie."

I stepped through the door with Flood at my side. Goldor bent his head forward again to indicate that we should walk ahead of him, and we stepped onto a thick carpet down a short hall. We heard "In there," and followed his directions. I saw we were coming into a long rectangle of a room, but it was too dark to see much else and I stumbled down a couple of short steps—a sunken room of some kind. Flood followed, stepping lightly without a misfire. Goldor came right behind us and turned some kind of rheostat on the wall—a soft orange light came from the corners of the long room and I could see a black leather chair with bare wooden arms and some other blocks of furniture. The walls were hung with heavy tapestries. We turned to face Goldor, who said, "Are you a police officer, Mr. Burke?"

"No, sir," I said earnestly.

"You work for them, perhaps?" still in that soft voice.

"No. I work for myself."

"And you are here on business? You have business with me?"

"Yes. And I—"

"Are you wearing a wire, Mr. Burke?" I said no with a laugh and held open my army jacket so he could see I only had on the red T-shirt underneath. I saw his hand come from behind his back and the Buck Rogers ray gun pointed at me and I started to smile when I felt the three tiny pinpricks bite into my stomach and chest before my brain could register *"Taser! . . ."* I felt red-white pain tear through my gut and I was on the ground and my body was trying to be anyplace else. My nerve tips were screaming in agony and my legs wouldn't work but I knew what I had to do and I willed my hands to pull out the wires.

But before I could reach for them Goldor must have squeezed the trigger again and I felt another jolt and I must have screamed—something came out of my mouth and I lay there looking up at Goldor.

He walked over to me, holding the Taser pistol—a little instrument that shoots three little darts attached to thin wires. When the darts make contact, one squeeze of the trigger and the batteries in the pistol's butt shoot a massive load of electricity into the target. When they first came on the market they were very popular because they weren't classified as firearms, but then the lawmakers got together and made them illegal. A lot of people thought the manufacturer went out of business, but I know that there's no shortage of buyers—Idi Amin used to buy them by the planeload for his secret police.

Goldor still spoke quietly, in control. "If you move or try to pull out the wires I'll hold the trigger down for a long time. Do you understand me?"

I groaned something that Goldor took to mean that I did, and he walked even closer to me. I couldn't raise my head, all I could see were the polished tips of his boots. He turned to Flood—she was standing there with her mouth open. "Get over here," he said, and Flood walked over. When she was standing next to him, Goldor bent down and spoke to me, clearly and distinctly, like you would to someone who's not too bright:

"Mr. Burke, you will crawl over to that black chair, and you will do it *slowly*. Your hands are not to come anywhere *near* the darts. And when you get there you will *back* into that chair until you are seated and facing me. Do you understand?"

I muttered something—he hit me with a short blast and I could feel him smile when I screamed. My own voice frightened me, so high-pitched and thin. I bit into my lower lip until I could feel the blood run—some of it came out when I muttered "yes."

Goldor moved in and I crawled ahead of him. He stayed close, never letting the wires get taut, pausing only to tell Flood, "You stay there," like she was a dog he was training, and I backed into the chair until I was seated, facing him like he wanted. I could feel the blood in my mouth but I couldn't taste anything—each time my muscles contracted the pain shot around my nerves. Goldor took my right hand and put it on the arm of the chair. He reached down and snapped something with one hand and I felt myself strapped down. He did the same with the other arm, then stepped back and jerked the darts out of my body. I lurched forward like I was trying to come out of the chair at him and he smiled, stepped toward me and backhanded me across the mouth. I felt the pain still going through my guts, and I felt the fresh stabbing in my mouth where he'd hit me. Yes, and I also felt the fat lipstick cylinder slap into my right palm. My brain was screaming at me, "You have to live!" but I didn't fire my one shot—I'd have to get him up close to be sure.

I slumped back in the chair like I was finished, watching him through half-closed eyes. If he came back with something to finish me off I'd have to talk fast, get him next to me, fire my shot, pull what would be left of my hand out of the straps, get the hell out somehow . . .

I must have gone under for a couple of minutes. When I came around, Goldor was sitting on what looked like a padded bar stool and Flood was standing in front of me. She looked dazed. Goldor was saying something to her. I tried to focus on his words and managed to catch the tail end . . .

". . . and there's another reason for you to listen to me. Your friend isn't hurt badly. When this is over he will be able to go away with you. I know what he wanted, and I know how to deal with him. I understand. Listen to me. He told you he'd get you a part in one of my movies, didn't he?"

Flood didn't respond, just stood staring at him, but Goldor went on like she had agreed. "He told you he'd make a lot of money, didn't he? Told you a lot of beautiful girls start out this way, true? Oh, I know him, I know people like him. They have no sensitivity, no understanding of how things really work. But I can't help you unless you *let* me help you. I *want* to help you, Debbie, but you have to talk to me. Do you see? Do you?"

Flood seemed to be struggling for control, trying to answer Goldor's soft-voiced stream. "Yes. But I don't—"

"Listen to me. Listen to me, little girl. Those movie parts are not for a beautiful young woman like you. This man is nothing more than a flesh merchant. He's your boyfriend, isn't he?"

"Yes. We were going to—"

"I know. I *know*. I know only too well. He doesn't have a job, does he?"

"He's a writer," Flood said with an appropriate trace of defiance in her voice, but still very shaky.

"He's no writer, my dear. He's a bad man."

"You *hurt* him," Flood moaned in a sad little girl's voice.

"I didn't really hurt him, my child. All I did was show him who is the master of the situation, that's all. He has to understand. Let me ask you—is the truth evil?"

"Well, no. No, I guess it's not."

"Of course not. And, Debbie, understand this . . . *pain is truth*. Pain can not lie—pain *is*, you understand? Pain is what it is and nothing more. It can start and it can stop, but it is always real. Pain is truth, and truth is good."

"But—"

"Listen to me," said Goldor, his voice getting quieter and stronger at the same time. A doctor's voice, a father's voice, a voice of truth and wisdom not to be denied. "I can show you the truth, and I can make you what you want to be with that truth. Your miserable little boyfriend sits there and he has no pain now. I took his pain away, even as I speak the truth to you right now. He has no pain now, only truth. And the truth is that he didn't want you to be in the movies, only to make money for himself. He came here with you to display you, to exhibit you to me as though you were a dog or a horse. That is the truth. That *is* the truth, isn't it?" he said, leaning forward on the stool.

"I don't know"—Flood's voice was a whine now—"I don't know why he—"

"Yes, you know. Get past what you *don't* know—get to the truth. Listen to me, Debbie. You want to be in the movies, don't you? You want to have nice things, you want to be somebody, don't you? Wouldn't you like to live in a house like this someday?"

"Oh, yes. I mean . . ."

"And I can do all that for you. That is the truth too. But you have to *see* the truth, *experience* the truth for yourself. Do you understand what I'm telling you?"

"What are you going to do?" Flood asked, fear and suspicion in her voice.

"I am going to ask you some questions. And if you tell *me* the truth, I will show *you* the truth. And you will get what you want. Yes?"

"Yes," said Flood, in a doubtful little voice.

"How old are you?"

"I'm twenty."

"Where were you born?"

"In Minot, North Dakota."

"How long have you been in the city?"

"It was a year last month."

"Have you ever been a prostitute?"

"No! I never—"

"That's all right," said Goldor in the same therapist's voice, "just keep telling me the truth, Debbie. What kind of work do you do?"

"I'm a dancer."

"And where do you dance, Debbie?"

"In . . . in bars and—"

"Take off your sweater," Goldor ordered, still with his soft voice. And Flood mechanically reached to her waist and pulled the jersey over her head, stood there in front of him. Her breasts trembled in Goldor's orange lights of pain and I could see a droplet of sweat fall over one of the high ridges and slide down toward a nipple and I knew that just surviving this wouldn't be enough for me now.

"Yes, I can see what kind of dancing you do, my child. Have you had any work done to them?"

"What?"

"Silicone, uplifts, surgery . . . you know."

"Oh. No, never. I wouldn't ever . . ."

"I see. And do you like pain, Debbie?"

"No!" said Flood, her voice going frightened and breathy.

"You answer too quickly, little Debbie. All girls like pain sometimes. I don't mean pain like your miserable little boyfriend over there. I mean pain where you *get* something for it, where you *learn* something. Pain *liberates*, you see? It sets things free, makes things happen. Good things, rich things . . ." Goldor's silk-and-cream voice was quite an instrument.

"You have good things inside of you, we all do. Some are bad things, some are good. But when they *stay* inside of you they all hurt you. They stop you from being *yourself*, you see? They hold you back, they keep you from the wonders that should be your own. I know you, I know women like you. I have made much of them, made them into a greatness, into perfection. I have made them into beauty. You don't want to dance in bars, do you? You don't want greasy little men pawing at you. You don't want those cheap clothes. You want only to please *one* man, don't you? Not just any bum with the price of a few drinks. You know you have to reach out for what you want, don't you?" he said as he reached his hand under one breast and bounced it in his hand. And Flood drew a harsh breath and said, "Yes," her eyes cast down.

"And you *used* to like pain, didn't you? You can tell me. I understand. When you were younger, yes? You understand. You did wrong things and you were punished and you knew the truth and you felt better, didn't you?"

Flood said yes again and kind of moaned, and I wondered if there was any way to shoot him with the lipstick so that he wouldn't die and I could finish him off myself.

Goldor kept on. "Do you want me to help you? Help you get the things you want, be the woman you can be? A *life*, a life of truth and beauty and richness?"

"How? I mean, what do I—"

Goldor's voice shifted pitch, got tighter and harder. "Go over to that table on your left, you see it?" Flood nodded that she did. "You'll find something on it. I want you to bring it to me, Debbie. Bring it over here to me."

Trancelike, Flood walked over to the table, bent and picked up something. She turned around and walked back to Goldor, holding a short whip with three separate lashes at the end. She bent forward slightly and handed the whip to him. He looked steadily at her, said, "Do you understand?" and she said, "Yes. The truth . . . to be free." Goldor took the whip from her and climbed off the stool. He stood to one side, holding the stock of the whip in one hand and the tips of the lashes in the other. Flood stood there watching him, hands clasped just below her breasts.

"Now, Debbie, I want you to bend over, turn your head to the side and put your face on this cushion." He indicated the bar stool.

"Can't I . . . ?"

"Debbie, you have to do this. I have explained it to you. I don't want to think you didn't understand."

"But first . . . I mean, shouldn't I . . . ?"

"What?" The barest hint of impatience crept into that controlled voice.

Flood said, "Can't I . . . ?" and reached down and unsnapped the button to the bottle-green pants.

Goldor's rich, dark-toned laugh boomed out. "Of course. Debbie, my child, you understand so beautifully. Yes—most appropriate. I'm so glad you *do* see."

Goldor patiently held the whip as Flood hurriedly jerked the pants down over her hips, hooking her thumbs so that her panties came down with them. She started to walk over to the bar stool, stumbled, let out a nervous laugh, and bent to unzip the white boots. She pulled off the boots, climbed out of the pants, kicked everything away from her, and walked to the stool again. Goldor saw the fire-scar on her rump and grunted in surprise—then smiled with teeth so perfect and even that they must have been false or fully capped.

Flood bent over the stool, flexed each leg like a ballerina warming up, and Goldor let out a moan like a man with stomach cramps and stepped toward her, raising the whip to his shoulder. I heard the whistle of the whip in the dead quiet of the room— Flood's right leg flashed in the orange light and I saw a whitish blur and heard a thump like a boxer's fist slamming into the heavy bag and Goldor went flying backward. He hit the floor like a bag of wet garbage.

Flood spun with the momentum of her kick like a kid's top gone berserk until she was almost on top of Goldor. Another spin and her foot shot into his throat, lifting his heavy body right off the ground. Then she whirled and ran over to me.

She unsnapped the straps from the chair's arms, crying and trying to talk at the same time.

"Burke, Burke, are you all right? Oh don't be dead, Burke. Burke . . ."

"Flood . . . I'm *okay*. Just help me get up."

She pulled me to my feet and we walked over to Goldor. Forget it. The maggot had finally found the truth. He was as dead as a junkie's eyes. When I put my fingers to the side of his neck to be sure, there was no pulse, no breathing. I felt along his chest—three or four ribs on the right side were just plain gone, probably right through his lung. I felt his throat too but I couldn't even find his Adam's apple in the pulpy mess Flood had left.

I had my legs back, if not my stomach. We didn't have much time. My watch said 9:22. Flood was out of it, still mumbling to herself—or to me, I couldn't tell. I grabbed her shoulders, made her look at me. "Flood, listen to me. He's gone. We can't talk to him now. Take this," I said, pulling a black silk handkerchief out of my pocket, "and go over *everything* we touched, understand? We weren't here, got it?" She moved away like a robot, mechanically wiping every surface in the place. She was out of it. I told her to put on her clothes and stand there while I wiped things myself. I didn't know how much time we'd have.

I ran through the house until I found the giant kitchen, grabbed a handful of cleaning fluids and some paper towels, and rushed back to the room with the orange lighting. I soaked the paper towels in the fluids, took out half a dozen cigarettes, lit them one by one, then put each burning butt inside a book of paper matches so that the fire would come in contact with the match heads when they burned down to the end. I loosely wrapped each little firebomb in the fluid-soaked paper towels, planting them all around the room. A final sprinkling of the fluid over the arms of the leather chair and the seat of the bar stool, a quick run to the kitchen to replace the fluid containers and wipe them down. I checked the room—Flood was still sitting there, a white-faced statue.

I pulled out my pocket flash and worked my way down to the basement. I knew I'd find what I needed down there . . . a complete set of barbells suspended over a stand used for bench presses. I wrapped the silk handkerchief around the heavy steel bar and carefully pried off the weights.

Back to the orange-lighted room. I dragged Goldor against one of the tapestry-covered walls, propped him up in a sitting position, took the steel bar in my hands, and swung from the heels, crushing his throat until his head was almost ready to fall off. Next I went to work on his chest and ribs until the skin broke open and his insides started to run onto the rug. When they did the autopsy the cops would tell the doctors about the steel bar—at least they wouldn't be looking for a martial arts expert.

Flood just sat there, watching me, holding the white boots in one hand. I grabbed her other hand and dragged her to the front door, still wiping off surfaces we could have touched or brushed against. I opened the door and looked out into silent darkness. The floodlights were dead—the Mole had done his work. I could hear the crackle of the flames behind us. We were out of time.

I slipped out with Flood right behind me and quietly opened the doors to the Volvo, whispering to Flood to throw her boots inside and help me push the car from behind her door. I did the same with mine, holding onto the steering wheel with my right hand. The Volvo rolled smoothly down the paved driveway and into the street, and I hopped in when it was moving too fast for me to keep up. Flood did the same a second or so after me. I slipped the stick into second gear, popped the clutch and it fired right up.

I crawled around the corner, took another turn, and flicked on the headlights, then drove out of the area heading north, piloting the Volvo like it belonged there, I hoped.

We passed other cars, but no cops. Route 95 was right where we'd left it. Flood started crying when we crossed into New Rochelle, looking straight ahead out the windshield with tears rolling down her face like she didn't know they were there. I kept to the exact change lanes through New Rochelle, hooked the Hutchinson River Parkway and exited toward the Triboro. I didn't say anything to Flood, letting her cry quietly in peace. It was too late for talking.

We were supposed to come away from this trip to the suburbs with an address for the Cobra. Instead we had netted one dead sadist, one homicide investigation, one possible arson rap, and a cold dead trail. By the time we neared Flood's place I knew I was starting to recover from Goldor's Taser attack—I could tell by the taste of blood in my mouth.

41

I FLICKED THE Volvo's shift lever to pull it out of gear and let it coast toward a parking space across from Flood's door. She didn't make a move to get out. I had to move fast, there were a lot of things to do before the sun came up on what was left of Goldor.

"Flood. *Flood,* listen to me. Look, you're home now. Come on." Flood looked over at her building but still didn't move.

"This is not my home," she said in a dead, blue voice.

"Flood, we don't have time for you to be fucking mystical. I'll talk with you later, okay? Just get out. I've got to do some work."

She still didn't budge, so I tried something else. "Flood, you want to come with me? Want to help me?"

"Help you?"

"Yeah, I need some help. I need a friend, okay?"

The tears were still coming but she had control of her mouth. A first step. She said, "Okay," and patted my hand like I was the one walking on the ragged edge.

I pulled the Volvo out and found a decent spot near where the Mole had left it the first time. I slipped into the parking garage like a burglar, but nobody was around—no problems. I found the Plymouth, fired it up, and rolled it down the ramps to the checkout point. I paid the toll and split. If the cops came around someday they'd have to get a subpoena and search the records. Even if they got lucky, all they would ever find is that I was checking into the garage about the same time Goldor was checking out. Okay so far.

Flood was standing in the shadows where I'd left her, but she was still too stiff as she walked over to the car door. She slid into the passenger seat, staying over against her door—not crying now, her breathing pretty good, but still a long way from being in control. I found a pay phone near the drive and called Pablo's clinic—I knew it would be open until at least midnight. I left a message for him to call Mr. Black at eleven that night. Then we got back into the Plymouth, heading for the phone I'd told him to call. I gave myself about a half hour—if Pablo called and I didn't answer it would take another couple of days for me to reach him. Me not answering was the signal that the wheels had come off someplace. He should connect that with Goldor, but I didn't want to chance it.

The pay phone for Mr. Black was in a converted storage shed near the back of Max's warehouse. The message from Mr. Black meant that we were in an emergency situation, so I had to be sure that the phone we used was absolutely reliable. The only way to do that was to make sure it wasn't used most of the time. I didn't want to bring Flood into that neighborhood but she was shredding all my choices with her behavior—all I needed was for her to run amok someplace and bring the cops back to talk to me.

Flood could do time, do it standing on her head. There's not too many guns in jail and without one even the toughest diesel-dyke couldn't make Flood blink. She'd go deep into herself and make it last for the whole term. I could survive in there too, but so what? By the time I got out all I had built up out here would be just so much garbage and I'd have to start all over again—I was getting too old for all that and I could feel the fear coming in closer and I didn't have the time to deal with it the way I was supposed to—so I pointed the Plymouth toward the warehouse and concentrated on driving.

We made it into the front entrance with a good ten minutes to spare. I told Flood to just sit there, stay where she was, and slapped my palm twice on the hood of the car as I got out in a see-you-later gesture, to let Max know there was someone else in the car if he was watching. If Max was there, Max was watching.

The number Pablo had for Mr. Black would ring in a pay phone in a candy store in Brooklyn, one of four in that joint. It was hooked up to a call-diverter which would bounce the signal over to the phone we never used in the storage shed.

The diverter was a mechanical thing and not really all that reliable, but if it didn't bounce the call and Pablo heard any voice but my own he'd hang up and know the Mr. Black signal was for real. Maybe he'd put it together and understand about Goldor and maybe he wouldn't—this was as close to him as I was willing to get until the crime lab people picked the carcass clean and the grand jury made its secret decisions.

I had time to open the door to the shed, check the dust to satisfy myself that nobody had been around since the last time, and light a cigarette.

And then Pablo called. I grabbed it on the first ring, reminding myself that the whole conversation had to be under thirty seconds. "It's me, okay?" I said.

"I hear you."

"The legal research I told you I'd be doing? The stuff you said you might be interested in yourself? Forget it. It's a dead issue."

"That is too bad, *hermano*. You are certain?"

"Dead certain."

"Adios."

It would be hours before I could get a paper, and even then I couldn't count on coverage of Goldor's death, so I'd have to be especially careful not to talk to people. Fortunately, that comes easily to me—practice makes habit.

I gave Pablo about ten seconds to clear the line, reached under the phone, and pulled out the little gadget that looked like a rubber-edged cup with push buttons numbered one to ten on its face. I placed this over the mouthpiece to the phone, checked to see the seal was tight, and punched in the number of the candy store—the same Mr. Black number Pablo would have written down someplace. When it answered I was connected to the dead line next to the first pay phone. They wouldn't answer that phone in the store—it had a permanent Out of Order sign on the booth. This hooked me into the diverter's code box, and I used the push buttons to signal electronically and set the diverter to forward all future calls made to the Mr. Black number over to a pay phone next to a gas station in Jersey City. That broke the circuit. Even if the *federales* had a pen register on whatever phone Pablo had used, they'd never work it back to this shed. When I had some time, maybe in a few months, I'd go over to Brooklyn and uproot the diverter and install it someplace else. I'd notify Pablo too when I got the chance. For now, I was more interested in burning bridges than in building them.

I walked slowly back to the warehouse, expecting to see Flood's blonde hair shining through the windshield, but there was nothing behind the glass. I glanced up at the balcony, couldn't see a thing—I still didn't know if Max was on the set. Then I heard a low moaning sound, flowing deep, ending with a grunt. Over and over, like someone working up the strength to do something ugly and then finally getting down to it. Flood—in the semidarkness off to the side where I'd parked the Plymouth. Flood—in one of those elaborate *katas* I'd seen her do in the studio, flowing between the hood of the car and the side wall, whirling, spinning, thrusting. Her body flashed white in the murky haze of the warehouse. I looked around without moving and saw the bottle-green pants and the jersey top on the floor where she had thrown them, and I knew she'd never walk in disguise again.

It was like no *kata* I'd ever seen. Flood backed away from the car in tiny, ankle-hooking steps and turned completely, moving her hands like she was sculpting a statue from smoke with her fingers. She flicked a leg toward the sky, rocked back on her heel, and clapped her hands against the upraised foot, like a child playing in the sun. She rolled her body toward the car's hood and leaned her back against it, pushed her hands down and raised herself until she was parallel with the ground, her legs straight out in front of her. She slowly lowered herself to the ground on her knees, then leaped to her feet and turned so she was facing the car again. She leaned forward, bent at the waist, wiggled her hips like a prizefighter rolls his shoulders, and the leg with the fire-scar lashed out—again and again like a pumping piston gone mad. And then she stopped and I heard the jet-stream of her nasal intake as she danced away from the car. I watched her kill Goldor over and over again and I thought she would never stop the death-dance. She was all alone.

I quietly opened the door of the Plymouth, reached over, and opened the other door too. I looked for the right cassette, fitted it into the player and hit the switch, and the solitary guitar intro rolled out of the speakers and into the empty warehouse.

Flood spun and slammed to a stop in the middle of her mad dance, whipping her hands into a defense against the music. But it flowed out and surrounded her anyway. "Angel Baby," by Rosie and the Originals, the high, clear voice of the girl singer reaching for something that would maybe never be there, but giving it everything she had. And Flood stood there—white stone in silk underwear, waiting.

I walked out of the shadows toward her, willing her to feel the music and be someplace else, my hands open at my sides. "Hey, Flood," I called softly, "remember reform school?"

She stepped into my arms like she was back at those dances they used to give in the juvenile joints where they would invite the bad girls from the training schools so we could learn the social graces. We danced like we all used to then—our feet hardly moved, we didn't cover much ground. At first she held me as rigid as a steel vise, but as the tape played through and another song from the fifties came on she loosened her grip, her hands moving up until they hung around my neck, her face buried in my chest. We moved together like that until the whole tape ran down and there was silence in the empty warehouse. I kissed her on the forehead and she put her arms around my neck and ground her hips into me like girls did back then. I felt the muscles in her back smooth out and she laughed deep in her throat and I knew she was past it, back to herself.

I held out my hand as if the dance were finished, she took it and we walked back toward the car to sit the next one out. On the hood was a pile of black silk. She seemed to know what it was. She put on the loose, flowing pants and the thigh-length robe with the wide sleeves. As she stepped into the black silk I saw the red dragons embroidered on each sleeve and I knew Max had been there.

We gathered up Flood's whore-clothes and threw them in an old oil drum—I knew they would disappear into ashes and she seemed to know it too. I got into the Plymouth. Flood slid in beside me, slammed in close to me, put her left hand on the inside of my right thigh and left it there while I backed out and pointed the car's nose toward her studio.

42

THE PLYMOUTH ROLLED silently through the empty streets, heading for the West Side. Flood was quiet until we got to the highway, but her hand on my thigh wasn't tense. When I went into the entrance ramp she looked over at me. "You got any more of that music?" and I reversed the cassette and we listened to Gloria Mann sing her "Teenage Prayer" and I guess we both thought about the things we wanted when that song was on the street. There was a lot of music in the juvenile prisons back then. Guys would get together in the shower rooms because the echo effect made everything sound better—it was all groups, nobody thought about being a solo artist. We only heard what came over the radio—it was no big racial thing, all the groups were trying for the same sound. The last time I was locked up for a few days there was almost a race riot—some of the white guys objected to the constant diet of screaming-loud soul music that they piped in twenty-four hours of every bleak day. Music was more participatory when I was a kid—you got three or four guys together and that was it. Whatever they sounded like on the street corner is what they sounded like on the record. Too many kids today don't seem to give a damn about music, they only envy the musical lifestyle—gold chains and limos and all the coke they can stuff up their noses. But the kids themselves haven't changed—the newspapers say they have, but they don't know the score. As long as you have cities you have people who can't live in them and can't get out either. As long as you have sheep, you have wolves.

Flood took her hand off my thigh, patted around in my

clothes until she found a cigarette. She found the wooden matches and lit one, holding it to my mouth for me to take a drag. Between Flood's kick and Goldor's backhand, my mouth was a little below par, but the cigarette tasted good. Or maybe it was just good to be smoking while Goldor burned.

I use the West Side Highway when I have to go uptown. It's not always the fastest route but it's the safest. The Plymouth might not be able to outrun anything on the road—although it will blow away any normal patrol car—but the special suspension gives it a real edge on a rough road and they don't come much rougher than the West Side Highway. I swung back towards Flood's studio and found a safe-looking place to park. It was the dead hour on the street—late enough for the predators to have retired for the night and not yet early enough for the first citizens to emerge from their fortresses to try to make an honest living. The sky looked reddish to me, but I couldn't tell if it was the coming sunrise or my blurry vision. Flood walked along next to me, but the bounce was gone. She walked straight ahead like a soldier—her hips never brushed against me like they usually did. She didn't understand yet, and I had to make her see what had really happened if we were going to flush a snake out of the urban grass.

Her key unlocked the downstairs door. The staircase was unlighted, and Max's black robes made most of her disappear ahead of me. I could just barely see the blonde hair and hear the whisper of silk. The studio was empty again. We walked past the marked-off section and into her space, and Flood sat down. She was still off her game—usually she would be throwing off her clothes by now and heading for the shower, but I guess she figured some dirt doesn't come off with soap. I took out a cigarette but she didn't stir, so I went and found something to use for an ashtray myself. I sat and smoked in silence while I thought it through. Finally I looked over at Flood. "You want me to tell you a story?"

She started to shrug like she didn't give a damn what I did, then gave me a half-smile and said "Sure" without enthusiasm.

I said, "Come here, okay?" and she got up and walked over to me. She sat down real close and I took her shoulders in my hands, spun her around like a top, the silk pants sliding smoothly on the polished floor until she was facing away from me. I pulled gently until she was lying on her back, her head in my lap, looking up in my direction—but not seeing me. I stroked her fine hair as I told her the story.

"I was in the can once with this hillbilly. Actually he was from someplace in Kentucky but he had lived most of his life in Chicago. They had two men in a cell then—the joint was overcrowded and the race situation was bad. Virgil was a good man to have in your cell—quiet, clean, and ready to take your back if he had to. He didn't look for problems, just wanted to do his time. In the joint you don't generally talk about your beef—you know, how you got there and all—but if you cell with a man, sooner or later you hear his story. Or at least the story he wants to tell.

"When Virgil arrived in Chicago to work the mills, he met this girl from his hometown and they fell in love and got married. Before she met Virgil, this girl had been with this other man from down south—a real evil, vicious freak. He had done time on a road gang for beating a man to death with a baseball bat. Virgil's wife thought she'd left this man behind her, but he showed up one day when Virgil was at work. He slapped her around, hurt her without making any marks—he knew how to do that. He made her do some things she didn't want to do. Then the freak told her he would be back, anytime he wanted, and if she told Virgil, he'd kill her man.

"And it went on like that, you know, for months and months. Virgil would go to work, and this freak would come around. Sometimes he would take the money Virgil left for his wife to buy food and all. Once he took some Polaroid pictures of her— said he'd show them to Virgil if she ever said anything— nobody would believe her now.

"Virgil got laid off at the mill but he still went out every day looking for work. And he'd leave money with his wife for food and other stuff for the house. One day, he comes home and there's no money in the place. She had given it all to the freak. Virgil got into a beef with his wife about it and she couldn't tell him what happened to the money, and Virgil had been drinking a little bit because he was down and out of work and she still wouldn't tell him anything—he got crazy and slapped her. That was the first time he ever hit her. And then she started to cry and it all came out and he told her he would make it all right and he was sorry he hit her. Finally he calmed her down.

"He told his wife he was going to speak to the police the

next day, and he left that morning like he always did. Virgil didn't know where to find the freak, but he knew he would come around sooner or later. He was patient—when he saw the freak go upstairs he followed right behind, but when he threw open the door the freak was trying to hold his stomach together from where his wife had stabbed him—she was holding a kitchen knife in her hand and going after the freak to finish the job. The freak just lay there on the floor while Virgil and his wife screamed at each other loud enough for the whole neighborhood to hear—she was yelling at Virgil to get the hell out and let her finish what she'd started and he was trying to make her get in the bedroom and she wouldn't go—Virgil finally just took out his own knife and gutted the freak like you would a deer you just shot. Then he went next door and borrowed a phone to call the police.

"When the cops came Virgil said he had killed the freak but his wife kept saying *she* was the one. They both got arrested, but Virgil made a deal and took the whole weight himself. He pleaded guilty to manslaughter, and his wife was waiting outside for him to finish his time so they could be together—she came every visiting-day . . . I had this little racket going with some of the cons and I had Virgil help me out with some of it—he sent the money he made home to his wife through a hack we knew was all right."

I looked down at Flood, still stroking her hair. Lying next to me, she was quiet as death but her eyes were focused and I knew she was listening.

"Anyway, one day the parole board came in to interview all the guys who were eligible for release. I used to make good money coaching some of the guys on how to act in front of those lames, and I went over the whole thing with Virgil to make sure he got it right—no prior record, crime of passion, a workingman, home and family waiting for him, roots in the community, regular churchgoer—he realized that he was wrong and was full of remorse, he would be a good citizen in the future. All that bullshit.

"Before you actually get to see the board you have to see this guy we call the I.P.O., that's Institutional Parole Officer. He does all the preliminary screening and most of us believed that the board would go with whatever he recommended. I went with Virgil to the interview and sat down at the desk right outside the I.P.O.'s office like I was the next case. It cost me twenty packs to get the seat but I wanted to make sure Virgil handled himself like we'd rehearsed. He did real fine, said everything I told him to say. But then the I.P.O. got to the crime itself. He asked Virgil flat out, 'Why did you kill that man?'

"And Virgil just told him, 'He needed killing.'

"That was it for the interview—it was over right then, you understand?"

Flood spoke for the first time. "I . . . think so. I don't know."

"Flood, how do you explain killing a cockroach? There's some things that shouldn't be on this planet, some things that are born to die, nothing else. Not *everything* fits in this life, baby, no matter what the ecology freaks say. Who needs rats? Who needs roaches? From the very second that two people sat together around a fire in the forest, there was another human out there who felt better in the dark. You understand? You're trying to sort out Goldor in your head and it won't work, right?"

"Yes."

"And it never will, baby. You keep a clean house, right? You don't sit around trying to figure out where dirt comes from—you just sweep it out of the way or vacuum it up or whatever you do. You just don't want it in your house—you already know it's no good for you. Goldor's just dirt, Flood. Don't make any more out of him."

Flood looked up at me. She started to talk slowly, but then the words ran together and she was talking like she'd never stop. "In that room, where he took us. First I thought you were dead . . . I thought he'd killed you with that space-gun thing. But then I could see you breathe and I thought about that lipstick thing you showed me once and I was afraid you would kill him if he came near you again and I wanted him to tell me about Wilson and I thought I'd play along with him and then it got all crazy and I forgot why I was there and I knew what I was going to do—I knew I'd never find Wilson if I did and I couldn't stop myself and I wished I could kill him some more, some more times, and I thought about the girl you told me about on that film—she was just as important as Flower and she had people who would kill Goldor if I didn't and I knew he was going to die anyway and I wanted to keep him talking— I knew you would take the pain over in that chair and wait and I knew I could take whatever he had and I'd live through it too—I wanted him to keep talking so he'd tell me something and I thought about tying him up like he did to you and making him tell us and I couldn't think of even *touching* him and then I . . ."

I was rubbing her face with the back of my hand and she was talking quietly and fast and the tears were rolling again. I talked softly to her, like a mother crooning her baby to sleep. "Flood, we *will* have him, baby, we have his face, we'll have his body . . . Flood, listen to me, I understand now about the sacred weapon, I understand, okay? I know why you wanted to wear that ribbon. Lucecita knows, baby—just like Flower will know. I wanted to cancel Goldor's ticket myself, even while I was strapped into that chair I was thinking that there must be a better way of killing him so it would mean more than just stepping on a roach. You did what was right . . ." I whispered, my voice trailing off as I patted her face, still wet with tears.

"The robes?" she asked, looking up at me.

"Yes, the black robes came from my brother, the one I told you about—the master. It was a message from him, from Max, to go and do your work. Your work with Goldor is over. Goldor's over. Lucecita is smiling down at you now, like Flower and Sadie soon will . . ."

"Burke, if you do that for me, I swear I'll never leave you."

"We'll do it—me for my reasons, you for yours. But you have to get past this, I can't do it by myself."

"I can't seem to get back to myself," she was sobbing again "—I'm trying . . ."

"I didn't think you were a coward, Flood—I thought you were a for-real warrior. My brother thinks so too. If you can't get back, if you left yourself in that room with Goldor, then he *won*. You want that? He was going to torture you for a few minutes to entertain himself. Does he get to torture you for the rest of your life? Reach down for something, damn it—and if it's not there you just hide in this little house and I'll go and do my work—"

"It's not *your* work."

"Yeah, it is. Dead meat brings flies. I stirred up too much already. Wilson has to go—if he's here, sooner or later he comes for me, or he does something, I don't know what. I put my money on the table and I paid to see the last card. You're spitting on the only good thing in this life—we survived. We walked away from that maggot's house. We're alive and he's not. And now you want to die inside so you're not a woman anymore, not nothing. I'm not going to be nothing. When I check out of this fucking hotel it won't be because I'm a volunteer—and you can bet your ass it won't be with the bill paid in full either."

Flood looked up at me, rolled over on her stomach with her head in my lap, hugging my legs hard. I patted her back, stroked her hair—waited for her decision. I'd said my piece with my mouth—but it was my mind screaming at her to stand up one more time. She muttered something, her mouth buried in my lap.

"What?"

"You're not so tough," said Flood.

On a new roll now, and not knowing how to handle that last, I weighed in with, "The winner is the guy who walks out of the ring, not the guy who won the most rounds."

"Still on that endurance thing of yours?"

"It's the best card I have to play."

Flood turned her head slightly so she could see me out of the corner of one eye. I couldn't see her face, but I felt her smile in my lap.

"Endurance means you can last a long time," she said.

"So? I lasted this long . . ."

Flood turned her head back down, opened her mouth so I could feel her hot breath between my legs. She put her teeth around me and bit down—not hard enough to threaten amputation, but close enough. She kept her mouth on me until she was satisfied with her work, then she flowed up into that lotus position facing me. "Let me take a shower. Then I want to see just how good this famous endurance of yours is."

She walked toward the bathroom, pulling the black robe from her shoulders as she did. I sat there and smoked another cigarette and felt the pain flow back into me and pulse around my mouth—and I knew she was going to stand up.

The shower stopped before I got through the next smoke, and a dripping wet Flood padded into the room, holding a towel partially around her waist. She smiled—it was a good smile this time—and crooked her finger at me in a come-over-here gesture and I stubbed out the cigarette and followed her back into her small space.

She dropped the towel and came to me, still damp and even

more of a handful than usual. Her kiss was sweet and tender, sucking the pain from my mouth. She pushed the jacket off my shoulders and pulled the T-shirt over my head, unbuckled my pants, and knelt to take them off after my boots. I kissed her and rubbed her and her body began to glow in the early morning light.

She turned and walked over to the little table, bent over and thrust her backside into the air, looking at me over her shoulder—telling me she was finished with Goldor's demons and she had herself back.

I climbed into her as she waited, carefully at first. But the woman warrior took my hands and put them on her breasts and rolled her hips until I was fitted to her. I took her soft neck gently in my teeth and tested my endurance.

43

IT WAS JUST past ten o'clock by the time I was ready to move out. Flood and I had been through what had to be done a few dozen times, and I could see she was finally ready to sleep. I told her I'd call when I had something and went out the door. I rang for the elevator, sent it back down to the ground floor, hit the switch to call it back to me. I stood there waiting, smoking another cigarette. When I finished I ground out the butt on the floor and slipped it into my pocket. Still dead quiet.

I took the stairs down and walked to the car—it looked different in daylight, streaked and dull like it needed a bath. By now the Volvo we had used to visit Goldor would be nothing but scrap metal. Still a lot of traffic on the street, but I couldn't wait for the night—too much to do.

The Plymouth found its way back to the office on auto-pilot. I locked it up, climbed the stairs, checking everything as I walked. Still okay. Pansy wasn't even impatient but she stalked out the back door and onto the roof readily enough. I picked up the desk phone, cleared it for hippies, and dialed Mama's—no messages.

Pansy rolled in the back door, I found her something to eat and I sat with her while she snarfed up the mess I'd made for her in her steel bowl—trying to think, and drawing a blank.

I went into the side room to the chest of drawers, made a hook out of a coat hanger, looped it around one of the handles on the bottom drawer, and gently pulled it out. The twin razor-tipped barbs shot out of the opened drawer like a striking snake, but they hit only air—I was standing two feet away. It wasn't really too likely that anyone would get past all the security devices and Pansy too, but if they did I figured they should pay a little extra toll for the trip. The spring-loaded barbs would stab through anything, even padded gloves, and the solution I'd carefully painted on each tip would induce dizziness and nausea in a minute or two after that. It wouldn't kill anybody, but it'd make them think of poison right away—and head for the nearest hospital instead of going on with their work. I only set up the bottom drawer—professionals always start that way so they don't have to close one drawer to go to the next one— saves a few seconds on each job. For a pro, a few seconds saved on a job can mean a few years saved somewhere down the road. You learn a lot of things in prison.

Part of my stash was there. I counted the bills a couple of times. This was my case money—for emergencies only, not bullshit like food or gas. More than enough to smoke the Cobra out of his hole, *if* it didn't take too long. I took some of the bills, replaced the rest, set the springs for the barbs, and carefully closed the drawer. I went back inside to the desk, got out a yellow legal pad and some felt-tip pens, pulled an ashtray close, and started to map out the campaign.

Pansy came over to me, slammed against my leg in what she thought was a friendly gesture, put her massive head on my knee and growled encouragingly. She was wasting her time— I wasn't going inside to watch television, I had to work.

An hour passed and the yellow pad stared up at me, laughing at my blankness. At this rate I'd have to wait for the dirtbag to die of old age.

I went back into the side room and took a shower, using the time to think. Still nothing. I took an old Con Edison uniform, one of those jumpsuit outfits they used to wear, climbed into it, and sat on the floor. Pansy came over and stretched out next to me. I patted her head absently, knowing I couldn't force it.

Finally I got up and went back to the desk, rummaged around until I found an old draftsman's compass and a piece of cardboard. I stabbed the compass point into the cardboard and drew a two-inch circle. I used my razor knife to cut out the circle, took it back into the side room, found an ice pick, and stuck the whole thing to the wall. Another couple of minutes and I found a little can of spray paint I'd used on a videotape surveillance camera in one of those luxury apartment buildings a few months ago. I held one palm flat against the cardboard and sprayed, using the open circle as a stencil. In a minute I had myself a round black dot stark against a white piece of wall.

I found a blanket, folded it over a couple of times, and sat down. Then I looked into that dot, breathing in through my nose, forcing the air down deep into my stomach and groin, holding it there, exhaling so that my chest expanded each time. I did it again and again, in slow, steady rhythm until I found myself relaxing, looking deep into the dot. It grew larger and its edges disappeared—I was going inside the black hole and using my mind to probe out ahead of me, looking for the Cobra. Black holes are dangerous—I took Find-the-Cobra with me instead of a mantra, and I went away from this earth for a while.

Pansy's snarl brought me out of it—something was thumping against the back window in the side room, softly but insistently. I could see an indistinct shape against the dark curtains. I got quietly to my feet, reached in the top drawer, took out the flare pistol I keep there, checked to make sure it was primed, and moved over to the window. Pansy was at my side and just ahead, on point and ready. I parted the curtains ever so slightly, leveling the gun.

It was a goddamned pigeon, trapped in the maze of wire I had built around the windowframe. Only one of his feet was caught—his wings were free and they flapped like insanity let out of a bag. If he had a bit more strength he would have triggered the electrical circuit and some wino in the alley below would have had a fried squab dinner.

I went back inside and threw the switch to the Off position—it's clearly marked On in case some clown got in the front door somehow and decided to leave by the window—then I reached out to spring him. Pigeons are nothing more than rats with wings—I've never seen a city or a prison without them—but they know how to survive. I held him firmly in a gloved hand but he didn't even try to peck at me. He looked okay, so I tossed him into the air and he fell like a stone for a few feet, stuck his wings out experimentally to break his fall and then banked into a river breeze and headed for another roost.

I went back inside, lit myself a cigarette, and praised Pansy for her vigilance. She probably knew it was a miserable pigeon all the time and just wanted to get me out of the trance. It took me a few drags of the smoke before it hit me. I had it worked out all the time—if you're going fishing, you need worms, right? Now there's about three good ways to get them: you can buy them from someone who's selling, you could dig around in the ground and hope you got lucky, or you could wait until it rained and the worms came to the surface and you could take your pick.

That's how I could find this freak—all three techniques, with the emphasis on the last one. Only I wasn't going to *wait* for it to rain.

I went back to the desk and sat down to compose a few ads for the Personals column of some local papers. I couldn't wait for the nationals, although it was easy enough to figure what kind of reading matter would be on Wilson's list. It takes three or four months from the time you submit the copy until you see it in print, and he could be long gone by then. I permanently rent a few post office boxes around the city for freelance fundraising, and they would do the job here too.

First, the old reliable *Village Voice*. "SWF, widowed, young-looking 32, petite and shapely, financially secure, with two lovely daughters, ages 9 and 7. Looking for a strong man with life experience, possibly ex-military or law enforcement, to take charge of her life. Can we meet and talk about it? Letter, with picture ONLY to Box X2744, Sheridan Square Station."

Then in the *Daily News:* "COURIER needed. Must be reliable, with prior military experience. Out-of-country work, must have valid passport. High pay and bonus to the right man." And another box number.

An ad in the *Times* for a general houseman, good driver, competent with firearms, to serve as chauffeur-bodyguard to two young children on a Westchester estate. With another box number.

A couple of blind drops in the S&M rags, looking for "military" or "police" types for "special work" and promising high pay and great opportunities, including European travel, to the right man.

I didn't know Wilson's mind completely, so I also prepared some ads for a school-bus driver for a children's camp in the Catskill Mountains and for a director of security for a private daycare center in Greenwich Village. Still another from a freelance writer looking for military vets who wanted to discuss their experiences with foreign child-prostitutes in exchange for a $300 interview fee.

I could have written lots of ads that might have eventually attracted the Cobra, but I wanted him under pressure and looking for a way out, not just hunting for new victims. I put the ads together in separate envelopes, addressed them using the Pantograph I keep for such occasions. The post office supplied me with the money orders I needed, and the ads went out. From past experience, I knew they would surface within a couple of days.

I wheeled the Plymouth toward the docks and started looking for some of my people. I prowled under the West Side Highway, the part that the environmentalists are still fighting about, near the blank sandy slab that's supposed to be luxury housing someday. Luxury housing in this city is perfect—they fill part of the river with garbage to make a foundation and then they fill the buildings with more garbage, only the new garbage pays rent. Nothing showed. I made the full run up to Fourteenth Street, turned around, and headed back downtown.

As I stopped at a light I saw a working girl sitting on one of the concrete bases that anchor the steel I-beams that hold up the highway. She had short reddish hair, a hard thirtyish face, dark lipstick, a quarter-inch of face powder. A rust-colored sweater bulged out over huge tightly cinched breasts, the ensemble finished off with a thick leather belt, faded jeans, black leather boots almost to the knee. She was smoking a cigarette, blowing the smoke toward the river—waiting. Her partner, a skinny black girl wearing a turquoise knit dress and apparently nothing else, was standing by, hands on hips. The black hooker was anxious to get working, jawing with every car that stopped, but the big woman sat like she was part of the concrete.

I pulled up and rolled down the window, giving the big pros a look at my face. She asked, "Want to buy some pussy?" in a half-asleep voice like she didn't give a damn one way or the other while the black girl ran her tongue around her lips.

"How much?"

"Twenty-five for the pussy, ten for the room."

"Hey, I want to rent it, not buy it," I told her, and the black girl giggled.

"I just want to talk to you," I told the white woman.

She looked at me. "No sale, pal. I'm self-employed."

"Do I look like a pimp to you?"

"You don't look like *nothing* to me," earning another giggle from her pal.

"You want to talk about it?"

"For twenty-five bucks in your car, thirty-five in the room," she said in the same monotone.

"Deal," I said, opening the door for her. She slowly pulled herself off the concrete cushion and walked over to the Plymouth. She was about six feet tall, had to weigh 170 pounds.

As soon as she stood up I knew who she was.

I drove down by one of the abandoned piers, killed the engine, and turned to look at her. She said, "The twenty-five, man," and I reached in my pocket while she fumbled in her purse, and I had my gun out before she came up with hers.

"Take your hand out of your pocketbook, okay? Nice and slow. Nobody's going to hurt you."

A resigned light flashed in her eyes for a split-second, but she didn't move. I cocked the pistol—the sound was harsh in the closed car. She took her hand out of her pocketbook, threw one massive thigh over the other, and put her folded hands on her knees where I could see them.

"You're not a cop, right?"

"Right."

"So you want this one on the house . . . or is this payback?"

"It's neither one, JoJo. Just be cool. Give me the purse."

"There's no money in it."

"I know what's in it."

She tossed the purse at me, right at my face. I didn't move—my gun didn't move. The purse slapped against my face and fell into my lap. I snapped it open and found the tiny .25-caliber automatic—I put her piece in my pocket and tossed her purse into the backseat.

"Not much of a gun, JoJo."

"I don't need much."

"You want to know what this is all about?"

"I figure I already know. Some sucker sent you, right? You don't figure to blast me right here, and you don't look tough enough to whip my ass, so I figure it's got to be about money."

"It's about money all right, but money *for* you, not *from* you. I want you to do some work for me."

"Twenty-five for the pussy, ten for the room."

"Cut the shit, JoJo. I know you run a one-woman badger game, okay? I'm not going to any room with you. I want to buy something and I'm willing to pay."

"You know about me?"

"Yeah."

"From where?"

"From around."

"Then you're around the wrong people."

"And you live in the suburbs, right?"

"I'm listening," she said.

"I'm looking for a guy, okay? I've got his picture, got his description. You turn him up, I pay you a grand in cash. That's it."

"How much up front?"

"What do I look like, a fucking commuter? I'm not asking you to go out of your way—just do your work. You happen to see him, you make a call, you get your money."

"I can get the same deal from the *federales.*"

"Bullshit. Don't be so cool—there's no way you're talking to the Man. I'll front you a quarter for the phone call, that's it."

"And if I don't?"

"You can haul your gigantic ass out of here and back under the highway."

JoJo sat there like she was thinking it over—like she had all the time in the world. She said, "Got a smoke?" and I nodded towards my shirt pocket. She reached one hand toward the pocket, bringing her face close to mine. There was nobody home behind her eyes. I brought the gun closer to her face.

JoJo plucked a cigarette from the loose pack and stuck it in her mouth. She patted herself like she was looking for matches, then let her left hand trail down my chest to my crotch and groped around, squeezed—the gun stayed on her face. JoJo took her hand away, leaned back against the seat cushion, fired the wooden match against the sole of her boot. "At least you don't get a hard-on behind sticking a gun in my face."

"I'm here on business, okay?"

JoJo took a deep drag of the cigarette. Her sweater looked like it was going to burst a few threads and I could see the outline of the wire-support bra—she must have been the only whore in the city who wore one.

"Show me the picture," she said. I watched her face for a clue to her mind and gave it up. I took the Xerox of the mug shot out and handed it to her.

JoJo studied the picture intently. Her eyes narrowed. "That

motherfucker, it's him! I find this cocksucker and he's dead. On the house. I don't need your fucking quarter. It's him . . ."

"Hey," I said, to snap her out of it.

JoJo swiveled in her seat to look at me. Her face was dead-white under the makeup, red blotches mottled her cheeks—her eyes were crazy. I spoke softly, gently. "Listen, it's okay. It's okay, JoJo. I want him too, all right? I know he's a bad guy. It's okay—there's a lot of people wanting him now. Relax . . . just relax."

I patted her rock-hard shoulder, stroked it—but I never moved the gun from her face. JoJo finally took a deep breath, handing me back the picture. "I don't need this—I'd know that cocksucker anywhere. I don't need you to tell me what to do. If you want him, you got him . . . dead."

"Look, I just want you to—"

But she went on like I hadn't spoken. "And if you're one of his freak friends, if this is a test, tell him I'll always remember, okay? He's dead. You don't like it you can just fucking blast away right now."

"JoJo . . . JoJo, listen, babe. I'm not his friend—I don't even know him, okay? And I *do* want him. Just call me when you—"

"No calls. I see him, he's dead."

"You want the grand?"

"Not if I have to let him live."

"I'll pay you a grand for his *head*, okay, JoJo? When you finish with him, just take off his head, okay? And call me. When I see his head, I'll pay you the money."

And JoJo smiled like a little girl with a new doll. "Yeah?"

"Yeah. Okay. We got a deal?"

"We got a deal, pal," said JoJo, and slid over to open her door, leaving the Cobra's picture and her purse in the car. As she was walking around the back to my side, I grabbed the .25 and popped the clip, jacked the shell out of the chamber, then worked the clip until I was holding a handful of bullets. When she came up to the window I gave her back the purse with everything inside. JoJo leaned in the window, shaking her rump for new customers like she was saying good-bye to an old one. She gave me a wink with one droopy eyelid, and I had the Plymouth in gear and moving even as she was turning away.

I got to the highway before she did and turned downtown, feeling the chills in the back of my neck like the time I had malaria. I put my gun back where it belonged, kneading my left forearm with my right hand to restore the circulation. I had been holding the piece like it was a lifeline—with JoJo so close to me, I guess it had been.

After a few blocks, I felt a stabbing pain in my chest and realized I hadn't drawn a breath for too long. I got my breathing under control, checked my hands for the shakes—I had them, all right—and started to look for Michelle.

44

I DREW A total blank for a while—then I spotted Michelle working the other side of the highway. I hooked the Plymouth into a rolling U-turn and watched her face as I wheeled up alongside her. As soon as she saw it was me she started to run to the car. I pushed the passenger door open and she was in and we were moving again.

"What's on, honey—somebody chasing you?" she asked.

"I got to talk to you. Not around here."

"I know a spot," she said, and directed me down by the Municipal Building—she sent us east like we were headed for the drive but told me to pull up short near Pearl Street. It was a big construction site with no workers around. No police patrols either, but lots of citizen activity a few blocks away. Safe and quiet.

I rolled down my window, offered a smoke to Michelle, who declined in favor of her own brand. She smokes these long skinny things with pink paper and black filter tips she gets from Nat Sherman's. I tried one once when I ran out of my own—they don't taste bad.

"You know JoJo?" I asked her.

"Everybody knows JoJo, baby. Why?"

"I'm still looking for that maggot, right? The Cobra?"

"So you went to *JoJo?* Are you completely bonkers?"

"Maybe I am. I know she's a rough-off artist. I never met her before today but I know her rep. I thought I'd run the thing by her, tell her about the bounty and—"

"What bounty?"

"A grand cash, no questions asked, no testimony needed."

"And you told JoJo?"

"Yeah. How could I know she'd go into the fucking Twilight Zone on me?"

"Burke, you didn't show her a picture, did you? Or an artist's sketch?"

"Yeah, I did. How did you know?"

"And then she just went off, right?"

"I *said* yeah. What's the story?"

"Sweetheart, I thought you knew about JoJo. Sometimes I don't see how you can do your work, ignorant as you are. JoJo used to be a sweet young thing. One of those country broads— got tired of the farm and turned tricks back home down in Cornballsville. So she comes up here to make money in the big city, right? And where do you think she decides to set up shop? Delancey and the Bowery, if you can believe it. And she's out there without a daddy, thinking those double-sawbuck tricks are major bucks, you know? Now there's nothing down here but *experienced* black ladies, honey, plus a few little white-bread runaways that the pimps are afraid to let work near the Port Authority because there's warrants out on them, and all.

"And the working girls don't tell her nothing about the Life, you know—they just try and pull her into one of their old man's stables. But JoJo's not going for that—she's going to do a solo act. So one night this freakmobile shows up on the corner—two punks in front, another pair in the back. Ain't no working girl with any smarts getting in *that* car—but the other bitches play like it's no big deal and old dumb JoJo goes for it and they take her away to some room one of them had and they keep her there for three whole days—tie her up and fuck her and do a bullwhip number on her and make her spread for some Polaroids—they just go the whole freako hog. And after they pull a couple of trains on her they send out for pizza and let the delivery man have a shot. They call up all their friends and invite them too. And when they're finally going to leave, JoJo's a bloody mess and she ups and asks them for the *money*. Can you believe that? Well, one of them just goes nuts behind that and he takes a baseball bat to her and when the cops find her half her skull is caved in.

"They take her to the hospital and put a steel plate in her head and get her patched up and then some detective comes in with one of those mug-shot books and shows them to her and she starts screaming, 'That's them,' and points to *all* of them and jumps right out of the bed and they have to knock her out with the needles . . . JoJo ends up in the psycho ward for a year or two until she learns how to play the game and they spring her. Now she just gets even—every day, every way. Baby, you show her anything that even *looks* like a mug shot and it's Psycho City."

"Yeah, yeah, I saw that for myself. She doesn't recognize any of the pictures?"

"JoJo doesn't recognize anything period. She runs a fifty-fifty blend of hate and crazy. I can't even *tell* you some of the things she's done to johns. You go into a hotel room with JoJo and you're not walking out under your own power."

"I think she's not waiting for hotel rooms anymore, Michelle—she's packing. I think she would've blown me away right in the car if she'd had the chance."

"It's so sad. I talk to her sometimes, Burke, but I can't help her. Those freaks put her on another planet, what they did to her."

"Pass the word on the bounty, okay?"

"It's for real?"

"You bet your ass," I said, opening the door for her.

"Baby, *please,* not for a lousy thousand dollars," said Michelle, stepping out of the Plymouth to do her work.

I set out to make a few more stops, spreading the word. I wanted every dope addict, every hustler, every take-off artist in our area to be looking to score on this one.

As I rolled back uptown I looked across the highway and saw JoJo, still sitting on the same piece of concrete, smoking her cigarette and waiting for her connection. I thought about the steel plate in her head and got another chill. I'd never show her another picture—of anybody—ever.

I found the industrial building on West Twenty-fifth Street, took the freight elevator to the roof, walked across to what looked like a pair of greenhouses stacked side-by-side. The hand-lettered sign on the door said PERSONALIZED GRAPHICS: SAMSON/LTD. I rang the bell and waited. I heard the click that told me the door was open, turned the knob, and stepped inside. Two men working at individual drafting tables—one in his late thirties, very short hair, tight tanned skin with prominent cheekbones and delicate clean hands, wearing a blue oxford-cloth buttondown shirt with narrow rep tie—the other, shorter and heavily muscled, long blond hair and an earring in his left ear. He was wearing a cut-off dungaree jacket with no shirt underneath, showing a giant tattoo of a daisy on one bicep. The clean-looking one said "Burke?" and I walked in and laid the photo of the Cobra on his drafting table. "He been in here?"

"I never talk about my clients."

"Neither do I."

He looked back up at me, down again at the picture, and said no in a quiet voice. I said, "Call me if he does," and walked out. One of the "personalized graphics" they did was passports.

The next stop was a print shop I know where they would let me use their machinery and pay for whatever I did without looking at it—they didn't want to know. One of the few legitimate things I'd learned in reform school was how to run a printing press. Making up some WANTED posters with enlargements of the Cobra's mug shot was no problem. The photo blew up nice and clean, hard to miss. I set the type so the posters read WANTED FOR GENOCIDE AGAINST HISPANIC CHILDREN in bold red type and added a long list of the Cobra's alleged rapes.

Pablo's people would put them up all over town, especially in Times Square. Una Gente Libre wouldn't put their own name on anything like this, especially after Goldor, but the word would get around and the Cobra would know there were some serious people on his trail.

I threw the bundle of posters in my trunk and bought a paper—nothing on Goldor yet, so I went to a pay phone and called Toby Ringer. I told him that I'd heard Wilson had snuffed Goldor so I was giving up my search for him. The harsh intake of breath at Toby's end told me that he knew Goldor was dead. My phone call would make sure there'd be an APB out on Wilson.

Over to another phone, where I called my preppie reporter pal and gave him the hot scoop on a genuine mercenary recruiting operation right in the middle of Manhattan—putting together a string of soldiers of fortune to fight in Rhodesia and South Africa. A terrible scandal and an affront to black people everywhere, he agreed. I promised to call him back in another day or so with names and locations and he said he would go

in there undercover and expose the situation for his readers.
Christ.

It was getting into the late afternoon by then, so I rolled
the Plymouth back toward the warehouse looking for Max
before I made the call to the phony gunrunners. I pulled in,
killed the engine, and waited. Before I was halfway through
the first cigarette Max dropped onto the hood. I vacated the
front seat and we went into the back room to talk.

I pulled the lapels of my jacket to show Max I was talking
about clothes, made the sign of something falling softly through
the air, bowed deeply to show my appreciation of the robes he
had given to Flood.

Max dropped his own head in the briefest of bows, flowed
into his own version of Flood's crazy *kata* and ended with a
two-finger strike, his hand darting in and out so quickly that
only the rush of the silk sleeve ripping through dead air alerted
me. He looked the question at me—could Flood do that? Could
she finish the job, or was she just a dancer? So I told him about
Goldor and the Cobra and what I wanted to do, how I wanted
it all to end—a hiss came from Max. He was warming up.

He followed me to the workbench where we cooked up
another stencil out of some cardboard we kept lying around. I
found a dozen or so of the little spray cans and pointed toward
the car, made signs to show all the doors opening at once and
people jumping out, walking down the street looking straight
ahead—walking like warriors. I explained what the spray cans
were for as Max smiled.

It was still about a half hour before six so Max and I got
out the cards and we played gin until it was time. My mind
was on other things but I still beat him—Max is too supersti-
tious to count cards like I had showed him. I hooked up the
on-line phone set and dialed the gunrunners. James answered
on the first ring—I guess he does all the public speaking for
the two. "Yes?"

"It's me. I have a proposition for you. I'll pick you up in
two hours, right where you are, and we'll talk, okay?"

"Certainly," he said, and I rang off.

I gestured to Max that we were going to meet the same
characters who had been in the warehouse before. He made
the sign of a man reaching for a gun and I told him no—it
wasn't going to be a duel, just more talk. Seated at the table,
I reached for an imaginary steering wheel and turned it a few

times as if I were peering through a windshield. I looked a question at Max, pointing first at him then out into the street. He nodded, he would get us a car. I pointed at my watch and Max held up one finger—it would take him about an hour.

Max faded out the door and I hooked up the phone again and called Flood. "Hi, baby."

"Hi. Are you working?"

"Working hard."

"Anything yet?"

"I got most of the ingredients, but . . . uh . . . the cake's not in the oven yet."

"That's good—I'm very hungry."

"Me too. I'll be working late tonight. Okay to come by when I'm finished?"

"Yes, call first. How late?"

"After midnight."

"I love you, Burke."

"You don't have to motivate me—I told you I was on the job."

"Don't be a coward—you can say you love me too."

"Later," I said, and hung up. I disconnected the phone, went back inside, and looked through the paper Max had left. I couldn't even concentrate on the race results. Stupid Flood.

45

THE ASHTRAY WAS filling up by the time Max roared into the warehouse at the wheel of a Blood Shadows war-wagon— a huge black Buick Electra four-door sedan. The Chinese street gangs prefer the four-door models so the maximum number of shooters can hit the street at the same time. The Blood Shadows all come from Hong Kong with burning ambitions and psychopathic personalities as standard equipment. Thirty years ago a Chinese street gang was about as common as a forgiving loan shark. But in one quantum leap the Hong Kong kids overtook their ethnic counterparts all over the city, passing up territorial warfare and gang rape for the more practical activities of extortion and homicide. Shaking down their elders with complete disregard for the consequences, these kids made the old Tong Wars look like a polite debate—the intensity of their disputes was always measured in body counts. The only time they killed Caucasians was by accident, so they weren't considered a major law-enforcement problem.

Chinatown was their base, but they were moving into Queens and Brooklyn, and they linked up nationally with gangs in Boston and D.C. and on the Coast. A few years ago they had made the mistake of asking Mama for a contribution. Since then Max the Silent had been their hero, especially after four members of their hit squad had been released from the hospital—the other one stayed in the morgue. The survivors told the police they had been hit by a train. When they weren't spending their extorted cash on fingertip leather jackets or silk shirts or 9-mm automatics they haunted the kung fu movies.

And when they moved out of the moviehouses into the darkness of Chinatown's streets they would argue among themselves about who was the greater—the celluloid warriors on the screen or Max the Silent.

Max flipped the lever into reverse and we backed out of the warehouse. As he drove up the East Side Drive toward the Thirty-fourth Street exit I began a systematic search of the car—in the glove compartment, behind the sun visors, under the seats. I felt a tug on my hand, looked at Max and he shook his head to indicate the car was already clean. Good. The war-wagon moved over the potholes like a rusty tank—the gang kids didn't maintain their cars, just their guns.

We found the block where the gunrunners would be waiting and Max drove carefully up to them—in his world, the insult Gunther had given demanded revenge. I couldn't explain to him that in their world there was no such thing as an insult, just profit and loss. James and Gunther were standing where they were supposed to be. I opened the front door, let them have a look at me. They climbed into the backseat without a word and the war-wagon rolled toward the Hudson River. We were silent in the car—Gunther and James because they were acting like they were afraid of microphones, me because I had nothing to say to them.

When we got to the pier Max pulled the Buick in, turning it so it was parallel to the river about twenty feet from the pier's end. The place was deserted. Gunther and James followed me out of the car. I reached in my pocket for a smoke, watching their faces. They didn't react. They were relaxed—greedy, not frightened. Good.

"You said you had a proposition for us?" James opened.

"Yes."

"Is this a good place to talk?"

"Why not?"

"What if someone comes by?"

I looked over to where Max was standing by the Buick, arms folded across his chest. They got the message.

"Here's the deal," I said. "I'll be honest with you. I need some of the guns for myself, okay? And I need some men, about twenty experienced men who want to make some money. Short-term work."

"Out of the country?"

"What difference does it make?"

"It's just if you need them to go international there are items like obtaining good passports—"

"I see you know your business. Ever done any spot-recruiting?"

"Some, in London. Maybe we had the same client?"

"If so he wouldn't want us to discuss it, right?"

"Right. You said a proposition?"

"I need two hundred full-auto long arms, preferably AR–16s, but I'll take anything close. Only in 5.56 caliber, nothing bigger. A thousand rounds for each piece. And a bunch of other field supplies I could buy right here with no trouble, but I'll let you handle it all if we can make it a package."

"Like flak jackets, helmets, standard ordinance?"

"Yeah, and some fragmentation grenades, some plastique—"

"You can't buy that stuff here."

"*Who* can't?"

"All right, we won't argue. You'd pay cash?"

"On delivery."

"To . . . ?"

"London's okay."

"Maybe to you it is—not to us. With all the IRA business, you can't move a bloody thing in London. No good."

"Two more choices, that's it. Either Lisbon or Tel Aviv."

"Lisbon's okay—the kikes have the right idea on South Africa but I don't like working with them, can't trust 'em."

"Lisbon it is. You know the airport setup? The old Biafra runway?"

"I heard about it but I've never done it."

"I'll get you the papers," I said, watching his eyes gleam and then quickly go flat again. Greedy bastard.

"What's the timetable?"

"You get me the men lined up first, and I want the stuff ready to roll within three weeks from then. Okay?"

"The stuff's no problem. But we're not set up to do recruiting here. That takes time—"

"Look, I told you I had a proposition. I know a perfect place you can rent, and I can use my connections to get you enough publicity so every merc in the area will be knocking down your doors. You stay open one week, no more. If you don't have the twenty men by then I'll pay you so much a head, take the string, and pick up the guns later. Deal?"

"How much a head? And who fronts for the office?"

"A grand a head," I told him, "plus a five-grand bonus if you find me any of three guys I'm looking for. Specialists."

"And the office?"

"You pay for everything and I'll handle the publicity. But I'll throw two grand up front for the first two guys, and if you don't get me the full twenty I'll do the original deal on the guns, hold my string, and call you when I've got all the men together."

"That's twelve thousand all together—ten for the guns, like we agreed, and another two for the men—"

"That's *two* thousand *up front*. I'm trusting *you*, right? For two grand—for two men. I haven't *seen* any guns, right? I'm supposed to get a Bill of Lading, F.O.B., like we said. When I get that . . ."

"Agreed," said James, reaching out his hand for me to shake while Gunther did his best to repress a grin at my stupidity.

The rest of the transaction didn't take long. I gave them the address of the office building where they could set up, asked them what name they used for their outfit, and promised to have all the printing done by the next day. Before I handed over the two grand we had a nice professional discussion about the specific men I wanted them to recruit for my big operation.

"I need an explosives expert, a night sniper, and a martial arts man," I told them. "I want real professionals too, not some guys who took a course someplace. We pay the going rate, two grand up front per man sign-up bonus, payable on arrival overseas to any bank they want, or just cash in their hands. Okay?"

"You said you had specific individuals?"

"Yeah, but no square names, just handles, right? The explosives guy calls himself Mr. Kraus. A tall, German-looking dude, wears steel-rimmed glasses, brush-cut, very clean-looking. He's worked Africa before—he knows the story. If he hears about you, he'll sign right up. The sniper, all I know about him is the name Blackie. Ex-Marine, did two hitches in 'Nam. I heard he had some trouble with ATF so he may be hard to find, but I think he'd like a vacation for a while. And the karate guy calls himself the Cobra."

I threw in Wilson's complete description, but not his right name. I wasn't worried about paying the five Gs bonus on any of the other guys—they didn't exist. And if they turned up the Cobra, he'd be worth the two grand I was fronting them.

When I handed over the money, James wanted to shake hands again. Gunther didn't move, keeping his eye on Max all the time, looking at his back. That's as close as he'd come.

"I'll meet you at the new office tomorrow afternoon, say around two, okay? I may have some more info for you by then, and I'll have all the printing done for sure. We run this thing for one week, maybe two at the most. Then we close the deal with whatever you have by then, okay?"

"Right," said James. Gunther still wasn't talking. Under other circumstances I would have been happy to leave them on the pier to find their own way home, but I loaded them back in the Buick and we drove them back to their personal pay phone. Gunther kept on staring at Max like he was going to twist his head off his spinal column. I watched Max's hands on the steering wheel—they looked like old, cracked leather stuffed full of steel pebbles. They were very still.

On the way back to the warehouse Max made a fist of his right hand, squeezing it tighter and tighter as I watched. Then he looked at the top of his closed fist like something slimy was oozing out, scraped it away with his other hand, and made a throwing-away gesture. Yes. I told him, that was the idea— put enough pressure on the Cobra and he'd ooze out like pus from a wound.

Back at the warehouse I got into the Plymouth and Max and I went off to do our separate work. While I drove over to one of my cold pay phones to keep the pressure on, Max would be meeting with the Blood Shadows and giving them their instructions and equipment.

I got to the phone, set up the machinery to meet with Pablo's people, caught the second call, and made delivery of the posters. Pablo agreed to handle the distribution. I gave him as many details as I reasonably could about Goldor's death without mentioning Flood, explaining that it was unavoidable. I told him I'd thought about leaving some sort of UGL calling card in Goldor's house but decided it was better not to—he said that I'd done right. I knew that—I'd never really thought about doing anything but getting the hell out of there, but I didn't want him to think I'd been ungrateful for the information and the trust it implied.

I left Pablo and found another phone. From there a previously reliable informant told a certain DEA agent that a man precisely answering the Cobra's description was going to be moving some major narcotics through either Kennedy or LaGuardia Airport in the next week or two. They'd listen— the last tip from this informant had netted them fifteen kilos of high-grade cocaine on the way in from Peru.

I checked my watch—just enough time to hit Times Square, make the last phone call of the night, and watch the Blood Shadows at work. I found a booth near Ninth Avenue and Forty-second Street, just around the corner from the national head-quarters of SAVE (Sisterhood Against Vice and Enslavement).

I told the young lady answering the phone that a very bad thing would happen to each and every member of that orga-nization if they didn't shut their mouths about all this kiddie-porn nonsense. The young woman gave the phone to their executive director, and I ended up threatening her with hideous mutilation if she didn't get off my motherfucking case. When she calmly asked, "Who is calling, please?" I told her, "The Cobra, you fuckin' cunt," and slammed down the phone.

Still holding down the hook, I unscrewed the mouthpiece and removed the encoder disc the Mole had made for me. It didn't so much disguise my voice as make it impossible to voice-print. I had a few of the discs, but there was no harm in using the same one for the SAVE people as I used for the DEA—no reason why a drug informant couldn't be a child molester too.

I was walking toward my car just as two of the war-wagons rolled past me and slammed to a halt. All the doors opened at the same time, discharging a cold-eyed cargo. The young Chinese marched down the wide street in military formation, looking straight ahead. They walked in silence—nobody barred their way. Their leader saw a porno shop on his left, pivoted on his heel, and entered. His men followed at his back. I knew what would be happening inside—the leader would engage the man at the desk in some polite conversation (like, "You don't move, please," punctuated with a 9-mm automatic leveled at the clerk's face), and the rest of the army would fan out through the shop. They would find an appropriate space on a wall, slap on the stencil we'd made up, take out a can of the spray paint and do their work. When they pulled off the stencil, the wall would say COBRA BE WARNED! THE MONGOOSE IS COMING! Then they would walk out—nobody would call the

cops, and if someone did a petty vandalism arrest with a guarantee that no complaining witness would ever come to court
wouldn't bother these boys. I could just see Blumberg defend-
ing this one on the ground that the Blood Shadows were en-
gaged in some citywide anti-porn campaign.

It would take the army less than an hour to cover the whole
area, then they would vanish. I'd given Max three hundred for
the job to cover expenses in case the kids asked—but I didn't
think they would.

I had a couple more things to do before I rested for the
night. First, another stop at the printer's to make up the stationery and business cards for James and Gunther, who'd decided to call themselves Falcon Enterprises—white paper, green
ink. While I was there I used the machine and made up a plastic
sign for their office door too. Nothing but first class all the
way.

By then it was almost ten-thirty so I headed toward the
Village. I had seen a meeting of the Boundaries Society ad-
vertised in one of the local slime sheets. The topic for the
night's meeting was Inter-Generational Sex, the new euphemism for child molesting. I had been to one of those meetings
before—all about how early sexualization prepares a child for
the realities of modern living. Most of the audience had been
male, some of them with their "wards." It was a long shot that
the Cobra would show up to greet his brothers, but still, a shot
worth playing.

When I got there the guardian of the front door said "No
police," and I looked around like I was frightened at the very
word but it was no go—I wasn't getting inside without a major
beef.

I decided it probably wasn't worth the hassle, but I still had
a job to do so I sat in the Plymouth listening to Judy Henske
for another two hours until the meeting disgorged its vermin
into the streets. I watched each face carefully. No Cobra.

It was almost one in the morning by the time I nosed the
Plymouth out of its parking space and headed for Flood.

46

I LET MYSELF into Flood's place, working the downstairs locks with my set of picks. It took about a minute—a very secure setup. I moved up the stairs, checking for feedback visually, then closed my eyes, regulated my breathing, and rechecked on audio. Nothing. I rapped on Flood's studio door with two gloved knuckles. No response—at least she wasn't a total idiot. I knew she'd be near the door so I called out, "It's me, Flood" just loud enough for her to hear and the door swung open into a darkened room. I turned as it closed behind me and caught a flash of Max's black robes. The light was dim inside, but I knew my way and I walked around the taped-off section of the floor over to Flood's private place. She was right behind me.

"That lock downstairs is a joke, Flood. Any halfass could work his way through in a couple of minutes."

"So how long did it take you?" sweet Flood replied.

"Don't be snappy, babe. When you spook a weasel out of his hole, he bites. If Wilson gets wise, he's coming for you."

"I wish he would. I'm sick of this . . . this hunting. If I knew where he was he wouldn't *have* to come for me."

"That's not the point, damn it. If someone can get in one door they can get in another."

"We're not trained to protect property, Burke. We aren't guard dogs. We protect ourselves, a small circle around ourselves. If anyone comes into that circle, locks or doors won't matter."

"And you were waiting inside the door to this place?"

"Oh, yes."

"So if he raps and raps on the door and you don't answer, you just let him walk away?"

"No. If he didn't try and work his way through the door I would answer him—I would sound scared, encourage him to force his way in and—"

"And be ready for him?"

"Yes."

"That door's made of wood, nothing but bullshit veneer over soft pine."

"So?"

"So a twelve-gauge blasts it right off the hinges. That's one barrel—the second would be for you."

"Maybe."

"Go ahead, Flood, pout some more—a perfect little baby you are. *Maybe*. Isn't that fucking cute. I told you before, when we find this freak, you can have your duel, okay? Until then, you just be a good soldier and follow orders."

"I'm not a soldier."

"You are in *this* army. Be glad you're a soldier—there's worse things."

"Maybe being afraid is a worse thing."

"Get off that train, Flood. It's going nowhere. Being afraid is a good thing, a smartening thing. You're not afraid, great—but that's not smart. We don't have *time* now, you understand? We're close to him."

"How do you know?"

"I know. That's my work, that's how I keep doing my work. He's out there and he's close."

She came over to where I was sitting on the floor. She sat down, put her hand on my shoulder, and looked into my face.

"Burke, I want to *do* something. I'm sorry—I have most of my training but I don't have the patience—not yet. When this is over I'll work on it, I promise. But let me *do* something with you on this. I can do some things—I helped you so far, didn't I?"

I didn't mention how she had helped with Goldor—what was the point?

"There's something you can do," I told her. "An acting job on the phone. It has to be done in a couple of hours, and we have to find a pay phone to do it from, okay?"

"Okay," she answered, brightening a bit.

"I'll go over it with you until you get it right—we won't get a second chance."

"And it will help bring him to us?"

"Look at the wall, Flood. You see it? Don't glare at me like that—*look* at it. Okay, now draw a square on the wall with your mind—a white square—the whole border is made up of tiny pieces of tile, all different colors, dark shades. Okay?"

A short pause from Flood, then, "Yes, I see it."

"We are going to make a mosaic, you and me. We're going to keep filling in the square, working from the corners in until the whole thing is tiled over, yes?"

"Yes," she said, concentrating.

"But no white tiles, all right? Only the last tiny little tile is white. That's him—that's the Cobra—and *his* tile doesn't go down until all the other tiles are on the board. That's the way it works. He sits outside the board holding his one white tile, deciding where to put it, running out of space. But our tiles keep coming down and the more he waits, the less space he has. He won't put it down until there's no other space."

"Maybe he won't put it down at all."

"He *has* to put it down. He's floating in the air above the board, Flood—he has to come down—the board is his whole world. There's no other place for him to go."

"If we just work from the corners in . . . if we work according to a set pattern, well . . . won't he know what we're doing?"

"Not for a while. And when he does see it, when he sees the walls coming in on him, he may put his tile down fast, make his move while he still thinks he has *some* choices left."

Flood looked at the wall, speaking in a faraway voice. "Yes . . . and if he puts his tile down while he still has some room . . . that's what you meant about him coming here?"

"Yes, baby," I said quietly.

"I understand. And the phone call you want me to make . . . ?"

"Another couple of tiles on the board."

"Let's do it, Burke," she said, turning to me with a chilling smile on her beautiful face—and we started the rehearsals together.

47

IT WAS ALMOST four-thirty in the morning by the time Flood and I finished our work. We left her place after the rehearsal and went to my office, let Pansy out on the roof, and gathered up some equipment. Then back into the Plymouth and over to the warehouse. I took Flood's hand and led her to the back, where I plugged in the phone set. I wasn't so much worried about a trace on the call, but we needed a private space to work and I didn't want some nosy citizen blundering into a pay phone at that hour. Or a cop.

I made the connections and switched on the microcassette to check the twin speakers for feedback. The setup worked perfectly, sounds of a nightclub at closing time filled the little room—glasses clinking, loud stupid-drunk voices, tinny disco music, a wall of noise. I played with the volume and equalizer controls until it sounded just right, slipped the encoder disc into the mouthpiece of the field phone, and punched in the number, handing the instrument to Flood.

We heard the phone being picked up on the third ring. "FBI. Special Agent Haskell speaking. May I help you?"

And Flood's voice came on, sounding cigarette-raspy and scared at the same time. "Is this the FBI?"

"Yes, ma'am, how can we help you?"

"I work at Fantasia, you know, in Times Square?"

"Yes, ma'am. And your name is?"

"My name is . . . no—wait! Just listen, okay? I'm not going to tell you that. There's a guy that was in here tonight. He was drinking, but not too much, right? But he was fucked

up, you know? His eyes were crazy—not like they usually get
here when they see the girls, *real* crazy. And he was talking
to himself. People would sit down near him and then they
would just get up and move away."

"Yes, ma'am."

"And . . . we have to . . . like, sit with the customers,
you know? It's the job. So he grabbed me and he wouldn't let
me get up. He told me that President Reagan was a miserable
traitor, you know? A Commie ass-kisser. He said Reagan promised he was going to invade Cuba and recognize South Africa
and all kinds of stuff I didn't understand."

"Yes, ma'am," said the agent again, but the twin speakers
finally revealed an undercurrent of interest in his voice. "Could
you describe this individual, please?"

Flood gave him a detailed description of Wilson, talking
fast and breathy—we knew the feds would be recording the
call. Then she hit him with the clincher. "And I'm calling you
because he said he's going to kill the president. He said people
wouldn't listen to anything else. And he has a *gun*. I saw it—
a big black gun—and he has this book, like a notebook, you
know? He said he works for the CIA and he's on a secret
mission to educate America."

Silence from the agent, but you could feel him willing Flood
to go on, not wanting to break the flow of her words. "I'm so
scared," said Flood, "he knows my name—he asked me if I
was a loyal American. I was scared to call the CIA because,
like . . . maybe he was telling the truth. Is he? I mean, do
you know . . . ?"

"No, ma'am." His voice was tense but controlled now. "We
know of no such individual as you describe. Did he tell you
his name?"

"He said I should call him the Cobra, like the snake on the
flag, whatever *that* means."

"Yes, ma'am. We would like to have an agent come and
speak with you. Are you still at your place of business?"

"Yes—I mean, no! I mean, I'm leaving now . . . I'm leaving. I just wanted to tell you because I think he really means
it, you know?"

"Yes, ma'am, we appreciate your call. Now if we can
just—"

But Flood was already hanging up. I disconnected all the
equipment, shut off the tape, and went back to the Plymouth.

We drove over to Forty-second Street, but on the East Side. I wanted to drop off a new ad for the *Daily News,* complete with money order. If things went as planned it would run tomorrow: COBRA! I UNDERSTAND AND I CAN HELP YOU WITH YOUR PROBLEM. PLEASE CALL . . . and then there would be a phone number. Whoever dialed that number would hear the phone answered with "Major Felony Squad, Detective So-and-So speaking," and I didn't think the conversation would go on long after that. But its effect would linger.

48

I NEEDED TO go to the Bronx to see the Mole, and I also needed Michelle to work this last bit. I figured I'd ask her to go along for the ride—Flood would have made the mixture too tricky. I told her we wouldn't be rolling until tomorrow, to get some sleep and be ready. I dropped her off and turned back down toward the docks.

For once I was running in some luck. I spotted Michelle daintily hoisting herself out of the front seat of a dark Chrysler sedan. I watched from a distance as she waved good-bye to whoever was inside, then I nosed the Plymouth slowly over to where she was standing.

She was fumbling in her huge pocketbook for something when I pulled alongside. She recognized the car, opened the door for herself, and climbed in next to me. I pulled away without saying a word.

Finally she extracted a tiny bottle full of some dark liquid from her purse, took a deep pull, swished the stuff around in her mouth, and rolled down the window to spit it into the night.

"Want some, baby?"

"No thanks. What is it . . . mouthwash?"

"Don't be so vulgar, Burke. It's cognac."

"I'll pass. You want to work tonight?"

"Baby, I *am* working—I just spit my last job out of your window."

"Something *else*, okay?" Sometimes I hate what she does to make a buck.

"Don't you snap at me, Burke. You're not my fucking parole officer."

"I'm sorry, you're right. I'm your friend, okay? And I'm taking you to see another friend."

"Who?" Still not mollified.

"The Mole."

"Oh, the poor child still can't call up and make his own dates?"

"Michelle, give me a break. We need to set up another office. I need Mole for the electronics and you for the phones."

"This has something to do with the job for Margot?"

"I hope you heard about that from Margot herself."

"Why?"

"Because otherwise the individual involved may know more than he should."

"Oh, Dandy knows from *nothing,* dear, but the Prophet's been doing his Armageddon number so I trust whatever's coming down will be here soon."

"As soon as I find this freak."

"Just you and me on this job?"

"And the Mole."

"Oh goodie. I *love* the Mole."

"Michelle, listen—don't drive the poor bastard any crazier than he already is, okay?"

"Can I help it if I'm attracted to intellectuals? After all, it's rare enough that a woman of my accomplishments can have a decent conversation with her peers."

"You know what I'm talking about."

"I'll be good," she promised with an evil smile.

We motored along sedately until we crossed the line to the Bronx. I found a working pay phone, reached the Mole, and set up a meet near the junkyard. I didn't want to bring Michelle inside—I was afraid she'd insist on some major interior decorating.

We sat there waiting. It was a quiet night, except for the occasional howling of a dog or a police siren.

"I'm on a dead fucking blank, Michelle. He *was* here, somewhere in the cesspool, but he's gone. I'm not going to find him now—he's got to come to me."

"You have to play the cards they deal you, baby."

"Who says so?"

"The Dealer," said Michelle. And she was right.

The Mole materialized now at the side of the car. I rolled down the window all the way.

"Mole, I need some work done in an office building—phones, lights, stuff like that."

"So?"

"So I need it tomorrow. In Moscow's building—the little place upstairs, okay?"

Before he could answer, Michelle draped herself halfway across my lap and fixed her luminous eyes on her target. "Well, Mole, don't say hello or anything!"

"Michelle—" was all the Mole got out before she was off and running.

"Now, Mole, it's not polite to just ignore people. Especially your friends."

"I didn't see you—"

"Mole, *please*. It is common knowledge that you can see in the dark. You wear some clean overalls tomorrow—I don't want you tracking mud all over my . . ."

I elbowed Michelle sufficiently to get her back on her side of the car, shrugged what-can-you-do? to the Mole, who just said, "Tomorrow morning," and disappeared.

Michelle pouted for a few minutes on the way back, then started to giggle. The Mole has that effect on her. We made all the arrangements and I said I'd pick her up tomorrow.

Usually I don't dream. That night I dreamt of a leering lunatic standing over a fiery pit, throwing in one child after another. I knew somehow that when enough kids hit the bottom of the pit, it would reach critical mass and explode in his face. But I woke up before that happened.

49

WE GOT TO the new office around ten in the morning. I had already called Moscow the landlord and confirmed that the clowns had paid him a month's rent in front for the two-room suite on the fourteenth floor. As soon as I heard that I sent Max over to see Moscow with the additional two hundred for the little room just above the suite. Two hundred for two weeks—that was the going rate with Moscow for the setup. He periodically rents the two-room suite on the fourteenth to one group after another. He has a long list of clients—I was just one of the list. When the wiseguys pull one of their bust-out deals on a garment center manufacturer or a restaurant they rent the suite as a front and take the little room right above it to have a place to go if things get ugly. And when some dingbat radicals decide to establish a new international headquarters, Moscow rents the little room upstairs to the *federales* so they can eavesdrop in peace and quiet. The little room upstairs isn't much bigger than a closet, but it has an attached bathroom and decent ventilation. You can be comfortable up there for days at a time—I know.

Michelle and I took the stairs to the top—she bitched all the way about climbing in spike heels. I set her up in the little room and told her just to wait and be cool. She opened her makeup case, took out a clutch of Gothic novels, and sat down without another word. I took the stairs back down to the unattended lobby, checked the directory but couldn't find Falcon Enterprises. Carrying my suitcase, I took the elevator to the fourteenth floor, knocked, heard "Come on in" from James, who was at the desk in the front room—I heard Gunther rooting around in the back. Nice-looking setup, all right—a battered wood desk with an old wood swivel chair for the front, a long table on shaky legs with two more wooden chairs in the back, linoleum floors, bare whitewashed walls, two windows in the back room that hadn't been opened since the Dodgers deserted Brooklyn. Moscow wasn't selling decor.

I shook hands with James. "I brought you some stuff," I said, opening the suitcase. He looked on happily as I brought out the letterhead stationery complete with cable address, envelopes, business cards, desk calendar, assorted legal pads, and ballpoint pens. Then I took out the Rhodesian army recruiting poster, and a black-and-white line-drawing of a soldier with his foot firmly planted on a mound of dead enemies. The soldier was holding a rifle in one hand and a grenade in the other. The poster said: "Communism Stops Here!" A couple of large maps of Africa completed the decorations, and we sat down to have a smoke. Comrades in arms.

Gunther strolled in, gave me what was meant to be a chilling look once he saw Max was not on the set. He grunted as he looked over my supplies but his eyes lit up when he saw the business cards. He immediately stuffed a bunch in his pocket—legitimate at last. I sat in the swivel chair, put my feet on the desk. "My man will be here in a while. He's got an in with the phone company so you won't have to wait for an installation. You give him a yard and by the time you get the first month's bill you'll be gone."

It was okay by him—they were still playing with my money.

Both were in excellent spirits, smiling between themselves. You could see the idea of a real office and a front appealed to them. James was walking around the place, scratching his chin like he was deep in thought. "It's going to work—work very well indeed, I can see that. But you know . . . it lacks something, some touch that would indicate the scope of our operation. Our dedication to purpose, so to speak."

Before I could say anything Gunther smiled and pulled out a matte-black combat knife—the kind where the handle is a set of brass knuckles so you can break bones or tear flesh. He stared at my face, and I could see he was still hurting from what we did to him in the warehouse. He walked over to the desk where I was sitting and slammed the knife into the top so hard the whole thing jumped. He slowly removed his hand, watching me all the while, the knife stuck halfway into the desktop.

James said, "Yes, exactly. Just the right touch."

Gunther glared over at me. "You said something about publicity?" He made it sound like a threat, and stalked off into the back room. Gunther was as tough to read as yesterday's race results.

"Is he okay?" I asked James, just loud enough for Gunther to hear.

"Oh, he's fine, Mr. Burke. Just nerves. Gunther's more a man of action, you might say. I'll handle the recruiting."

"Okay . . ." Like I really gave a damn. There was a soft knock at the door and the Mole entered, wearing his Ma Bell uniform, carrying a toolbox and sporting a giant leather belt around his waist full of enough gadgets to perform brain surgery on a rhino. Not on Gunther, though—the Mole didn't carry a microscope.

Without a word to anyone the Mole walked the length of the front room, his eyes blinking rapidly behind the thick lenses. He squatted down, pulled a couple of push-button phones out of his toolbox, and went to work. He put the white phone on James's desk and went back to put the red one on the long table. Gunther gave him a fearsome stare and expanded his chest—the Mole never changed expression, just went on with his wiring job. The whole number took him about ten minutes, after which he walked over to James and extended one damp, plump white hand, palm up. James seemed to be thinking it over for a split-second, then reached in his wallet, pulled out a hundred, and handed it over. The Mole turned and exited.

James looked over at me. "Your man's not much of a conversationalist, is he?"

"Try the phones," I suggested.

James sat down at his desk, hit 411, asked the operator for the number of the Waldorf-Astoria, got the number, dialed the Waldorf, made reservations for two in a suite for one week from then. I guess he expected his ship to come in.

I got up to leave. "You'll be hearing from this reporter I told you about. That should give you all the publicity you'll ever need. Call me at this number," I said, handing him a card, "and I'll be back in touch with you within one hour no matter what time you make contact, okay?"

"Certainly," said James, extending his hand. I shook it,

waved at Gunther, who glowered back, and walked out to the elevator.

A few minutes later I was climbing the stairs to Michelle's little room. As I got to the top step I saw the Mole standing in a corner, watching and waiting—even with his pasty skin you had to look twice to see him sometimes, he was so motionless. I waved him on and we went into the little room. Michelle was facing the door—she looked up from her book when she saw me and really flashed to life when she saw I wasn't alone.

"Mole, baby! How's things in the underground?"

The Mole blinked a few more times than usual, gave Michelle his best try at a smile, but said nothing, as usual. He began to empty out his toolbox with the sure movements of a professional. He didn't need to check out the room, he had worked this place before. Out of the toolbox came a square metal rig with all kinds of toggle switches on its face as well as two little lights, one red and one green. He plugged in a phone mouthpiece and receiver, then ran some wires over to a little box that looked like the face of a pocket calculator. He opened up the mouthpiece, screwed in one of the supressor discs, ran some wires over to the wall, snapped in some other piece of equipment, touched two wires together, took a reading, opened a tripod with a flat top, and put the phone unit on top of that. All the time he was working, Michelle watched him with hawk's eyes.

The Mole pulled out two more phone sets, plugged them into the major unit, and ran some more wires toward the back wall. All this took him the better part of a half hour. Michelle and I didn't say a word—this was complicated work and we knew the Mole didn't like kibitzers. He moved with assurance and grace—no microsurgeon could have been better with his hands. When he finished he played with the setup for a couple of minutes, wearing his rubber gloves, then finally turned to us. "When the red light is on you make no calls. Green light, it's okay to use. The left phone picks up downstairs. The next phone is incoming to you from all the numbers you gave me. You dial out only with this box."

"Thanks, Mole," I said, slipping him his money, which disappeared someplace into his uniform.

As the Mole turned to go Michelle said, "Mole," making

him turn to face her. "Mole, you remember I asked you to find out about that operation? The one for me?"

The Mole nodded, blinking behind his glasses.

"Would it work, Mole? Would it be what I want?"

The Mole spoke like he was reading from a book. "The operation is for true transsexuals—only for transsexuals. Biologically it would work. Assuming competent surgery and proper postoperative care, the only associated problems are psychological."

"You know what a transsexual is, Mole?" Michelle asked him.

"Yes."

"What?" demanded Michelle, looking intently at him. For her, I wasn't in the room anymore.

"A woman trapped inside a man's body," said the Mole.

"Do you understand that?" asked Michelle.

"I understand trapped," said the Mole, not blinking so much now.

"Thank you, Mole," said Michelle, getting up and kissing him on the cheek. I thought the Mole blushed, but I couldn't be sure. He faded out the door and was gone.

Michelle sat there for a long time, tapping her long fingernails on the cover of her compact. I lit a cigarette, smoked in silence. A tear gathered in the corner of her eye and rolled down her face, leaving its track against the soft skin. I lit another cigarette, handed it to her. She took it, held it absently for a minute, gave me a half-smile and pulled in a deep drag. She exhaled, shook herself. "I'm going to fix my face," she said, and went into the bathroom.

It was another couple of smokes before she walked out— fresh, new, and hard again.

"Let's go to work, baby," she said, and sat down in front of the bank of phones.

I called the preppie reporter, told him I had located the mercenary recruiting outfit but my info was that they would only be there for another day or so and he said he'd move on it that afternoon. He thanked me for the tip, said he would make it up to me.

Then I called the ATF—that's Alcohol, Tobacco, and Firearms, with heavy emphasis on the last—and told them I couldn't give my name but a guy answering Wilson's description was making the rounds of the after-hours joints offering a half-dozen .45-caliber machine guns, complete with silencers, for immediate sale. When I said "silencers" I could just feel the excitement build on the line—a silencer bust to the ATF boys is like ten pounds of pure heroin to the narcotics cops. They kept pressuring me until I finally told them, "Look, I said all I'm going to. This is a *bad* fucking guy, he's nobody to play with. You know who he is—the Cobra, right? He said he's dealt with you all before."

I broke the connection and headed to the restaurant, where I found Mama in the kitchen.

"Max here twice already. He come back soon, okay?"

"Okay, Mama. Thanks."

"You want some soup?" came the inevitable question.

"Sure."

I sat down, the waiter came and Mama and I had some soup and hard noodles, eating in silence, thinking our thoughts.

Max floated in from the back before we were finished. He bowed to Mama, who bowed back. Mama offered him some soup. Max shook his head no—Mama insisted, grabbed his shoulder, and pushed him into the booth. A faint smile twitched over Max's face as he submitted.

Max showed me the racing form and I shook my head to tell him I was under pressure. I made the sign of squeezing a wound—gritted my teeth to show I was putting on all the pressure I could, clenched my fist. Max understood.

I showed him my watch, moved my fingers to indicate seven o'clock, then showed him the Cobra's picture, shaded my eyes like I was looking into the sun, twisting my head from side to side. I made a want-to-come-along? gesture.

Max reached his hand behind his back, slapped himself hard—he wasn't interested in hunting the freak, but he would come along to watch my back. Okay. I tapped my heart to thank him—he did the same to say we were brothers and it was expected of him, no big deal.

I said I would pick him up later at the warehouse, but for now I needed some sleep. In the movies tough guys never sleep. Maybe Flood was right, I wasn't so tough.

50

BACK AT THE office I took care of Pansy by opening the back door and she took care of her business topside. The phone was still open and I called Flood. Told her nothing would be happening until tomorrow and I wouldn't be able to see her until then. Then I called Michelle, saying I'd stop by much later to bring her some food and spell her at the phones.

"Burke," she said, "the cub reporter made his move downstairs."

"Sound like he knew what he was doing?"

"Not hardly."

"That's my man. I'll call in later on, okay?"

"Okay, baby. Not to worry, everything's fine here."

I couldn't get to sleep, so I deliberately overloaded my brain, knowing I could force it to kick out and spin into overdrive that way. I loaded it with names, places, pictures, faces, schemes, plans, tricks, hoaxes. I used to try this in prison but it never worked there. In prison the world is narrow and you can hold all the information you need to survive in a small part of your brain. Out here it's different. I've tried to make my world as small as possible, but every once in a while someone like Flood comes along to screw it up. Soon I felt my eyes close and the room go away . . . When I woke up a few hours later I didn't feel any better but I knew the sleep would help me later. I dressed slowly, loading up with a bunch of bullshit private-eye gear. If we got popped by the police tonight I'd tell some story about working on a case for the father of the kid I'd delivered to McGowan. He'd back me up on anything less than a felony-in-progress charge. He's done it before.

Max was waiting just inside the warehouse. I showed him the picture of the Cobra again and he nodded to show it was already in his memory bank. Max wasn't so good with faces (did all us Occidentals really look alike?), but once he saw a man move he could pick him out of a crowd at fifty yards.

It was dark by the time we turned the Plymouth toward Times Square. Where else to look for a freak with no address? We cruised Eighth Avenue, from the upper thirties to the fifties. The cold neon flashed on and off across Max's face, his eyes hooded against the street's night glare, with the sun-shield Lexan film on the inside of the windows, you'd need X-ray vision to see inside the Plymouth. That kind of stuff is illegal on the Coast but it's okay here in New York. Cops hate it. It makes it hard for them to claim that the pistol (or bag of dope, or human head, or whatever) was in "plain view" when they stopped the car for a broken taillight.

We didn't expect to spot Wilson just bopping down the street. He was moving now—out of his hole and running hard. But I already had the government to watching the airports and the bus stations for me. I had to do something, at least be in motion.

Garbage floated all around the cruising Plymouth—teenage girls working the streets with their built-up shoes and their broken-down spirits; the younger ones, the children who hadn't had their first periods yet, they worked the inside—the massage parlors and the hotels. The older ones worked the bars and the clubs. Even the pit has its own sense of order—rough-off teams stalking the sidewalks and lurking near the corners, looking for an excuse to take a wallet or a life; gaudy pimpmobiles parked all around the Port Authority Bus Terminal, dumb iron horses that ate human flesh, waiting for the pilot fish in their zircon rings and fake-fur hats to bring them new little girls; the videogame parlors with their load of little boys waiting for the chicken hawks to come calling. Those little boys were just for rent—if you wanted to buy one for keeps you had to see a man in a brownstone office and pay heavy cash. No deposit, no return. Very little heroin for sale down here; uptown's the stop for that stuff. But the streets were full of dirtbags in long filthy overcoats selling their methadone from the nearby clinic, and young hustlers were hawking 'ludes and speed everywhere.

If you knew where to go, you could buy genuine prescriptions for Valium, or Percodan, or whatever travel ticket you wanted. The gold-buying shops stayed open late to accommodate the chain-snatchers. The gleaming windows of the electronics stores displayed giant portable stereos, the better to achieve self-induced retardation. And in the back rooms the same joints sold gravity knives and fake pistols to smooth the passage of the stereos from the retardates to the muggers. There were theatrical supply houses that would sell you all the goodies you'd need to disguise yourself if you were into armed robbery or rape. And little shops that sold "marital aids" that looked like tools for felonious assault. Bookstores sold crash-courses in achieving orgasm through torture, and films—documentary proof of things that shouldn't exist.

When I was a little kid I once saw a bunch of men get together on the street in Little Italy. There was this vacant lot with all kinds of old rotting stuff in it, and rats were living there right out in the open. One of them had bitten a kid. The men surrounded the lot and poured gasoline all over the place and then set it on fire. When the rats poured out, the waiting men formed a line and tried to hammer them all to death with baseball bats. They killed a lot of them but a lot more got away. One poor bastard hadn't been prepared—he hadn't dressed for the part. A shrieking rat ran up his pants leg and tried to rip its way to freedom with its teeth. When they finally pulled off the guy's pants there was only blood where his testicles should have been. If they ever started one of those fires down here it'd be worse than what happened to that poor guy.

No point in staying in the background any longer—too many people could catch wise by now anyway. Max and I hit the street with the Cobra's picture at the ready, without much real hope, but we had to give it a try. Who knew?

The street didn't look any better close up than it had from behind the car windows. Max and I stood near the corner watching the flow, me thinking of our next move, Max indifferent. I scanned the length of the block—the only living thing doing legitimate work was a seeing-eye dog that had no way of knowing his owner had 20/20 vision and a few dozen pills for sale in his tattered pockets.

I picked a dive at random. The side of beef at the door was wearing a skin-tight red muscle shirt under a pair of thick black suspenders and carrying a flashlight that did double duty as a night stick. He held out a beefy palm, and I gave him twenty to cover admission for Max and me. We found a table in the smoke-clogged darkness a few feet away from the long bar on which two tired-looking girls exposed themselves to music. It was about as sexy as a visit to the morgue, and nowhere near as clean.

The waitress took one look at us, saw we weren't citizens, threw us the single obligatory shake of the silicone, and brought us the two lukewarm Cokes that came with the cover charge we'd paid at the door. The joint was useless—the Cobra could be sitting ten feet away and we wouldn't spot him. I took out the picture, held it so the waitress would see it was something she was supposed to notice. She pretended to take a close look.

"Seen him recently?"

"Never saw him before, honey." A waste of time.

Max and I got up to leave. We approached the side of beef and I took out the picture again and held it up. "You know this guy?"

"Maybe," meaning, what's in it for me?

"Maybe yes, or maybe no?"

"Just plain maybe, pal. We don't like private cops asking questions in here."

"Look, my friend has something to give this guy, okay? Maybe he could just give it to you instead."

"You ain't giving me nothin'," he snarled. Max grabbed one of his hyperflexed biceps like he was feeling the muscle. The beef's face shifted color under the greasy lights, his hand went toward his back pocket . . . until he looked at Max's face and thought better of it.

"Hey, what is this? I don't know the fuckin' guy, all right? Lemme *go*."

I could see it was no use and signaled to Max. We walked out the door leaving the beef rubbing his bicep and muttering to himself.

We checked a couple of porno shops, admired the MON-GOOSE stenciling of the Blood Shadows, drew nothing but more blanks.

Over on Forty-fourth we ran into McGowan. He flashed his Irish grin, but his partner hung back, wary. A new guy.

"Burke, how's it going? And Max?"

I said, "Okay," and Max bowed. I showed McGowan the picture but he shook his head.

"Seen the Prof?" I asked the detective.

"He's around. I heard he had some trouble with a pimp, got slapped around a bit . . ."

"Yeah," I said, "I heard that too."

McGowan just nodded. He just wanted to be sure I had the information—whatever happened to a pimp wouldn't cost him any sleep.

Another two hours on the street and we could see we weren't going to score. We found the Plymouth, rolled over to the Village, checked a few of the leather bars, even the one that specialized in police costumes. Nothing. We tried a few of the sleazo hotels off West Street, but the desk clerks were their usual fountains of information. Even with flashing some fairly serious money, we kept drawing blanks.

But the Cobra was out there—I could smell him. He hadn't left. Not yet. Going underground was impossible for him—I lived there and he'd just be a tourist. But time was pressing against us and we weren't any closer. All he had to do was go hop a Greyhound to anyplace and he'd be out of our reach. My one hope now was that the cub reporter would do a newspaper number in his column by tomorrow's edition and Wilson would snap at the bait. He didn't have the credentials to work professional crime—no working thief would include a freak like him as part of a team. He'd need the VA money soon. Did he have a passport? And if the government bagged him before I did, could I work something out? Getting him canceled in prison was no problem, but it would be too long a wait. For Flood. For me too.

Max sensed my feelings, reached over, and put a hand on my forearm. He clasped his hands in front of his chest to say that patience should be my ally, not my enemy. Sure.

I was so depressed I hadn't even checked to see who was running at Yonkers that night. I hadn't played a number in days. The only thing I had to look forward to in the morning was a newspaper column by a kid who wouldn't know a mercenary recruiter from a polo pony.

I dropped Max at the warehouse, went back to my office, and called Michelle to check on things. Nothing happening, but she was holding strong. So I went up there, brought her a bag of food, spelled her for a few hours while she napped on the floor in the sleeping bag I'd brought. It was getting light outside when I left to buy a paper.

51

THE STREETS WERE still calm and quiet when I hit the sidewalk, heading down Fifth toward Twenty-third Street, looking for a newsstand. There's a little park right across from the Appellate Division Courthouse between Fifth and Madison. Usually it's packed with three-card monte operators and soft-dope dealers, but it was nearly deserted at that hour. I spotted an old man wearing four or five layers of clothing, catching a piece of sleep, guarding his plastic shopping bag full of God knows what. He opened his eyes as I approached, too tired and too weak to run, probably thanking whatever he still believed in that I wasn't a kid looking to douse him with gasoline and set him on fire for the fun of it.

The weather was changing, you could tell. In the country they look for the robins—in the city we look for the old men coming out of the subway tunnels into the daylight. Those abandoned tunnels are nice and warm, but the territory belongs to the rats and it's hard to sleep. Somehow the bag ladies can operate above the ground even in the winter, but the old men can't cut it. They have to go for the Men's Shelter down on the Bowery or the TB wards or the subway tunnels. So when they finally come up for air you know the good weather can't be too far behind.

I cut through one of the crosspaths in the park, walking slowly. When I stopped to light a smoke I spotted a youngish white man slouching on one of the benches. He was wearing an old army jacket and a light-blue golfer's hat, engineer boots, dark glasses. Smoking a joint. I knew the type—too heavy for light work and too light for heavy work. He was out there watching—a finger for some kind of operation, not a face-to-face man or a planner. I walked past him, puffing on the butt, hands in my pockets. I could feel his eyes focus behind the sunglasses, but I kept rolling along out of the park.

I found a newsstand on Twenty-third where I bought a copy of the late edition and the coming night's racing form. This was unfamiliar territory, so I turned and headed back through the park until I found a bench behind the punk in the army jacket, stretched my arms, and took a deep breath to give myself a chance to look around. The park was still quiet and empty. I opened the racing form, took out my pen, and started on the evening's handicapping. I wanted to have the form well-marked in case some strolling cop got inquisitive.

I was working on the fourth race, the newspaper still untouched next to me, when I felt something going down. I glanced parallel to the ground. Nothing. Everything was static, the park was still. And then I heard the rumble of the armored car as it pulled off Fifth and turned on Twenty-third, heading for the West Side. The punk was still on the bench but sitting straight up now. As soon as the truck was out of sight he got up and walked away fast, checking his watch. Amateur.

I'd seen enough. I wrapped up my papers and headed back to Michelle. I wasn't that impatient to see if the column was in the paper—either it was or it wasn't. I couldn't change anything by reading there in the park.

Michelle opened the door even as my soft tap was echoing in the dead-quiet corridor. When she saw the racing form in my hand her eyes flashed instant disapproval so I quickly held up the copy of the paper to show her I hadn't forgotten why I'd gone out. I sat down in the chair in front of the Mole's telephone unit with Michelle perched on the arm as I leafed through. Sure enough, next to the kid's smiling photograph was his semiweekly column. The thick black headline read UNCLE BIGOT WANTS YOU! Michelle and I went through it together.

Master Sergeant William Jones, a crewcut spit-and-polish veteran of the Korean and Vietnam wars, sits alone in his ground floor recruiting office in Herald Square, patiently waiting to explain the advantages of the "new" army to enough young men to make his quota for the month. Sgt. Jones is able to offer a truly staggering array of inducements to potential recruits—guaranteed choice of training, overseas or stateside assignment, a deferred enlistment program, an improved G.I. Bill, a college assistance deal where the army contributes towards tuition, and "more money than a captain used to make, including combat pay." His office is attractive, centrally located, and the atmosphere is friendly.

But business hasn't been too good for Sgt. Jones and his fellow recruiters around the city. Even with massive unemployment infecting the ghetto, young men are simply not opting for a military career these days. Sgt. Jones says the problem is the army's insistence on educational standards that are not related to the needs of a fighting force. For the "new" all-volunteer army, only bona-fide high-school graduates need apply. Says Jones, "When I went in the service, I hadn't even finished the ninth grade. So what? The army taught me how to fight, made sure I knew everything I needed to know, taught me to be a man. I finished high school in the service, the same way most of my friends did back then. Today, it's ridiculous. There's no such thing as simple patriotism anymore. The kids today want everything handed to them on a silver platter." When asked how today's all-volunteer army would fare in a combat situation, Jones just shrugged, but all observers agree that the goal of developing a "professional army" has fallen well short of expectations.

Meanwhile, a few blocks downtown, at 224 Fifth Avenue, in a shabby two-room office on the 14th floor, recruiting for a vastly different kind of army is going on. This army makes no promises of "training." Indeed, it expects to hire only fully trained and experienced men—no women or rookies need apply. And unlike the U.S. Army, this army is pointedly *not* an equal-opportunity employer. The location where the recruits will serve is not even disclosed at the time of enlistment. Pay is a flat thousand dollars per month, with additional pay for "specialists" and some unexplained "bonuses." Term of enlistment is "for the duration" and the only promise made is that all recruits will see action against the enemy, described by the recruiters as "terrs," short for terrorists. Yet the men who run the little office say business is booming.

The office of Falcon Enterprises hasn't been around too long, and the man in charge, a suave individual who identified himself only as Mr. James, freely admits that they don't expect to be in business too much longer. James and his associate, a hulking individual who calls himself "Gunther, no mister," will not discuss the purpose of their recruiting efforts, but they acknowledge that they are hiring "soldiers of fortune" to work outside the U.S. They don't advertise, saying that true professionals will have no trouble locating them. Both men are understandably discreet about their own backgrounds, but there are occasional references to "African work" and it is clear that their operation is a thinly disguised front for one or more outlaw operations being formed in and around Zimbabwe (formerly Rhodesia) to resist black national rule.

When a reporter asked James if the Rhodesian groups were similar to the KKK that sprang up in the South after the Civil War, James, speaking with a faint British accent, replied, "You Americans are so strange about such things. Do you remember that scene in your *Gone With The Wind* where a wounded Confederate soldier asks for a lift from a carpetbagger and his darkie friend? Remember the darkie says, 'You'd think *they* won the war'? The winners write the history books, and the history of Rhodesia isn't ready for you writers yet."

And his associate Gunther, pointing to a vicious-looking knife half-buried in the top of a wooden desk, flatly stated he didn't expect any picketing from "Communists." James was willing to discuss the Rhodesian situation at length, claiming that the blacks in power did not represent the true majority and that many "good coloreds" would prefer things as they used to be. But details as to his recruiting operation were not forthcoming. When asked what it would take to be accepted for enlistment, James said it would require a valid passport, military or law-enforcement experience, and "a certain something in a man—we know what to look for."

Sgt. Jones reports that enlistments are down for the past year, but the mysterious Mr. James seems unworried, even though "only one out of five applicants is good enough to meet our standards."

Makes you wonder.

I looked up from the column at Michelle. It was perfect—if this didn't bring the Cobra into the daylight, nothing would. The only way it could have been better would have been if the recruiters promised every new man the child of their choice to sodomize, but maybe Wilson would read between the lines and start thinking about the spoils of war. The column was all we could have wanted. I had to believe it—if the Cobra read the paper, he'd be coming around.

52

I LIT ANOTHER smoke and reread the column just to make sure there was nothing in it to spook our target. It stood up just fine—including the right amount of liberal outrage at the recruiting effort.

Michelle poked at my shoulder to get my attention. "Am I going to be here much longer, baby?"

"Not too much, I don't think. Why?"

"Well, I'm not staying here another day without some cleaning supplies. Honey, this place is a dump. I am accustomed to better. I don't need much—just some spray cleaner and some paper towels, maybe a dust mop. And some plastic bags for garbage. Actually a vacuum cleaner would be just the—"

"Would you forget that? Another day or so won't make any difference."

"Burke, I'm *telling* you—I don't like being in dirty places—not when I have to live in them. You know what kind of woman I am," she said, her eyes snapping.

"Just another day or so. I have to go out and dig up the Mole. He's going to stay up here with you for a while, set up some things for me."

"Does he play Scrabble?"

"I don't think so. Ask him to build you a ray gun or something. I'll call you by early this afternoon, see how things are going. If the freak doesn't bite in a day or so, we close this down, okay?"

"Okay, baby. Listen, I meant to tell you before. I saw Margot and she asked me to ask you if anything was happening on her case. She said you'd know what she meant."

"Yeah, I know. This comes first, then I'll see—"

"And I should tell her . . . ?"

"Tell her that you saw me and I was working."

I drove the Plymouth to the Bronx, found the Mole, and made arrangements for some work to be done on the car—remove all the paint and coat it with dull primer. If the cops ask you about the primer you just tell them you're doing the repainting yourself and the primer was as far as you got. You can see cars like that all over the city. But they're a bitch to see at night—the dull primer just eats artificial lighting. The Mole had some kind of paint-remover that worked in a flash. Every once in a while I try to get him to patent some of his stuff but he never wants to discuss it. Money doesn't race his motor. I told the Mole I wanted him to stay with Michelle until I called off the Cobra-trap—he just kept working on the car like he hadn't heard but I knew he'd do it.

Simba stuck his wolfish face into the shed where the Mole was working, checked me out briefly, and strolled over to a red metal box in one corner. The beast sat before the box, then slapped his right paw twice on the top, waited a few seconds, then slapped it twice with his left. The top of the box popped open and he stuffed his evil-looking snout inside and emerged holding a fat T-bone with pieces of meat still sticking to it. He looked up at the Mole, who nodded, then trotted out the door with his prize. I couldn't train Pansy to do that in ten years.

"Hey, Mole—how does the box know the dog's supposed to use first his right paw and then his left?"

"The box knows nothing. I know," said the Mole, directing my eyes to a pneumatic tube running the length of the shed's floor and then to a fat bulb near his foot. When the Mole was satisfied I'd made the connection he stepped on the bulb and the top of the red box popped open again. "I put the bone in there myself," he said.

"And Simba dosen't know, right?"

"Simba doesn't care," said the Mole, going back to his work.

While I was waiting for the car to be finished we talked about the Cobra-trap. When you talk politics with the Mole you have to speak in generalities. He knows there was this black guy in Africa who built a statue of Hitler and he has some vague idea that South Africa is one of Israel's biggest supporters, so it's narrow, tricky ground. I asked him once why he didn't just go to Israel where he could live in peace, and he told me that there was no sacred ground, that it was all a myth. The Mole said that the Jewish tribe was destined to roam the earth, not to settle down in any one spot. "Not in a concentration camp, not in a country," was the way he put it. In a way it made sense—it's tougher to hit a moving target.

As soon as the car was ready I headed back for the city and Flood's street, from which I phoned that I was coming. She was waiting downstairs. When we got into her studio she started to pace like a caged beast. Like the polar bears in the Bronx Zoo—they don't want to get out, they want to get you in there with them.

"Flood, sit down, okay? I got a lot to tell you."

"What?"

I handed her the copy of the newspaper, then quickly realized it was folded open to the evening's racing entries. Flood slapped the paper out of my hand. "Burke!" It was a wail, like she was a little lost kid and I'd let her down. Flood wasn't too keen on strategy. Combat was her style and she wanted to get on the battlefield—fuck the travel arrangements.

"Come here, babe. Listen to me. We've set the trap, all right? The freak may walk into it today, maybe tomorrow. I don't know. But soon. If he doesn't, he's either gone to ground or he's gone south, you understand?"

"Yes. You mean it's almost over for this place, one way or another?"

"Right. Now listen, we've got to play this like it's going to work—assume it's going to come off, yes?"

"Why?"

"Because if it does and we're not ready, it's all for nothing."

"I just want—"

"Hey, Flood. Fuck—I *know* what you want. I don't have to hear it a thousand goddamned times. Just get your stuff, okay? You're coming with me."

"My stuff?"

"Whatever you need if you meet up with him." Flood nodded and started putting some things in a blue-and-white vinyl duffel bag. When she got it all together she threw it over her shoulder.

"Burke . . . tell me it's really going to happen. Please?"

"It's going to happen, Flood."

And the sunburst smile came out on the face of this plump little blonde girl who was hoping, finally, to get her chance to fight to the death.

We drove to the warehouse—slowly, carefully, no need to attract any attention right now. As the Plymouth hummed and I felt Flood's warmth beside me, I was thinking how fine it would be for me to be taking her to the racetrack instead. Or the zoo. I get enough pain in my life from other people—I don't need to put any on myself, so I stopped thinking like a fucking citizen.

I pulled the car right into the warehouse, all the way up to the back wall. The door closed behind us before I turned off the engine, and I knew that Mama had reached Max.

"Come on, Flood," I said, extending my hand for her to take. She held out her hand as trustingly as a child. A soft, slightly damp chubby little palm—and on its other side, two enlarged knuckles with a faint bluish tinge. Would her hands be like Max's someday, when she finished her training? I pushed that thought into the part of my mind that dealt with questions like that, questions like my father's name.

Flood followed me into the back room. I motioned her to sit down on the desktop, lit a cigarette, and waited for Max. She opened her mouth to ask me something and I told her to be quiet.

Max the Silent materialized in the doorway wearing a black silk *gi*, a duplicate of the one he'd given Flood. Flood came off the desktop without moving her hands, flowed to her feet, opened her hands to Max, bowed. Max bowed in return, deeper than Flood.

I told Flood, "This is Max the Silent—my brother. He knows what you want and he has agreed to allow his temple to be used for your ceremony."

Flood spoke without taking her eyes off Max. "Tell him thank you, Burke."

"Tell him yourself, Flood." And Flood brought her two hands together in front of her face, bowed over her hands, saying thank you as clearly as any speech.

Max pointed at Flood, curled his pointing finger into a fist, tapped his head. Flood nodded yes. They were of the same school. Then Max pointed at me, turned the finger back on himself, curled into the fist again, tapped his heart twice, half-smiled. Flood understood that too.

Max turned and we followed him out of the back room around to the stairs. Up one flight, then another. We came to a door covered only with a bamboo weave. Max pushed the bamboo aside for Flood to enter, and we were in Max's practice room. The rough wood floor was hand-sanded and bleached so it was clean as an operating table. Flood didn't have to be told to remove her shoes. The floor was slightly rough to the touch. Against one wall was a giant mirror, against another were Indian clubs, long wooden staves, a pair of fighting swords. A heavy bag like prizefighters train on was suspended from the ceiling in one corner.

Max approached the center floor, arms at his sides. He swept his hand to cover the surroundings, bowed toward Flood with an after-you-please gesture, and Flood knelt in front of her duffel bag and brought out the robes Max had given her. She shucked off her outer clothes, stuffed them into the bag, and put on the black robes.

She sprang onto the floor, spun into a *kata* that vibrated with grace and power. Her kicks became hand-thrusts so smooth that I couldn't see the transition—her breaks were as clean as surgery. She worked against the mirror as she was supposed to, finishing in a deep bow to Max. No change in breathing, like she was at rest. A lioness returned to the jungle, and glad of it.

Max bowed in respect. He opened his hands, caught Flood's nod and stepped onto the floor. He knife-edged one hand, blurred it toward his own neck and pulled it to a dead stop maybe an inch away. He bowed again to Flood, motioned her forward to him.

Flood stepped onto the floor, twisting her neck from side to side to get loose. Max moved his hands in gently waving patterns in front of his face and chest—like he was carefully gathering cobwebs. He held one leg slightly in front of the other, bent at the knee.

Flood danced in on her toes, twisted her body to the side and faked a left-handed chop, then spun into a kick from the same side, her foot darting like a snake's tongue. Max took the kick on the outside of his thigh and moved behind her in the same motion, firing a two-finger strike at her face. Flood fell forward, her hands caught the floor and she back-kicked at knee height. Max flowed under the kick and his elbow whipped back with the power of a piston, stopping a millimeter from Flood's temple. Finished. Real duels between top *karateka* don't take more than thirty seconds—except in the movies. They move too fast and there's no margin for error. If Max hadn't pulled his last strike short, Flood's skull would have been crushed.

They both got to their feet. Bowed. Bowed again. Flood's face was flushed with joy—Max's eyes were bright with approval. He held out his hands, palms up. Flood put her hands in his and he turned them over, examining closely. Max drew his hand across his waist, patted his legs, nodded emphatically. Then he held out his hands, nodded again, but with reservations.

Flood said: "I know. My kicks are better. My teachers have told me that I'm lazy. That I work with what works for me, not with what doesn't."

Max pointed to my wristwatch, and Flood understood. It was too late to learn new tricks—she'd have to fight the Cobra with what she had. Flood was ready. She went back to the duffel bag and brought out the picture of Sadie and Flower, the piece of silk, and the candles. I handed over a copy of the Cobra's mug shot, and her quick flashing smile told me I was on her wavelength. For a change.

Max left the room and came back with a low red lacquered table that had tiny dragon's claws for legs. He placed it in the far corner so the mirror would reflect the icon no matter where you stood.

I left Flood and Max in the temple and went downstairs to hook up the field phone and check in with Michelle.

53

MICHELLE ANSWERED THE phone on the first ring, her voice all breathy and excited, not like her at all. "Burke, is that you?"

"What is it?"

"He hit the hook, baby. He sent a kid—"

"Don't say anything more. I'm on my way."

I ripped the phone from the connectors and sprinted for the Plymouth. Flood would be safe with Max, and if anyone hit the top floor looking for Michelle they'd have to get past the Mole. Everything was locked in place now, and phone conversations weren't going to help.

The Plymouth slipped through the light traffic like a dull gray shark. The smaller fish moved aside, and it took only minutes for me to get back uptown. I rolled into the parking spot, waved my arm to attract the attendant, and slipped him the ten bucks as I was locking up. The lobby was deserted— the indicator said one elevator car was on the eleventh, the other on the ninth. I hit the Down switch for both cars and charged up the stairs.

Still quiet—still empty as I went along. I timed my breathing so I had a burst of oxygen left at the end of each flight— you don't want to be out of breath if you meet unfriendly people. I sucked in a nasal blast before each flight, let it out as I was climbing. I stopped at the top floor, waiting for my blood to settle down and listened. Nothing. I approached the door, tapped softly. Not a sound. I tapped again, said, "It's me, Michelle," and the door swung open.

I moved inside and found myself facing the Mole hunched over some kind of plastic box glowing ruby-red from its insides, a slim metal cone pointed directly at the door. The Mole looked at me, blinked, took his hands out of the box.

Michelle was sitting in a corner, a petulant expression on her face, like she was being punished for something she didn't do. She opened her mouth to say something and the Mole held up his hand to silence her before she got a word out. "She went out," the Mole told me in his soft voice.

"You *what?*"

She bounded off her perch, came over to me, glaring over her shoulder at the Mole. "He sent a kid, Burke. A little kid. We got the whole thing on this hookup the Mole has here. Some little kid walks in downstairs and tells them he needs the phone number for his older brother. Like his older brother doesn't want to come in *personally,* right? He says he wants to establish contact—like he memorized the words. So the jerks downstairs, they give the kid the new number for their operation and the kid just walks out. Can you believe it?"

"And . . . ?"

"So I ran downstairs and followed the kid when he came out of the elevator."

The Mole began in an injured tone, "I told her not to leave—"

"You don't give me orders, Mole!"

"I could have followed him."

"Cut it out, Mole—you couldn't follow your nose," Michelle shot back. I could see the two of them were prepared to spend hours over this, so I finally asked the key question. "What happened?"

Michelle preened her feathers before she answered, the little kid in school who had the right answer all along and had her hand up and was finally getting called on by the sluggish teacher.

"The kid was a street boy, you know? A real chicken-hawk's special. Sweet little face, maybe ten years old. He looked like one of those Colombian kids they sell in the adoption scams— just a baby. He stops for a hotdog a couple of streets down from here. I thought he might be going to one of the flophouses or something. I was just going to get the address, that's all."

"Did he hook up?"

"He sure did, baby—but let me tell it. The kid bobs and weaves, the little clown. Takes a bus uptown, walks around near the park, then just starts to bop down Broadway like he doesn't have a care in the world. Never goes *near* a phone. Finally he goes into Happyland. You know, that videogame arcade on Broadway? So I go in there after him and he meets up with a guy at the Space Invaders game in the back. And he gives him a piece of paper—it had to be the phone number."

"Was it our man?"

"Honey, there is no doubt in my mind. He's the same freak," she said, holding up her Xerox of the mug shot.

"What did they do then?"

"Wait a minute, baby, slow *down*. It's him, all right, except he's dyed his hair blond. Can you believe it? But he's the one. I even saw the tattoo. What a freak—he just stands there patting the kid on the back of the neck and whispering something to him. He gives the kid money and the kid starts to play the machine and this creep just stands there watching the kid play. He keeps trying to pat the kid on the ass and the kid just wants to play the game. You know that place—nobody gives a shit what happens as long as you put the money in. Times Square, right? So I made sure it was the same guy and I got to a phone and called the Mole and he told me something was coming down and to get back here and I did."

Michelle finished her story, smugly looking at me for approval. What she got was, "You dizzy broad . . . that freak would put you down as easy as stepping on a roach if he saw you following him. The Mole was right."

And before Michelle could answer that one the Mole said, "He called."

"What?"

"He called. While Michelle was outside playing. I have the tape," and he flipped a switch without saying anything else.

I heard the ringing on the phone through the speaker, and then I heard James's confident voice. "Falcon. James speaking."

In response, a voice with a threatening top edge. "I heard about your operation. You people on the level?"

"Certainly, my friend. What can we do for you?"

"I want some work. Overseas."

"You are familiar with our standards?"

"Look, I'm a decorated combat veteran, all small arms, qualified jumper. And I'm a black belt in karate."

"Do you have a valid passport?"

"Yeah, yeah, I got all that."

"Well, my friend, we'd surely like to speak with you. Shall we make an appointment—say at four this afternoon?"

"No daylight for me, understand? I got problems here—nothing with the law, but I just came off a special operation and I don't want to be walking around. Tonight, okay?"

"If you insist. Are you ready for immediate work?"

"Mister, I'm ready to leave anytime—sooner the better."

"You understand that we can't reveal the departure point until you've cleared our interview?"

"Yeah, yeah, how long will that take?"

"It depends on your references. But if all goes well you can expect to leave within the week."

"Good. I'll see you anytime tonight. Meet me at the—"

"I *am* sorry, my friend," James said, "but you know how these things are. You come *here*. And you bring your passport and proof of military service with you. There are no exceptions."

A pause from the other end. Then, "Yeah, okay—about nine tonight?"

"That will be satisfactory."

"You need my name?"

"That won't be necessary. As you know, we allow all our recruits to select the name of their choice upon enlistment. You understand the conditions?"

"Yeah, yeah, I understand everything. I'll be there around nine tonight. You'll be there, right?"

"As we said," replied James, and rang off.

I listened to the tape over and over. It had to be the Cobra. Who else would have the phone number? By the time it got listed with Ma Bell the operation would have folded its tents and vanished. You can get a new listing from the operator, but not the same day the phone's installed—and the phone company wouldn't have this one anyway. The Cobra wouldn't wait, and he was too sly to just walk in. Nine o'clock, the scumbag had said. My watch said it was already past three. Now was no time to start alienating my troops.

"Mole," I said, "that was perfect. And Michelle, you shouldn't have gone out like that but I believe you've made the whole thing work," and I reached out to give her hand a squeeze.

Michelle flounced over to the Mole, hands on hips. "See,

smartass Mole," she sang out, but the Mole just blinked at her, still annoyed.

"Okay, Michelle. Pack your stuff—you're leaving, okay? You did your job. If you see the Prof on the street tell him to go over to Mama's and wait for a call. Mole, you go with her, take all this stuff with you. Make it like nobody was ever here."

Michelle and the Mole started to clean up, not speaking to each other but working well together. The Mole would snap together some electrical connections and box them up, and Michelle would be right behind him with the paper towels.

"Mole," I asked, "can you take out the elevators?"

The Mole refused to dignify such a question with an answer, but Michelle piped right up. "Are you serious, Burke? The Mole could take out NASA if he wanted to." And I caught the ghost of a smile crossing the Mole's face, which immediately vanished when Michelle said, "And *I'm* not leaving either. Not until this is finished. I want that freak too, Burke. You should've seen the way he was—"

The Mole had turned to Michelle and was speaking in his softest voice, the words coming slowly and evenly spaced, like from a talking machine with a heart. "Michelle, I am sorry I yelled at you. You were very, very brave to follow like you did. I was just . . . worried. You should go now. The work we have to do now, it's bad work. Not for you."

And this got the Mole a quick kiss from Michelle, who picked up her makeup case, said, "You let me know" in a warning voice to me, and was out the door.

"You're a charmer, Mole," I said, and it looked like he blushed, but it was hard to tell in that lousy light.

The Mole said nothing, just busied himself with the rest of the equipment. I snapped out the final instructions, in a hurry now like never before.

"Mole, hook up something so you can be signaled from the lobby. When you get the signal, take out the elevators. Where will you be?"

"Basement."

"Okay, now listen. After the elevators go down, get ready to move out—don't leave anything behind. You see this?" I showed him a tiny airhorn powered by a tube of compressed air. The Mole nodded. "You know the sound it makes?" He nodded again. "If you hear this go off it means we've got problems. So knock out as much of the electrical power in this area as you can in a minute or two and get *out*. Okay?"

"Okay." We shook hands. I wouldn't be seeing him for a while. If I was busted he'd hear about it and see the people who had to be seen for me. It was a lot to ask of the Mole— not blowing things up, that was just a day's work—but talking to people . . .

I got into the street fast. I had to see a lot of people before it got too dark. I left the Mole in the little room, his fat white fingers flying over the machinery.

54

THERE ARE SOME citizens who will tell you that all big cities are alike. Those people are born chumps. Where else but in New York could you find a Prophet sitting in the lobby of an empty office building in the early evening, poised over a shoebox and looking for all the world like an elderly black man just trying to pry a few coins loose from society. Or a warrior from ancient Tibet without the power of speech but with the strength of a dozen men standing still as a statue on the second-floor landing of that same building? And could you find a little round man with an underground complexion and a brain that understood the cosmos sitting in the basement of the same building, waiting to make electrical systems magically disappear? It was all there in place as I strolled into the Fifth Avenue lobby that night, dressed up for the role in a belted leather trenchcoat, soft suede snapbrim hat, tinted glasses, carrying a pigskin attache case and a .38, some anesthetic nose plugs, a can of mace, and a set of handcuffs.

I caught the Prof's eye as I entered the lobby, raised my eyebrows behind the glasses. He flipped the cover of his shoebox to show me the Cobra's picture taped inside. The portable radio sitting next to him wasn't playing, but the Mole would hear its song when the Prof sent him the message. The elevators had a neatly printed sign: CLOSED FOR REPAIRS, PLEASE USE STAIRS.

I walked past the lobby entrance and climbed the stairs. Max was in position. I held up one finger, moved my lips like I was speaking, pulled my fingers away from my mouth to show words spilling out. Max nodded—we'd talk the freak out of the building if we could. He could come easy or he could come hard. But he was coming. Max would watch—if he saw the Cobra and me leaving together he'd wait a beat, then slip out so he'd be in the front seat of the Plymouth before us. If Wilson panicked when he saw me on the stairs and tried for the door he'd find it locked. If he smashed his way past that, the Prof would pull his just-released-from-Bellevue madman act on the sidewalk to give us another clear shot. So if Wilson, a.k.a. the Cobra, stepped into the lobby, he was going to be leaving with us one way or another.

I checked the time—21:01 on the face of my genuine Military Assault Watch ($39.95 from a mail-order house). I thought it was a nice touch. My mind wasn't open to the possibility that the Cobra wouldn't show. If that happened I'd have to use Michelle, track down that kid in the video joint . . . too much to think about and I had to get into character for the meet . . .

I heard the Prof's voice. "Shine, suh?" and no response. But that was the signal. And when I heard a muttered "Fuck!" I knew the Cobra wasn't happy about the stairs. Some soldier of fortune—his idea of jungle warfare was probably blowing up a few African villages at long range and then moving in to mop up. But when I heard his footsteps coming up at me I knew he wasn't a complete phony—he had the light, patterned steps of a martial arts man moving toward an objective, and his breathing sounded correct.

When he came up to where I was waiting against the wall, I took a flash-second to decide—the gun or the game—and then there he was, right in front of me. The Cobra—a little taller than me, thin and hard-looking, his nose and earlobes both too heavily tipped, just like they were in the mug shot, the acne scars in place. Wearing a fatigue jacket so I couldn't check for tattoos, but it was him. His hair was longish in the back but cropped close up front, and blond, like Michelle had told me. His mouth opened when he saw me and I saw the fear flash in his eyes. I spoke first—calm, level—reassuring. Just a man doing a job. "Sorry about the elevator, my friend. Mr. James insisted—security, you know. You're the appointment for twenty-one-hundred hours, I assume?"

"Who're you?"

"My name is Layne. I work for Falcon."

"You American?"

"Sure. The limeys are just the recruiting end, pal. At our end it's all the U.S. of A."

He stood facing me in a karate stance, slightly modified so it wouldn't be too obvious—keeping both hands in sight. I didn't like that—it didn't mean he wasn't packing a gun, just that he thought his hands were enough to do the job. If he decided to take me out, Max wasn't close enough to stop him. He would never get out of the building alive, but that was no comfort. Revenge was Flood's game—mine was survival. I kept both my gloved hands clasped on the handle of the attache case, holding it in front of me.

The seconds slipped by as the Cobra eyed me. It was like the staring contests young bloods would get into on the yard when I was in prison—the kind of game you can't win. If you drop your eyes, the other con thinks you're weak—and a weak man in prison doesn't stay a man for long. If you lock eyes for real, you've got to fight. And if you have to fight, you have to kill. Once you're on that slide, you can have a decent life for yourself inside the walls . . . but you can never get out. I had to end this part fast.

"You know me?" I asked him.

"No," he said softly, "I just wanted to see . . ."

"See what, pal? You did this before, right?"

"Yeah . . . right," but his eyes never shifted and he didn't move.

"All right, let's get rolling. I got some contracts for you to look over and we got a place for you to stay with the other guys until we move out."

"Where is this place?"

"It's downtown, near the docks. Come on, pal. I don't want to stand in this goddamned stairwell all night, okay?"

And I walked past him like there was nothing for him to do but follow me, deliberately leaving my back exposed to anything he wanted to do—but finally getting myself out of the line of fire between him and Max.

I heard the sharp intake of breath through his nose as I went past. He wasn't relaxed—wasn't going for it yet. I kept walking, talking over my shoulder about the "operation" like he was right next to me. When I got to the bottom of the first flight of stairs, I turned around and looked back. The Cobra had moved down a few steps, but he wasn't coming along—just staring down at me.

I turned to look up at him, now holding the attache case in one hand while the other was comforted by the feel of the revolver in my coat pocket. With twenty feet between us the odds had changed: between my pistol at his front and Max the Silent at his back, he was deader than disco if he moved wrong.

The Cobra seemed to realize he'd lost the edge, and he started toward me. I shrugged my shoulders elaborately, calling up to him:

"Hey, pal, you in or you out? I got a rendezvous at oh-two-hundred over in Jersey and two other men to pick up. What's your problem?"

"Let's go," he said, flashing his snake's grin for the first time, and staring down toward me.

I turned and went down the next flight, like I expected him to catch up. I was part-way down when I heard movement behind me—he was coming. The muscles in the back of my neck tightened as I concentrated on the sounds. An amateur would try to rush up behind me and knock me down the stairs, but the Cobra would want to get close and do it right.

Now he loomed up silently on my right side, lightly touched my arm. "Can't be too careful, right?" he hissed, and fell into step with me. I could only see his right hand—the left was somewhere behind me. The Cobra was back in control, he thought.

One more flight to go. I still couldn't see his left hand. When he spoke he turned to look at me and his body got closer—it wasn't an accident.

"How long's this operation going to run?"

"Hey, you know how it works, it runs until it's over. You're in for the duration, right? You draw a month's pay up front in cash, the rest goes to wherever you want it sent."

"Yeah, right . . ." It was like I'd thought: all he knew about mercenary work was what he'd read in magazines.

We got to the lobby together, walking past the Prof, who tried another "Shine, suh?" which got no response from me. The Cobra, in character, said, "Shine this, nigger," hawking and directing a blob in the Prof's general direction. The Prof ducked his face behind the shoeshine box, and the Cobra smiled his smile more brightly now that he figured he was among friends. But when he glanced over at me and I kept my face deadpan he seemed to realize that he'd made a mistake: real men didn't spit at niggers, they blew them away. He shifted his shoulders and I knew what was on his mind. "Forget it," I told him, "we've got better things to do."

He nodded and we went out the door into the street, about a block from where the Plymouth sat waiting dark and quiet, only a whisper of smoke from its exhaust. Max was already there.

Another block to go. I had to keep him off balance, stop him from thinking.

"Got your passport with you?"

He tapped his breast pocket, saying nothing. We were at the Plymouth—I walked over and opened the back door, climbing in myself so that it wouldn't remind him of the last time he got busted. But he stayed quiet, slid in next to me like he was supposed to, and pulled the door closed.

It was dark in the car. Max didn't turn around—with the black watch-cap over his skull and the canvas gloves on his hands he looked like anybody else.

"What's with him?" the Cobra wanted to know. "I thought you'd be alone."

"I do liaison work, friend—I don't drive the cars, okay?"

The Cobra moved slightly away from me and reached his left hand across his body to roll down the window on his side.

"Don't," I told him. "From this point on the mission's rolling. We're in a gray sector here and we don't need any attention, right?" The Cobra nodded, looking pleased, glad finally to be among true professionals like himself. The Plymouth rolled away from the curb with its catch.

The Cobra leaned back and we both lit cigarettes. I kept talking to calm him, but there was no place for him to go now—the back doors couldn't be opened from the inside.

"You ever work before?"

"I did some jobs, local jobs—not in Africa, though."

"How'd you know this was an African operation?" I said, sounding surprised.

"I know these things. I just read between the lines," he said, grinning his winning snake's grin.

"You do combat or penetration jobs?"

"Either one, man. Either one."

"You got your choice with this operation."

"You got a lot of guys signed up already?"

"We got ten men besides you already on-board here in New

York, another fifteen in Houston. I understand our people on the Coast are doing real well too. You got any particular specialty? They pay extra for that, you know the scene."

"Interrogation," said the Cobra. No smile this time.

I nodded, then told him, "You'll have to bunk with us for a few days until we're ready to shove off. The accommodations are pretty good, we got food, TV, access to phones. We even bring in a whore or two every couple of nights."

"I get my own," he said quickly.

"Yeah, well, once you're in we can't have people just walking around the streets, right? Security. We bring in what the guys want."

"Yeah . . ."

I figured he was thinking he didn't know me well enough to ask me to bring him a kid for him to practice his specialty on.

55

THE WAREHOUSE LOOMED in sight. Max rolled in the front, slipped out from behind the wheel, and went back to close the door, all in one continuous motion. I knew he'd be hitting the switch to tell Flood the cargo had arrived.

Max opened the door on my side, I slid out, he walked around the back of the Plymouth, and opened the Cobra's door. Wilson climbed out, stretched himself, yawned. He looked at Max, said, "He's a zip . . ." in a surprised voice. I shrugged my shoulders in a what-can-you-do? gesture and pointed to the stairs. The Cobra started to climb, seemed to hesitate when he heard something, then realized it was just a radio. Hearing Hank Williams sing "Your Cheatin' Heart" seemed to add a spring to his step. As he completed the first flight I slipped past him to show him the way to the second, where Flood would be waiting, leaving Max behind him. The Cobra was in a box, but not the box where he belonged—not yet.

I got to the door of Max's temple and we couldn't hear the music anymore. I pushed aside the bamboo so the Cobra would precede me, and we all went inside—

And there stood Flood in the black robes, in a room lit only by the flickering candles on the altar.

"What the fuck is . . . ?" He spun around to face me. He saw the double-barreled sawed-off leveled at his chest, and stopped. He glanced at Max and saw the warrior, now wearing the same black robes as Flood.

"Give me the passport," I said, "and if your hands touch anything else you're chopped meat."

The Cobra reached slowly for his breast pocket, saying "Hey, look . . . man, look. I *got* it. It's here. What's going on . . . ?"

He placed the passport gently on my open palm. Flood stood watching—still as stone. I held the passport in one hand, slid my thumb inside and flipped it open to the first page. There was his picture—and MARTIN HOWARD WILSON in government lettering. A valid passport, just like he promised. I nodded to Flood and Max.

The Cobra stood with his hands at his sides, waiting to see if he'd passed the test. I prodded him forward with the scattergun until he was close enough to see the little red table. Close enough to see the metal spike with the dark wood handle wrapped in red silk. Close enough to see the picture of Sadie and Flower—to see his own photograph. Then he knew.

Max and I stepped back, away from him. I spoke to him in a calm voice—no more mystery. "Look, pal. It's a job, you understand. This lady has a beef with you and she hired us to bring you here. Now it's between you and her. We're out of it. Only you don't leave until it's settled. That's it."

The Cobra stood there, staring straight ahead—his mouth was open, his breathing was bad. Then Flood spoke up, her voice thin and clear, without a tremor. "Martin Howard Wilson"—like a judge handing down a sentence—"you killed that child. Flower. Her people are dead. I am of the child's blood and I want yours in payment—"

"What is this *shit*—"

"Shut up," I told him, moving the shotgun for emphasis.

Flood went on as if nobody had spoken. "I will fight you. Now. In this room. On this ground. We fight to the death. Only one of us leaves this room. If you defeat me, you will be free to go."

The Cobra looked at me. I nodded. "That's the deal, pal. One of you leaves the room."

"I beat this cunt and I leave? No problems?"

"No problems," I said, and stepped back.

56

FLOOD BOWED TO MAX, bowed to me, and turned to bow
to the altar she had made. The Cobra unbuttoned his fatigue
jacket with one hand, slowly, so as not to provoke me into
blowing him away. He was wearing only a black T-shirt under
the jacket, the butt of a small automatic protruded above his
belt.

"Your choice," I said, stepping slightly to my left. Max
moved out of the line of fire.

The Cobra used only his thumb and index finger to pull it
out—a nasty little .25-caliber Beretta, more than enough to
do the job at close range. He held it by the butt and gently
tossed it in my direction. It bounced off my thigh—my eyes
never left him.

Still watching me, he knelt and unlaced his combat boots,
took off his socks, put them on the floor. A look of profound
disgust flashed across Max's face.

I walked toward the Cobra: the scattergun backed him away
until I was between him and the boots. A glance showed what
I expected—a sheath stitched up one side of the boot, with the
knife handle sticking out the top. I kicked the boots away and
stepped back.

He looked over at me, giving it one last try. "Can I talk to
you?"

I shook my head. He looked at Max's face, saw his future,
and turned to face his past.

Max and I faded back against the walls, leaving the Cobra
and Flood alone on the deck. Flood shrugged her shoulders,

causing the lovely silk robe to fall to the floor behind her. She faced the Cobra wearing a black jersey top with accordion folds in the shoulders over flowing white silk pants. Around her waist was a white sash, tied so that its tails revealed two black tips.

Flood flicked her foot and the discarded robe flew off the deck and came to rest against the altar. She spread her arms wide to the Cobra—and bounced toward him on the balls of her feet.

The Cobra ran to meet her, shifting his upper body so it was parallel to the ground and firing a sharp roundhouse kick off his right foot. Flood flowed under the kick without changing her position, and he whipped the left foot back to the ground and lashed out with the right—Flood wasn't there.

I looked over at Max—the Cobra was quicker than I thought he'd be, and he was fighting her correctly. An amateur would try and use his greater upper-body strength against a woman, but his longer legs gave him more power with less risk. Someone had trained him well—his concentration on Flood was total. Max and I weren't in the room for him anymore.

Flood still hadn't moved. The Cobra faked a chop with his left hand, spun into a tightly controlled back-kick, and used the forward momentum to fire three quick chopping strikes in one burst. The first two missed—Flood took the last one on her elbow, spun into it, and twisted her hips to launch an elbow at his exposed face. The Cobra leaned back, his lips parting as her arm shot by, but Flood kept spinning, aiming an eye-dart that just missed, raking the side of his face. First blood. The Cobra rolled to the floor and lashed up at her ankles with his heel, supporting himself with his palms.

Flood shot past the Cobra's leg and exploded into the air, dropping down toward his face with one leg punching out like a piston.

The Cobra, true to his name, slithered sideways on the hardwood and aimed a powerful chop just as Flood's foot flashed past him. She took it on the outside of her thigh, grunted, hit the floor with one leg and lashed back at him with the other. She caught him square in the ribs, but he was off his feet when it landed. He flew backward, hit the floor, and spun back up—his hands had never touched the deck.

Flood stepped back, circling her face with her hands, weaving a tapestry of death from the air. The Cobra's mouth was bloody where he had bitten into his lip. He feinted to his left, pivoted on his right foot, firing another kick in Flood's direction—but she hadn't moved. Her back was to the door—all the fakes in the world wouldn't get him through the opening.

He advanced on her with an extended left hand, thrusting it in and out, circling to his left, not letting her get set to kick. He knew where the danger was—her feet, not her hands. He switched hands in a blur, his right fist shooting forward. Flood threw up her forearm in a block but it wasn't clean—there was a sharp crack and her arm dropped down for a split-second as she spun away.

He knew what he had to do now. He moved in again, hands out. Flood kicked at his midsection but he was ready—twisting with the force of her kick, he brought his hand out and around in a full spin and caught her just below the eye. It looked like an open-handed slap—Flood's head snapped back with the blow, but she instantly blasted him full in the chest when he tried to follow up. He staggered back, losing his balance, and she was on him, blood streaming from under her eye. But the staggering was a fake—the Cobra caught her coming in and landed a three-finger dart to the same spot—his hand came away bloody. Flood hissed, hooking clawed fingers at his face with both hands, but he was already backing away, breathing smoothly.

The Cobra was dancing now—up on his toes, shaking his wrists to get full circulation, relaxed. Flood stood as though rooted to the hardwood, one side of her face covered with blood. One eye was closed, but the other was clear and cold. I glanced over at Max—his face was composed but the cords of his neck stood out like high-tension wires, and his forearms were knotted steel. He was looking only at Flood. I knew what he was thinking—she'd never quit. Flood was wedded to the Cobra until death did them part.

I silently screamed at her: "Flood, he'll never leave this room alive no matter what. You don't have to die too . . ." But I knew it was useless—there was nothing in her mind but the Cobra's blood on Flower's grave.

He came in behind a cat-stance, offering only a snake's shadow for a target. He fired an exploratory left leg but Flood stood dead-still. He spun in a full circle, driving the edge of his hand across his body right to the point where her neck met her shoulder.

Flood hit the floor as though driven by the Cobra's strike, but she was moving just ahead of his hand—she hit the floor with one palm and her own leg lashed out, the toe shooting toward his kneecap. I heard the crack before I saw him crumple and go down on one leg, the other twisted behind him—useless now. He clawed at her pants to bring her to him but she spun away and swirled to face him head-on—a blonde ghost—too quick for a Cobra to catch.

Now it was the Cobra who was rooted to the ground, but his fangs still worked. Flood danced in, stepped past his hand-strike, and caught the side of his head with a spinning kick. His neck twisted with the kick, but he brought his hand around again just quickly enough to block her next shot. The room was so quiet I could hear my own heart—and the Cobra's raspy mouth-breathing.

Flood moved back over to him, set herself, rocked back on her right foot, and the left fired kick after kick—a heel to the side of the head, a toe to the neck, her powerful leg flashing inside the silk pants. He blocked some—but not enough. Flood was a graceful surgeon, cutting away flesh and bone to get to a tumor.

Then she stepped right into his grasping fingers, looking down as he clawed up toward her groin—and kicked the other arm at the elbow joint. Another crack and he was down, face to the floor.

She turned her back to him and went to her altar. She bowed deeply, reaching into the red silk folded on the little table. And when she turned again, the long metal spike was in one hand.

As she approached the Cobra her body flowed into a crouch. She leaned forward, reaching out with her left hand, the spike held next to her hip on the right. The Cobra looked up at her, brought his hand out from under his body and held it out palm up. In surrender.

Flood rocked back on her heels, a puzzled look on her face. And the Cobra struck. Scrabbling like a super-speed crab, he pushed himself off the floor with his one good leg and fired both hands at her throat.

Time stopped. I was watching the whole thing as if the room were full of crystal-clear Jello—everything in slow motion. His body was flat to the ground, his spine arched backward, his hands just about at her face when she brought her right hand around her hip and up into his exposed throat. Up on her toes now, but still in her crouch—the force of her strike lifted his upper body off the ground, where she held him, suspended, with her one hand.

Time froze them like that until her thighs flexed and she slowly straightened up—the Cobra, his throat still connected to her right hand by the spike, slowly rose with her. It seemed forever until Flood's right arm shot forward, pulling the Cobra up like a rag doll, then flipping him straight back. His head hit the hardwood, and he was flat on his back—the handle of the spike sticking out of his throat.

I looked down at what was left of Martin Howard Wilson— his face contorted, locked forever into his last thoughts. The spike must have gone right through the throat and into his brain. The snake would never crawl again.

Flood was out of gas. I started to move to her before she fell, but Max quickly stepped forward, shaking his head no at me—she had to finish this herself. Max bowed his head and so did I—looking down at the dead Cobra—but not out of respect. I could see the muscles tremble slightly in Flood's thighs, in spasm from the strain. One arm hung loosely, prob- ably broken. Her expression: half-warrior who had survived a battle to the death, half-schoolgirl who had just gotten her heart's ultimate desire.

Time passed. Flood's breathing smoothed and her legs stopped trembling. She worked her head from side to side, ignoring the blood flowing down one cheek, then held out her hands and Max and I came to her and each took one.

We turned and walked to the altar. Flood knelt, took the Cobra's mug shot, and I fired up a wooden match and handed it to her. She held the burning photograph in her hands, ignoring the fire as she had so many years ago in that room with Sadie. Only when the picture turned to paper ash did she rub her hands together. She wiped her hands on the red silk, wrapped the picture of Sadie and Flower inside its folds, and put it in her robe. She knelt again, said something in Japanese, I think. When she got to her feet her face was a bloody, discolored mess and her hands were burned—but the tears in her eyes were pure joy.

She bowed deeply to Max, spreading her hands as wide as they could go to show him the depth of her gratitude. Then she reached to her waist and pulled the bloody black jersey over her head. Standing naked from the waist up, she threw the jersey at the Cobra's body, then took Max's robe from her altar and handed it back to him. Max held his hands up, palms out—he spun his hands in a circle, refusing the return of his robes, telling her to put them on. Flood bowed again and wrapped herself in the robes. She searched through her duffel bag, found her own rose-colored silks, bowed to Max, held them open. Max took the robes with one hand, touched his heart with the other. They didn't need words—he would no more wear her robes to dispose of the Cobra's body than she would wear his to fight him.

Flood looked around the temple once more—taking it all in, memorizing it for life. Max clasped his hands together, closed his eyes, and leaned his head against them. It was time for Flood to rest. She nodded and flowed into the lotus position on the temple floor, Max's robes draped around her shoulders, pulling everything inside her.

Max and I left her there while we went to throw out the garbage.

57

I MADE A bed for Flood in the trunk of the Plymouth—she couldn't go to a hospital, and I didn't want some inquisitive cop noticing her anywhere near the scene where the Cobra vanished. It didn't look like a problem . . . he'd been carrying all kinds of weapons but he hadn't been wired.

When I opened the trunk again inside my garage Flood was curled up like a baby, one arm cradling the other. It probably was broken but she never made a sound. I got her upstairs, let Pansy out to the roof, and went in the back for my medical kit. When I came back into the office she was sitting on the desk in the lotus position, looking at the door.

"Flood, get up and take off your clothes."

"Not now—I've got a headache." She smiled, pointing to her battered face. But the smile was weak and the crack fell flat.

I threw the cushions off the couch, pulled a flat piece of plywood out from behind it, and laid it against the springs, then folded over some blankets to make a cover and put a clean sheet over the top. Flood hadn't moved.

"Flood," I told her as gently as I could, "you have to work with me now, okay? Put your legs over the side of the desk. Come on."

She slowly unwrapped from the lotus position and did like I asked. I eased the robes from her shoulders and took the bad arm in my hand. The skin was bruised but not broken. "Can you move it?" She rolled her arm from side to side. Her face stayed composed but some pain flashed in her eyes when she brought her hand toward her shoulder, flexing the bicep. At least it was a clean break, if it was broken.

I motioned to her to climb off the desk and untied the white sash as she stood in front of me. The silk pants came next, falling to the floor in slow motion. She stepped out of the pants and kicked them away, then stood there in the morning light as I went over her body as carefully as I could. The flesh over one elbow was gone, a lumpy discolored knot was on the outside of one thigh, and the two smallest toes of one foot were already dark with clotted blood. She let me move the toes without protest—they weren't broken, just bleeding under the skin. Like a patient child, she opened her mouth and allowed me to probe around—all her teeth were intact, the damage was on the outside. Her pupils looked okay, and she wasn't talking like someone who had a concussion, but I didn't want her to fall asleep for a while just in case she did.

I took one of the pieces of aluminum in the medical kit that looked like a good fit, tested it against her forearm, bent it into the right shape. I put the aluminum splint against her forearm and wrapped it into place with an elastic bandage. It didn't look pretty but it would work well enough if she didn't jump around, and let the bone set properly.

I swabbed out the open wounds, packed them with Aureomycin, and covered them with gauze bandages. Then I walked her over to the couch.

"Which is better, Flood? Lying on your back or your stomach?"

"Depends on what you have in mind."

"Flood, I don't have the patience for this crap. You don't have to convince me you're tough. You're going to be fine, okay?"

"You looked so scared, Burke . . ."

"Maybe you *did* get a concussion. I'm not the one who got mangled."

"I know. I'll be good. Whatever you say."

I put her on the couch lying on her back, folded a pillow under her head, and covered her with another sheet. I got the splinted arm supported by a folded blanket, kissed her forehead, and went back to the desk to put things away.

"Burke," she called out.

"What is it? Just relax, I'm not going anywhere."

"My sash . . . the white sash with the black tips . . . ?"

"Yeah?"

"It's for you. To keep, okay?"

"Okay, Flood, I'll keep it." By then it was obvious she didn't have a concussion—but she was running on the fumes in her reserve tank.

"Keep it here . . . for me, okay?" she said, and was drifting off to sleep before I could ask her what she meant.

58

ALMOST A WEEK went by like that. Max brought over all kinds of strange-looking gunk from Mama Wong's kitchen for Flood to eat. It looked like molten slag to me, but Flood seemed to know what it was. Pansy tried some too, but she didn't like it . . . no crunch.

I watched her get stronger, watched the swelling go down until I could see the other eye, watched her flex the arm experimentally, practice her breathing.

I didn't go out much, but Max stayed with her when I did. Pansy stayed to guard her when I went downstairs for the papers in the morning. I would read the stories to Flood until one morning she told me to stop. The headlines just sounded like body-counts, she said, so I stuck to the race results. I still watched the horses, but I didn't feel like making any bets—with Flood getting better every day I sensed my luck was about to change, and I didn't like the feeling.

One morning she was already up when I came back upstairs. She was wearing an old flannel shirt of mine—unbuttoned, it hung on her like a robe. She was working her body: hard now, not tentatively like before. A modified *kata* in the narrow office, but the kicks and chops and thrusts looked clean and sharp. She was back to herself. Her pain was leaving, and mine was on its way.

I tried not to show it. "You want one of these bagels?"

"You have any pumpernickel?" Flood wouldn't eat white bread.

"Yep. New York Fresh too."

"What's New York Fresh?"

"Less than two days old."

She grinned. Except for what looked like a monster black eye, she was as good as new. The splint was on the couch—she twisted the bad arm behind her and touched the back of her own head. "See?" Like a little girl showing off. I saw.

I took my bagel, cream cheese, and apple juice and sat down in the chair behind my desk to read the morning paper in peace. Flood wasn't having any of this—she plopped herself in my lap, nuzzled my neck. "Let's go out today, okay? I feel like I'm locked up in here."

"You sure you're ready?"

"Yes, yes, *yes*," she squealed, squirming around in my lap until I gave up trying to read the paper.

I finally got to the paper while Flood was taking a shower. I started with last night's race results, like I always do, but I wasn't that interested. I still had almost all of Margot's money, and pretty soon it would be time to earn it. I'd been working out a plan in my head but needed to run it past Flood first.

She bounded out of the shower, water still glistening on her white skin, smiling an angel's smile. I knew she hadn't forgotten—I couldn't keep her here much longer. She walked to the back door to let Pansy out.

"Put some clothes on first."

"Who's to see up here?"

"Just do what I tell you. I can't explain every little thing to you."

She saw the look on my face and sweetly went back for a towel while Pansy waited patiently. Good—I didn't feel like telling her about the kind of people who watch. I was listening to one of those radio psychologists on a talk show late one night on a stakeout: she was saying how people who like to watch are really harmless: repressed, sad perverts, more annoying than dangerous. Once when I was being held waiting for trial the guy in the next cell told me he watched women to see if they had a message for him. Something about the way they dressed themselves before they went out—it sounded like the guy belonged in Bellevue instead of the House of Detention, but it wasn't my problem. They took him off the tier later that night. One of the guards who knew me from the last time stopped by my cell and slipped me a pack of smokes through the gate. I figured he just wanted to talk—the nights get lonely for them too.

"You hear about Ferguson?"

"Who?"

"The guy next door, the one they took out before."

"He never told me his name."

"He tell you anything at all?"

I handed him his pack of cigarettes back through the bars. "You know better than that. You trying to hurt my name?"

"Hey, I didn't mean nothing, Burke. The cops don't *need* any fucking info on that guy. Don't you know who he is? Fucking Ferguson—he killed seven women. Cut 'em to fucking *pieces,* man. They found all the stuff in his apartment. And listen to this . . . he told the D.A. that they all *asked* him to kill them, that they gave him a fucking *message* to do it. Can you believe it?"

"How long you been working here?"

"Yeah, I guess you're right. But every time I think I've heard it all . . ."

"What's in the paper?" Flood wanted to know.

"I thought it all sounded like body-counts to you."

"Today's different. I feel so *good* . . . like I want to dance."

"As long as you don't sing."

"Why?" she asked in a threatening tone.

"Oh, it's not on *my* account. It's Pansy—she has real sensitive ears."

"Is that right?"

"Honest to God. I'm sure if she heard you sing like you did in the shower this morning she'd be strange for a week."

Flood felt too good to care about my musical critique. I was just glancing through the paper before going up on the roof when the headline jumped off the page at me: "TERRORIST BOMB KILLS TWO IN MERCENARY RECRUITING OFFICE." The story went on to explain how the back window of a Fifth Avenue office had blown out "yesterday afternoon in a blaze of red fire. Police arriving on the scene found the mangled bodies of two white males, neither as yet identified, and most of the office still smoldering in flames." No fewer than four separate phone calls had been made to the media claiming responsibility for the bombing, ranging from a known black liberation group to some folks who claimed the recruiters were endangering the African environment with their proposed jungle warfare. The story said the investigation was continuing—good luck to them, I thought. Well, so much for my big plans about making a rich score from Gunther and James.

I'd never know the true story, and I wasn't about to burn my fingers prying into it. No way the investigators would be able to trace the phony gunrunners back to their fleabag hotel—they'd probably moved as soon as they scored the front money from me anyway. And if they did, all they could find to connect to me would be a name and a phone number. So what? The Prof had promised to check out their hotel room and pick it clean, working in his hall-porter costume, and it was a long twisted trail back to me no matter what. And I had my usual alibi.

I tossed the paper aside, looked over at Flood. "I've got a debt to pay to someone who helped me with the business we just finished. It's a one-acter, won't take long. You up to it?"

"Sure"—she smiled—"as long as it's *outside* someplace."

"Sure. First stop, at least, New York fresh air." I needed to assemble my people for this last piece, and I didn't want to call from the hippies' phone. "So get dressed," I told her, "we're going out."

We spent the day at the Bronx Zoo. They have this re-creation of an Asian rain forest right inside the cyclone fencing—Bengal tigers, antelopes, monkeys, the whole works. You ride through it on an elevated monorail, and the driver tells you what's happening over the loudspeaker. We did the whole place—everything but the Reptile House. When we got to the bear cages everybody was gathered around the artificial ice floe where a mother polar bear and her cub were basking in the sun. The mother bear looked balefully at everyone. One little kid asked his mother why the bear looked so mean—she told him it was because it wasn't cold enough for them. Flood turned to the woman, smiled her smile, told her, "It's because she doesn't belong here—this isn't her home." We left a puzzled woman in our wake, but I knew what Flood meant, and it hurt. I pushed the feeling aside.

Afterward, as the Plymouth moved through the burnt-out hulks that were once apartment buildings in that part of the Bronx, I felt sorry for any of the animals that might work their way through the fence and get out. . . .

It wasn't until late that night that we all got together in the warehouse: me and Flood, Mole, the Prof, Michelle, and Max. I had the floor plan of Dandy's apartment Margot had drawn for me spread out on a bench, and Mole was using one grubby finger to indicate how he'd work his end of the deal.

It looked easy enough, provided Margot came through with the set of keys like she promised. If she didn't the whole deal was off and she could go to the Consumer Protection Agency for her money.

"Michelle . . . any problems?" I asked.

"Don't be funny, honey. My piece is a breeze."

"Mole?"

"No."

"You got all the stuff?"

"Yes." The Mole was really being gabby. Usually he'd just nod.

"Prof?"

"His mind is on crime but his ass shall be mine. Revenge tastes even more sweet than a virgin's—"

"Cool it, Prof," said Michelle, "there's ladies present."

"I was *going* to say 'than a virgin's kiss,' fool. What on *your* mind?"

"If it was the same as yours, it'd make me a lesbian."

"That's enough," I told them. "Michelle, can't you get along with anyone?"

"I get along with Mole," she said, patting his hand.

The Prof looked like he was going to snap back but some glint from behind the Mole's thick glasses must have convinced him that playing the dozens could be a dangerous game when you let lunatics participate. He let it slide.

"Flood, you're sure you're up to this?"

A brilliant smile, glowing even in the dim warehouse. "I'm looking forward to it."

"You know what you have to do?"

"Burke, we went over and over it. I have it down pat."

There was no reason to ask Max if he was ready—and not because he couldn't hear the question.

"Okay, this is Wednesday. We do it Friday morning."

"Say, Burke," said the Prof, "you really going to use that damn dog of yours?"

"Why not? Pansy's perfect for the part."

"That beast is a *monster*, Burke. It makes me nervous just to be in the same *neighborhood* as he is."

"As *she* is."

"You mean that dog is a *bitch?*"

"Sure enough."

"Well," shrugged the Prof, "I guess that makes sense, when you think about it."

Thinking about it wasn't something I wanted to do right then.

59

FRIDAY WAS A muggy, dirty morning on the Hudson River docks. A Jersey smog-fog was rolling in. It was break-time for the working whores—the truck-driver traffic finished for the morning, the first citizen-commuters not yet on the scene. Peddlers were setting up their stands on the hoods of their parked cars, free of the wolf-packs who were gone now—back to their dens, the roving bands dispersed with the coming of daylight.

The Plymouth was parked near the pier next to a standing pay phone. I was listening to Judy Henske on the tape, trying not to think about tomorrow. Flood was lying with her head in my lap. Pansy slept in the back, unconcerned.

I looked down at Flood's lovely resting face. She was living well within herself now, at peace finally—another fucking club I couldn't join.

The phone rang, I reached out the window to pick it up, and heard the Mole say, "Moving. Now," and I knew it would take the mark only a few minutes to get on the scene.

Soon after, the black Lincoln Town Coupe pulled up and I saw the weak sunlight glance off the sheen of nylon and the flash of a red scarf as Margot exited Dandy's pimpmobile. Time to go to work.

Flood knew her part. She bounced out of the Plymouth wearing some new white vinyl boots over dark stockings topped by a pair of white hotpants and a brilliant orange silk top. Her blonde hair was in pigtails on each side of her clean fresh face, a face marred by the Cobra's fangs only a short time ago. She switched over to the highway, to all eyes a piece of juicy young stuff who had just gotten a lesson from her pimp and was now working off the debt.

Her big butt looked even more so in the white pants, and her skin looked too small for all the flesh underneath. Heels clicking on the pavement, her body swayed and bounced like it was moving slower than her feet. She reached into her little plastic clutch-bag and pulled out a big pair of dark glasses.

The timing had to be right—we had been watching Dandy and we knew he didn't hang around long after he dumped Margot off every morning. But Flood was right on the money— her path crossed Margot's and she walked just in front of the Lincoln's hood like she was going back to work. I watched Margot keep on walking and disappear into the shadows—and Flood stop and whirl around, hands on hips. When the Lincoln crept slowly forward, I knew Dandy had taken the bait. It's not every day a quart of vanilla ice cream falls into your lap. I couldn't see much from where I was, but the Lincoln was standing in place, smoke still burbling from its exhaust.

Then Flood swivel-hipped her way around the front of the black car and climbed into the passenger's seat. The Lincoln slithered away and the game was on.

I didn't have much time. Flood would keep him talking for a bit, maybe ask him to buy her some coffee, but sooner or later Dandy would try to make her end up in his crib. I fingered the key to his lobby and the key to his apartment that I'd gotten from the Mole. Margot had supplied us with the plastic impressions from the kit I'd given her, so I was sure they'd work.

As the Plymouth pulled away Pansy momentarily stuck her head up, saw there was no work to do, and rolled over on the backseat. I only had to get to the West Twenties, a short run. The Plymouth swung into a lazy U-turn, split the shadows over the highway and picked up speed. I reached over and rolled down the passenger-side window. As I slowed for the turn onto the uptown road, a canvas bag came flying through the window, immediately followed by a moving shadow. Max. The fucking showoff—there was plenty of time for me to have stopped the car.

Pansy sat up, sniffed the air briefly, growled. Max put his hand into the backseat. Pansy sniffed again, licked his hand, and went back to sleep.

Dandy's block—quiet and peaceful. I drove its full length

until I saw the white Dodge parked where it should be, Michelle at the wheel. She spotted the Plymouth, kicked over her engine, and pulled out, leaving me an ideal escape space. I reversed into the spot, hit the protection systems, and we all climbed out. Pansy bounded out to me and I snapped on the short leash, handing it to Max. The Prof was working the front, picking through a week's worth of trash in a curbside dumpster. When he saw Max and Pansy move toward the back where the Mole would be waiting to let them into the basement, he shouldered his collection bag and followed.

I opened the front door, saw a couple talking in the lobby, and lit a cigarette to wait them out. Finally I walked in, pushed Dandy's buzzer, and used my lobby-key without waiting for a response. I knew where he lived—second floor, rear. The Mole's key opened the lock.

I went through the place quickly. A small bedroom used as a giant closet for all Dandy's threads, a larger bedroom with a round bed, built-in stereo, giant-screen Sony complete with Betamax. Huge collection of records and tapes. On the dresser, a vial of cocaine, a gold coke spoon with a diamond chip in the handle, half a dozen Krugerrands. Inside top drawer, a pearl-handled .32-caliber Colt Astra. The bottom of the closet revealed a bunch of shoeboxes full of Polaroid pictures. Some of Margot, some of women I didn't recognize. Three pairs of leather handcuffs. A thick leather belt with holes punched all through it, no buckle.

No more time to search. I pocketed the Krugerrands and picked up Dandy's green Princess phone. No dial tone. "Mole?" "Here." "Let's go," I said, and hung up.

The door opened and Max walked in, holding Pansy's leash. The Prof was with him. "Time's short," I said, and everybody went to work: Max opened his bag, started pulling out his gear. I took the phosphorescent paint and the thick brush, called Pansy over to me, and generously lathered her fangs with the stuff—I opened the container of pork fried rice I'd brought with me and left it on the floor so she wouldn't notice the taste of the phosphorus. In the dim light of the apartment her teeth took on an unearthly, menacing glow. Pansy seemed to relish the thought, letting loose a few experimental growls that rumbled against the plaster walls until I told her to shut up and go lie down behind the plush purple velvet couch.

Max was exchanging his faded jeans and sweatshirt for a

set of green silk robes. He checked himself in the full-length mirror in the second bedroom, nodded in satisfaction, and then took a hideously carved teak mask from his bag. The mask was hinged on each side of the jaw, an ugly thing with slits for eyes and a slash where the nose would fit—the eyes tipped with dark green paint and the rest just a shiny, smooth surface of dark wood. As Max fitted the mask to his face his ancestors smiled in approval from somewhere in the mountains of Tibet.

The Prof pulled off his ragpicker's clothes. Underneath was a pristine white linen suit, the kind plantation owners used to favor years ago. He looked dazzling.

We worked together in silence, even Pansy. I got out the leather belt from Dandy's drawer, showed it to Max. He took one end in each hand and gave it an experimental tug, nodded behind his mask to show me it would be okay, no problem.

I set up my instruments on the kitchen table. It wasn't really clean enough for an operating room, but then again, I wasn't going to be working on a human being. The syringe was full of liquid Valium, the fresh new hypodermic spike still in its plastic case. I screwed them together, squirted a bit of the Valium to make sure it was working. Next I checked the anesthetic nose plugs—and the gym sock full of fresh aquarium sand just in case we wanted to do the job quickly. The bedroom window opened easily onto an alley in the back of the apartment, just like Margot had told us. Finally I checked the three smoke canisters the Mole had left behind in the apartment, spaced equally around the bedroom. I worked rapidly in the thin rubber surgeon's gloves—fingerprints weren't going to be an issue in this case.

The phone rang once. Stopped. Rang again. They were on their way up. Pansy stayed where she was in response to my hand signal, the rest of us deployed like we had rehearsed.

A key turned in the lock, and Flood came walking through the door, Dandy right behind. A tall thin dude sporting a short afro, early to mid-forties. He was clean-shaven with a mouth full of good teeth. Flood strolled over to the purple couch and perched on the edge of the cushion. Pansy smelled Flood on the other side and gave out the tiniest of growls, inaudible unless you were listening for it. Flood stayed on the couch while Dandy paced the floor, rapping his rap. "Baby, if you choose in New York you choose for good. That's the way it is. You working those tricks by yourself, you was *bound* to get yourself hurt. You need a man. That's the Life, that's the trade, that's the deal. Only way to deal is to be for real."

"You said you had some dynamite blow," Flood piped up.

"Baby, I got the best coke, the best of everything. I don't be like some of those halfass simps. I'm a *player*, you understand? I don't work a string, got no bottom woman. In fact, I been thinking about letting my woman go for some time now. Saved enough money for her to open her own boutique."

"Really?" said Flood in a voice full of wonder, her dreams coming true.

"Square business, girl. I ain't lying. Of course, she was willing to run the fast track, do what she had to do. There's got to be some pain in the game, little girl, some pain in the game. You got to pay the cost to be the boss, you understand?"

"I don't like pain," said Flood in her little girl's voice. "I like to party but I don't like that other stuff."

"Bitch," said Dandy, walking over to Flood, "you don't know what pain is."

"*Hey*," gulped Flood in a soft frightened voice. She jumped off the couch and ran into Dandy's bedroom, the pimp strolling calmly behind—taking his time, all the time in the world. After all, where could the little bitch go?

Flood dashed into the bedroom, saw there was no escape, and whirled like a doe at bay before the hunters. Dandy was right behind her, reaching out a languid hand for her arm— when Flood's white-booted foot slammed into his solar plexus like a dart of lightning. As the air exploded from Dandy's lungs Max leaped from behind the door and had the pimp's throat in his hands before he hit the ground—a quick squeeze of his hands and Dandy went limp.

I came out from under the round bed, holding the needle at the ready. Max ripped the pimp's jacket from his shoulders, tore away his shirt, snapped off the gold chain with the heavy medallion and tossed it to me. Max's steel fingers closed on Dandy's flaccid bicep, causing the veins in his forearm to stand out in bold relief. I tapped a nice one near the inside of the elbow, slipped in the needle and gently fed him the liquid Valium. Then we all stepped back to check on our work. Dandy slumped to the floor, his breathing shallow but regular. He was in no danger—from the Valium.

We propped him up in a chair in the corner of his bedroom, moved the smoke canisters into place, and summoned Pansy.

It would take about twenty minutes for the Valium to begin to wear off. We only wanted him dopey for the second act, not unconscious.

Flood went into the other bedroom to change her clothes while I searched the rest of the apartment. If Dandy was working the bondage-photo racket he had to have some money someplace, and it wouldn't be a safe-deposit box.

It took me almost a full twenty minutes, and all I could come up with was about a thousand or so in bills, some more coke (which I scattered all over the place to throw the dogs off the scent), and some more jewelry. I tried thinking—the Krugerrands kept popping into my mind. *Sure.* I went over to Dandy's limp body and started the search. It didn't take long—the thick moneybelt came off his waist without a struggle, and I found myself looking at forty perfect pieces of South African gold, each one individually wrapped. More than fifteen grand, even with the exchange problems. I put back the empty belt. If pimps were getting into gold coins, I could see the makings of a lovely scam somewhere down the road . . . but Dandy was ready for business.

When I saw he was coming around I snapped the tops off the smoke canisters and stepped out of the way. It wouldn't do for him to see my face. I took up my position behind him and watched the thick greenish smoke fill the room. I had left the windows tightly closed, so none of it would get out until we were ready. Dandy moved his head, grunted something I couldn't make out, and then his neck went rigid as he saw Max the Silent standing in front of him, wearing the teak mask and holding the broad leather belt. Dandy lurched to his left, looking for a way out. Pansy snarled, her fangs glowing in the green haze, and lunged at his waist. Dandy fell back into his chair— obviously none of this nightmare was adding up. To his left was an unknown horror in a warrior's mask, to his right was death in a beast's body. And through the middle came the Prof, clad in his white linen suit. Standing between the mad dog and the masked man, with the green smoke billowing—the Prophet's finest hour. And then he spoke:

"You have offended God. You were warned and you ignored the warning. You trade in the Devil's work. In pain. It shall be no more." Max then stepped forward, holding the leather belt before Dandy's glazed eyes. Max took one end of the thick belt in each hand and pulled it apart like it was wet Kleenex, tossed the two ends contemptuously to the floor, and stepped back, his hands disappearing beneath his robes.

And the Prophet now said, "Your life in filth is finished. Ashes to ashes, dust to dust, garbage to garbage. I have spoken."

Max advanced slowly on Dandy—Pansy could barely restrain herself from burying her fangs in his flesh. The pimp didn't resist when I stuck the nose plugs into the sockets. Two more gasping breaths and he was out again.

Max pulled off his mask and the green robes, the Prof donned his ragpicker's outfit over the white linen suit, Flood packed everything away, including her whore-clothes. The smoke canisters were almost empty, warm to the touch—all went into the big suitcase. One last quick spin around the place to check everything, Pansy lumbering after me, growling her frustration. I'd have to take her down to the training compound and give her an agitator or two to play with.

All done. From the back pocket of his jeans Max pulled a green plastic garbage bag, the super-giant size. He snapped it open, gave one end to Flood and the other to me. We held it open and Max picked up Dandy like a load of rags and dropped him inside. I pulled the nose plugs out of Dandy's face and we twisted the top closed, using three of the wire tags. The pimp would be out another minute or two—long enough.

I pushed the heavy curtains aside to check the back alley. It was still empty. Flood and I stood on either side of the window and shoved it open, then watched as Max tossed out the garbage bag. It sailed through the air, then hit with a dull thud. Green smoke started to billow out of the window and we slammed it shut.

I phoned the Mole that it was time to go. Max and the Prof went to the basement—the Mole had his own car parked nearby and he would take care of dropping them off. We walked to the Plymouth, me now wearing a different hat and Flood looking like a different woman in her pleated slacks and wool jacket.

Pansy went back to sleep, half on the floor and half on the seat. Flood held my hand in both of hers, and we drove back to my office.

60

WE WERE IN Flood's studio, she was packing. There had been nothing in the morning papers or on the radio about yesterday's action, but the afternoon edition of the *Post* had the coverage. Flood perched on the arm of the chair as I read aloud:

PIMP SAYS HE SAW GOD
IN PLASTIC GARBAGE BAG

A man with a history of convictions for pimping was discovered early this morning unconscious, injured, and wrapped in a green plastic garbage bag, police said.

The man, whom police identified as James Tyrone Simmons, 41, was taken to Bellevue Hospital, where he reportedly told doctors a bizarre story of how God and several fiery devils appeared to him inside the bag. He could not explain, however, what he was doing there.

Simmons was listed in good condition, suffering from a broken ankle and wrist and multiple contusions. He was being held for observation, according to a hospital spokesman.

"Except for some broken bones, he's fine physically," said Dr. Ito Kumatso, the hospital's chief psychiatric resident. "But the story he told us is something else.

"He talked about having a vision from God. He said God told him to change his ways, and then sent down monsters and wolves with fiery fangs. There was also something about green smoke.

"It sounds like a TV horror movie, but his terror seems genuine enough," Dr. Kumatso said, adding that Simmons will remain in the hospital under observation for at least several days.

Simmons's only request, Dr. Kumatso said, has been for a Bible.

Sergeant William Moody of the 10th precinct said that it was unclear whether Simmons had been assaulted. If there was an assault, Moody said, robbery was not the motive.

"There was money in his wallet and he was wearing jewelry when we got to him," Moody said.

Simmons was discovered by neighbors in an alley behind his apartment at 704 West 26th Street.

"I hope they find him a psychiatrist who talks English," I said to Flood.

"What are you talking about, Burke? If the doctor doesn't speak English how could he work with patients—?"

"Flood, this is New York City, not Disneyland. Half of the shrinks they use in the city hospitals are from out of country. They can't get a license to practice over here so they either work in some Medicaid mill or work for the city. I was investigating a case once for this Puerto Rican family. Their kid was bopping down the street listening to his new portable radio. You know, the giant-sized jobs the kids carry today? Anyway, a couple of punks tried to rough off the kid's radio and one of them got himself stabbed. So they had this kid in detention and we're working on a self-defense case. Meanwhile, they send the kid to see this Pakistani psychiatrist—to interview him and make his report to the court. When I come into the court there's this doctor up on the stand telling the judge that the kid is sexually disturbed. He says that the kid has a fantasy that he has a woman's vagina on his shoulder—and that his reality-testing is so bad that he keeps insisting on it. So the judge asks the psychiatrist how he came to that conclusion, and the Pakistani tells the judge that the kid keeps saying, "I was bopping down the block with the box on my shoulder . . ." and he goes on in that upperclass Paki accent of his:

"'I am most familiar with your American idiom, sir. And it is common knowledge that the word *box* is a synonym for the vagina.'

"Well, the judge about had a kitten. He was no legal scholar but even *he* knew the kids call a ghetto blaster a box."

"What did he do?" Flood wanted to know.

"About what you'd expect—he thanked the doctor for his time and remanded the kid for another psychiatric exam."

"You think that pimp will get a shrink like that?"

"It doesn't make much difference—he's sure as hell crazy by now. Anyway, Margot's well away, and that was the deal. I pay my debts."

"I know you do," said Flood, bending to kiss me.

"We have to leave for the airport," I told her.

"There's enough time," she said. And that was true.

61

TWO HOURS LATER I nosed the Plymouth through the parking lot at JFK, looking for a soft spot. I carried Flood's little bag in one hand, held her waist with the other. She bumped against me softly.

"Burke?"

"Yeah?"

"The last time we made love. In my studio. I thought about having your baby—in Japan—raising him there."

"And you decided not to, right?"

"Yes."

"I know," I said. And I did.

We walked to the departure lounge. I didn't have a ticket so the JAL people said I could only go so far. I already knew that—I've heard it before.

I put my thumb under Flood's square chin and tilted her lovely face up to me. I grabbed a look at those clear big eyes for the last time, the little tic-tac-toe crosshatch scar now almost invisible under the Cobra's fading bruises. I kissed her. My heart died.

Flood looked deep into my face, said, "I'm for you, Burke," squeezed my hand and turned to go. I watched her walk away—and I knew it was the truth.